Love, Lies and Café au Lait

Lynn Forth

CROOKED
CAT

Discover us online:
www.crookedcatbooks.com

Join us on facebook:
www.facebook.com/crookedcatbooks

Tweet a photo of yourself holding
this book to **@crookedcatbooks**
and something nice will happen.

To David, Stephen and Andrew,
Rosie and Fiona,
Ben and Barney, Molly and George
I love you all

Acknowledgements

Actually sitting down and writing a book is a solitary occupation. However, like most authors, I have a lot of people to thank for encouraging and supporting me through the process.

So, thank you to the wonderful RNA (Romantic Novelists' Association) who believe that what we do is important, as well as fun. Without the robust guidance offered by its New Writers' Scheme, my first book would never have been accepted by my publisher Crooked Cat. Especial thanks must go to Jules Wake who not only critiqued my first book, *Love in La La Land*, but also offered helpful ideas on this second novel, *Love, Lies and Café au Lait*.

Thank you also to The Birmingham Chapter of the RNA who are always there with fun, friendship and many snippets of advice, as is my small local group of authors led by Morton S Gray. I am deeply indebted to her and the other vibrant writers, especially Janice Preston, Alison May, Georgia Hill, Liz Hanbury and Lisa Hill for their reassurance through the inevitable self-doubting times.

My gratitude also to my editor Maureen Vincent-Northam and to June Davis for her eagle-eyed diligence. Heartfelt thanks to my publishers, Laurence and Stephanie Patterson at Crooked Cat. The warm sense of community they foster amongst their writers is exceptional.

Thank you to all those friends who have supported me, and, having read my first book, still cheered me on to write my second …and third and ….

All my love to my warm, loving family who are always there with encouragement, understanding and support.

Above all, my thanks must go to my long-suffering husband, David, who has patiently read and re-read all my books, and is always ready with faith in whatever I do….and a welcome cup of tea.

I suppose I should also thank the city of Nice. It was there in a real café that, like Annie, I had a moment of sheer bliss, an epiphany that became the inspiration for this novel.

About the Author

Lynn went to live in Accrington when she was 11 and still has the accent to prove it. She now lives in Worcestershire where it doesn't rain as much.

Like most authors, she wrote stories from an early age and continued this fascination with words and people, by studying English and Psychology at University. Later, as a lecturer at the local College, she enjoyed teaching and transmitting this love of words to students of all ages. Perhaps she succeeded a little as, in 2007, she was presented with a national award as an Outstanding Teaching and Learning Practitioner at a glittering Star Awards ceremony in London. A very proud moment.

However, this demanding career, together with bringing up two sons, left little time for her to write down all the ideas whirling in her head.

She escaped and in 2015 she joined the wonderful RNA and now writes in a room with a view.

Love, Lies and Café au Lait

Chapter One

'So does that mean you've got four weeks before you become redundant?' Sophie asked, as she tapped her empty glass.

'Yup. Oh, Sophie what am I going to do?' Annie was trying in vain to open a new bottle of wine. If ever she needed to drown her sorrows, it was now. Sophie, watching her struggles with the corkscrew, came to her rescue with a sigh.

'Give it 'ere.'

Surrendering the bottle to her friend's far more experienced hands, Annie pleaded, 'So…any ideas, Soph?'

Annie flung herself back into her chair as Sophie topped up their glasses. She knew if anyone could come up with ideas, it would be her best friend. Taking a hefty gulp of wine, she sat back and waited expectantly.

The soft September sunset was glowing off the surrounding rooftops. Through the open windows the distant drone of traffic came humming up to her third floor flat like the deep, lazy hum of bees. On the sofa, Sophie, her long legs tucked elegantly beneath her, was idly twirling a lock of her tawny blonde hair as she pondered the problem.

Glancing down at her old M&S jeans and baggy navy T-shirt, Annie inwardly sighed in envy. Sophie's jeans were moulded to her legs and her silky white top exuded class.

Annie still marvelled at the transformation. Since entering the world of work, her scatty school friend had shown a single-minded determination. She had vowed never

3

to be poor again, to travel widely and to find a rich husband before she was 30.

She had done all three.

Although not sure whether to be amazed, appalled or intimidated, Annie was trusting her friend's single-minded focus would help solve her impending jobless predicament.

Sophie fixed her hazel-green eyes on Annie. 'Look, what job would you really like, if you could? I'm not sure you ever were your typical librarian.'

'Oh, don't start that again.' Annie could do without that familiar argument. 'As I've said before, there're a limited number of things you can do with an English degree.'

'True. But it's not just the job I object to. It's what it's done to you. Where's your sparkle gone? You were so much fun at Uni. Think of the social life we had. All those parties. We never stopped laughing...and so many friends.' Sophie sighed nostalgically. 'Do you remember that night we pulled Hamish and Mac?'

Annie blushed, 'It was a great night. They were so lovely. Especially Hamish.'

'Yes, poor lad, he didn't know what hit him. You were on top form that night. I'll never forget how funny and flirtatious you were.'

'Hey, you were on full wattage as well, don't forget.'

'True. We were a great team weren't we? That's the Annie I remember so vividly. You saw him, you fancied him and he didn't stand a chance.'

'Well, it wasn't quite like that, not really.'

'Annie, admit it. You were a real Flirty Gertie back then. You dazzled 'em. I don't think you realised just how...well... magnetic you were. And now look at you. From dazzling to dull in eight short years.'

Annie flinched. That hurt.

'Sorry, Annie love, perhaps that was a bit brutal. But surely you miss the buzz? You must miss all that fun?'

'Yes, of course I miss it. But what choice did I have? Suddenly life got serious and I had to grow up.'

'I know you felt your mum needed you. But so did

Hamish. You two were so good together. She never did know what you'd given up, did she?'

Annie kept her head down so her friend wouldn't see the pain in her eyes. 'Aberdeen was a long way away and Hamish had just got a good job so he couldn't really move down here. It just wasn't practical.'

'But the last thing your mum would have expected, or wanted, was for you to sacrifice your life for her.'

Annie tried to keep the emotion out of her voice. She really didn't want to talk about this again. 'I know. But once I found out about her illness, I just had to go back to Accrington, didn't I?'

'Yes, of course. Sorry, Annie. I'm a horrible person. I wouldn't have done it for my mum, but then she's not as great as yours.' Sophie's tone was bitter as she topped up their glasses before continuing, 'Look, I know you've had a shitty time over the past year so maybe losing your job is a blessing in disguise.'

Annie choked. Even for upbeat Sophie, this was going some. But her friend was in full flow. 'You need time off, need to treat yourself. You need to rediscover the fun you.' Her face lit up with inspiration. 'I know. You could go on a gap year.'

'What?'

'Why not?'

'You're mad. Where would I go? And what on earth would I do for money?'

'Well, you've got your redundancy pay.'

'That pittance.'

'And you could rent out this flat for a year. This area of Manchester is becoming quite desirable. That would cover the mortgage and the bills.' Sophie was warming to her theme. 'Lots of people get jobs when they are away and I've heard the living is dead cheap in India.'

'India!' Annie gasped. 'In that heat. With my colouring. Red hair and freckles are not meant for—'

'OK. OK. Perhaps not India but...'

'You can stop right there, Sophie. I'm way too old for a

gap year.'

'Well, perhaps you are upper end…'

'I'm thirty next April.'

'All the more reason to do it now. A sort of last fling before middle age sets in.'

'Thirty is not middle age.' This was exasperating. Although she might be too old for a gap year, she wasn't *old* old.

'But the boring way you live now, it could very well be. You have definite stick-in-the-mud tendencies.'

'I have not'.

'Yes, you have. Get out there, get a life, get yourself a fella. The ones you've had since Hamish haven't been up to much.'

Although Annie was used to Sophie pulling no punches, she could still be shocked by her bluntness. 'OK, Miss Hot Lips Sophie Saunders. I know they might not have been up to your luscious lover standards, but they've all been perfectly decent…'

'Decent. Oh my god, save me from *decent* blokes. You need a good dose of *indecency* before you are old and grey. Remember Hamish. You need to rediscover all that passion. Lots of steamy, headboard-banging bonking would do you the world of good. You need to live a bit.' Sophie gave a salacious grin.

'There speaks someone who has lived a lot.'

'Oh yes…and loved every sex-filled minute of it.'

'Luckily Philip doesn't know the half of it,' Annie commented quietly.

'Thank goodness. But I'm going to settle down and be a good girl from now on. Honest.' Sophie did a scout's honour sign. 'Anyway, no time for passion now, I'm saving all my energies for the wedding planning.'

Annie rolled her eyes to the ceiling. Boy was Sophie planning. For the first time, the prospect of going away somewhere seemed attractive. For how much longer could she feign the excited interest expected from her role as chief bridesmaid.

'Another top up?' she asked, 'and help yourself to nibbles.' She gestured at the crisps and stuff she had managed to pick up at the corner shop on her way home from work. Knowing Sophie was coming, she had arranged them in little fancy dishes hoping they might look more sophisticated and more tempting.

Sophie wrinkled her nose in refusal. 'Not worth the calories, darling.' With a gleam in her eye, she pondered, 'OK, maybe a gap year is a bit too much, especially at your age.' She grinned as some pretzels winged past her ear. 'But you could have a break, a sort of mini-gap. Where would you like to go?'

Annie knew instantly.

And so did Sophie. 'France, of course. I should have guessed. I still can't believe you've never been.'

'I know. I tried to get Mum to go during her last years but she always came up with an excuse: too far to drive, too much money, hated flying, hated trains. In the end I realised she preferred to live in France in her imagination rather than visit the real place again.'

Sophie nodded. 'Do you remember that time when we couldn't go on the school French trip because our mums couldn't afford it?'

'Yes, and so she did us that French weekend at home.'

Sophie's eyes were dreamy. 'She taught us how to make cheese soufflés, and Tarte Tatin...'

'Which you said was just an upside down apple pie.'

'She was most affronted, wasn't she? 'It's not. It's a Tarte Tatin', she insisted. And we listened to all those French records and wafted around saying 'Ooo la la' and speaking everything in a sort of 'Allo Allo' French accent.'

'Yes, and when we asked her what the French was for something, she made up these Franglais expressions like *'il pleut des chats et des chiens '* for 'raining cats and dogs.'

Sophie convulsed, 'Oh yes. And let's *frapper la route* for 'hit the road' as we set off somewhere. I actually believed some of them. When I used them at Uni, they all laughed at me. But it was a wonderful weekend.' She sighed, misty-eyed. 'As you know, it was then that I decided to learn French properly. Get a job using it, travel there. That weekend changed my life.'

Too full of emotion to speak, Annie nodded.

'Your mum was always so glamorous,' Sophie continued. 'I'll never forget her standing at the school gate with her long, dark Juliet Greco hair…'

'Dyed as you know. She was really mousey blonde.'

'I know that now. But back then she was so dramatic in her big sunglasses and floppy straw hat in summer, and red beret and red lipstick in the winter. And always smoking those Gauloises cigarettes.'

'Hateful things,' Annie said bitterly. 'I'm convinced they are what killed her. You know, even when she knew she'd got cancer, she still wouldn't give them up. 'If I haven't got long, I may as well enjoy it while I can.' Even at the end, in the hospice…' She choked at the memory.

'I know, Annie love. There was nothing you could do. She was one hell of a strong character. I'm sure she would love it if you went to live in France for real…if only for a short while?'

'I must admit I'm tempted to see what it's really like, having heard so much from Mum for all those years.'

'Although be prepared. Your mum's version of France was pretty dodgy… as was her French.'

'You mean it's not all…'

'Garlic and Gauloises,' they said, laughing in unison.

Annie grinned, 'Yes, I had gathered that.'

'So where would you go, do you think?'

'Silly question.'

'Of course. Nice. Where else?' Sophie groaned. 'Although you do know going there would be a wild goose chase, don't you?'

'Yes. I know.'

'OK.' Sophie sighed, 'I suppose if you go, at least it will get it out of your system. And the jobs will still be here when you get back…or not. In fact, if you improve your French, I could perhaps get you a job in my company. It's a thought isn't it?'

Annie wasn't listening. She was lost in a vision of the long promenade in Nice, lined with palm trees as seen on a faded postcard. Of tall old buildings in faded ochre climbing up a hill with a pencilled arrow pointing to narrow alleyways and hidden squares.

Then reality crashed in.

'This is stupid. No way is Nice remotely possible. The south of France is supposed to be awfully expensive. I couldn't afford to stay there for even a few days, let alone live there. What a silly idea.'

It was Sophie's turn to have a faraway look in her eyes.

'Come on, Sophie, what are you thinking?'

'Nothing, nothing.'

But she clearly was. And would be drawn no further.

Chapter Two

'It's all sorted,' Sophie announced, waving a bottle of Fizz.

Annie wasn't really in the mood for dramatics after a fraught day at work. In theory, as someone who was being made redundant, she should have little work to do, but bloody Brian had been off again with some spurious stomach bug, which tended to coincide with Aintree race days. Normally she loved her job at the university library, but simmering resentment had spoiled any pleasure as she rushed around, single-handedly sorting the whole reference section.

The last thing she needed was an excited Sophie on her door step.

'OK, come in. What's sorted, Sophie?'

But no details were forthcoming till the bottle was popped open and glasses were frothily filled.

'Here's to your trip.' Sophie clinked glasses.

'Look, Sophie, it's just not possible. I've thought about it, I really have but...'

'Oh ye of little faith. You should know me by now.'

'True. But not even you could conjure up a cheap trip to Nice and—'

'Well, I have, so there.'

Annie drew a deep breath. Then waited. Not for the first time, she was uncertain whether she was going to like one of Sophie's plans.

'OK.' Sophie took a long swig of her prosecco and a deep breath. 'I've got a French cousin by marriage who lives in Nice, a bit ancient I think. I'm supposed to have met her when I went there as a kid, but I can't for the life of me remember what she looks like. Anyway, she is looking for a member of the family to live in her flat and look after her little dog. It's a Chihuahua, I think. She's off for the winter, going south somewhere…um…possibly South Africa to visit her sister…or friend.'

Sophie paused for effect. 'Anyway, I've told her you will do it.'

'Wait a minute. Do what?'

Sophie looked exasperated 'I've just told you. Live in her flat and look after her dog.'

'For the whole winter?'

'Yes. Like I said, while she goes away. Six months. End of September to March, I think.' Sophie looked as if she was waiting for applause, or at least an outpouring of gratitude.

Annie just kept opening her mouth like a goldfish.

Clearly a little annoyed at this lack of appreciation, Sophie patiently spelled it out further. 'She only trusts members of the family with all her precious objects, and, of course, her soppy old dog, so I've told her you are a cousin of my dad's and how responsible you are, and how much you love dogs and how good your French is…'

All Annie could do was gasp at these blatant fabrications.

'And it's all sorted. You leave in a fortnight.'

'What? What? What?' Annie at last found her voice as she realised the finality of the arrangement. All decided without one iota of consultation.

Sophie had moved on. 'But first you have got to look the part for a classy place like Nice. And look the part of one of my dad's posh relations. We will have to go shopping.'

'Never mind the clothes, Sophie. What about speaking French and telling me more about—'

'But you'll have to go on a crash diet. The French like their women wafer thin.'

'Sophie,' Annie protested, aghast at the imminence and apparent finality of the plan. 'I can't just up and leave my flat in a fortnight. And what about the finances? I will need a job.'

'Yes, what you need is a capsule wardrobe,' mused Sophie, who hadn't heard a word Annie had said.

'Stop. I can't give up work just like that.'

11

'Course you can,' said Sophie airily. 'You are going to need all the time you can get at the gym to hone up your body. And you've got to get on with your grooming regime.'

'Grooming regime?'

'Not to mention practising your French,' Sophie added ominously. 'I'm just steeling myself to iron out the vagaries of your Accrington French to resemble something that would be comprehensible in the sophisticated circles of the Côte d'Azur.'

Annie was just trying to find a way of stopping the Sophie steamroller before it went too far. 'But I've got to serve at least another month at the library.'

'Oh no, you haven't. You said how uncomfortable the atmosphere is there and how they are working you too hard. If you are sodding redundant, then let them realise how sodding much you do. I can't believe you didn't just flounce out the day they told you. I would have.'

'I can't leave them in the lurch.'

'You aren't, you stupid woman. *They* are the ones who have left *you* in the lurch.'

'It's not really their fault. It's only because I'm the last one in, so with all the cutbacks, I'm the first one out.'

'I know, you've told me. Yes, and I know, if you had still been festering away in Accy library, this wouldn't have happened. So, in a way this is all my fault. I was the one who wrenched you away from your dull comfort zone.'

'It wasn't—'

'Don't you dare tell me it wasn't dull,' Sophie said fiercely.

Annie said nothing. Perhaps her friend was feeling guilty after all.

'I had to do it, Annie. I had to do it for you. I couldn't bear to see you mouldering your life away.'

There were tears in her eyes. This was the real Sophie peeking through. Beneath the fierce ambition was her true friend. A friend who had dropped everything last year when, after a long fight against cancer, Annie's mum had died.

Numbed by grief, Annie hadn't known which way to

12

turn. Although expected for so long, her mum's death had still hit her hard. Sophie had been there, offering comfort and hard-headed practical support. She had also seized the opportunity to prise her grieving friend away from all that was cosy and familiar. Unable to think clearly, Annie had taken the line of least resistance. She had given in and sold her mum's terraced house, her childhood home.

'Don't look back; look forward,' had been Sophie's relentless mantra.

Which is how, six months later, Annie had found herself living a new life, a more vibrant life, and one she was beginning to enjoy. She had used the money from the sale of her mum's house to get a small flat with a manageable mortgage in the middle of Manchester. New friends and a new job at the university library had given her a buzz and stimulation sadly lacking in her old life.

She hugged her friend. 'Thank you, Sophie. Please don't feel guilty. You were right. And I do love this new life. I hadn't realised how much I was missing. I owe you…'

'No you don't.' Sophie pulled away from the hug, fierce again. 'I owe *you,* Annie. I owe you for rescuing me from those dreadful school bullies and befriending me when no one would talk to the new posh kid. You were the only bright light in my life back then. You and your mum. You made me laugh and I began to think that maybe I could survive the crap after all.'

'No, Sophie, honestly I didn't do anything, I just—'

'Shut up and listen to me,' Sophie's intensity silenced any more protests. Her tawny eyes were still full of tears. 'For once in your life let someone do something for *you.* You are the only person in my life who has never let me down. I have sorted this trip to Nice and you *are* going.'

They sat holding hands for a long moment while Sophie recovered her composure.

'So you *are* finishing at work whether they like it or not. If they don't, you'll just have to go off sick.'

'But I've never had a day's sickness yet.'

'Hmmn, but you could rick your back carrying heavy

books, couldn't you?' Sophie eyed her significantly over the rim of her glass. 'Anyway, serves them right. Keeping on that deadbeat Brian and letting you go.'

Annie felt a stirring of rebellion. Brian's smug grin *was* beginning to infuriate her.

Sod it. Perhaps she would go. Then they would see who did all the work.

Go to Nice. The thought played around her head before bumping into the reality of her common sense.

'But hang on. OK, that's the accommodation sorted but what will I live on?'

'Told you. Rent out this flat. I've already mentioned it at work and I've got a couple of takers.'

'What!'

Sophie had the good grace to look abashed. 'Well, you can't let the grass grow. It's a nice couple. You can trust them. They know it's only for six months but they want to live in this area while they suss out somewhere to buy.'

This was going too far, too fast. Sophie was steam-rollering her again. Annie grasped at anything to slow her down.

'But hang on. You need me. I'm your chief bridesmaid. You need me to help with your wedding planning and… stuff.'

Her protests were met with a loud laugh.

'Annie darling, I love you, you know that, and you know I wouldn't have anyone else as my chief bridesmaid. But you're absolute rubbish at it.'

'I'm not. I've looked at all those table decorations, all those um…favour whatsits…all those colour scheme pieces of material thingies.'

'Swatches. They are called *swatches*.' Sophie's tone was not patient.

'Yes, them. And all those wedding dress designs…and… and chair back bows…'

'As I said, you are rubbish. You try, I'll give you that, but you glaze over within ten seconds. You have no taste or discernment, you just like *everything.*'

Annie had to admit she did.

'Then of course you just keep gasping at how much everything costs.'

'No bloomin wonder. Come on, Sophie, four thousand pounds for a measly red...'

'Burgundy...it was burgundy...how many times...not red. *Burgundy.*' Sophie's voice had risen by several octaves.

Chastened, Annie thought it wise to change the subject. She tried another tack.

'Anyway I can't go and just look after a dog for six months. What will I do all day?'

'Um, well...' Sophie had calmed down but had the grace to look embarrassed.

'Oh no. Don't tell me. You've got that sorted as well.'

'Come on, Annie love. It's my job to sort stuff. Believe me, this is nothing to what I have to do every day for sodding Adam.'

Sophie's high-flying job as PA to an arrogant, demanding boss, Adam Jarvis, meant she worked long unpredictable hours, juggled with multiple time zones, jetted off around the world at a moment's notice and, despite the odd moan, she clearly thrived on the pressure. She also made no secret of the fact that she loved the high salary and lavish lifestyle.

With a sigh of satisfaction, she launched into yet another aspect of her masterplan.

'Right. Ages ago, Adam told me he'd found his granny's diaries in the attic and he always reckoned they would make a great book. She was a bit of a racy character, a flapper in the twenties; she mixed with a very louche set. Her handwriting is tiny and he's tried to decipher it and has just given up. Anyway he has often talked about getting them typed up. It would have to be by someone trustworthy as some of the stuff could be confidential. I think he suspects his dad was really the son of some Lord or other...'

'Wait...what are you saying?'

'So I said I knew someone who could do it...for a hefty fee, of course.'

'Sophie!'

'Well, why not you? You could sit there in the sun...take your laptop, type it up onto floppy discs. Post them back to him at regular intervals... Money for old rope.'

Annie was about to protest when Sophie said nonchalantly, 'And of course, while you are there, you could keep an eye out for your French dad.'

That's what clinched it.

She was going to Nice.

Chapter Three

Annie looked at her watch then scanned the bustling Manchester crowd again, looking for Sophie. She was definitely not looking forward to this day's shopping trip. Her heart sank even further as she saw Sophie approach with outstretched arms and a wide grin. She could tell by her greeting that her friend was in one of her *Ab Fab* moods.

'Annie, Darling. Mwah mwah.'

From the gleam in her eye, Annie knew this was going to be a long day. Sophie's stamina when it came to shopping was phenomenal.

'Right, let's hit the town. I've been giving a lot of thought to your capsule wardrobe. You've got to live for six months from one suitcase, but it can be done if you've got the right combination of outfits. I know just the clothes and colour schemes you need. And where to get them.'

Annie quailed. This had happened before and it had never been that easy. Her friend's taste was miles away from her own. As was her spending power.

Her fears were confirmed immediately.

'What we are looking for is the right combination of silk tops and cashmere jumpers. Perfect to take you through the Rivera autumn and winter.'

'Sophie, there's no way I can afford—'

'Nonsense. Don't give me that look. I know what I'm doing, so just do as you are told.'

'Yes, Miss Bossy Boots.'

Sophie grinned. 'You haven't called me that in ages. You may as well give in now, you know.'

Annie grimaced. It was true. So she trailed after her friend in mute compliance.

However, after what seemed like hours of trying on different clothes, Annie mutinied.

'I'm not looking at any more bloody beige.'

'And which of these garments would you describe as *beige?*' asked Sophie, a steely glint in her eye.

Annie wilted a little. 'Well...I suppose some of them are more sort of brown.'

'That one's *taupe*, that's *caramel* and this *brown* one,' she uttered the word with exaggerated distaste, 'is in fact *marron.*'

Annie looked blank.

'OK, chestnut to you. You really must get a more sophisticated colour vocabulary if you are going to France.' She sighed in exasperation.

'Sophie, can't I have blue? You've always said I look good in blue. I don't mind what sort of blue, sky blue, pale blue...um, royal blue... um...' Annie was running out of shades of blue without mentioning her favourite, the one that Sophie derided the most, 'a very nice navy'.

'I thought we were going shopping for blue. I like blue,' she finished lamely.

'In autumn! You can't wear pale blues in autumn.' Sophie's shock was palpable.

Annie's rebellion died in the face of her friend's obvious horror.

'Look, Annie love, forget blue. You have got to play to your strengths.'

'Which are?'

Sophie had always said her blue eyes were her main asset, which is why she had made blue the staple colour in her wardrobe ever since their first shopping spree as they prepared for Uni ten years ago.

'It's your colouring. Your hair will be so unusual in France. Lots of French woman try to do auburn but yours is so obviously the genuine article it will be your...um...U.S.P.'

'What?'

'Unique Selling Point.'

Annie wasn't too keen on the selling angle.

'These *browns* as you call them,' Sophie indicated a rack of silk blouses, 'coupled with a sprinkling of the right sage green...such a difficult colour for anyone else...will really look classy. Mmm...it's a pity your skin isn't paler. That really would be dramatic. Pale skin, red hair, blue eyes. Wow, you really will stand out amongst the Mediterraneans. Yes, ideally, pale skin would finish the look, but you do have freckles...and a regrettable tendency to blush...'

Annie blushed.

'So I think we will go for a light fake tan. Should blend in your freckles a bit.'

She looked at Annie with an expert eye and draped an ivory silk blouse against her friend's face.

'Look, Sophie. I appreciate what you're saying but I don't feel comfortable in pale colours. I like to be unobtrusive.'

'You are not wearing bloody black again. Or 'very nice navy' either.'

Annie opened her mouth to protest. Then shut it, feeling ungrateful.

She had to admit Sophie always looked good. In her role as PA to an alpha male boss, she looked classy, assured and took no nonsense from him, or anyone else.

'Just trust me will you?' She was growing impatient. 'In fact, you *can* have some other colours as well as bloody beige...I've decided you definitely need some pink.'

'Pink? But...' Annie tried for one last time. These clothes were going to cost a fortune and she would have liked some say in the matter.

'Umm...definitely some pink,' grinned Sophie. 'After all you know what they say about it.'

Annie didn't. So Sophie gleefully enlightened her.

'Pink is called the old maid's last chance.'

'What?'

'Because everyone looks good in pink, even old spinsters.'

'You cheeky bugger. I'm not an old maid.'

'You will be if you don't get a move on,' Sophie warned.

Annie gave up. Reluctantly, she went to try on another load of pale, expensive garments selected by Sophie. Including a pink silk scarf. As she surveyed her image quietly in the mirror away from her friend's badgering, she began to tune in to this new look. Yes, she had to admit she did look surprisingly good in some of the outfits. More sophisticated perhaps.

By the end of the morning, with compromises on both sides, a capsule wardrobe was purchased. The cost of it all put paid to her redundancy money and a chunk of her savings.

As they retired thankfully to a nearby wine bar for a much needed drink and shoes-off session, Sophie glowed with satisfaction.

'You've got a classy wardrobe now which will attract classy blokes.'

'I'm not sure classy is what I'm looking for.'

Sophie was shocked. 'Don't be silly. You can't beat a bit of money, class and old fashioned courtesy.'

'Hmmn. What about a sense of humour, rugged good looks and the bonking ability of a bull?' Annie countered, grinning.

'Look', Sophie sighed, 'it's a fallacy that women want a bit of rough. It's OK when you're young and still exploring. But you are nearly thirty. What we are talking about now is husband material, and that is totally different from shagging skills.'

Annie was about to protest.

'Look, I should know,' Sophie continued sadly. 'Jean-Pierre was fantastic in bed, gorgeous, charming, and perfect in every way, except one. The most important one; he just wasn't faithful. Yes, it broke my heart to walk away. But at least he only broke it once. If I'd stayed with him, I'd have ended up like my mum – bitter, twisted, divorced and penniless.'

She stirred her coffee and glanced at her expensive engagement ring.

'I know Philip isn't going to set the world, or even my

bed, on fire. But he's good and kind and reliable.' A guilty grin crossed her face. 'It helps that he's also wealthy with a large, rambling, ancestral home in the best part of Cheshire which has the most important feature of all...a pony paddock.'

Annie laughed, but she knew the history behind that apparent throwaway line. When Sophie's philandering father broke up with her mum, they had to move out of her spacious home to live with her gran in a small house in Accrington. He was clever enough to hide his income and assets, so the divorce settlement eventually bought just a small terraced house, two streets away from Annie's. The whole experience was traumatic for Sophie. But it was the loss of her beloved pony, Starlight, that seemed to cut the deepest. Seeing Sophie's terrified bewilderment when she arrived at a tough comprehensive after her posh, private school, all Annie's protective instincts had kicked in and she befriended her instantly.

Now, twenty years later, although very different in every way, the friendship bond was still as close. She gazed at her friend fondly, knowing her apparent confidence and toughness hid deep fears and insecurities.

Hence the safe choice of Philip, her wealthy, somewhat staid, fiancé.

'Right, now for the underwear.' Sophie, revitalised by the lunch and wine, gathered together their posh garment bags.

'What?' squealed Annie, very aware of just how much all this had cost, and totally unprepared for a further clothing tussle.

'Look, if you are after a man you have got to have decent underwear.'

'You mean indecent,' giggled Annie.

'Precisely,' Sophie agreed. 'You cannot shag a Frenchman in Marks and Spencer drawers.'

'I wasn't aware one of my aims in going to Nice was to shag a Frenchman.'

'It is and you will,' asserted Sophie. 'You'll be like catnip to…er…cats. Now, I know just the place for some very sexy furbelows. Follow me.'

'Yes, Miss,' grinned Annie, meekly. It was just easier to go with the flow. She had learned to save her resistance for the things that really mattered. Besides, she could see how much Sophie was enjoying this. And if she was really honest, so was she.

'Out! Now!' Sophie commanded. 'Come on, show me what they look like.'

Annie cowered. She couldn't emerge from the silk festooned changing room dressed, or rather undressed, like this.

'Now!' Sophie's voice brooked no opposition.

Annie reluctantly drew back the curtain in her cerise lacy balcony bra and silky matching knicks.

'Wow! You look terrific. That is soo sexy. Why on earth haven't you been flaunting that for years? I can't believe you have wasted all that luscious body hiding it under baggy librarian jumpers. Remember, it's all heading south soon, so make the most of it now.'

'Thanks, Sophie, for once again hinting I'm nearly past it.'

'No, not exactly past it,' Sophie said with a grin before adding briskly, 'but you will never look as good again. Those undies will get those Frenchmen salivating all over you.'

'Ugh, not an image I want in my head, Soph.'

'Well, you know what I mean. You've got to accentuate your gorgeous curves.'

'Can't I rely on my natural alloouer?'

'Your what?'

'My alloouer.'

'What's a loouer?'

'You know…the French for sex appeal, attraction… um…'

'Oh my god. You mean *allure*.'

'That's what I said…alloouer.'

Sophie looked horrified. 'I give up. All those French

tapes you've been listening to, all those talking exercises I've given you, and you *still* speak with the most atrocious English accent...actually, it's not even English, its Accrington.'

'Just 'cos you now speak posh, Our Sophie. You used to speak dead common like me.'

Sophie gave a mock shudder. 'Darling, I never spoke as common as you.'

True. She had tried to blend into school life by rapidly acquiring a strong Lancashire accent but had shed it just as fast once she left.

Sophie paused and gave Annie an appraising look.

'Seriously, Annie, looking like that you should never again fear you have no alloouer. God help me, but your pronunciation of alloouer does have a sort of come-hitherness about it. Oh sod it, whatever it is, you've got it in spades.'

She turned to the matronly saleswoman who was watching the interaction between them with benign amusement.

'She's having two sets of those. Yes, those two colours. And two of those she tried on earlier. Put them on my account.'

Annie began to protest.

Sophie waved a hand. 'My treat. Just a little going away present.'

Annie rushed to thank her with a hug.

'We'll have none of that, thank you. Not while you are wearing these skimpy nothings. What will people think?' laughed Sophie.

'Actually, I would have thought it would be every man's fantasy,' winked Annie.

Chapter Four

'Two days to D-day. Departure day.' Sophie clinked their celebratory champagne glasses.

They were having their last girls' night in before the launch of the new and improved Annie onto the unsuspecting inhabitants of Nice.

Sophie had arrived with some of her expensive Italian handbags to complement Annie's new outfits, and a variety of designer scarves to add a splash of classy colour.

Annie stood in front of the mirror trying on each silky soft scarf in turn. 'These are gorgeous. But you shouldn't have. You really are too good to me.'

Sophie was having none of it.

'I pick up these scarves at every airport I go to. Shopping is how you pass the time, and don't forget I get some of it on expenses anyway. Have to look the part, you know. Talking of which, as a supposed relation of my dad's you have got to *look* classy, even if you don't sound it.'

'I actually thought my French was improving.'

'Stop fishing for compliments you ain't going to get,' Sophie said flatly. 'Right, your place is let from next week and the money will go into your account every month so should give you some spare after it has covered the mortgage and bills.'

She then opened a faded, paisley-patterned canvas bag. 'Here are Adam's granny's diaries. There are ten of them as you can see.'

Annie took the battered leather notebooks and peered inside the first one. She had been curious to see what they would be like.

'Oh crikey, Sophie, have you seen this writing? It's tiny.

I'm never going to be able to decipher this.'

'Yes, you will,' said Sophie airily. 'I couldn't at first, but I can now pick out the odd word or two.'

'Odd word or two! If I'm going to transcribe these, I need more than the odd word or two.'

'You'll soon sort it out. And it might make interesting reading. Adam's a bit of an arrogant swine, as you know. Apparently his Grandma Nina was always hinting at some big secret in her diaries. I think he's hoping to find some scandalous connections to royalty, or at least the aristocracy. As you know, you are sworn to secrecy about what you find.'

Annie nodded, mainly worried about deciphering the tiny scrawls.

'Anyway, I've told him how difficult the work will be so managed to screw him down to a good price so it should help with your living costs.'

It was a surprisingly generous amount. Annie often wondered just how legit Sophie's boss was and whether she had got something on him.

'Now about your French...'

Annie sighed. She had been extensively coached by Sophie over the past weeks and felt her schoolgirl French had been revitalised. A view not totally shared by her teacher.

'Your understanding is quite good and you've got a good latent vocabulary. But your verb tenses are rocky. And your accent...' Sophie sighed, 'well...it is so...well... unashamedly Lancashire. I give up. I just hope they understand you.'

Annie hung her head in shame. Her two main sources of French were her mum and her French teacher and both were Accrington born and bred.

'They might find it endearing, I suppose,' Sophie said, looking doubtful. 'So you must practise it all the time. That's the only way to get good at it. Don't get sucked into the English ex-pat community out there. You must act as if you really *are* French so pretend you are *at all times*, even if people talk to you in English. I expect you to be fluent when you get back and I'll be cross if you're not. Do you

25

understand?'

'Yes, Miss.'

'Don't come the simpering idiot with me.' Sophie tried to hide her grin. Then became serious. 'Come on, Annie, don't let me down. This really is a golden opportunity for you to shake off your Accrington shackles and emerge as a new you.'

'Yes, I know and I really am grateful.'

'I don't want your gratitude. I want you to enjoy it and come back as the fun-loving old Annie I used to know. Oh, and try to find a fella, will you? A classy fella. All those clothes and underwear, please don't waste them.'

Annie grinned and was tempted to give her usual 'Yes, Miss' response whenever Sophie got dictatorial. But she could see her friend was really sincere.

'OK. I'll honestly do the best I can…at least on the French front. I promise I will speak French from the moment my foot hits French soil. By the time I return I will have so much savoir faire you won't know me.'

Sophie suddenly looked worried. 'You will be careful out there, won't you?'

'Yes, of course.'

'What I mean is…well, you are bit unworldly, you know.'

'I'm not.'

'Yes, you are. I know you have read all those books and think you know the world through their pages, but real life is not like that.'

'I know…'

'No, you don't. You are a romantic at heart; you believe the best in people all the time. You are too nice, you know. I wonder if you are just too nice for Nice.'

Annie spluttered, 'Too nice for Nice?'

Sophie laughed. 'OK. Just try not to look like an innocent abroad. It can attract the wrong sort of bloke and…'

Annie hugged her friend. 'Don't worry about me. I'll be fine.'

'I hope so. I'm travelling all over the place, as you know, so phoning might not get me. But email me. Let me know you've got there safely and what it's like and stuff.'

'I will, Soph.'

'And, Annie love, I know you are holding out a hope of finding Fabien, but really, it's a needle in the haystack. You know that, don't you?'

'Yes, I do. And will you stop worrying about me.'

'OK. Just concentrate on going somewhere your mum never got to go. Enjoy it for yourself as well as her.'

Both a bit emotional, they raised their glasses.

'Here's to Mum and France,' Annie said and Sophie clinked her glass, echoing her toast.

'Anyway, my work is done.' Sophie cleared her throat as she seemed to survey her handiwork with satisfaction. 'At least you now look the part. You have a new stylish wardrobe and hairstyle. You are expensively shod, dressed, groomed, manicured and spray tanned. If you act as sophisticated as you look, you should be OK.'

Annie gave her friend a reassuring grin, hoping to hide just how much the prospect excited and daunted her in equal measure.

She would be all on her own in a foreign country. All winter. She couldn't return to England, not even for Christmas and birth of the new century, the millennium no less. She must stay, come what may, to look after a dog she'd never met. What a responsibility!

But the idea of acting French excited her. Could she create a new vibrant personality, someone not weighed down by all the drudgery and responsibility of the last few years? Sophie was right. Going to Nice was a unique opportunity. Despite what she had said to Sophie, she really had high hopes of discovering Fabien and then learning if he really was her father.

Could she really be half-French?

Chapter Five

Internet Café, Nice. October 1 1999

Chère Sophie

Well I've arrived. As you can see, I am not writing in bloomin French. Too much to tell and, if my spoken accent makes you wince, my written French will make you weep. But just to show willing I will intersperse French bon mots wherever the opportunity arises. OK, I know I will enjoy doing it more than you will enjoy reading it, but what the heck...or tant pis as I believe the locals would say.

Found an Internet Cafe at last and the usual slightly nerdy twelve-year-old to show me the ropes. First of all, thank you, thank you, for sorting this wonderful opportunity. Whether I find my French dad or not, it's still a fantastic way to start my new life, the new me. New century, new me...well, that's the plan.

It's a cliché but where do I start? I suppose, as I'm in France, you are going to get impressions... (Geddit?)

Well, my alloouer was obviously on full wattage and I got chatted up on the plane by a very nice, rather distinguished, older man. He gave me his card and offered to take me out for dinner. I said Ta. No intention of going, but it did a girl's ego no end of good to be propositioned like that by a man of obvious taste and discernment. Proves the makeover has worked, doesn't it?

Don't snort.

Little did he know that the moment my foot touched French soil, with a Wonder Woman twirl, I would be transformed from a diffident English rose to, tarraaa...Franglais Woman...a subtle and alluring blend of

28

English charm and French sophistication, mixing savoir faire with Northern grit and unable to utter a single word of English till she once again boards the plane for home.

At least that's what I have promised myself, and you, and I intend to keep my word. It's just the charm, sophistication, and savoir faire bit that is going to be difficult.

To start with, can you believe it was raining as I landed in Nice!! Not quite an Accrington deluge because it was warmer than the Lancashire stair-rods we know so well, but, nevertheless, it was a substantial downpour. Not at all what I was expecting from the Côte d'Azur, so I hadn't got my brolly handy.

Also, as I came in on the bus from the airport, I couldn't really see much of Nice through the steamy windows, but what I saw, to be honest, didn't look that great. I got off at the designated stop but it took me a while to find Madame Dumont's building. When I finally found it, I discovered it was a lovely iced cake of a building, fin de siècle, tall, white, and elegant with small round balconies and just one street back from the swanky Promenade des Anglais, just as you said it would be.

Trouble was, I was soaked and felt like the proverbial drowned rat. Really fed up, as I wanted to make such an elegant impression on your second-aunt-in-law-twice-removed, (sorry, Sophie, but you know I have trouble working out her exact relationship to you). I announced my arrival on the intercom and thought I'd have chance to straighten myself out before I got to her door. But oh, ma chère amie, as I heaved my suitcase up two long flights of stairs, red-faced, puffing and panting and dripping and cursing, she was waiting for me at the top of the stairs.

Her look spoke volumes. I don't know what you told her about me but I was very obviously **not** what she expected.

She, on the other hand, was exactly as you described: petite and immaculate. Dark hair elegantly pulled back in a French pleat (what else!) and yes, I noted the shoes as instructed, Sophie, classic brown leather (crocodile??) with kitten heels, and totally unscuffed...in fact the exact opposite *to mine.*

Anyway, whatever the French is for something the cat dragged in, that's how I felt at that moment. All your careful grooming and training oooomph out the window (long... French...with shutters).

You know how your French pen-friend, Marie, can make you feel so uncomfortable with that cool appraising stare as she scrutinises you head to foot, well, I have to say that ain't nothing compared to what I got. Laser eyes!

Still, give her credit, I wasn't exactly at my best and she did actually let me in to her hall to drip on her rug (Afghan, with a silk fringe).

She invited me to avail myself of her bathroom (roll-top bath in the centre of room, gold ornate taps, beautiful smelly soap and white fluffy towels) to tidy up, which I did as best I could before being ushered in to her lounge.

Wow. I know you haven't ever been in her apartment, but I can tell you the room itself is beautiful: large, a high ceiling with decorative mouldings, wonderful chandelier in the middle, two long French windows leading to small wrought-iron balconies, patterned Turkish rugs all over the marble floors.

But it is stuffed...and I mean stuffed...to the gunnels with...stuff. This I could see in spite of the pervading gloom of a rainy afternoon and the fact that the only illumination was provided by small pools of dim light cast by dotted ornate table lamps swathed in pinkish scarves or gauze. (A fire hazard?)

Sophie, I can't convey to you the rising panic with which I peered at every surface in the room. All the cabinets and the little occasional tables had loads of carefully arranged, mainly china, objects on them. Up north we would call them knick-knacks; I suppose the French would call it bric-à-brac. But Sophie, oh Sophie, she soon made clear to me they were her collection of Limoges!!!!!!! and Sevres porcelain!!!!!!!!!

Eeeeeeeeeeeeeeeek.

I froze. I knew if I moved I would knock something priceless over and I could see from her face she was thinking bull...china shop (taureau......magasin de porcelaine).

I sat down tentatively and soddenly on the edge of her chaise longue (what else!) while she went apprehensively to make me a cup of coffee.

All this time she had been clutching her Shiatsu!!!! (Not a Chihuahua as you told me. Not that it makes much difference). She put him/her down as she went out of the room and to be fair he/she didn't yap too much at me, although there was no way I was risking my fingers for a stroke.

The coffee arrived, of course on a silver tray in small delicate cups...with saucers! I can't remember the last time I negotiated a saucer. Even you, in your best Hyacinth Bucket mode, have never risked giving me a saucer. Sophie, I have never felt so large and clumsy.

Anyway, she had clearly decided what can't be cured must be endured, and began firing off a load of instructions about the flat, the dog, everything. It was a haze of rapid French... Vet's phone number & address...sheets...laundry / Monday / dog food / tablets / walks / heating / key / concierge. Strictly no external phone use unless it's an emergency. And overnight visitors definitely forbidden, said with meaningful look.

I murmured something about offering to do the cleaning. She was aghast at the prospect and I was relieved to find that the concierge would continue cleaning the place twice a week.

Either she doesn't trust me to do it properly or she doesn't trust me at all, and she wants the concierge to keep an eye on me. And I've found out since that this concierge, of course, has a key...and snoops. She's called Madame Lafarge, large lady with an ample, undivided bosom, forbidding face, suspicious eyes, and monosyllabic utterances. I think her last job was sitting knitting by a guillotine. She also has a dog (the invisible, never-walked variety) which she has obviously taught to bark every time anyone leaves or enters the building.

Your aunt-in-law is clearly besotted by her little aged

Shiatsu and was worried about my ability to take proper care of her. Yes, the bow in the topknot should have given it away; it's a her, called Pimpernel. She's getting on a bit so strict instructions about her diet, her evacuational habits and precisely how many kilometres she has to be walked each day.

(I've called her Pimpy ever since and she now recognises her name...and my accent...and walks are invariably longer than those specified...so you **can** teach old dogs new tricks.)

I reassured Madame and made friends with Pimpy who is, in fact, very sweet-natured and not half as neurotic as her owner. She has turned out to be good company, snoozes noisily every afternoon and I find myself practising my French on her. She understands every word I say. Honest.

Anyway the rest of the first evening was a bit of a blur of rapid French with me clinging to the odd familiar word and fighting down a rising tide of panic and trying to read some dimly seen instructions she'd prepared for me. She doesn't seem to use the chandelier and all the little lamps are so delicately swathed in pink and lilac silk scarves that the whole room is perpetually, if flatteringly, shadowy.

I have since taken off most of the drapery, if only so I can see not to knock things over. But in fact when unveiled, it's not much better. The bulbs inside are about the wattage I thought hitherto only available to seaside landladies.

I'm sure the concierge, nosy Madame Lafarge, is scandalised by the sacrileges I immediately wrought in the apartment but my nerves couldn't cope with all that china in the pinky gloom. I carefully put away the most obviously fragile stuff and have since noticed that even she is gradually tidying away a lot of the Limoges into cupboards, which obviously makes her cleaning job a lot easier and suits me down to the ground. One of my first purchases is going to be a reading lamp for the main room and the bedroom, as you simply can't see to read in the evenings or to decipher those bloomin diaries.

Anyway to return to my first night. After a frugal salady meal followed by some very smelly cheeses, Madame said to *my mystification, I must help her with the 'click clack'. This turns out to be a sort of Put U Up bed. As it's only a one bedroomed apartment there was nowhere else for it but a tiny space in the corner of the main lounge. How I didn't knock into something as I sorted the bedding, is a miracle.*

But I decided that night...both literally and metaphorically...I've made my bed so I've got to lie in it. But it was an uncomfortable and sleepless first night in Nice.

I thought, this is another fine mess you've got me into, Sophie.

Madame Dumont's taxi arrived early next morning. With a swish of perfume, extravagant kisses to Pimpy and a perturbed glance at my rumpled sleepy self in the corner, she was elegantly gone.

Fret not, my flower, since then all is well. More than well, in fact, bloomin ecstatic.

I set off with Pimpy later that morning to explore Nice under bright cloudless skies.

And kapow! Sophie, as I approached the seafront, the intense blue of the sea took my breath away. I just stood and stared. It really was the Baie des Anges, the Bay of Angels.

I had one of my epiphanies.

I know you laugh when I call them that, but some moments are so special, so mind-blowingly overwhelming, they make me gasp. All my senses tingled in delight. The long elegant curve of the white buildings round the bay, the sea so blue with sun sparkles glittering as far as the eye could see, the warm wind on my face, the slow dragging sounds of the waves pulling back the pebbles and the drifting smells of brine and garlic and other strange indefinable scents...so very French, I could almost taste it. And the awareness that I am here, experiencing this and will be living in this beautiful place for the next six months. Unbelievable. I just laughed out loud.

People moved away.

Sorry to let you down and that super cool image you tried so hard to foster in me.

Confession time. Not long after, I had another one. Yup,

another ecstatic moment, another epiphany. You don't have one for ages, then blow me, two come at once.

After a long morning of wandering aimlessly in heightened delight at everything I saw, I noticed a café in the corner of the market place in the sunshine. Someone was just leaving a table at the back, so, very bravely, I decided to go for a coffee. Feeling a bit conspicuous, I picked up Pimpy so that they would think I was French, and boldly grabbed the table. It was the perfect vantage-point to see everyone busying themselves in the market and I got so absorbed I didn't see the waiter at first. So I was a bit flustered when I ordered my coffee, in perfect French of course, 'Café au lait, s'il vous plait' and he gave me the most amazing smile. Our eyes met and...no, I'm not going all mushy but I really did feel a connection. Went a bit hot all over. Anyway when he brought my coffee, it had a plate of hot, sugary, crunchy sort of eggy fried bread with it. It was delicious...and free.

Sitting there in the sunshine with the sights and sounds of the market, crunching this bread, sipping real French coffee, Sophie, yup, you've guessed it, another epiphany.

Everything just felt so right somehow; I felt my shoulders relax. I realised I'd had a funny fluttery feeling in my stomach for weeks...half excitement...half full-blown fear of the unknown. Suddenly it was gone. I had an overwhelming feeling of contentment, a feeling of all's well with the world. I was starting to live.

I think I must have been grinning like an idiot, because my gorgeous waiter caught my eye and he grinned back. He seemed to know what I was feeling. And that somehow made me feel I belonged there.

Perhaps I am half French after all.

Thank you, Sophie – whatever happens from now on, it was worth it for those special moments. I felt another me was emerging. The me I could be. Don't know who she is yet but...

Merci, merci, merci.

Mwah Mwah

Moi

Chapter Six

Annie paused. How much would Sophie really want to know about how she was settling down, what she had seen. There had only been a brief reply to her last two emails. Just how interested would her much-travelled friend be in her descriptions of Nice? Outside the dingy internet café, the sun was streaming on to a gleaming cavalcade of cars. Pimpy was snoozing in her shopping basket at the side of the grubby, coffee-ringed computer desk.

But she simply had to tell someone about the whirlwind of sights and sounds of her first days in France. So she began yet another email to Sophie.

Internet Café

Chère amie
I forgot to ask last time (shows how caught up I was) how are the wedding plans? Has Philip come round to the full morning coat and cravat ensemble? Can't see it myself, but I know all too well your powers of persuasion, don't I? How else would I have landed up here, not knowing a soul, for six whole months, even missing Christmas and the whole millennium stuff at home?

Still, you'll be pleased to hear it's not taken long for me to settle in...almost in a rut now (she said with a nonchalant Gallic shrug of her scarf-bedecked shoulders). At first I had to jouer à l'oreille (play it by ear...our old favourite Franglais phrase, but in case you had forgotten). But now I have a wonderful routine, which I suppose I have imposed on myself, almost as a security blanket because, in spite of my little epiphany in the café, I did feel very vulnerable and rootless at the beginning.

*But if it turns out I **am** half French...just saying it makes me feel peculiar...then I must get used to this way of life. I still don't feel in any way French, but I suppose it's early days. At the moment I'm just trying to absorb the atmosphere before I start any real searching for my possible father.*

However, I do keep an eye out for the name Fabien on office plaques and shop signs and have composed a list of locations where I've spotted them. Quite what I do with them, I have yet to work out. But baby steps with the whole thing at the moment. A bit daunted to tell the truth.

Anyway I suppose its old hat (ancien chapeau) to you but I have to say I love the setting of Nice. Love the beautiful, white, elegantly proportioned buildings lining the long expansive curve of the Promenade. And what a Promenade. So wide. Love it. But something I hadn't expected was the extent of the traffic along the front, three lanes either way creates so much noise. I thought romantically it was the sea I could hear all night. It was, of course, the cars.

As instructed, I found the flower market. Wonderful. You were right, so very different from English markets and a world away from Manchester. The smells, cheeses, piles of colourful fruit, strange bunches of floppy green veg, offally meat products and a stall with a formidable woman slicing up crazy portions of a large flat round pancakey thing to give to a queue of locals. The sign said 'World Famous Original Socca'. It was delivered by a man on a noisy scooter with a round metal pan on the back. Looks fattening, but I will try it another day when I dare to speak a bit more French.

Quite a few English voices, all seem quite loud and confident and definitely with long southern vowels, not a short 'a' to be heard. Mainly more mature persons of classy demeanour. Good job I promised you I would only speak French as I'm sure a touch of Lancashire English would have them reaching for their sneers faster than you could say Accrington Stanley.

Any road up, I walk Pimpy every morning along the Promenade des Anglais which is often windy and blustery but

36

always sunny and, so far, warm.

I love the Promenade for the people and conveyance watching. I am trying to count how many different combinations of wheeled contraptions I have seen. There are always cyclists, some with children on their backs, in harnesses, in tandem bikes or towed in buggies. Then, of course, loads of skateboarders, then roller skaters or swish bladers, some being towed by dogs, some even towing young children behind them. There are always some sleek Yummy Mummies roller blading along pushing a baby in a buggy. Then there are some weird stand-up bike things with two big wheels and a handlebar they steer with, called Segways I think. They are inevitably ridden/driven by super-posey blokes who pretend to be unaware of the fascinated speculation they leave in their wake.

Sophie, you should see them. All these means of transport share one thing in common, no matter what the age of the user, they are all slim, tanned, fit, confident and use their conveyances with accustomed ease. They weave in and out of the mere walkers with grace and style. I've never seen anyone practising uncertainly. Are they born knowing how to use them?

As I am walking miles every day (so much further than mere kilometres), I bought a sort of wheeled shopping basket for Pimpy at the market so I don't have to carry her. She wasn't sure at first but then took to it comme un canard sur l'eau (duck to water...tee hee) and now loves it and peeks out of the top in quite an endearing fashion. But I have never quite managed the bow in her hair properly and she can look a little deranged at times. Tant pis. I get a few smiles round the market but, from what I've seen, there's a long tradition of eccentrics down here so I don't even figure on the scale. And I keep kidding myself they will think I'm French anyway.

No spluttering, Sophie! It's not ladylike.

The old town is a maze of streets. First time I got lost. But I love it as I weave amongst the outdoor displays of ornate plates and crockery or designer clothes-racks selling leather coats or cream linen dresses. And there are café tables

37

crammed into every available corner with menus offering all manner of offal and the testicles of every known ruminant on the planet.

I have to negotiate paths also blocked at intervals by racks of bright blue and yellow tablecloths. I know with your impeccable taste, you would think it terribly kitsch, but I'm a sucker for popping in to browse round these Provencal shops with their colourful linen and tableware and fake crickets chirping in the doorways.

And what about the pasta shops. I had no idea pasta could come in so many shapes and stuffed with so many different things. I am determined to try them all.

Every now and again as you emerge from a packed little street, you find yourself in a small square dominated by a church, and tall faded ochre buildings with dilapidated shutters. Very Italian somehow.

And then there're the smells: lavender, coffee and always, but always, the pervasive wafts of garlic-soaked cooking. And I smelt a Gauloises this morning. So many memories of Mum it made me cry.

I'm not getting sentimental, but I do feel Mum is watching over me.

Gotta go. Not done to cry in these places. Will write again soon.

Love to hear from you.

Oodles of love,

Annie

Chapter Seven

'Oh, look, Our Pimpy, it's bloomin raining. Huh, I didn't come here for rain. I can get that at home. So I suppose you'll have to wear one of your little coats. Now let's see, which one do you fancy...this rather classy green tartan one? Or what about this cheerful little number in red. Oops, or is it burgundy, as Aunty Sophie would call it?'

Annie sighed. How she longed for a good old chat with Sophie. But she wasn't allowed to phone her from the apartment and in spite of constant hinting emails, Sophie hadn't phoned her.

'So, my little *chien*, I'm stuck here on my bloomin own talking to you. In theory, I should be talking, even to you, in flaming French, but I've got fed up with it and decided today's an English day. You understand me, don't you?'

Indeed, Pimpy cocked her tufted head to one side and eyed her quizzically as if listening to her every word.

'Let's find your lead. I wonder what exciting adventures we are going to have today.' She sighed. 'Oh sod it. We'll not go far. Let's face it, been there, seen it, done it. All the museums, art galleries, train rides along the coast, all wonderful, but fed up of doing it on my own. There's not an inch of the old town left unexplored so we're not going there in the rain. I suppose it's back to the bloomin market for more bloomin cheap veg...or should we try yet another bloomin pasta shape. Be still my beating heart.

'Talking of beating hearts, we will have to call in and see Jacques, won't we?'

She stopped fussing over Pimpy for a minute to think about her dishy waiter. Tingling all over, she remembered so clearly his grin when he obviously noticed her epiphany moment in the café. She knew now from overhearing people, his name was Jacques. Was it her imagination, but he always seemed particularly pleased to see her? If he was not too busy, and the grumpy Patron wasn't looking, he would stop and have a bit of a chat. The wonderful thing was she could understand his French really well, and he certainly had no problems with hers, unlike some of the market traders.

Confiding in Pimpy as she tied on the dog's little tartan coat, she realised the prospect of seeing Jacques had made her insides flutter a little.

'He is rather dishy, isn't he, Pimpy? I confess I find him very sexy and rather fanciable. Is it that tight white apron round his waist, emphasising that pert bum? Or those broad shoulders. He really has a wonderful physique. And the way he holds up his tray on those long strong fingers…'

She realised she was blushing. This wouldn't do at all.

'What will Aunty Sophie think? I know she said I must get myself a fella, but she definitely wouldn't approve of me fancying a waiter. But then again, between you and me, Pimpy, she is a bit of a snob.'

She giggled guiltily.

'The person she *would* approve of is my distinguished older gent, Monsieur Xavier. Obviously quite wealthy and very polite. It was lovely getting to know him and I have you to thank for that, Pimps, my little moppet. He really makes a fuss of you, doesn't he? And we have a nice chat, unless he's with one of his very glamorous daughters. I think they are a bit snooty so he doesn't talk to me if they are there.'

She paused to ponder for a moment before squatting down to confide in the attentive little dog.

'Listen here, Our Pimpy, I have a cunning plan. He's the right generation and, once I pluck up courage, I intend to enlist his help. He just might know a fifty-year-old bloke called Fabien who went to the Sorbonne in Paris in nineteen sixty-nine and knew a girl called Grace Makepeace. As Aunt Sophie said, it's a long shot, but well worth a try.'

Just as she picked up her brolly, a flash of sunshine came lancing through the window. Looking at the sky, she saw the rain had stopped, leaving the pavements gleaming in the late autumn brightness, so she began to divest Pimpy of her tartan coat.

'You won't need this now the sun's come out. Do you know, I actually think that rain made me feel a bit homesick? Huh. Here I am, living on the bloomin French Riviera and I'm really longing to be back in Lancashire. That's it,' she said with laugh, 'I really have gone mad, talking to a dog and longing for rain.'

Shaking her head, she went to change her raincoat for her swish jacket and carefully selected a matching silk scarf. Picking up Pimpy's lead she grinned.

'Come on. Let's see if Monsieur Xavier is there. At least chatting to him is good for my French. And Jacques' smile is good for my…well, is just good for me. But I really must try not to blush.'

On arrival at the café for her morning coffee, she was disappointed to see that Monsieur Xavier was with one of his highly-perfumed, raven-haired daughters, so she only got a discreet nod of acknowledgment. Jacques was busy. Although she still got a special smile and a nice plate of hot, crunchy bread, there was no chat.

Crestfallen, she trudged back to the apartment and as the weather had become overcast again, she decided to continue her work on Adam's granny's diaries.

After a while she stretched and yawned. 'Crikey, Pimpy, this writing is doing me head in.' Bending over the tiny scribbles in the black notebook, she informed the dozing dog. 'I'm earning every flipping penny here.'

But the entries were fascinating. What a life this Nina had led. Full of liaisons and flirtations with…well, who? Everyone had a nickname or just initials. If Sophie's boss had hoped to find links with the rich and famous, then a lot more digging would have to be done to decipher quite whom his grandmother had slept with.

As she tapped away on her laptop, Pimpy suddenly lifted her head and Annie too became aware of voices and the

41

clippy-cloppy sounds of high-heeled mules on the marble floor upstairs. Although she couldn't hear what was being said by the occasional boomy male voice and the frequent chattery female one, from the cadence and tone she knew it was English.

'Listen to that then, our Pimpy. Does that sound like English to you? Bit close for comfort. Eh. Got to remember my promise to Aunty Sophie, no speaka da English till I get home. Apart from to you of course.' Annie scrubbled the top of Pimpy's head and she gave a little bark of happiness.

For the rest of the afternoon, both she and Pimpy were very aware of the clippy-cloppy sounds going back and forth up and down the stairs outside. Pimpy was very intrigued by the frequent yapping of a small dog and went to the front door and replied with small woofs of her own.

'Now don't get excited, Pimps. That's an English dog and you wouldn't understand him. Although of course you do understand me, don't you?' Pimpy always knew from her intonation when she was being asked a question and cocked her head to one side in a most endearing fashion.

The little dog really was a lovely, loving companion. Walking her every day was an enjoyable excursion. Annie never ceased to be surprised by the number of people who would stop and pet Pimpy, especially other dog owners. As a result she had acquired a whole new doggy vocabulary and a few acquaintances. In the evening she would curl up with Pimpy and watch fast-talking TV programmes in an attempt to improve her French. When her brain could no longer cope with the torrent of alien words, she would find guilty solace in reading dog-eared English novels bought from a tatty second hand book shop she had found down a side street.

Next day, with a cool wind blowing, Annie abandoned a planned excursion to Monaco on the train and did a routine trip to the market for food. Unsure of how her finances would stretch, she was having to eke out her money. Food shopping was expensive and so she existed mainly on the wonderful vegetables from the market. She frequented one stall in particular and could now chat easily with the stall holders, but it was always about food and cooking. Not wanting to be typically English, she always avoided talking about the weather, which was getting colder. These simple exchanges, while pleasant, were no substitute for the proper conversations she craved.

She desperately wanted to chat with Monsieur Xavier so she could broach the subject of her search for Fabien. He was about the right age and certainly seemed to know everyone. Although he always got an effusive welcome from the café Patron, she noticed Jacques was just stiffly polite. Curtailing her saunter round the market, she set out to watch for Monsieur Xavier's arrival at the cafe. It would be best if he were there first so he could beckon her to his table, rather than looking a bit forward by inviting him to hers.

To her increasing disappointment, there was no sign of him. Eventually she could loiter no longer and when her usual table became free she sat down facing the market so she could see him arrive. When she enquired of Jacques if he had seen Monsieur Xavier lately he was strangely unforthcoming. All she got was a very sexy Gallic shrug and, of course, her plate of hot, fresh, sugary bread, which she now knew was called pain perdu, lost bread. Jacques had explained earlier that it was stale bread dipped in beaten egg then fried in butter and sprinkled with sugar.

Thoroughly disappointed, she returned disconsolately to her apartment. As before, her afternoon diary session was punctuated by clip-clopping sounds from upstairs…but this time, no voices.

Chapter Eight

Monsieur Xavier didn't show the next day either. And when she asked if Jacques had seen him recently, there was a surprised look and very curt 'Non.' And no helping of pain perdu either. She had come to look forward to the generous helpings, usually served by Jacques with a conspiratorial wink when the stern-faced Patron wasn't looking. But not today for some reason.

Crestfallen, she entered her apartment building and was too preoccupied to be aware of a presence at the top of the stairs.

A tell-tale tapping sound made her look up. She recognised the source of the clip-cloppings immediately. They were gold, high-heeled mules attached to darkly-tanned, red nail-varnished feet. Annie's eyes were drawn upwards to the animal-patterned, cropped leggings and a skin-tight, gold, strappy top showing heavily gold-bangled scrawny brown arms. Mrs Clippy-Cloppy was a petite peroxide blonde of over fifty, heavily made up and smelling of heady perfume with a pervasive undertone of cigarette smoke. But she had bright friendly eyes and a warm smile. She wasn't wearing a coat so Annie had the distinct impression of an ambush. Clearly she had been watching Annie come and go and was lying in wait for her.

'Ooh allo,' said this figure in mock surprise. Her accent reminded Annie of 'EastEnders'. 'Is this your flat? Thought so. I'm your new neighbour upstairs.'

In a flash, Annie realised she was trapped. Her wonderful bubble of Frenchness was about to be burst and she did so want to carry on pretending. Panicking, she found herself responding in heavily accented English.

'Aaah bonjour, Madame. 'Ow do you do.'

'Oh.' The brown eyes widened in surprise at Annie's accent. 'You don't look...I mean, I didn't realise you were French. Can you speak much English?'

'*Comme ci, comme ça*,' mumbled Annie, desperately.

The woman just looked puzzled.

Oh no. This was going to be harder than she thought. So she conceded, 'Oui...a leetle.'

'Oh good. Let me introduce myself. I'm Reen.'

Consternation. What could she say? Annie was such an obviously English name.

'Um...I am called Marie-Ann.'

'So pleased to meet you, Dahling.' Reen beamed. 'What a relief you speak some English and can understand me. I'm no good at speaking anything foreign at all. I can manage a bit of Spanish you know, ordering in a bar, that sort of thing, but nothing more. So have you lived here long?'

Annie realised she was in for a friendly but determined interrogation so in halting English, and in an accent which owed a lot to Inspector Clouseau and a bit to 'Allo Allo', she explained she was looking after the flat and *chien*-sitting for an aunt who had gone away for the winter to South Africa.

In return, Reen told her that she and her husband, Ted, were refugees from the Costa del Sol, forced to flee while their villa was being renovated.

'We're having a new terrace with a jacuzzi attached to our pool outside. Then inside, all new en-suites...you know with one of them sunken whirlpool baths. So, while we were at it, we decided to have the whole thing done over by one of these interior decorator fellas. He's quite camp and Ted's not too sure of him, but he's done a lovely design.

'Trouble is, it's going to take a while and the place will be mess...which I can't be doing with. And all the builders' dust, it ain't good for my lungs. Cough me guts up I do. But I'm sure it'll look dead classy in the end. You know, like one of them places you see in the magazines in the hairdressers.'

Yes, thought Annie, I can just imagine it.

'Anyway,' Reen continued, resolutely blocking Annie's

way into the apartment, 'we've had to move out while it's being done up, so a friend of a friend offered us this flat upstairs here. It was empty for the winter, so he said we could have it till we got sorted. Very posh isn't it?'

In spite of this evident poshness, Reen's tone implied she was uncertain whether this had been such a good idea after all.

'We could have gone back to stay with the family in England but it's a bit difficult with our little Pugsy, you know.' She indicated her little pug dog waiting at the top of the stairs. 'And anyway I can't stand the English winters no more, not with me chest, an all.'

Her throaty smoker's voice gave evidence of compromised lungs. With a lurch, Annie was reminded of her mum.

Reen was obviously enjoying the chat, albeit a bit one way, and continued as if still justifying the wisdom of the move to Nice to herself. 'We could have stayed with friends on the Costa, but it's always a bit dodgy staying with friends, especially when you don't know how long for. I'd hate to impose on anyone. Anyway I've always fancied seeing the French Riviera so here we are. Though I thought it would be warmer than this. I've been frozen since I came.'

I'm not surprised, thought Annie, eyeing Reen's golden strappy top and her bare be-muled feet. Definitely the wrong clothes for a winter in Nice. In fact wrong in every way for a classy place like Nice.

But she warmed to the bright eyes and chatty openness of the talker and realised she was enjoying listening to colloquial English. Reen bent down to make a fuss of Pimpy and introduced them both to her pug dog, Pugsy, who had descended the stairs and had been circling the group uncertainly for a while. The two little dogs sniffed each other with interest and Reen squatted down to utter warm endearments to the waggy pair.

Annie saw her escape route to the apartment door open before her and was just about to start edging towards it, when Reen straightened and smiled. 'Would you like to come up for a cuppa?'

In spite of herself, Annie was jolted. Somehow the very Englishness of the word 'cuppa' made her homesick with longing for a cosy chat over a mug of tea. Suddenly coffee seemed an alien drink.

She almost succumbed…but knew she would have to turn down the invitation, no matter how tempting. What possessed her to deny she was English? How stupid. An increasing feeling of guilt crept over her at deceiving such an open-natured person as Reen and she certainly didn't trust herself to keep up her French pretence for any length of time.

Besides, would a real French person have understood the invitation?

Flustered, she refused, 'Alas, Madame Reen, I must visit un ami…how you say…a friend.' She scooped up Pimpy and muttering something about getting her 'diner' she let herself into the apartment, leaving Reen looking a little hurt and disappointed.

'Bloody stupid,' Annie said to herself, closing the door on Reen's crestfallen face. How could she be so silly sticking to an idiotic idea to live as a French person? And now she had started the French charade, she was trapped. How could she suddenly become English without making an utter fool of herself?

What a mess.

But then, she rationalised that Reen was hardly her sort of person and they would have nothing in common. Annie had heard all about the Costa del Crime and she fantasised that Reen with her obvious East End accent might even be a gangster's moll.

But she still felt mean.

Bugger. Bugger. Bugger.

Nothing was going right. She was lonely, and the only person who had extended the hand of friendship, she had churlishly turned down.

Chapter Nine

'Is that Reen going out?'

Pimpy cocked her ear at the door, mimicking Annie's behaviour.

'Yup, there go the clattering mule sounds. Crikes, Pimpy, I don't know what we'd do if she ever reverted to trainers,' Annie whispered, feeling huge pangs of guilt.

'This is so silly isn't it, especially after you and Pugsy got on so well, but I really must avoid Reen if I can. Sooo embarrassing that encounter. How on earth can I let on I'm not French now? What a bloomin mess. I haven't heard a male voice for a bit now so I assume Mr Reen has gone to rob a bank to pay for the renovations to the villa, or to see his underworld pals in jail.'

Dashing over to the window, she watched the slim, shiny, Reen-shaped silhouette disappear round the corner.

'Right, we can leave now. Where's your lead. But we'd better keep an eye out. Let's see if Monsieur Xavier has turned up this morning. It's strange he hasn't shown up now for a couple of days.'

As she was doing her morning shopping in the market, Annie again kept an eye on the café. Still no sign of Monsieur Xavier. As Jacques had been distinctly cool the last time she was there, she couldn't face her usual coffee. She trudged home for an early lunch in a despondent mood, with her rejection of Reen preying on her mind.

The weather had also taken a turn for the worse. The skies were still a brilliant blue but there was a bitingly cold wind, which seemed to penetrate even the warmest clothes. The famous mistral wind, Annie thought. She had heard about it. Legend had it that it could drive folks to murder by its insidious freezing infiltration of every nook and cranny.

Plodding home in the bitter wind, just in front of her, she saw the slight frame of Reen emerging from the brightly-lit casino. The frail figure hunched her shoulders against the cold and clutched her thin, shiny jacket tightly around her. She then hoisted a little dog up in her arms and turned dejectedly, clip clopping her way in the direction of her apartment.

The loneliness of this figure tugged at Annie's heart. Impulsively she scooped up Pimpy and rushed after her. Before she really thought about it she had greeted Reen with a cheerful, 'Bonjour, Madame.'

The delighted look on Reen's perma-tanned face told her she was right; Reen, too, was feeling lonely and dejected.

'Oooh bonjour, Dahling. Lovely to see you. How are you? Isn't it cold? My fingers are frozen. Here, have a feel.' And with that she put her icy little fingers up to Annie's cheek.

With the endearing homeliness of the gesture, Annie lost all her intended formality. It reminded her of her grandma who also always felt the cold. And always had cold hands, but a warm heart.

Annie bent her head to listen as, all the way home, Reen talked non-stop, giving full vent to her pent-up loneliness.

Of course there was no way Annie was going to get out of an invitation to a share a 'cuppa'. As they climbed the stairs to her apartment, Reen turned to her and confided in a lowered voice, looking around in case she was overheard, 'You know, Dahling, you are the nicest French person I have met here. And even though I say this as shouldn't…cos it's speaking against my own…all the English people here aren't very nice either. Everyone I've tried to talk to has been really snooty.'

To hide her sharp spasm of guilt, Annie asked, 'Ow is this 'ere 'snooty'?'

'Bless your heart, Babe…you know…well, sort of snobby. Toffee-nosed.'

'*Ah, oui. Je comprends*'. Annie hid a smile, thinking of a

real French person trying to make sense of that explanation.

Reen's borrowed apartment was a minimalist dream, stark white walls, sparse gleaming chrome tables and a few muted beige soft furnishings.

Annie could see Reen hated it.

It had obviously driven her to venture out to the casino for warmth and colour. There were not even any rugs on the pale, marble floor. No wonder Annie could hear the clip-cloppings from below; they reverberated off these bare walls. Annie gave an involuntary shiver and for the first time thought fondly of the overstuffed cosiness of her flat downstairs.

Reen was watching Annie's reaction.

'Yes, Dahling. It's a bit bare, ain't it? Not my style at all, but,' she continued in an effort to be fair, 'I expect it's lovely and cool in the summer.'

She shrugged off her little shiny jacket. 'Anyway, how's about a cuppa to warm us up. Oh, and let the pooches get to know one another a bit better.'

And so Reen fussed around her and made her feel welcome and fed her, (and the dogs), chocolate digestives with her tea.

'They're a real English delicacy you know. My eldest son always brings us a load of these proper biscuits when he comes to visit.'

Annie was discovering that Reen was a self-chatting person and not a lot was demanded of her in the way of response other than a '*oui*' or '*non*' or an exclamation or two. This assuaged her anxiety about her French subterfuge and she began to really relax and enjoy the tea and company.

Reen nattered on about her family and her husband, Ted, who had gone back to Spain to sort out a problem with the builders.

'He phones me all the time. He's 'aving a right old game with it all. I'm beginning to wish we never bothered. 'Ere, I'll get you a picture of it.'

And she was gone into the bedroom returning with several framed photographs.

'This is my Ted outside our villa.'

The photo showed a good-humoured, heavily-built man, brown face, open red shirt, hairy chest, smiling proudly outside ornate gold wrought-iron gates leading to a large, whitewashed house subtly named Tedreen Villa.

'See…it's named after us…you know, our names joined together…geddit?'

Annie couldn't trust herself to speak, so she just nodded.

'And these are my boys,' said Reen, proudly showing Annie a much-thumbed photo from her handbag of three tousled-haired, bright-eyed boys grinning at the camera. 'That's Tyrone, that's Tarquin and that's my youngest, Troy.'

Annie gulped at the names. 'Tyrone, Tarquin and Troy?' she repeated forgetting her accent in her amazement.

'Yes…we looked in a book for names beginning with 'T'' because we thought it would be nice if they all started with the same letter as my hubby's name, Ted.'

Annie nearly blurted out, 'Ted? Surely that's shortened from Edward, so it should be an E', but refrained, thinking instead of those poor boys going through school with names like those.

'Of course, this was taken when they were much younger…but it's my favourite photo,' said Reen, fondly gazing at the three cheeky faces. Annie, looking at their expressions, caught the sense of bravado that had made the names not only survivable at school, but also probably a source of pride. Those boys could obviously handle their wonderful names. She looked at her new friend and felt like hugging her.

'Look, Dahling, would you like to stay for a bit of lunch? I'm a hopeless cook but I've got some tins of soup I can warm up. I can't find a toaster…but I've managed to find some nice English bread we could have with it.'

Annie knew Reen was desperately trying to prolong their conversation and as she was enjoying the company too, she happily agreed. She was not finding the French deception too hard to maintain as very little was demanded of her apart from the odd acquiescence and lots of nodding and smiling which came naturally to her.

It was tinned cream of tomato soup, which took Annie straight back to her childhood. It was her favourite, so was always a treat after she'd been to the dentists. And it was years since she tasted the spongy cotton wool of a sliced white loaf. She loved it and made many murmurs of appreciation.

Eventually and reluctantly, she took her leave after hearing all about the family scrap metal firm which had funded their present lifestyle, and lots of gossip about people she didn't know from the Costas.

She was descending the stairs after a perfumed hug, when, to her consternation, Reen called after her, 'Tell you what, Babe, let's go out somewhere nice tonight to eat.'

Oh no, Annie thought. Oh Bugger.

It was one thing pretending to be French with just Reen, but quite another amongst real French people, even if it was only waiters. She would be expected to chat, converse and even translate Reen's idiomatic English. The thought made her go cold. How could she be so stupid? Fancy befriending a needy English person. Now she would be revealed as a fraud. It would mean she would have to confess to her new friend and completely humiliate herself.

Reen clearly misinterpreted Annie's look of horror.

'Oh no, Babe. It's my treat; it's on me. You won't have to pay for a thing. It's my way of saying thank you for a lovely natter.'

Annie couldn't have felt guiltier.

Out of desperation, came inspiration.

'*Mais non. C'est* my turn. You must come to me tonight and I weeel cook for you. We weel 'ave, 'ow you say, a dinner and a 'girls' night in'.'

'Oh, I couldn't possibly put you to all that trouble, Dahling.'

'It weeel be my pleasure.'

'Oh, ta very much. It's very good of you but only if I can come and help, although I've told you, I'm not much cop at cooking.'

'OK. Zat is *pas de problème.*'

'Oh, Marie-Anne, Dahling, that would be lovely. And you can show me how to make something French for my Ted when he comes back. He'll be so tickled. That's such a lovely idea. What time do you want me?'

'I weel see you about seven of the clock, *n'est-ce pas*?'

Even to her own ears, Annie's accent was excruciating, but Reen seemed delighted with the plan.

As she regained her apartment, Annie was weak-kneed with the thought of a crisis averted. But not a moment to lose. She left a sleepy Pimpy and hurried out to the market deciding to blow the budget and get whatever food she required.

She realised she was looking forward to the evening. It would be fun to eat with company for a change. But she must remember to be French.

Chapter Ten

On the dot of seven, there was a tap on the door and there was Reen, dressed up to the nines in a silver sequinned top, chunky gold jewellery and gold lamé leggings. She was expertly holding two bottles of wine in one hand, and bottles of gin and tequila in the other. Over her arm was a clinking bag full of various bottles of mixers with a jar of bright red glacé cherries on top.

'Just brought a spot of lubrication. Not sure what your favourite tipple is but I've got vodka and rum and brandy I can fetch from the flat, if that's your poison.'

'Non. Non,' Annie laughed. 'Zat should be more zan enough.'

She loved the way that Reen had no idea how idiomatic her English was…and how incomprehensible she must be to most foreigners.

After Reen had exclaimed with joy at the apartment, which she thought was soo classy and so French, she offered to make tequila slammers while Annie instructed her in the art of making a Tarte Tatin for pudding.

They had a wonderful time. It was true, Reen had no culinary expertise whatsoever, but she was quick to learn and thoroughly enjoyed the girlie closeness of the enterprise.

Muting her French accent somewhat, Annie asked her how she had brought up a family without being able to cook. Reen said where she lived in London they had always been surrounded by various takeaways and cafés. Besides, she had been so busy working alongside her Ted on the family scrap-iron business, it never seemed worth it, flogging over food that was gone in a flash.

'Their gran used to live just round the corner and she

looked after them while I was at the yard. She fed 'em proper food and we always went round to her for a Sunday roast so the kids never suffered. It might have been different if I'd had a daughter...it would have been nice to do things like this together. I suppose your mum taught you to cook?'

Annie suddenly sensed she was going to have difficulty fending off searching questions about her home and family and so diverted Reen's energies into beating the egg whites for the cheese soufflé.

It was a thoroughly enjoyable, and very tipsy, evening. Her guest kept up a steady supply of drinks so they giggled together over silly things and Reen had bawdy fun with the conical shapes of the soufflés in a way that reminded Annie of herself.

As the meal drew to its drunken finale, the up-ending of the Tarte Tatin was executed very carefully by a distinctly unsteady pair of hands. Reen never ceased to marvel at Annie's culinary prowess. And Annie had to admit proudly to herself, it was all delicious.

As the booze flowed, Annie knew her accent fluctuated wildly and at times she was aware that it was a cross between Welsh and German, then Indian and Italian. Towards the end when the second bottle of wine and Reen's tequila slammers really kicked in, she often forgot to have any accent at all, apart from her basic Accrington one.

If Reen noticed she didn't say anything. She was definitely better at holding her drink than Annie. At the end of the evening, Annie was vaguely aware of Reen helping her stagger into the bedroom, and tucking her up in bed.

'God bless, Dahling,' she heard Reen whisper as she quietly let herself out of the apartment.

Next morning it was only a whimpering Pimpy that made Annie raise her throbbing head from the pillow. Oh no, she would have to take her out.

She struggled out of bed, fully clothed, not daring to open the shutters. Looking down at her crumpled clothes she knew she couldn't go out like that, so began hunting round for her old floppy tracksuit to pull on.

Of course. It was in England. Sophie hadn't allowed her to bring anything as tatty as that. She was just cursing vehemently to herself when there was a tapping on the door.

Bugger. Bugger. Bugger.

It would be Madame bloody Lafarge come to clean the sodding apartment. Well, she could bloody well buzz off and take her snoopy little nose…

'Annie, it's me,' said Reen's voice through the door.

Annie tottered to the door and opened it to a perfectly groomed Reen with Pugsy under her arm.

'Thought so.' She grinned as she viewed Annie's unkempt appearance. 'Bless your heart, Babe, you ain't used to the drink are you? My fault. Would you like me to take Pimpy out for you?'

Annie could have hugged her. Instead she staggered to one of Madame's elegant chairs and flopped down as Reen found the lead and, smiling broadly, quietly escorted Pimpy out of the apartment.

Annie got a long drink of water and went back to bed.

Cleaning up the kitchen much later in the day, Annie suddenly froze.

Did Reen call her Annie or Marie-Anne when she knocked on the door?

If only she could remember what was said towards the end of the evening. She knew there had been a real heart-to-heart session, but what it had been about, she hadn't a clue.

At some point Reen had stroked her head, but why and when? No. It was no good, it was all a blur and, in the end, Annie was too bleary to worry about it anymore.

Pimpy was returned to her in the early evening by a still smiling Reen.

'Look, I won't come in, Babe. You need an early night. I just want you to know I haven't enjoyed myself so much in ages. Really. It was so very different from my normal nights out drinking in a bar and stuff. Told my Ted all about it and he said you sound a dahling. I loved all that cooking and our girlie talk. Can't tell you how special it was.'

And to Annie's surprise she leant forward and gave her a big hug and a kiss. Then turned and clip-clopped back up the stairs.

Chapter Eleven

The next day, still racked with uncertainty about what she had revealed to Reen, Annie once again listened for sounds on the stairs so she could time her excursions to avoid meeting her upstairs friend. This was going to be so complicated. She was just going to have to play it by ear and listen to whether Reen called her Annie or Marie-Anne.

But, she realised with a thud, Reen tended to call her Babe or Dahling.

And as she spoke in the same colloquial way to everyone, there would be no clues there.

Well, Annie decided, she would just have to continue the 'French pretence' until something obvious was said. And then she would just have to own up. But she didn't fancy the humiliation of confessing. There was something so open about Reen which made her deception even worse.

'Serves me right for breaking my promise to Auntie Sophie,' she muttered to Pimpy, who looked longingly up the stairs for her canine companion.

She would just have to put off meeting Reen for as long as possible. Fancy coming all this way to France and bonding with a perma-tanned refugee from the Costa del Sol. Shame really, because she liked the vulnerable and obviously soft-hearted Reen.

Bugger. Bugger. Bugger.

As she approached the market a polite, 'Bonjour, Mademoiselle,' made her look around.

Monsieur Xavier was just about to enter one of the posh restaurants along the Promenade des Anglais.

'Oh, Bonjour Monsieur Xavier.' Annie was delighted to see him again as he was always so courteous to her and made such a fuss of Pimpy.

'You are going to the market, perhaps.'

'Oh yes, I must buy something for my lunch. Are you well? I haven't seen you for a while at the café.'

'No, it is a little chilly to sit outside even for me. When that mistral blows all sane people go inside. In fact I am just about to go in and have a drink before lunch. Perhaps you would care to join me.'

'Oh, that's very kind, Monsieur, but...'

'No, please, Mademoiselle, be my guest. It is more pleasant to share with someone and I find your company most agreeable.'

Annie felt herself go pink with pleasure. How could she refuse such a gracious invitation?

'Can I bring Pimpy in with me?'

'But of course. We French are very civilised about our dogs. I know you English are supposed to be nation of dog lovers, but, in fact, we French own more dogs per head of population...so we accommodate them better.'

Annie sighed. She had always spoken French to Monsieur Xavier but he had apparently sussed her out. 'So you know I'm English then.'

Monsieur Xavier laughed. 'But of course, Mademoiselle. You are delightfully English in so many ways.'

It was said with such a twinkle in his eye, Annie felt herself blush again.

The waiters clearly knew Monsieur Xavier well, and guided them to an elegant small table at the back of the restaurant.

'What would you like to drink, my dear?' asked Monsieur Xavier in impeccable English.

'Oh no, please can we continue to speak in French. I sort of promised my friend I would keep practising.'

'But of course. You have a charming accent. Your friend is here in Nice?'

'No, no. Sophie's in England, but she speaks fluent French and she thinks my accent is atrocious.'

'I can assure you it's definitely fascinating. Now, I'm

having Ricard. Would you like one too, or perhaps a Kir Royale.'

'Is a Ricard the aniseed one with water?'

'Yes, have you tried it before?'

'Well, I've sipped a friend's at a party once. So yes, I would like to try one if that's OK.'

'But of course.'

Monsieur Xavier turned to give his order.

Close up, he wasn't as old as perhaps she originally thought. Although his hair was greying at the temples, he had attractive smiling lines around his intelligent eyes. He was immaculately dressed and had well-manicured hands. Definitely he had been very handsome in his youth and was still good looking. Very French, Annie thought. Very distinguished.

'Allow me,' he said as the drinks arrived. He poured some iced water from a small pitcher into her clear drink, which became a cloudy, caramel colour. He then added two small ice cubes from a dish. The smell was definitely aniseed. It tasted quite strong but was teasingly warming as she sipped it.

A tray of olives and small tapenade appetisers had appeared. Monsieur Xavier gestured for her to help herself then settled back in his seat.

Obviously intrigued by what she was doing in Nice, he proceeded to politely delve into her reasons for being there. He seemed quite interested in why she was on her own. So she told him about her dog sitting and a bit about herself. She found the need to talk impelled her to more fluency than she thought she possessed. The Ricard also seemed to help. Before long Monsieur Xavier had gestured for another.

As she sipped her drink she hoped it would give her Dutch courage to ask for his help. But first she had to find out about him and whether he really would be a source of information.

In answering her queries she found out the most important answer first, yes, he had always lived in Nice. He used to own a fashionable clothing company, but he had tired of the frantic pace of commerce so left most of the running of the business in the competent hands of his son.

Annie got a distinct impression he was wealthy. From the attentive way he treated her, he obviously liked the companionship of women. She wondered if it was because of his attractive daughters. They certainly seemed a handful whenever she had seen them. Tempestuous and very striking, strange in a way he hadn't mentioned them. She must ask about them at some point. But the atmosphere between them was so relaxed; she just let the conversation flow. The café was warm and cosy and it was just lovely to chat, albeit on her side at times rather stiltedly.

It seemed as if Monsieur Xavier was enjoying it too, because he called for the menu and insisted she join him for lunch. The drink had gone to her head a little so she didn't take much persuading. But it was an expensive menu and Annie wasn't sure what to order. As if sensing her uncertainty Monsieur Xavier said, 'I can recommend the foie gras mousse for starters perhaps, then the Sole Meunière is always very good here.'

'Oh yes, that sounds delicious.'

Oh how starved she was of nice food after all those cheap veggie soups she had been existing on.

'And I think a good bottle of wine also. Yes?'

The food was excellent. Small quantities, excellent presentation with lots of plate twirls of intensely flavoured sauces. She would have loved to mop them up with bread, but felt this wasn't quite the right thing to do, given the classy clientele who surrounded her.

As she relaxed more, Annie was lulled into confessing how much she missed her friends and conversation since she had arrived in Nice.

'It was very brave of you to come somewhere where you know nobody at all.'

'I suppose so.'

'But you are in touch with your parents? You phone them often.'

'No, Monsieur They are both dead.' It sounded so stark in

French.

He patted her hand in sympathy.

'But your friend, Sophie is it? She phones you often no doubt.'

Annie looked down. She didn't want to give the impression that Sophie didn't care. 'She is getting married and is very concerned with all the arrangements. And she has a very busy job, flying here and there.'

'Of course. Of course.' Monsieur Xavier nodded as if he totally understood.

'And you have been here how long?'

'Over a month now.'

'And you still know nobody?' He seemed very concerned by this.

She couldn't really count Reen upstairs, or the brief chats with Jacques, so she just nodded.

Once again he patted her hand sympathetically. Was he a little lonely too? Is that why he asked her to share his lunch.

Changing the subject, he asked her about her impressions of Nice. Enthusiastically she embarked on eager descriptions of the art galleries she had visited, the long exploratory walks around the old port and the old town, the amazing views from the high park by the Chateau, the walk along the full five mile length of the Promenade des Anglais, the bus trips to the hill villages and all the train trips along the coast. It was so good at last to share her excitement at all her visits. He was a good listener.

The meal was coming to an end and Monsieur Xavier had called for coffee. This was it, the perfect opportunity. If she didn't ask him now, she would kick herself.

So emboldened by drink and the intimacy of the surroundings, Annie braced herself to broach the subject of Fabien.

Chapter Twelve

Nervously, Annie sipped her remaining wine. 'This may seem a little impertinent but I wonder if I could ask for your help in a matter that is…well…it's rather complicated, but quite important to me.'

A slight frown appeared above his eyes, but he urged her to go on.

'You see, I'm looking for someone.'

'Yes.'

'Someone called Fabien.'

His eyes flashed cold, 'A boyfriend?'

'Oh, no. Far from it. In fact I think he might be my father.'

'Your father?' The coldness had left his eyes but it had unnerved her a little. Was that a flash of jealousy there? Surely not.

For a moment she wondered whether to proceed.

'Please, Mademoiselle. Do continue.' He smiled his usual courteous smile and waved his hand in encouragement.

So she cleared her throat and began. 'I'm afraid it's a bit of a difficult story. When my mother died earlier this year…'

'My commiserations, Mademoiselle.'

'You are so kind, Monsieur. She'd been ill for quite some time so… But it was a shock when it finally happened.' Annie paused. It was still difficult to talk about but she must try to damp down her emotions if she was to continue with the story.

Monsieur Xavier waited sympathetically while she blinked back the tears that threatened to overwhelm her. With an effort, she shrugged and tried to formulate a coherent story. Without thinking, she lapsed into English.

'When I was going through her things, I found a small blue box I had never seen before hidden in her bottom drawer. Inside, tied with a pink ribbon, were two postcards of Nice and a strip of four black and white photos, you know the ones you used to get in a photo booth.'

Here she paused and took another sip of wine. Monsieur Xavier was listening intently.

'I wish I'd brought them to show you. I knew that Mum had been to Paris in the summer of nineteen sixty-nine when she was eighteen. But the postcards indicated that she had met someone from Nice there, a student called Fabien.'

'Fabien who?'

Annie sighed. 'That's just it, I don't know. He was studying at the Sorbonne and lived in Nice. That's about all I know.'

'And the postcards say he was your father?'

'No, not exactly. In fact not at all. But the postcards are from him and are very passionate and they obviously had an affair. None of which I knew about.'

Monsieur Xavier looked puzzled. He clearly couldn't see the point of all this. Somehow she had to convince him of their significance.

'In the first postcard, Fabien talks about what a fantastic summer they had in Paris and how he is longing to see her again. The second one asks when she is coming to visit him in Nice. Oh, I know it seems silly and probably it's just me putting two and two together and making five. Sorry, that's an English expression. It means I could be making too much of all this and jumping to the wrong conclusions.'

'That's OK, I understand perfectly. I think I have spoken more English in my life than you have French.' Monsieur Xavier smiled benignly and judging from his impeccable accent, this was probably true. But he still looked puzzled by her quest. 'So why do you think he was your father? Did you grow up always wondering and looking for a father?'

'No. Until I found that box I always assumed the man who was my father, was my father.'

'You did have a father?'

'Oh, yes. My mum wasn't a single parent. Piecing together what I have found out, I know she started studying French at university. But then had to leave in the first term because she was pregnant with me and so she had to marry my dad, who was her school boyfriend. It was all a bit hushed up of course, but I came along six months after the wedding so...'

'But you don't think he is your father.'

'I don't know. This is beginning to sound stupid, isn't it? My friend Sophie says it's a wild goose chase, sorry, another English expression.'

'Perhaps you could tactfully ask your father. Or did you say he wasn't around anymore?'

'Yes. My father was killed in an accident at work when I was seven so I don't really remember much about him. He worked nights so I only saw him at the weekend. I do remember I had always to be quiet and couldn't play with anything noisy or have friends round. He and Mum were very different personalities, I think. Everyone always said I took after her, in my colouring and my love of reading and...'

Annie stopped. She didn't want to bore her companion with all the reasons she now had doubts about her parentage. She had thought about little else since she found the contents of that hidden blue box. It was difficult to express the impact it had had on her.

She had read, avidly, a small cheap notebook she had also found in the box. It listed all the things her mum had seen in Paris and the restaurants she and her friends had visited, what they had eaten etc. It was clearly a brief factual record of the trip in the summer of '69. But then her writing had changed as she described meeting this sexy student, Fabien, who had clearly swept her off her feet. Within days she seemed to have ditched her friends and gone off with him to his student room. And there it ended. There were no more entries after that as if she had no time, or no need, to record anything after that. Or perhaps it was just all too intimate.

But it was the two faded postcards of Nice from Fabien that really interested Annie. One, postmarked September, showed the beautiful Baie des Anges, and the palm trees on the Promenade des Anglais. In it he said how he had enjoyed their time together in Paris and how he longed to show her his beautiful city by the sea. The other, postmarked October, displayed the market and had a faint pencilled arrow over the old town. He had written how he hoped she would like where he lived when she visited as she promised she would.

With the notebook and two postcards was a strip of black and white photos taken in a photo booth. They showed a Mum she had never seen before, young, shiny-eyed, laughing and looking adoringly at the handsome dark youth by her side. Fabien was smiling at her in a way that gave Annie butterflies in her stomach. They looked so in love, so good together.

The postcards showed he cared and hoped for their relationship to continue.

But it clearly hadn't.

Since discovering them, Annie had become obsessed with the significance of what she had found. Gradually she had evolved the theory she now outlined to Monsieur Xavier.

'You see, I wonder if Mum got pregnant with Fabien, then married my dad to cover it up. She obviously had a passionate affair during that summer in Paris and the dates are right. It explains why my mum and dad never seemed to fit together. And why I never had much of a connection with him. It would account for why Mum always longed to be French. I just wonder if...'

'Hmmn. If you don't mind my saying, dear Mademoiselle Annie, it all seems a little...doubtful.'

'I suppose so.' Annie knew how flimsy her case was. Sophie had said as much. But her belief had niggled since she had seen those postcards and it had brought her to Nice to try and find the answer. And Monsieur Xavier could be a route to finding Fabien, if only she could convince him to help. 'You are probably right. But I would love to trace him, and then perhaps it would lay my doubts to rest...or perhaps confirm them. And I would be most grateful if you would help me.'

Monsieur Xavier looked at her for a long moment with a

calculating expression that Annie couldn't quite decipher. Was he weighing up the difficulty of the task or was there something else?

'Of course, dear Mademoiselle. I will see what I can do. You understand that just a first name will make it very difficult. That is, if he still lives here.'

'Oh, yes, I know. But I would really appreciate it if you could make some enquiries.' Annie sighed with relief and beamed at her new friend. 'So we're looking for anyone called Fabien who once studied at the Sorbonne. He would be about fifty by now, I think, if he was a student in 'sixty-nine.'

'I do know some Fabiens, but none that fit that description. But of course I will make enquiries. Very discreetly of course.'

'Oh that's wonderful of you. I do know it's a long shot and I mustn't get my hopes up but...'

Monsieur Xavier patted her hand. 'I will make no promises. But I can see how important this is to you.'

'Thank you.' Annie squeezed his hand and was rewarded with a wide smile.

'No, that is quite enough gratitude. It has been a most interesting story and a most interesting lunch. We must do it again, I think, sometime soon.'

'Oh yes, I would love that.'

'But now, I'm afraid I must leave you. I have an engagement elsewhere.'

'Oh yes, of course. I'm so sorry to have kept you.'

'No, no, not at all. It has been most pleasant.' Monsieur Xavier waved an elegant hand for the bill.

Looking round, she saw most of the other diners had gone. 'I'm so sorry. I hadn't realised how late it was.'

'Don't worry, my dear. As I said, I have enjoyed your charming company very much.'

As they got up to leave, Annie thought she saw a dark-haired figure at the door.

'Is that your daughter looking for you?'

'My daughter?'

'Yes, you know, those two beautiful girls I've seen you with in the café.'

For a moment Monsieur Xavier looked disconcerted. Then he recovered, 'Ah no, Mademoiselle. I have no daughters. They are my nieces.'

'Oh, sorry.'

He patted her hand again. 'You English, always saying sorry.'

'I know. Sorry about that.' Annie laughed. 'Oops. Yes, I see what you mean. From now on I will go back to French then. I shouldn't really have been speaking in English at all. Sophie will be most cross.'

'Then you mustn't tell her,' said Monsieur Xavier with a wink reverting to French again.

'No I won't.' So in her best, most courteous French she said sincerely, 'I must thank you for a most delicious lunch and for allowing me to take up your time with my story.'

Monsieur Xavier bowed, 'As I said, my pleasure. I look forward to seeing you again when we can continue our most interesting conversation.'

'But of course, Monsieur. That would be charming.' Annie couldn't help but thank him again as he turned to go. Feeling thrilled and very pleased with the way the whole lunch had gone, she set off home. Her quest had begun.

Chapter Thirteen

It was a restless afternoon followed by a sleepless night. She had drunk far more than usual. Those Ricards were deceptively strong. Also her brain kept mulling over everything that had been said during the meal with Monsieur Xavier. Try as she might, she couldn't suppress her excitement at setting the ball rolling in the search for Fabien.

Next morning, with Reen's footsteps clattering above her head, she quietly crept down the stairs for her usual walk to the market. For how much longer could she avoid her chatty neighbour? What a stupid dilemma to get herself into.

Buying her usual array of veg, she thought longingly of the delicious meal yesterday, enjoyed twice as much because it was such a contrast to her usual economical fare.

But she would treat herself to a coffee this morning, and a chat with Jacques, if possible. In spite of herself, her heart gave a quick spontaneous flip at the thought of seeing him again.

The fresh wind made it too cool to sit outside so she ventured into the warm, steamy interior, hoping to spot Monsieur Xavier. He wasn't there, but Jacques came over to greet her with a slightly concerned *'Ça va?'* before escorting her to a tiny table near the kitchen. Annie realised with a flicker of pleasure that he must have noticed she had missed coming in for several days.

Jacques was busy as usual but was it her imagination or did he hover attentively near her even after she had her coffee? And that was a particularly generous helping of lovely warm pain perdu.

She was tucking in to her second slice when, from her vantage-point at the back, she spotted Monsieur Xavier enter.

She was just about to wave when Jacques came and blocked her view and started to talk to her about the weather.

Surprised and a bit miffed at missing Monsieur Xavier, she didn't really concentrate on what she replied. She was even more surprised when Jacques continued to block her view and carried on talking to her about the coolness of the temperatures at the moment.

Politeness forced Annie to concentrate on her answers to the figure standing in front of her in a most determined fashion. And it hit her afresh, just how good looking he was and how she couldn't suppress the flare of attraction she felt every time she saw him.

As she replied to his comments, she remembered the special smile he had given her the first day during her epiphany moment. It had made her heart race and heat had permeated her body in a most disturbing way. Since then she was acutely aware of a flutter of excitement as she approached the café at the prospect of seeing him. Whenever she was seated at her table, she tried not to follow him with her eyes as he wove deftly between tables. Always in vain. She couldn't help but notice the way the cut of his long white waiter's apron accentuated his slim hips and taut jean-clad thighs. Was it just that all French men exuded a certain sex appeal? Was it something in their gestures, the way they shrugged their shoulders conveying a sort of nonchalant insouciance?

Over the weeks she and Jacques had exchanged pleasantries as he delivered her coffee. Did he seem to give her special attention or was that wishful thinking? Whenever she asked him the odd question about the market or about an obscure item of food, he seemed to linger and his keen blue eyes looked into hers in a way that sent tingles up her spine. His grin was certainly mischievous as he kept a wary watch for the eagle-eyed Patron who obviously discouraged too much chatting to the customers. Was he flirting with her? At the time she felt a definite spark between them, but afterwards castigated herself for her foolishness. Making someone feel special, surely that's just what all waiters did with their customers to encourage them to return?

But today something about the way he was standing in front of her made her look at him more closely. Seated as she was, he towered over her with broad shoulders and long lean legs. His chestnut hair was bleached a little by exposure to the sun and his tanned skin accentuated his bright, blue eyes and his warm, open smile. His white shirt was rolled back at the cuffs and revealed brown muscular arms and strong capable hands.

His French was so easy to understand it gave her confidence to respond easily and, increasingly, fluently. But never before had he initiated such a prolonged conversation. Surprising also, as she had supposed only the English talked about the weather. He grinned and nodded at her reply about the cold wind before glancing over his shoulder and moving away to attend to another customer.

She was aware she had blushed a little as she had been talking and hoped he hadn't noticed.

As she regained her composure, she saw that Monsieur Xavier had sat down near the door with his back to her. He was engrossed in talking to another distinguished looking gentleman. Should she walk the length of the café to talk to him? Would he think her rude if he turned round and she hadn't acknowledged his presence, especially after their close conversation over lunch yesterday? Was he even now making enquiries about Fabien? She was just debating whether or not to join him when Jacques came up to talk to her again. In wonderment she watched him pull out a chair and sit down opposite her. The other waiters were busy watching for customers so she assumed Jacques was on a break.

He asked in his careful French, '*May I sit here with you*?'

Slightly flummoxed, Annie replied, '*Bien sûr.*'

He settled down, smiling at her surprised look and continued in his wonderfully comprehensible French.

'*What part of England do you come from?*'

Annie sighed and gave up. It seemed in spite of her best efforts, everybody French knew she was English.

'*I come from a town in the north of England.*'

'Ah oui. What is it called, your town?'

'Accrington.'

There was a sharp intake of breath *'Aaah, Accrington Stanley.'*

Annie was surprised and very impressed. She hadn't realised that even the French knew about the town's football team, and said so.

He laughed and continued, *'Et, Accrington, is it near to the town of Oswaldtwistle?'*

Now Annie really was astonished. She said how impressed she was that a Frenchman's knowledge of English geography was so *formidable. 'How do you know of it?'*

He was now grinning so broadly Annie thought his face would crack, but he recovered enough to say in perfect Lancashire English, 'Cos I come from Oswaldtwistle.'

There was a stunned silence as she tried to compute the impossibility of this statement.

'But you're French...' she stammered. Then realised, of course...that's why she could understand his French so well, it had a Lancashire accent just like hers.

'How stupid am I?' she gasped but he was laughing so much at her astonishment, she just had to join in. In fact the more the realisation of how blindingly obvious it all was, the more she laughed.

As their laughter subsided, he apologised for the deception. He had actually thought she knew and, like him, was determined not to speak English. 'I'm highly flattered that you really thought I was French.'

'But you have a most magnificent Gallic shrug.'

He looked slightly bashful. 'Ta, I've been practising in the mirror.'

They both realised they had lapsed into English.

'Oh crikes, I promised I wouldn't speak English whilst I was here, but ...oooh...this is so nice.'

'I know. I miss it as well, especially the Lancashire sort. Most of the accents round here are very southern.' He grimaced. 'Hang on a minute, the boss is back. I'd better go and serve but...' and here he bent low and whispered in her ear, 'watch out for old Bluebeard over there,' and he nodded his head towards Monsieur Xavier.

'What?'

But he had whisked away to serve a customer.

How puzzling. So, his blocking of her view hadn't been accidental. Looking back at her, he gave a twisting motion with his hands to indicate something dodgy and a look of warning, which she understood. Mystified, but slightly alarmed, she surreptitiously changed her seat so she had her back to the door so if Monsieur Xavier turned round she wouldn't catch his eye.

'All clear,' Jacques murmured a few minutes later as he passed her table. 'He's gone.'

Glancing swiftly around, Annie saw the elegant back of Monsieur Xavier leaving as the Patron held open the door for him.

'Look, we can't really talk here,' Jacques muttered. 'The Patron would have my guts for garters. I finish at five. Do you fancy a natter? An English natter?'

Sod my promise, thought Annie, and she nodded enthusiastically.

'OK. How about we meet outside here just after five and we could go for a walk and perhaps a drink? Hope you don't mind but I'll still be in my waiter scruff because it would take too long to go and get changed.'

Annie beamed 'That'll be fine. I'm dying to talk and know about...well...everything.'

How intriguing. How exciting. She walked home, tingling in anticipation from top to toe. And puzzling over Monsieur Xavier.

Chapter Fourteen

Annie spent the afternoon smiling to herself, both at her past stupidity and at the prospect of an evening spent breaking her promise. She had tried to speak nothing but French, she really had, but events kept conspiring against her. First Reen, then telling her story to Monsieur Xavier and now Jacques.

In fact, Jacques was obviously Jack. And from Oswaldtwistle, a town not five miles from the Accrington of her youth.

'Well, I'll go to the foot of our stairs,' she said to herself as she got ready to go out. 'I wonder what that would be in French. *Je vais au pied de l'escalier, peut- être?'*

It would be fun to bounce off some of her Franglais with Jack. Oh, how she was looking forward to chatting…and in English. And Jack really had noticed her, seemed to like her. Their relationship was now going to go beyond customer and waiter.

But perhaps the connection between them was just because he knew she was northern English, like him. Perhaps he had been just indulging in what he saw as a mutual game of play acting. Had he lost some of his allure now she knew he wasn't an exciting Frenchman and just plain Jack from Oswaldtwistle?

Her feelings about him were now all confused. And what about his warnings about Monsieur Xavier? What on earth did he mean?

It was with a mixture of apprehension and anticipation that she set out to meet him.

Jack's tall, lithe figure approached with a cheery wave and broad grin. Annoyingly, she felt a spike in her heart rate. This wouldn't do, at all. OK, he was definitely dishy, but he was a waiter from Oswaldtwistle for goodness sake.

Returning the wave, Annie suddenly felt unaccountably shy. Although she had dressed up a bit, until this moment she hadn't really considered it a date. But out of the context of the café, was it?

'Hiya'. His greeting was so Lancashire and so familiar she just laughed, all diffidence forgotten.

'I take it we're not speaking French then,' she grinned.

'Well...we can if you really want to.' But he looked disappointed.

'Nah. Let's not. I need a good fix of my native tongue.'

'Me too.' His tone was even more heartfelt than hers. 'Do you fancy a stroll along the Prom before we go for a drink? It'll be nice to stretch my legs properly instead of dashing around. And I'm not right bothered about being in yet another cafe for a bit.'

'Suits me. I love the Prom.' She had never before thought of the grand Promenade des Anglais as just the Prom.

'I suppose we should be terribly English and introduce ourselves formally,' he suggested using an upper-class accent. 'I'm Jack Hudson.'

'So charmed to make your acquaintance.' Annie smiled, turning to give him a small formal curtsey while extending her hand mockingly for the obligatory hand shake. He took it and gallantly raised it to his lips and bestowed a small kiss on the fingertips. Despite the obvious fun in the gesture, Annie felt a delighted shiver go through her body and blushed at her thrilled response.

To disguise this, she laughed, 'Oh no, you can't be plain Jack after a gesture like that. I've always called you Jacques in my mind and Jacques you shall remain.'

He grinned. 'Fine by me. And now you, Mademoiselle.'

'It's Annie, Annie Roberts.' On a bold impulse as he extended his hand for the mock formal handshake, she surprised herself, and him, by raising it to her lips. Giving him a flirtatious look, she kissed the back of his hand in return.

Wow. This time a definite shock of electricity passed

75

between them. Startled by this reaction, Annie turned away, embarrassed.

Too fast. Far too fast. What was she thinking?

Did she hear a catch in his voice as he suggested a little gruffly, 'Should we cross the road here to get to the Prom?'

Somehow negotiating the steady stream of traffic calmed the atmosphere down a little.

'Right, you first,' Jack commanded as they began sauntering side by side down the curve of lights that outlined the familiar sweep of the bay. 'How did a young lass from Accy end up all sophisticated and elegant with a little pooch and time to sip coffee every morning in the sun on the glamorous French Riviera?'

'Wow. Is that how I look?' Annie was astonished. And delighted. The picture he painted dazzled her. She had so wanted to look like that, but never in her wildest dreams did she think she had succeeded.

'Well, yes. You are classily dressed and can clearly afford to live here for weeks without working. Most of the Brits who do that are at least twice your age…and definitely don't come from our neck of the woods. I've been trying to figure you out for ages.'

Annie was thrilled. So she obviously had an air of mystery. The temptation to prolong this feeling of being a woman of intrigue was too strong. She hesitated. The image Jack had of her was so enticing she couldn't bear to reveal the boring truth just yet. Trying to retain her enigmatic air, she tossed her hair in a fantasy of allurement. Catching Jack's startled look as he edged away, she stopped. Ah…more practice obviously needed in hair-tossing techniques.

Partly to cover her ineptitude, and partly to reassure him she wasn't having a fit, she had to confide the truth.

'In fact, I'm really very boring and living off a shoestring. Can't you tell from all the bloody cheap veg I buy from the market?'

'I just thought you were vegetarian. Although I've noticed how you wolf down the pain perdu every morning. It doesn't touch the sides.'

'So much for my alloour,' sighed Annie.

'Your what?'

'Never mind. It's a long story. I'd much rather hear yours.'

'Oh no, you don't…ladies first.'

Annie hesitated. It was so good to stroll companionably along in the mild evening air and chat. The tall figure by her side was grinning down at her, waiting expectantly. It was far too soon to venture into anything deep about her mum or her search for Fabien. And how could she avoid mentioning them if she embarked on her tale?

Raising a dramatic hand to her brow, she declared in a quivering voice, 'Alas, I am far from elegant and glamorous. I am, in fact, jobless. The only thing keeping me from a life of penury and starvation is looking after that little French pooch you see me with.'

She gave an exaggerated sigh.

Jack grinned. 'OK, nice performance but come on, our Annie, spill the beans. What's the real story?'

'OK, but it's dead boring really.'

She'd had time to think about her story. One that avoided anything too deep. So she embarked on a no-frills summary of the immediate events that led her to Nice. She concentrated on telling him about her redundancy which gave her the opportunity to have a little time off and how she ended up dog-sitting for her friend, Sophie's distant relation. It was a carefully edited version. She tried to imply the trip was a watershed point in her career and a chance to perfect her French for some possible future employment.

'All these posh clothes are at my friend Sophie's insistence so I could pass muster as a classy relation. In fact all the extras, handbags, scarves, and accessories are courtesy of her. She's got a mega good job, jetting round the world and so picks up lots of expensive stuff in airports. This is far from my usual mode of dress, believe me. It's taken me a fair while to get used to them. Still not sure they are quite me.'

He was nodding as if it did solve a mystery. Perhaps that's what puzzled him. The mismatch between the clothes and the real person.

'OK, Annie, that explains a lot and, I'll have you know, the real story was far from boring. I think it's a bit bold to come over here knowing no one, leaving Manchester and all your friends. Why here? And what do you do all day?'

She hesitated. No, still too early to talk about her mum, her death, and her subsequent search for Fabien. It was all too deeply felt and she worried she might get upset. This would make the conversation far too serious and she wanted to retain the lightness between them.

'Well...' she began hesitantly.

Something in her face must have alerted him to her reluctance to delve into deep issues.

'Sorry... Sorry... Sorry. How rude of me. I can't believe I was so blunt. That's the trouble with us Lancashire folk, we are just plain nosey.' As he continued to apologise profusely, she realised he thought he had stumbled upon a story of heartbreak and rejection.

'Oh no, I'm not here to escape from a bloke,' she reassured him.

But Jack, clearly embarrassed by the impertinence of his prying, changed the subject and asked her if she had been to any of the places around Nice.

She instantly warmed to his sensitivity and followed his lead by telling him about all her museum visits, her trips to art galleries, her forays into the hills and train rides along the coast.

But this diversion into generalities seemed to have caused a slight distance between them. Wanting to restore their previous bantering relationship, she joked, 'Enough of this boring travelogue of mine. Come on. I want to hear all about you now. And I warn you, this Lancashire lass has won prizes for nosiness. Stop me if I start shining a light in your eyes and giving you the third degree.'

He laughed, clearly relieved that he hadn't offended her by his questions.

'Look, my mother and my aunts could give the Spanish Inquisition lessons, so I'm used to it. But it's getting a bit chilly out here. Should we go somewhere warmer to talk?'

'Eeee, lad, tha's gone soft living down here. But if you insist, I suppose we could find somewhere cosy. But you're not getting out of your turn to talk, so think on, young fella mi lad.' She giggled. 'Isn't it nice to talk proper, for a change?'

'Yup, it's right nice.' He grinned as they made their way across the road to get to a bar he had indicated.

Ensconced in a corner of the softly lit bar, Annie sipped her glass of red wine and waited eagerly for Jack to begin.

He laughed. 'It really isn't very interesting you know.'

'Oh no?' countered Annie. 'A lad from Ossy, even more the back of beyond than Accy, ends up totally at home in a small exotic corner of the Côte d'Azur, tanned from the sun, gliding effortlessly from table to table with trays laden with outlandish comestibles, able to banter in the local patois with the natives, and,' she added meaningfully, 'passing himself off as French born and bred.'

'Only to folks from Accrington.' He grinned. 'All right. But it's not half as glamorous as it sounds. I have to work long hours for a pittance for a slave driver of a boss and...'

'Stop,' Annie cried. 'These are classic procrastination techniques. I use them myself so I recognise what you are doing. Get on with your story, and if you are a good boy and tell me *everything*,' she lowered her voice and said in mock seductive tones, 'I promise, I too, will reveal all.'

'Ooooh,' he sighed gazing into her eyes, 'Promise?'

Yes, there was a definite flare of attraction in those laughing blue eyes. Annie blushed at her boldness. What are you doing? she said to herself. You don't know him well enough to be this suggestive. But in her heart she knew she did. She hadn't felt this good about herself since the fun days at Uni. So what was wrong with flirting with a gorgeous bloke with roguish blue eyes, a wicked smile and a very fit body?

Anyway she was enjoying it. And from the grin on his face, so was he.

Chapter Fifteen

'Are you sure you want the *whole* story?' Jack looked over the rim of his glass.

'Yup, start at the beginning and I'll tell you when to stop.'

He grinned. 'You do realise I will demand the same from you.'

'Ooops, although I may plead the third amendment…or is it the first? You know the one where you are not obliged to incriminate yourself?'

'You mean you have done incriminating things?'

She grimaced, knowing just how boring her life had been, but said defiantly. 'You never know, I might have.'

'Hmmn. You mean you are really a well-known cat burglar forced to flee to the Riviera to escape the long arm of the law?'

'You, my friend, have been reading far too many second-rate detective novels…and believe me, I am an expert on those.'

'Really? Are you a writer?'

'Huh, I wish. No, I'm a reader…but enough about me. I've told you, it's your turn. Get on with it.'

'OK. Good job I've got a thing for masterful women.'

He gave one of his wicked grins and her insides turned somersaults. Phew. She felt the sudden hot blush seep from her face down her body till it reached her curled up toes.

His eyes sparkled with mischief. He knew exactly what he was doing and the reaction he was having. Clearly he thought that two could play at the flirting game.

She had to concentrate on her wine for quite a while before she dare look up again.

'OK.' She smiled, 'I'm waiting.'

'Right. You're on. Where to start?' He took a swig of his beer and thought for a moment, then said quite seriously, 'Well, if you really want me to start at the beginning, I suppose it's all my gran's fault. She lived in Ossy all her life but always wanted to travel. Obviously that generation wasn't well-off and she never even owned a passport but I remember she always talked and sang about foreign places. She had a sort of wistful look when she sang her favourite song.' A nostalgic expression came over his face as he remembered. 'It was all about faraway places.'

The hairs stood up on Annie's arms as she recognised a song her mum used to sing with a yearning look on her face. 'I know that one too.' She gasped in astonishment.

'Fancy that. How amazing.' Another moment of intense intimacy seemed to pass between them as they locked eyes.

It was almost too much so Annie tried to laugh it off. 'I suppose it's only natural that people from our rainy corner of the world should dream of escaping.'

'Suppose so.' But he too seemed very aware of that shared closeness between them.

Taking another contemplative swig of his beer, his shoulders seem to relax as he leant forward eagerly to continue. It was as if the floodgates had opened.

'All my life I've been interested in places, and the land and rocks and hills and…and…well, geography really.'

She listened as Jack talked of his childhood enthusiasms. He, like her, was an only child and they shared the trials and tribulations of their single status and the sheer weight of expectations unconsciously placed on their shoulders by their parents.

'They were so chuffed when I got a place to study Geography at university.' Jack ran his hands through his hair as he confessed, 'Secretly, I would have loved a gap year first, to travel and explore, but I couldn't disappoint them. And I knew they would have been far too worried to let me go far. The only child thing I suppose. A bit too protective.'

Annie nodded. That had been true of her early years also. 'Me too. That's why I only went to Manchester.'

'It was Lancaster for me, which was great. I joined the hiking club, the canoeing club, and all the outdoor stuff I could. There were always trips to the Lake District at the weekend or the Dales or the Peak District.'

He grinned. 'Places with lots of geography. Anyway at the end of the three years I'd decided to have a complete break and go and explore some of the faraway places I'd sort of learned about.

But the best laid schemes et cetera...' He gave a wry smile. 'At the end of my last year, a company contacted my university tutor about a job in G.I.S.'

'G I S?'

'Sorry. Geographical Information Systems, sort of maps and computers. My tutor recommended me for the job. As it was in Manchester, it looked ideal for me and, to my surprise, I got it. But I took it, with the clear intention of staying only a couple of years, paying off my student loans, saving up a bit, then off on my travels.'

He paused to finish his drink. Annie guessed what was coming.

'Nearly ten years later I was still there.'

'Yup,' Annie sympathised. 'Something similar happened to me. For various reasons I had to go back to Accy and one of my mum's friends worked in the library and got me a job there till I found something else. And I stayed there 'temporarily' for years.'

'Ah, hence your expertise on detective stories.'

'Oh yes. I used to have to choose books for some of my housebound readers and they were very specific about what they wanted. I was the fastest skim reader in the business. I could go on Mastermind, specialist subject cosy crime and clean romances.'

'So you are a librarian?'

'Yes, it always sounds quite stuffy doesn't it?'

'Well, I have to be honest; you don't fit the stereotyped image.'

'No, but that's because I've left my grey cardy, my rimless glasses and pursed lips at home.'

'Thank goodness.' An appreciative gleam in his eyes, once again made her heart give a quick flip.

'Yes, my grey cardy and I stayed in the library for over eight years, till...well, until a while ago.' She desperately didn't want to reveal it was only her mum's death and Sophie's insistence that had got her out. She was enjoying this evening too much to cloud it with unhappy memories.

He was watching her face keenly and seemed to sense there was much unspoken stuff. 'But at least the redundancy freed you, didn't it? Would you still be there if it hadn't happened?'

Annie nodded, he was half right, the redundancy had freed her. She waved her hand, not wanting to take the focus from Jack's story. 'Never mind me. I'm retaining my air of mystery. Remember, it's still your turn. You haven't revealed all yet.'

'Well if it's the full striptease you want, I'm going to need another drink. Same again for you?'

'Yes please, but it's my turn to get them.'

'That's OK,' he said, rising to go to the bar.

'No, my turn,' she insisted. 'You said you only got paid a pittance.'

'And you said you were so poor you could only eat mouldy veg.'

'I didn't say mouldy.' Annie protested at his retreating back. But she was pleased he'd remembered the veg reference. He had clearly been paying attention to what she'd said.

She watched his animated face as he ordered the drinks and chatted to the barman. He was so easy to talk to and had a similar sense of humour. How could she feel so close to someone she had only known a few hours? The fact that he was dishy made it easy to fancy him, but it was something more than that. Certainly he caused her heart to flutter, but he had done that before she knew he was English, now it felt deeper somehow. Was she imagining it or was there a deeper connection?

She really must find out more about him. Was there a

lurking girlfriend? Was she misinterpreting a harmless flirtation as something more? She waited impatiently for him to return from the bar.

Chapter Sixteen

Smiling, he carried the drinks back and settled down to resume his story.

'Ready?' he asked.

'Steady. Go.' she replied.

'OK. So there I am in the buzzing metropolis of Manchester, quite enjoying my job; quite enjoying the lifestyle; enough money to save up and get quite a decent pad; so life quite good really.

But I still hadn't been anywhere. OK, I'd had holidays with my mates, you know the usual stuff, Ibiza, Megamuff. Then the last couple of years I went on posher holidays with my girlfriend, Emma, to Cyprus and northern Spain and Portugal.'

Girlfriend. Annie was suddenly alert. Of course, a gorgeous bloke like him would have a girlfriend. It hit her unexpectedly hard. How stupid to assume he was free. Just as she was really, really fancying him more than anyone she had met for ages. She felt cheated somehow.

Did her face betray her, because glancing at her, he explained. 'Emma was my girlfriend in the Sixth Form but we split up when I went to Uni. Then she got a job in Manchester and we sort of hooked up again.'

He frowned into his drink. 'She came to live with me in my place and it was fine but I still had a bit of a wanderlust so I tried to choose more interesting places to visit. But if it didn't have a pool, she didn't want to go. And then when we got there I wanted to explore and she didn't. She just wanted to lie by the pool and read…well, not actually reading, not books anyway, just sort of glossy gossip magazines. Sounds awfully snobbish doesn't it?'

'No,' said Annie simply. She too could not contemplate *life* without books, let alone a mere holiday.

'It was during these holidays it really came home to me how much I wanted to see more of the world. And I worried that if I tied myself down to someone who didn't, would I always feel restless and sort of unfulfilled?

'And thirty was looming, and although I had a quite nice life, I still hadn't done any of the things I sort of thought I would have done by that age. I somehow felt if I didn't do them by the time I was thirty then well…I never would. Silly really that a birthday should mean so much.'

His hands were clenching and unclenching round his drink.

Annie felt shivers up her spine. They really did have a lot in common. 'I absolutely know what you mean. My thirtieth is next April and it has definitely focused my mind on what I want from life.'

'Really? You don't think it's silly?'

'Nope. I've realised I've never really lived and, like you, my thirtieth is a sort of looming event. Although I still haven't a clue about the big picture, I know I've got to be more adventurous and seize life a bit more. OK, Nice isn't exactly adventurous, but doing it on my own has felt quite daring.'

'I agree. I think it's called pushing the envelope.'

They gazed at each other in mutual understanding. He lifted his drink. 'Here's to seizing life before the dreaded big Three O.'

As they clinked glasses, he gave one of his engaging grins.

Her somersaulting heart pleaded, 'Oh, please don't let him be taken.' She leant forward, eager to discover what happened to Emma.

'More,' she commanded.

Jack started to rise. 'OK. Same again?'

'Oh crikes, no. I didn't mean booze, I meant story.'

Jack seemed surprised and obviously flattered by her evident interest. 'Are you sure?'

'I'm agog!'

'A what?'

'Agog,' she grinned and said by way of elucidation. 'You know...full of agogment.'

'I thought we'd agreed to speak English.'

'OK. OK, guvnor you've got me bang to rights. I do make up words sometimes.'

'And yet you studied English, didn't you?' he said accusingly.

Just then, to her embarrassment, her stomach gave a very audible rumble.

He grinned. 'OK, never mind agogments, it's time for food. I'm starving as well. There's a good Italian place just round the corner. Do you fancy pasta or something?'

He stood up and reached for his jacket.

'I'd love one,' she replied, standing up also, 'but on one condition, we go Dutch and I buy the wine.' Her determined tone was somewhat undermined by another enormous tummy rumble. 'Bloody veg,' she grumbled, trying to retain her composure in the face of Jack's obvious delight in her mortification.

'No,' he said sitting down again. 'We go Dutch on *everything* or we don't leave until your stomach is evicted by the Noise Abatement Society.'

'OK, you win.'

'But just before we go, do you mind if I just phone Lucien, the guy I share an apartment with. I ought to let him know I won't be home for a meal. He won't bother, he'll go out or to his family. It's just that sometimes his sister, Nicole, comes round and I'd hate to inconvenience her. Is that OK?' He pulled out his mobile phone.

'Sure, go ahead,' and Annie turned away so he wouldn't think she was listening to his rapid French conversation with his friend. And she didn't. Not really. Until he lowered his voice a bit and she caught snippets about '...une fille tres intéressante … … Oui tres drôle … … Ah oui, très jolie aussi.'

Wow. She could live with that description. Interesting.

Funny and pretty.

It sounded as if Jack fancied her as much as she fancied him.

This promised to be a great evening. As long as girlfriend Emma wasn't still around.

Chapter Seventeen

'Right, should I push the bateau out and have a steak bravo.' Annie pondered aloud as she scanned the extensive menu.

'Steak Bravo?' enquired Jack searching the lists.

She grinned. 'Sorry. Pardon my Franglais.'

Realisation dawned. 'Oh, a steak 'well done'. God, that's dreadful.'

'I know,' she beamed happily.

Then to her consternation another stomach rumble rent the air.

He laughed. 'Whatever we have, it had better be quick. Let's have a starter. I fancy pushing the bateau out as well. A pasta starter first? A nice bottle of red. Then two steaks it is. And maybe even a pud later?' He glanced at her, his eyes twinkling with enticement.

She couldn't believe her ears.

'Are you a pudding man? How wonderful. All the men I know are strictly savoury types and never even glance at the dessert section.'

'Yes, I confess to a sweet tooth. In fact, thanks to my sedentary job in England, I was in danger of getting quite tubby at one stage. The wonderful thing about eating French style and having an active job as a waiter is that I sit before you the lean and hunky shape I am now.' And he patted his torso and threw out his chest in mock-heroic fashion.

Nice chest, Annie thought. Very nice chest indeed. I would definitely like to get acquainted with that chest and the rest of his body too.

His preening was cut short by the arrival of a cheerful waiter and the meal and wine were expertly ordered.

Over a delicious plate of hot ravioli, egged on by Annie's

repeated promise to 'reveal all later', Jack continued recounting the events that led up to his present situation.

'Well, as you know, I was feeling restless and trapped. I knew I'd got the travel bug, or wanderlust as my gran always called it. So I started planning my escape.

'I contemplated my original intention of having a gap year and going to Thailand, Australia and New Zealand. Then I realised that the world had moved on and now all the eighteen-year-olds were doing that pre-university. I knew I wouldn't be on their wavelength and thought they might think I was a bit old and sad.'

'Exactly my thoughts,' Annie burst in, 'when my friend Sophie was persuading me to have a break. Her first suggestion was a gap year in India. I rejected it for all the same reasons as you. Also that heat would have done for me. And,' she lowered her voice, 'I couldn't face the toilet facilities, or rather, lack of them.'

He poured them both another glass of wine. 'Yup, know what you mean. I confess, I didn't exactly want to rough it. Anyway it suddenly hit me one day at work. My job involved mapping Europe. Here I was, a twenty-nine-year-old geographer who knew everything about so many places in Europe, apart from what they looked like. I had never actually seen the roads I was mapping, the towns, the hills, mountains and rivers.'

He stopped and downed a glass of wine. His eyes gleamed with excitement, obviously remembering that special moment.

That was his epiphany, Annie thought.

He continued eagerly. 'I remembered the delight I used to feel as a kid watching the places on the map appear before my eyes as we drove around. I knew we'd be approaching a railway line, or a bridge, or a river so I'd look out of the window for them. And down the side of some roads on the map there was a green line showing they were picturesque. I'd always beg my parents to drive down those if they could.' He grinned, embarrassed by his enthusiasm. 'Sounds proper nerdy doesn't it?'

'Not at all. Sounds fantastic.' Annie wished she had felt the same excitement about their yearly summer holidays to a caravan in Borth.

He looked relieved by her reassurance. 'So it suddenly struck me, that's what I would do. I would follow the map around Europe, driving along the roads with the green lines down them showing they were pretty.'

Annie loved watching his animated face as he told her how he had planned his trip. But his eyes showed the strain as he told how first he had to finish with an uncomprehending Emma. He felt it was only fair as the relationship was going nowhere. Running his hands through his hair betrayed his emotion as he revealed it had been more difficult than he expected.

'She was really upset and couldn't really understand. She kept asking what was wrong with her. And there wasn't anything really. I just knew I wanted more from a relationship, more in common, more excitement…more love, I suppose. But I didn't want to hurt her by saying all this, because I did care for her, so I don't think she really understood. She wouldn't, couldn't believe it was over, and kept thinking we would get back together. Finally she seemed to accept it and moved out. I think she thought I would miss her. And in truth, I did. Suddenly my life seemed so empty. I kept wondering if I was doing the right thing. It seemed so selfish. All our friends shunned me, thinking I was a right bastard. I felt really alone and isolated.'

Drained by recollecting his troubled dilemma, Jack sank another glass of wine. Annie had rarely met a fella that could agonise quite like this and she was touched by the honesty of his reflections. And very flattered that he was indeed 'revealing all' to her.

In a gesture of sympathy she automatically reached out and held his hand across the table. His answering clasp was strong and electrifying. He looked startled by the connection, as if, like her, he was wondering where this was leading.

The waiter coughed discreetly as he brought their steaks and they self-consciously pulled apart.

'Another bottle?' Jack enquired eyeing their empty glasses.

'Why not?' she said gaily. 'Penury here we come.'

'Oh, it's not so bad,' he said. 'I quite like stale bread.'

'And I can make a lovely thin gruel from old cabbage stalks,' she offered.

'Gruel?!! Gruel?!!! Luxury,' Jack retorted.

As they tucked into their steaks with gusto, Annie relished the unfamiliar flavour of meat. She had long ago determined she wasn't a vegetarian, and this meal confirmed it.

So between mouthfuls of food and wine, Jack continued, obviously happier now the painful part was behind him.

'Giving up my job gave me a huge sense of release. I hadn't realised how old and respectable and staid I felt in my straitjacket of work and routine. Don't get me wrong, I loved the job and will probably go back to something like it one day. It had just happened too early for me. Right job, wrong time.'

With a jolt, Annie realised that's how she felt about her job in Accy library. The university one had been much more vibrant and busy and stimulating. Sod's law that, as she discovered she wanted it, it didn't want her.

'Oh, Annie, I can't tell you how much I enjoyed planning my trip. It made me feel carefree, like I had when I first finished my degree, with so many possibilities before me. I knew it was make or break time. So against everyone's advice, I sold my flat to fund my adventure. Then I thought, if I'm going, I might as well go in style. So I bought Elspeth.'

'Elspeth?'

'A game old girl,' he teased.

'OK. Have I got to guess?'

'You can try.'

'Hmmn, Elspeth the elephant?'

He roared. 'Now that would be great. Ambling around Europe on the back of an elephant.'

'Well, I figure it has to be something beginning with e.'

'Yup, you're right.'

Chapter Ten

On the dot of seven, there was a tap on the door and there was Reen, dressed up to the nines in a silver sequinned top, chunky gold jewellery and gold lamé leggings. She was expertly holding two bottles of wine in one hand, and bottles of gin and tequila in the other. Over her arm was a clinking bag full of various bottles of mixers with a jar of bright red glacé cherries on top.

'Just brought a spot of lubrication. Not sure what your favourite tipple is but I've got vodka and rum and brandy I can fetch from the flat, if that's your poison.'

'Non. Non,' Annie laughed. 'Zat should be more zan enough.'

She loved the way that Reen had no idea how idiomatic her English was…and how incomprehensible she must be to most foreigners.

After Reen had exclaimed with joy at the apartment, which she thought was soo classy and so French, she offered to make tequila slammers while Annie instructed her in the art of making a Tarte Tatin for pudding.

They had a wonderful time. It was true, Reen had no culinary expertise whatsoever, but she was quick to learn and thoroughly enjoyed the girlie closeness of the enterprise.

Muting her French accent somewhat, Annie asked her how she had brought up a family without being able to cook. Reen said where she lived in London they had always been surrounded by various takeaways and cafés. Besides, she had been so busy working alongside her Ted on the family scrap-iron business, it never seemed worth it, flogging over food that was gone in a flash.

'Their gran used to live just round the corner and she

'OK. Zat is *pas de problème*.'

'Oh, Marie-Anne, Dahling, that would be lovely. And you can show me how to make something French for my Ted when he comes back. He'll be so tickled. That's such a lovely idea. What time do you want me?'

'I weel see you about seven of the clock, *n'est-ce pas*?'

Even to her own ears, Annie's accent was excruciating, but Reen seemed delighted with the plan.

As she regained her apartment, Annie was weak-kneed with the thought of a crisis averted. But not a moment to lose. She left a sleepy Pimpy and hurried out to the market deciding to blow the budget and get whatever food she required.

She realised she was looking forward to the evening. It would be fun to eat with company for a change. But she must remember to be French.

'Emu?'

'Oh god. I suppose I'd better tell you. Elspeth the E-type.'

'E-type what?'

'You peasant,' he grinned. 'Elspeth is a car, a lovely, classic old e-type Jaguar. Maroon, convertible, and born the same year as I was. And without her temperamental nature, I wouldn't be sitting here talking to you now.'

'Well, in that case let's raise a toast to Elspeth.'

He clinked glasses, 'To Elspeth.'

'So you are going to have to explain her role in all this.'

'OK, to cut a very long story short, I know not very short, but don't forget you asked for it, I spent most of this last year meandering through France. I started in the north and, as far as possible, followed those roads with the green lines on marking the scenic routes. I decided on France because I could remember quite a bit of French I learned in school so I bought myself a 'Teach yourself French' tape which I played in the car to refresh myself. And, like you, I have tried not to speak English at all. And most people seemed to understand me.'

He gave a teasing grin. What was he implying?

'They understand me as well,' she protested hotly.

'Yes, Annie love, of course they do.'

Did he realise he had just called her 'love'? She daren't look so just kept her head down and carried on with her meal.

After a pause, Jack just picked up his story from where he left it.

'I really enjoyed the freedom of all that travelling and exploring – for a while...'

Did he, like her, find visiting places on your own vaguely unsatisfactory? Had he longed to share everything with someone, just like she had? Was he her 'soul mate'...thinking and feeling like she did?

'Sorry, I'm taking ages to get to the point aren't I? So eventually I arrived in Nice and was just driving out along the Corniche to go to Monte Carlo when Elspeth broke down in a puff of smoke and fumes. She was towed into a local garage but, because she is a specialist car and a bit ancient, they had to send off for the parts. It would take over a week for them to arrive. I got talking to the garage bloke, same age as me, called Lucien, who was great, very friendly, so I asked him about somewhere to stay. Well, of course, he knows everyone in Nice, they all do. He soon got me fixed up at his uncle's small hotel near the port. The family was great and sort of took me to their bosom.'

He smiled shyly at the memory and sighed. 'It was so nice to stop for a while and talk properly to people, and be involved. I hadn't realised how fed up I was with just travelling and spectating. You sort of feel you are only skimming the surface of life.'

There it was. Another example of 'soul matery'. Annie could only gasp and nod vigorously in agreement. 'Tell me about it.'

'Well, by the time Elspeth was repaired I'd made friends with Lucien, the bloke at the garage, and I loved Nice and decided to stay for the summer. Lucien needed someone to share the rent in the apartment he'd just found so he asked if I would like to move in with him. I jumped at the chance and we get on great.'

Here he lowered his voice and looked around, 'Reading between the lines, I think he wanted to escape from the family a bit so didn't want to share with a brother or cousin. His family can be a bit overpowering, probably a bit controlling. But they have been great to me. They have sort of adopted me and, because I needed to eke out my savings, they fixed me up with that waiter job with yet another uncle – Albert, who owns that café.'

'The sour faced Patron.'

'Yes, he's not one of nature's rays of sunshine, is he? Runs a tight ship as you have probably noticed. I wasn't sure at first because I'd never done anything like that before and wasn't sure my French was up to it. But...well, I've been there all summer and had a great time. And Uncle Albert hasn't sacked me...yet, and he's tough so he would if I wasn't any good. Which is why I didn't dare stop and really talk to you the last few weeks.'

Somewhat shame-facedly, he grinned, 'But I think I've more than made up for it now. Can't believe how much I've rabbited on. You shouldn't have been such a good listener.'

He sat back with a sigh. 'Anyway that's more or less it. So, right, Mademoiselle, your turn.'

'Whoa, hold your horses for a minute. You can't just stop. Wait till I've asked you about…'

'Oh yes, I can. And oh no, you don't put it off. My mother warned me about girls like you, teasing me on, promising to reveal all, then…'

Blushing, Annie laughed. 'OK, but can we order a pud first?'

'And you accused me of procrastination! But, clever little minx that you are, you have obviously found my Achilles heel. OK, let's see, Crepes Suzette, crème caramel, ice-cream. Oooh, my favourite, a Tarte Tatin.'

'I do a very good Tarte Tatin,' boasted Annie. Then eyeing him coyly she leant forward, 'You'll have to come up and see it sometime.'

His eyebrows shot up with glee. 'Oh, you temptress. See what I mean about promises…promises.'

She just gave what she hoped was a sultry smile before returning to the menu.

'Crepes Suzette for me,' she decided.

'Well, it was going to be Tarte Tatin, but perhaps I should save myself for yours, so I'll join you in some crepes.'

Thrilled, Annie ducked her head down over the menu. He had just confirmed that they would definitely meet again. If only to eat a Tarte Tatin. Was he as attracted to her as much as she was attracted to him?

Having ordered, he sat back, folded his arms and gave her a look that brooked no opposition. 'So your turn. Reveal all.'

'Well, not *all*, of course, a girl has to retain some vestige of decorum.'

He snorted.

'OK, here goes.'

Hmnn. She had promised to reveal all, but definitely didn't want to spoil the happy atmosphere by venturing into the Accrington part of her life. And the probably silly search for Fabien was all bound up with her mother's death so she would give that a miss…for now.

'I hate to say this after all my enticements, but there's not much else to reveal. I've already told you about my redundancy and how Sophie got me this job in Nice. She's a right bossy boots and organised everything, even down to taking me shopping for an appropriately sophisticated capsule wardrobe. And, in spite of all my protestations, she was obviously right in her choice of attire because you were convinced I was a classy bird, even if you guessed I wasn't French.'

'Yes, but I much prefer who you really are, to that image you projected.'

'Thanks, but are you insinuating I'm not a classy bird then?'

His lips twitched. 'Of course not, but…'

'Well, just what about me isn't classy then?' Annie enquired sweetly, tilting her head provocatively.

'Ooh that's a difficult one to answer. Could it be the thunderous tummy rumblings? The atrocious Franglais phrases? The dreadful double entendres? Not to mention the voracious appetite. The bread mopping of the plate for the last vestiges of sauce. And then there's the sheer speed of the pudding consumption. Should I go on?'

'Curses, Moriarty, you've seen through my clever disguise.'

'But someone else hasn't,' he said mysteriously.

Annie looked puzzled.

'Bluebeard.'

'You mean Monsieur Xavier?'

'Yup. I think he definitely has you in his sights.'

'What do you mean? He's just a sweet, lonely old gent given the run-around by those petulant nieces.'

'Oh dear. Sorry, Annie, that's the last thing he is.'

Chapter Eighteen

Jack looked serious and took another swig of wine. 'If that's what you really think, it's a good job I rode to your rescue. At first I thought you knew his game and you were playing along. But then the more I saw of you, the more it didn't add up and I began to think you really were an innocent abroad.'

Annie flushed, annoyed at this description. That's not how she felt about herself at all.

He leant forward and lowered his voice. 'Those aren't his nieces. They are his…well…his girls, his employees. Um… he runs a sort of very discreet agency, which puts well-off men of a certain age in touch with girls, women who will… um…entertain them…for a price.'

'You mean Monsieur Xavier is really a Madame? A brothel Madame? I mean a pimp,' she gasped, wide-eyed.

'Well, I'd never really thought of it quite like that, but yes. Although it's very up-market stuff. More of an escort or introduction agency, I suppose.'

'But he never imagined I was a girl like that, surely?' She was horrified at the prospect. 'And you…you surely never thought I would…?' she paused, appalled.

'No, of course not,' he reassured her. 'And it wouldn't have happened in an obvious way. From what I've heard, I think he would have proceeded quite slowly at first and taken you out for the odd expensive meal and perhaps bought you the occasional little gift that you wouldn't have liked to refuse. He would then have introduced you to one or two friends of his, probably older, cultured men like himself who would enjoy listening to your lovely English-French accent and looking at your…um…abundant charms.' He looked down at this point, blushing a little.

'Anyway, I'm guessing that one of these men would have shown a particular interest in escorting you around but would have eventually demanded payment...in kind...for the expensive nights out. And you, being a nice girl, perhaps wouldn't have realised till that point what was happening.'

Annie sat stock-still, her face pale. He was right! She was so trusting, gullible, and lonely. She would have fallen for it. She knew she would.

She had to a certain extent already. When she thought back to the lunch she could now see how cleverly Monsieur Xavier had ascertained she had no friends or family around her. He knew she was lonely, and perhaps a bit skint; perfect innocent prey for his plans.

He had skilfully enticed her into accepting an expensive lunch and discreetly plied her with drink. She went hot thinking that perhaps the waiters in the restaurant knew his game. Did they think she was...?

Rigid with shock, her mind raced forward to imagine the dreadful scenario Jack had outlined. All too likely. What a fool she was. Sophie was horribly right, she was naïve. What was her phrase? 'Too nice for Nice'.

She groaned and put her head in her hands.

'Sorry,' he leant forward. 'I didn't know all this to begin with, but I've sort of kept an eye out for you ever since that first day when you smiled at me. I could tell that sitting there in the café in the sun was somehow special for you.'

'It was an epiphany,' she said, lifting up her head and remembering that moment so clearly. She had seen Jack look across at her and smile. So she was right, he had recognised it was an important moment for her.

'Right,' he said, doubtfully. 'After seeing your...um... epiphany,' he hesitated, clearly hoping it wasn't rude. 'I knew you were, well, a nice girl. So,' he continued, 'when I saw Monsieur Xavier strike up an acquaintance with you, I sort of asked around about him. I knew he was a regular with a lot of glamorous women friends, but the more I heard, the more I didn't like it.

'Then, when you didn't show up for these last few days, I

thought something had happened to you. I was so relieved to see you today, especially on your own. But then I saw you wanting to make contact with the old lech when he came in. So I just had to stop you, but discreetly. Apparently, Monsieur Xavier is quite an influential man hereabouts. It wouldn't do for him to see me thwart his plans.'

Annie nodded, still slowly piecing it all together. Dare she reveal that she had already been enticed into one expensive meal? No, she couldn't. She already felt naïve and foolish, which was especially galling in front of Jack. To tell him about her lunch time encounter would only reinforce this 'innocent abroad' image.

No, she would definitely have to keep it to herself. Now she knew Monsieur Xavier's intentions, she would steer clear. But it was a close shave.

What was worse was the fact that she had trustingly enlisted Monsieur Xavier's help in searching for Fabien. That was something she definitely must keep hidden from Jack.

His concerned gaze was fixed on her face. He seemed to be very aware of how stunned she was by his revelations.

Topping up her wine, he apologised again. 'Sorry, if this is a bit of a shock to you. I knew I must give you a gentle general warning. And look what's happened. I didn't expect to be enticed into a full three course meal, including pudding, and the remains of what I suspect is our third bottle of wine.'

Annie realised it was.

She gave a shaky grin, still all too aware of what might have happened but for his intervention. 'You're my knight in shining armour. You have saved me from a fate worse than death. You have delivered me from dishonour. How can I ever repay you?'

'Umm, you can stop all that for a start.'

'Yes, there were rather too many clichés there. As an English specialist, I should be heartily ashamed. Nevertheless,' she said seriously, 'it's all true. And I am very grateful.'

'Right. You can show your gratitude by finishing your story.'

'I have told all,' she protested, taken aback.

'Oh no, you haven't. You have carefully avoided answering every time I've asked you what you do all day. I'm sure Pimpy doesn't take up all your time.'

'Ah, bugger,' Annie moaned. 'The man's no fool. He's noticed. Can't a girl retain any air of mystery?'

'Not a hope. Not when she promised all night 'to reveal all'. Although seriously if you don't want to tell me you don't have to.'

'You have got to be one of the most considerate blokes in the whole wide world.' She beamed, vaguely aware that she might be slurring her words a little. 'But now, my prince, the dance of allurement is over. I will reveal all. Be prepared for the discarding of the seventh veil.' She wafted her white linen serviette suggestively in front of her eyes, before letting it drop seductively on to the table.

At least that was the plan. It was unfortunate that this theatrical moment was spoiled as the waving serviette flicked her half-full wine glass and knocked it over. Their waiter, who had been eyeing her movements with bewilderment, leapt forward to fish out the crimson, sodden serviette and try to prevent the red wine spreading across the rest of the white tablecloth.

As Annie apologised profusely, she realised she really was drunk. What she had hoped was an alloouering gesture, probably looked stark staring bonkers to anyone watching.

'Look, I'd better go to the ladies and powder my nose.'

She got up with exaggerated care and was just about to walk carefully to the loos when she saw Jack gesture for the bill.

She turned, bent and hissed venomously in his startled face, 'Don't you dare pay that while I'm gone!'

She then proceeded very slowly to the loo. Aiming for the door took a lot of concentration.

Chapter Nineteen

She was a long time, but eventually emerged less shiny-faced and a little less slowly, having in fact powdered her nose. She had also cupped her hands to drink copious amounts of water from the tap. As perhaps could be deduced from the drenched front of her jumper.

Jack *had* paid the bill but succeeded in getting her out of the door before she protested too much. He was also a little unsteady on his feet and seemed to crave the fresh air as much as she did. Linking arms, they clung on to each other as they negotiated the corner of the street with its lethal knee-high bollards.

Annie gasped as the cold air hit the soaking wet patch on her jumper. She needed to steady herself a bit more so, pointing at a bench on the Prom, she suggested, 'Shall we just sit over there for a few minutes. Then we can sort out how much I owe you.'

Safely seated facing a bright moonlit sea, Jack steadfastly refused all attempts at payment.

'I'm not that hard up. Anyway I haven't enjoyed myself so much in ages. Like you, I didn't realise how much I missed speaking silly English and you are very easy to talk to. It's been a great evening.'

'I agree and the very least I can do to repay you for the best meal I've had in ages and for saving me from a fate worse than death is…ta daah…to finally to reveal all.' What was she burbling on about? But she was enjoying his company so much, she just wanted to prolong the evening for as long as possible.

'It's a bit chilly for that, isn't it,' Jack seemed a bit worried about what was coming next. Perhaps he thought the drink might lower her inhibitions just a bit too much.

'No…No… You deserve the truth about what I do all day.'

'Oh right,' his relief was so obvious she was a bit insulted that he hadn't wanted her literally to 'reveal all'.

'It's not very interesting. In fact, I'm deciphering some scandalous diaries from the nineteen-twenties about a free spirited socialite.'

'Decipher? Like breaking codes?'

'No, not really. I say 'decipher' because her writing is so tiny and she does use lots of abbreviations which I have had to deduce from the context. Also she disguises the names of the men she sleeps with by initials or nicknames. She has bonked everywhere, several stately homes, backs of taxis and even in the House of Lords. I'm getting quite engrossed.'

'Sounds fascinating. Is she a relation by any chance?'

'Oh, no way. Far too posh. No, they belong to my friend Sophie's boss. They're his nan's and I'm sworn to secrecy about what I find there. I type them up on my laptop, transfer them on to floppy discs and post them off about once a month. He's paying me quite well. I suspect Sophie twisted his arm to get a good price.'

'Sophie sounds a formidable woman.'

'Oh she is, on the surface. But we've been friends for nearly twenty years and she's been wonderful to me. Oh yes, she's an interfering old bag at times, I grant you. Always so certain she knows what's best for me, but to be honest, she's usually right.'

With chagrin, she remembered again Sophie saying she was an innocent abroad, and so it had proved. Jack had said the same thing. Despite knowing her for such a short time, he seemed to know her so well.

Lost in thought, she gazed out as the sea restlessly glinted under the patchy moonlight. It was so companionable sitting close to Jack's protective presence. But suddenly she shivered as the wind became stronger and colder.

Jack obviously noticed. 'Come on, Accrington Annie, time to go home,' he commanded, hauling her somewhat unceremoniously to her unsteady feet. His warm comforting arm wrapped round her waist as he followed her directions to her apartment block.

All the way there, Annie deliberated whether to invite him up. Would it seem too keen, or too obvious? She felt instinctively, in spite of the obvious attraction between them, that somehow he wouldn't make a move to suggest it, so it was up to her.

She was right. There was an uncomfortable pause outside the entrance. She was just about to offer a cup of coffee when she heard a familiar clip-clopping sound coming towards them.

Reen! Oh no. She'd forgotten to tell Jack about her French pretence and how she had deceived her English neighbour. She daren't risk getting into conversation. But how to stop Reen greeting her and all the ensuing embarrassment?

With no time to think, she swiftly lunged at a surprised Jack. Throwing herself at him, she pinned him against the cold marble wall and plunged into a deeply passionate kiss.

Wow. For a minute she was bowled over by the definite electricity shooting between them. Keenly aware of his long, hard body pressed tightly against hers, she wound her arms round his neck. His lips were firm and hot against hers and she longed to lose herself in exploring his mouth, his body.

But she was acutely aware of the presence of Reen just behind her. Keeping her mouth firmly clamped to his, she listened intently as Reen seemed to be searching for her keys in her bag. It seemed to take ages before she extricated them and inserted the correct one in the lock.

All this time Jack's eyes were open and locked on to hers in amazement. She was just beginning to run out of kissing breath when she finally heard the door open.

'Night, night, Dahling.'

Reen was obviously chuckling and Pugsy gave a little acknowledging bark as he was hauled over the threshold. With relief she heard Reen's feet retreating towards the stairs.

She let Jack go. Bemused and still panting from the kiss,

he exclaimed, 'Whoa. What happened there?'

'Oh help, she's coming back,' Annie hissed. 'Look, whatever happens, speak French.' And she once again flung Jack against the wall in a passionate embrace.

'Ouf,' she heard his breath escape in surprise.

She sensed that Reen had emerged from the door and seemed to be waiting politely for a suitable pause.

There was nothing for it. The sheer embarrassment of pinioning a man she had not long met, against a cold marble wall eventually overcame her. As she released him, she heard him frantically sucking air back into his compressed lungs.

'I'm sorry to interrupt you, Dahling, with your young man,' Reen began, gazing with frank curiosity at a rumpled Jack, 'it's just I've been trying to get in touch with you all evening to ask you a big favour.'

Flustered by the awkwardness of the whole situation, Annie could only mumble, 'Oui?'

'My Ted phoned to say there's been some problems with the Jacuzzi. He can't get the one we wanted in quite the right colour. Well, you know how hopeless men are with colours; he doesn't know the difference between soft cream, peach or Mongolia, so I daren't let him do it on his own. So, he wants me to come home for a day or two to help sort it out. There's a flight I could get early tomorrow morning, but...,' here she hesitated, seeming genuinely uncomfortable under the uncomprehending gaze of the entwined young couple. 'No it doesn't matter really. I hadn't realised you had got a young man. I really shouldn't have disturbed you.'

She turned to go in.

'Non...pardon, 'ow can I 'elp?' Annie was mortified at putting on such a fake French accent.

Jack shot her a surprised look but said nothing. He was clearly enjoying her discomfiture and intrigued by the connection between her and this mule-clad, over-tanned, mock-ocelot coated, Essex-speaking woman.

'Well, it's Pugsy you see. It doesn't seem fair to take him all the way there and back for a couple of days. He hates flying. It upsets his tum and he...well...' here Reen lowered her voice and leant forward to whisper so the patiently waiting Pugsy wouldn't hear his mistress discussing his condition in such frank detail, 'well, he shits for days.'

Jack's hoot of laughter was transformed into a series of coughs by Annie's dig in his ribs.

'I was going to ask you if I could leave him here with you. Not,' she added hastily, 'to live in your apartment. He'll be quite happy staying in his basket upstairs, but I just wondered if you'd mind taking him out when you take Pimpy and popping in to feed him. I'll leave everything ready for you.' She paused, seeing Annie's hesitation and added winningly, 'He won't be any bother and he's really taken to you, and Pimpy.'

Annie remembered Reen's kindness in looking after Pimpy when she was feeling bad from her hangover and couldn't find it in her heart to refuse.

'*Mais*, of course, Madame Reen, *avec plaisir.*'

'You're sure it won't be too much trouble. I mean if you are too busy…' and here she shot a meaningful look at Jack.

'*Pas de problème, Ma chère amie*', Annie said hurriedly. She was worried Reen might want an introduction to Jack, which would complicate matters considerably.

Reen still looked unsure, so Annie assured her again that it would be a *'plaisir'*.

This time, at last realising Annie meant it, Reen gave her a big smile of relief.

'You are such a treasure, Babes,' she said emotionally and Annie could see one of Reen's fierce hugs coming so extricated herself from Jack just in time.

'She really is a dahling,' Reen said to Jack, who nodded. 'I'll pop the key and instructions under the door in the morning, um…er…just in case you're not up when I go.'

And with a final twinkling smile at them both, she was gone, rapidly clip clopping across the hall.

Jack just stood there, a quizzical eyebrow raised.

'OK…OK, I can explain everything,' Annie began.

'Did she really just say Mongolia instead of magnolia?'

'Yup, she really is a mile a minute. She lives in Spain and

loves what she calls 'flamingo dancing'. You know with castanets and stuff. Why don't you come up and have a coffee while I explain.'

He looked a bit embarrassed.

'As much as I'd love to, do you mind if I don't. I'm on the early shift tomorrow and it's a fair walk home.' Perhaps sensing her feeling of rejection, he joked, 'Look, it's already well past my bedtime but I'm dying to know the story behind all this intrigue. Tell you what, they owe me some time off so I'll finish late morning. Then how about a drive. I could introduce you to Elspeth and show you some of the places I've found in the hills around here.'

'That would be wonderful. I really hate visiting places on my own and I'd love to explore some more.'

As he arranged to pick her up at 'their bench' on the Prom, he pulled her to him. Lacing his fingers behind her back, he bent over and kissed her softly. Her knees buckled slightly at the intensity of her response.

Pulling away, he murmured. 'Till tomorrow, Our Annie, when I expect to hear all about your French pretence, 'flamingo dancing' and your interesting friend.'

She grinned. 'I will reveal all...again. Promise.'

Chapter Twenty

Annie awoke slightly bleary next morning. She had passed a somewhat fevered night. Whether that was the memory of Jack's kiss or whether it was the results of the wine, she wasn't sure. But considering how much they had drunk, she didn't feel too bad. Clearly wine was kinder to the system than Tequilas.

Thinking of which, just what had she promised Reen?

She padded to the door. Sure enough, Reen's key and Pugsy instructions had been discreetly pushed under the door. Dressing quickly, she popped upstairs to bring Pugsy down to her flat and fed both dogs together while she showered, warmed up a quick croissant from the freezer and got ready.

Feeling very French with two little dogs, she promenaded on the Prom. It was good to be out in the fresh, late-autumn sunshine. The cool wind raced across the surface of the sea causing it to glint and sparkle. The sight of the restless blue sea always enchanted her and lifted her spirits. And this morning as she walked, it gave her a chance to mull over the events of the previous night. There was so much to think about.

She shivered again as she contemplated her naivety about Monsieur Xavier. How cleverly he had sussed out she was on her own, knew no one, and was pathetically glad of his company. It was so obvious now.

The scenario Jack had painted seemed all too terribly possible and she was cross again with herself for her lack of worldly wisdom. But then, if Jack hadn't sensed her innocence, he wouldn't have felt impelled to warn her. They wouldn't have met and had such a wonderful, funny, chatty evening. Would she have eventually sussed he was English like her? She laughed. She really was an idiot in so many ways. But she felt buoyed up. This was all coming good in the end.

She couldn't decide what she felt about his disinclination to come up for coffee. Did she feel rebuffed? No, not really. Was he just a really nice lad who didn't believe in going too far, too fast? Or did he just not fancy her? She was certain he liked her, but how much and in what way? Was that a friendly kiss last night, or something more?

Did she want it to be something more? She certainly fancied him. And there were real sparks flying when they flirted. But was it just the relief of finding a like-minded English person after weeks of being starved of company?

Would she really have invited him up and then gone to bed with him on their first date? That was not like her at all. She hadn't even done it with Hamish till a few dates later, and she was much younger and bolder then. Looking back, thank goodness he refused. The awkward next morning scenario was too excruciating to think about. She blushed at the thought.

She must calm down and see how things developed. But although she hadn't really been able to concentrate on the kisses last night, she had definitely enjoyed them. Perhaps next time, he might take the lead.

Tumbling all these thoughts in her mind, she did her usual round of the market stalls, nodding 'bonjour' to several familiar people.

She decided not to go for a coffee. She was not sure how she would react if she saw Monsieur Xavier. However, her heart gave a leap as she glimpsed the lithe frame of Jack holding a laden tray aloft as he snaked between the tables.

Wanting to give herself time to consider her wardrobe for their afternoon outing very carefully, she hurried the dogs back home. Two dogs were definitely slower than one; each one had to stop and sniff at different smells and in the end she dumped them both in the wheeled basket which they both good-naturedly shared. She supposed being 'lap' dogs they were used to being conveyed in all sorts of contraptions.

Once home, they settled down in their respective baskets and she knew they would contentedly snooze together for the rest of the day.

What to wear took a time to decide. The days were becoming decidedly cooler, despite the bright sunshine, so one of Sophie's warm cashmere scarves was definitely needed. As were her posh leather gloves.

At the appointed time, she waited patiently in the sun at the little pull-off point near 'their bench'. A maroon convertible pulled in with its top down. As car ignorant as she was, even she gasped at the long, lean, sexy shape of an E-Type Jag.

He grinned at her look of admiration.

'Get in quickly before we're deafened by the hoots from these cars behind us.'

Smiling, she hopped in and settled into the shiny leather seats. Jack roared away, clearly enjoying the throaty sound and the resulting stares of passing onlookers. He looked impossibly raffish, his blue linen shirt open at the neck and the wind ruffling his chestnut brown hair.

She felt the sexy throb of the car's engine pulsate through her body as Jack confidently changed gear with his strong tanned hands. His well-cut jeans hugged his long lean legs as his feet danced over the pedals, changing gear and weaving in and out of the busy lanes of traffic. Glancing across at her, his blue eyes were alight, obviously sharing her thrilling response to it all.

So intense was her exhilaration at the speed, the noise, and the wind in her hair, that she had trouble catching her breath. She was aware that her pulse was racing at the sheer physical sensation of the car...and the driver. Heat surged through her body and suffused her face in a warm glow. Luckily Jack was so engrossed in the jostling driving conditions that it wasn't until they hit the outskirts of Nice that he was able to talk. By which time, she had recovered her composure a bit.

Although it was sunny, it wasn't warm, so she wrapped her cosy soft scarf tightly round her and snuggled down in the seat. Having the top down meant she could see everything better. The rocky promontories reared up all around them as they reached the surrounding hills.

Turning to Jack, she was unstinting in her admiration.

'What a fabulous car. What an animal roar it makes.'

He grinned and did a tiger growl that sent ripples through her stomach.

She laughed in delight. 'And I love that big wooden steering wheel, and all those dials and stuff. It's so wonderfully old fashioned; it's like something from a Ladybird book.'

He looked surprised.

'Oh no, that isn't an insult. I meant it as a sort of tribute to how it feels.'

'Don't worry, that's how I took it.' He patted the side of big maroon car affectionately. 'Silly really to feel so much emotion about a car, but she's my pride and joy. A bit past her prime maybe, but she's a classy old girl.'

As they roared further up into the hills, she recognised some areas she had explored before. But how different it felt now. She told him about her earlier ride on a little train, which had taken her on a magical journey up these hills on a soft misty day.

'It was a wonderful trip, but I really missed having someone to share it with. If you see something you always want to say to someone, ooh look at that. Well, at least I do.'

'Yes, I felt the same about my journey down through France. It was fine at first, then I too wanted to share it. Does something have to be shared to be fully experienced do you think?'

'I suppose lots of people, explorers and travellers don't feel that need. I suppose it says something about us, if we both feel the same.'

He shot her a look of pure recognition.

Feeling elatedly in tune with Jack and her surroundings, she burbled on ecstatically, happily enthusing about every new thing that caught her eye.

Joining in with her delight, Jack told her how he had

driven Lucien's sister, Nicole, around this self-same route and even though she enjoyed the hills, they were so familiar to her, she hadn't viewed her surroundings with the same intensity as he had.

They gasped in unison as they rounded a bend in the road and saw a beautiful golden-stoned village perched on a hilltop. Below them, in the distance, shimmered the vast blueness of the sea.

'Even the air smells different. I'm in love with this place,' he said. 'The hills here are so different from home.'

'Yup,' agreed Annie. 'And it's not raining.'

'Let's stop here for lunch. Look, I can park over there and we can sit outside that café in the square.'

'OK. As long as you agree it's my turn to pay.'

He sighed. 'We are not going to have this argument again, are we?'

'Of course not, because this time I will brook no opposition. OK?' She gave him a hard stare.

He grinned. 'I love it when you are so forceful.' Then looked abashed as if embarrassed by his remark.

Secretly thrilled at what he had said, and the way he said it, Annie followed him across the cobbled square as they were both drawn by the cooking smells emanating from a small rustic restaurant nestling in the sun.

Sitting outside at a corner table with a bright yellow tablecloth, they perused the menu.

'I fancy the set menu, don't you?' Annie remarked. 'But not the cassoulet. All those beans wreak havoc with my… um…innards.'

'Yes, but once we start driving again, I'm sure you will be able to…give vent with impunity.'

'What. I wouldn't dare, not in Elspeth.'

He grinned. 'Thank you, I'm glad you appreciate the classiness of the old girl. I think I'm having the mussels. How about you?'

'Nope, too much fuss. When I'm hungry I just want to tuck in and get on with it.'

'Hmmn, I've said it before, you are such a peasant,

Mademoiselle Annie. It seems you can take the girl out of Accrington, but you can't take Accrington out of the girl.'

'Yup. This girl is going to have meat and chips, bavette and pommes frites, followed by a pud. What's not to like?'

It was a delicious meal, simple but full of flavour. And afterwards Annie sat back contentedly and looked around. 'It's just all sooo French.'

'And how do you define French?'

'Do you know, I can't quite define it? How do you encapsulate the smells, sights and feeling of Frenchness? Here we are, sitting in a golden-stone village, neat and ancient with gaily coloured shop signs, pavement cafés and coffee smells in the air. It's the colours, the ambience…it's… I know…it's worlds away from Accrington.'

He roared in agreement. They both felt the same and knew that what this place wasn't, was as important as what it was.

Chatting comfortably during the meal, Annie had at last recounted the history of her dealings with Reen. And shamefacedly confessed to her French subterfuge.

He loved it. 'How do you get yourself into such pickles?'

'I know,' she sighed. 'I panicked because of my promise to Sophie to improve my French. I had to speak only French, be French, and not get embroiled with the English ex-pat set. Mind you, right now, I'm so glad I broke all of them.' She cast a sidelong glance in his direction.

He grinned, 'So does Reen still think you are French?'

'I don't know. I just wish I could remember what I said that night, and whether she called me Annie or Marie-Anne next morning.'

He suddenly snorted with laughter. 'Sorry. I just remembered your face when you heard her footsteps last night. I wondered what was happening when you launched at me…' Tears were running down his face, 'and then…' he choked, 'when she came back, you lunged at me again.'

'Oh god I know; I'm so sorry.'

'I couldn't breathe. You threw me against that cold wall with such force you winded me, and then you wouldn't let me come up for air.'

'Oh don't. It's just I could feel her waiting behind me. I really am sorry. It's just I didn't know what else to do.'

'Stop apologising. It's not every day a fella gets pressed tightly against a wall by a passionate, flame-haired temptress.'

She blushed. Is that how he sees me? Wow.

Just then the peace of the square was disturbed by the high-pitched hornet whine of a manic moped. A young lad hurtled into view, whizzing past the café and careering towards the side of the parked Elspeth.

Jack leapt to his feet. The moped missed scraping the Jag by a hair's breadth, then raced down the steep street opposite.

'Bloody hell! That was close.' Looking very pale, he warily resumed his seat. 'Look, are you ready to go? I'd quite like to move Elspeth in case any more demented mopeds frighten her out of her wits. And I think the old girl could do with a bit of glamour after all these winding roads. How do you fancy finishing the day off in Cannes?'

'Ooh how posh, Our Jack,' she gushed, fluttering her eyelids in mock wonder.

Grinning, they set off for the style capital of the Côte d'Azur.

'I'm having a *c*up of *c*offee on the *C*roisette in *C*annes.' Annie deliberately clicked the 'k' sounds, loving the alliteration of it, as well as the experience itself. She looked around as if trying to believe this was really happening to her.

'You look like you did that first time you came into the café.' Jack grinned. 'I could tell from your face what you were thinking 'cos I've had moments like that myself. I feel special in France in a way I've never felt in England. And it's not just because I'm different, being a foreigner. I've been in France for nearly a year now and I still wake up in the morning with a tingle of excitement. I'm really thinking of getting a proper job here and settling down.' He blushed as he said it and looked intently into his steaming coffee.

Annie didn't quite know what to make of this. Is he

113

hinting? Surely not. It's far too early to be thinking of settling down together. Besides, as much as she loved France, she wasn't sure she wanted to stay forever. Would her French ever be up to the standard of her English and could she go the rest of her life communicating in a language other than her own?

On the other hand if Jack wanted to stay...

Stop. This was stupid. She knew she felt the same initial flare of attraction for Jack as she had felt all those years ago for Hamish. These were the only two times in her life there had been such a strong instant tug of emotion. But just because they seemed to have a definite rapport, it didn't mean she should be imagining a future relationship between them. Yes, she fancied him like crazy, especially when they were roaring around in Elspeth. And something about the throb of the car, definitely gave her the hots for the driver. But she must definitely nip any other thoughts in the bud.

Their shared childhood memories of their home towns seemed to be a safe topic of conversation so she embarked on tales of going to discos up at the neighbouring town of Great Harwood, (always nicknamed Mucky Herrod by the locals).

Jack joined in with memories of drinking Dandelion and Burdock while watching football up at the Accrington Stanley ground.

One of Annie's student holiday jobs was temping at a tiny plastic coat-hanger enterprise run from a couple of back-to-back houses in his hometown of Oswaldtwistle. When she returned to Uni no one could believe the name of the place, let alone such factories existed in this day and age. So she had enjoyed embellishing this experience into a Dickensian tale of waifs at the door holding out their hands for a pittance in recompense for the hardship and privations endured in back-breaking manual labour in the gloomy Victorian hovels of a dark, down-trodden mill town.

'Why does it not surprise me that you made it into such a melodrama,' Jack laughed.

'And don't get me started on clogs and shawls,' Annie warned.

They both were aware that all this was a long way from the sunny sophisticated view from their table in Cannes.

It was late afternoon when they arrived back in Nice. As they drove along the Prom, Jack suggested, 'How about I drop you off at your apartment, then I'll take Elspeth back to park her in Lucien's garage. Sorry, but I don't like leaving her out anywhere. Then, if you fancy it, I'll come back and we can perhaps go out somewhere for a meal.'

'That sounds great.'

'Perhaps we should go somewhere different from last night.'

'I can't think why you would suggest that,' Annie said, all innocence.

As he let her out of the car outside her apartment, she reached over and gave him a swift kiss.

'Thank you for such a smashing day.'

He grinned, 'I've loved it too.' Then he roared off.

Annie sighed and hugged herself. He was gorgeous. But did he feel the same way about her? So far the signs were very promising. Very promising indeed.

Chapter Twenty-One

There was a buzz at Annie's apartment intercom. It was Jack, much earlier than she expected. She buzzed him in and he arrived somewhat breathless from his run up the stairs. Luckily she was nearly ready. Sometimes not having many clothes was a bonus. It saved the dreadful indecision about which outfit to wear. But definitely something low-cut was in order if she was to entice him up afterwards. He was clearly not immune to her charms.

Secretly she had packed a few of her own favourites in amongst what she called 'the posh stuff'. And she had deliberately selected her favourite royal blue top. It was an old one from her Uni days. She had been wearing it the night she met Hamish and since then, she had saved it for special occasions. She felt good in it. It was a little low cut, but it had elicited so many compliments, it always made her feel confident and definitely alluring.

'Time to bring out the big guns,' she murmured, turning sideways to admire her bosom in the mirror. Sophie's sexy underwear choices were going to get a run for their money tonight.

But Jack was in such a rush to tell her something, he didn't even look at her or at the hastily uncluttered apartment that she had ensured was meticulously, but nonchalantly, tidy.

'Very sorry about this,' he panted. 'Of course I blame myself; I should have remembered but I was so enjoying our time together it slipped my mind. I should also have taken your telephone number.'

'Woah, take a breath.'

'Phew, it's further back here than I thought. I've really had to leg it. Sorry but I had clean forgotten it was André's birthday party tonight. He's Lucien's brother, and of course

I'm expected to go. I've explained about you, so you're invited as well, if you would like to come.'

It sounded exciting but she was vaguely disappointed. She was looking forward to an intimate tête à tête with Jack, followed by... She hadn't let her mind dwell too much on that, but she had, of course, changed the sheets on the bed. And made sure there were precautionary essentials in the bedside drawer. Just in case.

He seemed to sense her reluctance. 'It should be fun. It's at another uncle's restaurant so I know the food will be great. But all the family will be there. There are dozens of them I've met, but even more I haven't. Really, it's a great honour to be included so I can't not go. I'd love you to come and meet Lucien and his family. They've been very good to me. But I'll quite understand if you don't fancy it.'

'It does sound great.' She felt a bit mean. 'If you're sure they don't mind me coming with you.'

'Absolutely not. Nicole, Lucien' sister, especially said how much she wanted to meet you.'

'But is this outfit OK?' she asked.

She could see from his eyes that it was more than OK.

Feeling pleased at her choice, she flung her jacket on and they set off at a fast pace across town.

A wave of noise hit her as Jack pushed open the restaurant door. So many people, all talking animatedly at once. In spite of Jack's comforting hand on her arm, she quailed.

A slim dark-eyed man approached her with outstretched arms, and a very engaging, distinctly sexy, smile.

'*Enchanté*, you are Annie, I think.' His bright eyes signified his obvious approval of her to Jack. As he bent to kiss her on both cheeks, she was aware of his frank admiration of her low cut neckline.

'This is Lucien, my good friend,' Jack returned his warm two-cheek-kiss embrace, 'and don't let him flirt with you too much.'

'Flirt? What is this flirt?' Lucien grinned wickedly and

raised his shoulders in mock incomprehension.

Neither Jack nor Annie had a chance to answer as they were then swept up into a round of introductions and kissing, all in rapid, noisy, animated French. Jack beamed and seemed to be able to hold his own. Indeed, he seemed to assume a different persona, more relaxed, his body movements were more gesticulatory and his face more expressive. It suited him. Made him even sexier somehow.

At first Annie was overwhelmed and just smiled and nodded at everything and everyone. Which wasn't difficult as Jack was right, they were a lovely warm family. And the buffet food was copious and delicious with generous quantities of good wine. At first she concentrated on not looking too imbecilic as she ate and drank and grinned and agreed with everything said to her in accented French she only half understood.

Eventually she squeezed next to Jack and found a good vantage point with which to view the room. Instinctively it seemed, Jack put his arm round her waist but was engaged in animated conversation with one of the uncles about the relative merits of French and English football.

Her eyes were drawn to Lucien and his immediate family. From her questioning of Jack as they hurried to the party, she learned there were four brothers, André the oldest, then Jean-Marc, then Paul and Lucien the youngest. All of them were very good looking in a dark-eyed Mediterranean way. They stood out from the rest of the packed room by being taller and slimmer and moving with light-footed grace amongst the tables, topping up drinks and joking with everyone, especially with the females. But it was Lucien's progress round the room that kept drawing her attention. He was definitely the most charismatic of the lot, clearly a favourite with his infectious laugh and engaging banter. Was she imagining it, but he did seem to be catching her eye often, giving her an especially teasing grin and once even a conspiratorial wink.

After this wink, Annie determined not to look his way again. She didn't want to encourage this loose-limbed

Lothario.

Suddenly Jack leapt up and caught a very attractive woman by the arm and steered her over.

'Annie, this is Nicole. She has been especially wonderful to me.' He gave Nicole an unusually warm smile that instantly worried Annie.

Nicole gave Annie one of those looks French women give to other women. A slow appraising gaze that takes in everything from top to toe. The eyes were critical and cold. They robbed Annie of any confidence she was feeling in how she looked.

Feeling distinctly discomfited, Annie found herself stammering, 'Bonsoir. Thank you for inviting me. It is such a lovely party.'

There was no answering warmth from Nicole, who just nodded coolly and said politely she was welcome.

Seemingly unaware of this frisson, Jack began chatting to Nicole about the food and the party.

It gave Annie a chance to take a good long look at someone she immediately thought of as her rival for Jack's affections. It was a gut instinct.

She could see Nicole had obviously been stunningly beautiful in her youth and she still shared her brothers' dark good looks. She looked a bit older than Annie and was impeccably dressed in an expensive, beautifully-cut dark-red dress that showed off her figure to perfection. Annie immediately felt cheap and obvious in her bright blue top. How she wished she had brought one of Sophie's designer scarves to wrap nonchalantly around her shoulders.

Nicole was turning towards Jack, asking him something in a low voice, so that he had to lean towards her to hear it. He then eagerly rushed off in search of a glass of sparkling water for her. Left together, Annie tried to engage in conversation but it was hard work as the noise in the room made it difficult to hear Nicole's muted and monosyllabic responses.

She was relieved when a young child of about six rushed into Nicole's arms to tell her something. From her responses,

Annie realised it was her son. The child soon wriggled out of his mother's embrace and, with a small apology, Nicole got up and followed him. When Jack returned with her water, he seemed disappointed at her absence and his eyes quested for her in the room.

Annie deliberately drew back his attention. 'Do you mind if I have that water, Jack? I need to dilute the wine a little.'

Offering the glass to her with a smile, he said, 'No. Not at all. Very wise. They are certainly being very generous with the drink tonight.'

'Can I ask? Was that Nicole's son she went off with?'

'What? Oh yes. It would be.'

Annie waited for more information, but none was forthcoming. Intrigued by this seeming reluctance, she pressed on with her queries.

'So, is Nicole married then?' She tried to keep her tone neutral, but she couldn't dispel a little niggling voice of concern about the way Jack had looked at this cool, dark-haired beauty.

Jack looked around and taking her to a quieter corner, began in a low voice, 'No, not married. As far as I can make out, in her early twenties, Nicole fell for a married man. The affair lasted for quite a few years and seemed to become an open secret, known to most of Nice. As you can imagine, the family were not happy about it. Apparently there were lots of angry rows trying to force her to break it off. Possibly in an attempt to force him to leave his wife, Nicole became pregnant. But, inevitably, he chose to remain with his wife and children. So, to the family's dismay, Nicole became a single mother. That's it in a nutshell.' Jack hesitated. 'I think Nicole is a very strong character so Lucien didn't really want to say much more about it.

But as you can see, the child, Sébastien, is much loved, even a bit spoiled in my opinion,' Jack shrugged. 'But the whole affair did cause a bit of a scandal in what I think is still a deeply conservative corner of Nice society.'

Annie's stirrings of unease increased as she watched his eyes follow Nicole around the room. She hoped it was just that he felt deeply sorry for her plight.

'But she's a very beautiful woman, surely she could get a husband if she wanted.'

'Oh yes, I think there have been offers, but for some reason, none of them have been right. She gets lots of help from the family so possibly she's contented with her life.'

Annie felt a definite urge to change the subject away from Nicole. Looking around, she realised she recognised some of the stall owners from the market.

'I think I know quite a few faces here.'

'Oh, you will. It's a big family and they have a finger in every pie in Nice. Loads of the stalls, cafés, restaurants, shops and garages of the town are run by uncles, aunts, and cousins. It's a pretty tight-knit community.'

He indicated the party, 'I know it's a bit noisy and loud but are you happy to mingle some more?'

'Yes. I'm beginning to tune into the accent. Let's go.'

Jack grinned and, to her delight, held her hand as they launched again into the animated throng. But they were soon separated as Jack was dragged off to talk to someone about his car.

She found herself chatting to an older group of women who wanted to know all about her. She kept it simple saying she was house-sitting her aunt's dog for the winter while she did some writing. They nodded approval. Nice was famous for writers they said. She felt a little guilty at passing herself off so grandly but it was a convenient explanation.

Inspiration suddenly struck her. 'Perhaps you could help me.'

Good-natured nods indicated their interest.

'I have a French character I was thinking of naming Fabien. I just wondered if that was a common name in France. For example,' she rushed on, 'are there any Fabiens here tonight?'

'Oui,' said a large lady Annie had seen on the market. 'There's Uncle Fabien over there.' Eagerly, Annie's eyes looked at where the lady was indicating.

'Um…which one is he?'

'The old gentleman sitting in the corner.'

'Ah, oui.'

Annie quickly dismissed him as the wrong age range.

'Any more Fabiens here?'

The group looked a little bewildered.

'My character is about fifty and quite good looking,' she explained.

'I wish,' joked one fair-haired woman.

'So no one here like that?'

'Little Fabien is only eight, and here is a Fabien who is not very good looking at all,' the fair-haired woman remarked with a twinkle in her eye.

Everyone laughed.

'Which one?' asked Annie, rather too hastily.

'My husband,' said the young woman rather puzzled. 'Here he is chatting to your Jack.'

Looking at the Fabien who had come to join them, she could see he was too young but he was very handsome. She joined in the laughter and decided she couldn't enquire any more. Fabien's wife looked at her a bit suspiciously and moved away to reclaim her spouse.

She hoped Jack hadn't overheard the conversation. He knew nothing as yet about her search for Fabien. She knew she was putting off telling him because it was all linked into the death of her mother and would be very upsetting to talk about. Was their relationship up to that yet?

But 'your Jack', the woman had said. She liked the sound of that. Out of the corner of her eye, she could see that Jack seemed to be getting some good-natured ribbing about her. Although she didn't understand a lot of the teasing, it was obvious that they were being paired up in a romantic way. Although he seemed a bit embarrassed, he was not displeased, so clearly the idea of them as a couple was not unwelcome.

She relaxed and determined to enjoy this wonderful insight into Nice society, beginning to appreciate why Jack loved being part of it.

Perhaps her misgivings about Nicole were unfounded.

Chapter Twenty-Two

Eyes alight, Jack came to stand next to her.

'Are you enjoying it?' he murmured, close to her ear, sending tingles along the nape of her neck.

'Very much. And you are obviously part of the family, aren't you?'

He looked pleased. 'Yes, I don't know why, but they seem to have accepted me. I feel very lucky to have landed amongst such a warm-hearted group of people.'

Some instinct told Annie she was being observed. Looking across the room she could see Nicole in deep conversation with Lucien. They both glanced over at her and Jack for a moment before separating.

But with his arm about her waist, Jack was guiding her towards a boisterous group of mainly young members of the family. He introduced her around and they all immediately welcomed her. As she joined in the chatting she noticed all four brothers were flitting in and out of the conversation as they replenished their guests with wine. She was aware that her glass was being frequently topped up and she found her fluency increased in proportion to the drink taken.

It was a fun group and, as the evening wore on, she gained more confidence to join in with the joking and banter. She noticed the group listened intently to what she was saying and obviously found something about her conversation fascinating. She wasn't sure whether it was her accent or her expressions but she was clearly amusing them. Lucien often hovered near her and on one occasion was convulsed like the rest of the group by something she said. She turned to Jack for explanation but he too was laughing too much to tell her so just hugged her instead.

Oh well, she thought, it can't have been that bad. And judging by the fact that the group were egging her on to more faux pas, they were all clearly enjoying it.

In a quiet moment, she whispered to Jack to ask him if she was making a fool of herself. He gazed at her with laughing eyes and said fondly, 'No, they just love your accent and find your quaint expressions utterly charming. And sometimes mystifying. You have a wonderful knack of translating English idioms straight into French. You do know that they haven't a clue what 'raining cats and dogs' is, or 'just the ticket'. And I'm not sure what they made of to put *'un chat parmi les pigeons'* although I suppose they could guess what a cat would do among pigeons. Probably your style is a little racier than what they are used to from the English people they usually meet, so I'm glad you gave up on 'getting your *pantalons* in a twist'. And it even took *me* a while to realise 'une douleur dans le derrière' is a 'pain in the bum.'

Annie grinned, 'But it's just Franglais. Everyone else I talk to like that understands me.'

'Oh, really. Who for instance?'

'Er...well.' She was stumped for a moment and then remembered who had been the main recipient of her French over the past weeks. 'Well, Pimpy understands every word I say.'

He roared, 'Of course she does. For goodness sake don't stop, I'm loving it just as much as they are.' And he hugged her again, and his arms drew her in closer as they laughingly parried Franglais expressions between themselves.

Feeling his arms entwine around her, she snuggled into his chest for a brief moment. But, seemingly out of nowhere, a loud passionate argument had erupted in their group and they called on Jack to contribute. It totally lost her as it became even more heated. Worried by its vehemence, and that something she had said may have unwittingly caused it, she slipped off to the loo.

It was cool in there. Whether it was the noise, the wine or the increasing closeness to Jack, but she needed time to steady herself a little.

As she returned, she noticed all was calm again. Almost as if waiting for her to emerge, Lucien was immediately by her side offering to top up her glass. Anxious about what had caused such a heated flare-up, she asked him about it. He looked surprised at her concern and told her it was just a normal disagreement between friends.

She couldn't believe it. 'Normal!'

Lucien laughed. 'We French are more honest than the English and discuss things more passionately and openly. I have noticed that you English are too polite to express real opinions. You are too frightened of hurting someone's feelings and always try to keep the peace.'

Annie had to admit there was a certain truth in what he said. 'I think you are right. I can't remember the number of times I have said 'I don't mind' when every fibre of my being *did* mind. But I suppose I was brought up not to make a fuss.'

He nodded. His twinkling brown eyes travelled up and down her body in frank approval and somehow enticed her to go further.

'Right,' she said boldly, 'I'm going to start making it clearer what I want from now on.'

Seeing the wicked glint in his dark eyes, she realised he assumed she meant she wanted him. Blushing fiercely she turned away. This man really could flirt.

She found Jack and noticed his face lit up when he saw her. In one sinuous movement he snaked his arm round her waist, sending yet more heat to her face. Was he a little tipsy? He was certainly enjoying himself.

'It's great isn't it?' He nuzzled into her neck sending all the little hairs on her body aquiver. Laughing she clung to him and just nodded, the music and noise levels making it hard to converse anymore.

Holding her close, Jack began to sway in time to the music. Laying her head on his chest, she was just about to close her eyes when she saw Nicole grab Lucien again and stare meaningfully in their direction. What was it about them that was causing Nicole to pay them so much attention?

Her initial qualms about Nicole had lessened as the party progressed and Jack had become more openly affectionate towards her. Although a bit shy at the beginning, now his glances were full of smouldering intensity that caused her pulse to quicken and desire flame along her limbs. She curved her body into his, and felt a corresponding tightening of his hold around her.

He was just about to say something to her when Lucien approached to fill up their glasses. Despite his protests, Jack's glass was laughingly filled up to the brim. Feeling slightly unsettled by their earlier encounter, Annie refused the top-up. Lucien filled it anyway and winked. Then proceeded to drag Jack away for another car-related conversation. Exceedingly irritated by this deliberate intrusion, Annie put down the unwanted drink and decided to go in search of water.

Returning, she couldn't find Jack at all. However, Lucien was hovering nearby and was just closing in on her when he was accosted by a slim mousey blonde who put a determined hand on his arm. Annie tried to remember her name from an introduction earlier in the evening. Monique, yes, that was her name. With a shrug, Lucien accompanied her over to the other side of the party where Uncle Albert from the café was holding sway about some political issue or other.

The young group beckoned her over and began asking her about some of the strange expressions she had used earlier, but Annie had lost the mood for linguistic fun and games. Although she did join in with the odd remark, she was mainly glancing round the room searching for Jack.

Eventually she excused herself and quartered the room, growing increasingly concerned. What could have happened to him? Surely he wouldn't leave her at a party where she didn't really know anyone.

Eventually, with relief, she discovered him slumped on a chair in a corner, being clucked over by a group of indulgent older women. He had a fixed glazed look and was smiling beatifically at all and sundry. It was getting late, the party was winding up, but he was clearly in no fit state to walk her home, or anything else for that matter. His eyes closed and his head lolled to one side.

She looked round anxiously. Everyone was departing. It was a long walk back across town and she wasn't too sure of the route.

Luckily an older couple she had been talking to earlier were just leaving and seeing the situation, kindly offered her a lift. She accepted gratefully.

Turning to go, she saw Nicole and Lucien bending over the sleeping Jack. They seemed to be laughing.

Chapter Twenty-Three

It was a restless night as the flirtatious figure of Lucien flitted in and out of her dreams. Her skin prickled as she remembered the lascivious way he looked at her.

But her dreams were also filled with the sensation of Jack's arm around her waist, his hot lips in the nape of her neck. She awoke with burning thoughts of desire, and by the ardent glow in his eyes, she was sure he felt the same.

But the evening had ended with crushing disappointment. What had happened to get him so drunk? She couldn't help suspecting Lucien was actively involved in the process. And Nicole. But why?

Lucien had definitely flirted with her. Had she unwittingly given him cause to think he stood a chance with her? She fervently hoped not. And surely he could see that Jack and she were together. With an involuntary thrill she wondered if they were now 'an item'. Certainly Jack's behaviour indicated it, and most people at the party seemed to think so.

Still puzzling, she got ready to go to the market. And to see Jack. As she approached her usual vegetable stall, she recognised Jean-Claude and his sister Isabelle from the party the night before. They greeted her warmly with two kisses and chatted as they effortlessly served their many customers. Annie had frequently noted their friendly repartee with their regulars and now, to her delight, she was included in their banter. Her order of grapes was surprisingly generous, and cheap, and the bag included a couple of un-requested oranges. As she made her way around the market she experienced nods and smiles from people who she vaguely recognised from the night before.

It was a lovely warm feeling.

To her surprise, even the usual unsmiling Patron, Uncle Albert, came over and greeted her as she sat at her usual table. He informed her with a wink that Jack was a *peu malade* this morning but he came over personally to bring her a coffee. An honour indeed. Although she was bitterly disappointed not to see Jack.

Sipping her coffee in the surprisingly warm winter sun, Annie noticed the arrival of Mousy Monique, the girl who had engrossed Lucien's attention at the end of last night. She kissed Uncle Albert and a fleeting moment of body language and resemblance made Annie suspect that perhaps she was his daughter. Come to think of it, she had seen Monique there often, sometimes chatting to Jack and the other waiters and sometimes the regular customers, including Monsieur Xavier.

Speak of the devil. He was approaching her now. She froze.

'May I join you?' His request was, as ever, courteous and charming. In spite of herself she smiled her assent.

There followed a polite exchange in which they caught up with the usual subjects of weather and health.

In his usual amiable way, he soon noticed she now had two dogs peeking out of her basket and asked to be introduced. Annie did the honours for Pugsy and he made an equal fuss of both little excited bundles.

As she explained Pugsy's presence, Annie realised it was an opportunity to show that she now had friends and a social life. The portrait of the absent Reen was therefore skewed somewhat to show a caring, motherly figure who had taken Annie under her wing. Which, she realised with a shock, was probably not far from the truth.

He listened, smiling, but something about Pugsy evidently puzzled him and he asked how old he was. Annie remembered vaguely and told him.

'But if he is so much younger than Mademoiselle Pimpernel, why does his name begin with the same letter, a P?'

Annie was flummoxed by the question.

'Surely they were registered in different years?' he persisted.

Mystified by all this, she enquired about the significance of the name.

Gradually it emerged that in France all the pedigree dogs born and registered each year were allocated the next letter in the alphabet from the previous one. All their names had to begin with that letter. So you always knew the age of the dog from the first letter of their name. He assumed it was the same in England.

He was as fascinated to discover the lack of any system in England as Annie was to learn of this regimentation in France. They went on to laughingly discuss the national differences this perhaps reflected.

'It's ironic that yours is the nation that invented the term laissez–faire. Our language had no equivalent so we have had to borrow it from you,' she observed.

'Absolutely,' he laughed, 'and we have to borrow terms of time from you like *le week-end.*'

Annie was in her element as they discussed their respective nation's borrowed phrases. She was thoroughly enjoying herself and was nearly caught off guard as he casually asked if they could continue the conversation over dinner, as he was very sorry but he would have to leave in a moment for an appointment.

'I would like to show you a very unusual restaurant. No doubt you have seen our very famous hotel, the Negresco, with its outrageous pink dome and wonderfully amusing decor. Well, in spite of the perhaps ostentatious architecture, the restaurant serves superb food and I would be delighted if you would accept an invitation to dine there with me. I do enjoy our conversations so much. Perhaps you are free this evening?'

If Annie hadn't been warned she would have leapt at the chance to visit a place that she had often stood longingly outside, trying to glimpse its world-famous Baccarat chandelier. Intimidated by the liveried footmen at the door, she had never dared venture over the threshold in spite of the guidebooks saying it was a must-see experience.

Flustered by her awareness of his motives and not sure what to say, she hesitated before she could come up with a reason to refuse.

Monsieur Xavier was waiting, smiling benignly at what he perhaps thought was her embarrassment at such a wonderful offer.

'Thank you so much, Monsieur Xavier...' she began.

'Oh, call me Henri, please. If I may call you Annie?' and he smiled into her eyes as he reached for her hand and brought it gently to his lips.

Oooh, he's a smooth operator and no mistake, thought Annie.

'I'm afraid I can't make it this evening. I have a new friend who has invited me round for supper.'

'Oh.' He looked a little surprised and displeased.

'This new friend...?'

'Isabelle,' Annie invented.

He seemed pleased it was a girl's name. Blast, thought Annie, I should have invented a boy's name, but it seemed a bit presumptuous to say she had a new boyfriend called Jack.

'How do you know her?'

'She lives in the same apartment block as me.'

'Oh good. I am pleased for you. Perhaps another time then?'

'Monsieur, pardon...Henri, I wonder if you have made any progress on finding Fabien.'

'Alas no, Mademoiselle. But rest assured I am trying.'

With a courteous nod, he was gone.

Relieved, Annie sank back in her chair. That was a narrow escape.

If only she could tell Jack about this encounter. But she had no idea where he lived and didn't even have a phone number. Dare she ask Uncle Albert for information? He was standing in the doorway, as always, closely observing everything that happened in his domain. No doubt he had taken in everything about her meeting with Monsieur Xavier.

I wonder how he has interpreted it. I suppose I could

approach him and chat a little before making enquiries about Jack. Annie looked across at the imposingly rotund shape hoping to catch his eye rather than traversing the café to meet him.

No. In spite of his previous welcome, Uncle Albert still exuded a slightly forbidding air, so she just waved at him as she left. He nodded.

Despite not seeing Jack, Annie strolled back home feeling happier than she had for ages. She had deflected Henri Xavier, had made friends in Nice and was beginning to feel part of the place instead of just a visitor. And she had a man in her life to occupy her thoughts and fantasies.

In the end, she was pleased with how she had handled Monsieur Xavier as she didn't want to alienate him completely in case he did discover the right Fabien. But she had let him know she now had two friends, Reen and the mythical Isabelle, so he might not pursue her any more. But, just in case, she must find a different excuse for if he persisted. Probably lunchtime meetings would be safe. It was the evening ones she should be wary of.

Hoping Jack might pop round, she sat out on the rather chilly balcony half-heartedly typing up deciphered notes on her laptop. She had dressed ready to be surprised, wearing something chicly casual, as she kept an eye out for his familiar lithe figure walking along the street. The afternoon and evening wore on, but no such luck.

A bit despondent in spite of her good day, she took the dogs for a slightly longer last walk. She wanted to peek into the Negresco at night. Yes, she sighed; it looked just as sumptuous at night and the Baccarat chandelier could just be glimpsed through the elegant foyer. Well, never mind, perhaps Jack might be persuaded to take her. She would suggest going Dutch of course.

But just the prospect of seeing him put a spring in her step and she realised she was smiling as she walked home.

Chapter Twenty-Four

Next day at the café, a slightly shame-faced Jack greeted her with a grin. He pulled out her chair with a flourish and bent to whisper. 'I'm not exactly in Uncle Albert's good books after missing yesterday, so daren't stay and natter.'

His breath on her neck caused an involuntary shiver of excitement. He rested his hand briefly on her shoulder, before a swift caress of her back. Then he was gone but not before he had turned and winked at her.

Returning with her coffee and a mound of pain perdu, he bent low and murmured, 'Do you fancy a drink tonight and probably a bite to eat?'

'Yup, love it but…'

'I know… going Dutch. Meet at the usual time at the usual place?' He nodded his head towards the spot of their first rendezvous.

'Okey dokey.' Annie smiled. How lovely to have a 'usual place'.

The sun was setting like a ball of fire over the sea creating a glimmering rosy pathway to the horizon. Annie sighed. This place was beautiful and as she waited for Jack to arrive she reflected how lucky she was to be here. How her mum would have loved it. Did she have the same fluttery anticipation as she waited to meet Fabien? More and more she was tuning into her mother's feelings all those years ago in Paris. Certainly she knew she was experiencing a range of emotions she had never felt before. All day Jack had filled her thoughts and she had difficulty concentrating on anything else.

His now familiar figure hurried across the road to greet her with a beaming smile and a lingering kiss on both cheeks, French style, which set her pulse racing.

Immediately, they both launched into intense chatter

about the party and the people. He was mortified by how much he had imbibed that night and told her of his tremendous hangover and the inevitable teasing he had received ever since.

'I was fussed over by those aged aunts. Apparently they couldn't believe how floppy and silly I was. I'm so sorry about deserting you like that. Fancy not seeing you home. I heard you were well looked after. Monsieur and Madame Salas are lovely, aren't they? What did you think about Lucien's family? Aren't they as welcoming as I said they were?'

He launched again into enumerating all the wonderful things the family had done for him, especially Lucien.

Annie didn't dare voice her suspicions that Lucien had deliberately got him drunk, because she couldn't figure out why he would have done that.

'Usual place for a drink?' asked Jack indicating the bar across the Prom.

'Yes, please.'

He reached out to put his arm round her and she tucked into his shoulder as they crossed the busy Promenade. It was a great feeling.

The bar was cosy and crowded but they found a table in the corner, where, knees touching, they continued their conversation.

Annie smiled. 'I have really noticed a difference since the party. Everyone in the market is so friendly. And, shock news, even Uncle Albert said a few words as he served me my coffee yesterday morning.'

'Wow, an honour indeed,' he laughed. 'But I'm not surprised. You were a tremendous hit, you know.'

Annie dimpled with pleasure. 'Really?'

'Oh yes, Nicole wanted to know all about you...well... they all did. In fact I'm under strict instructions to arrange another get-together as soon as possible.'

Although surprised, Annie replied, 'Oh right. That would be great.'

Later, over a meal in their 'usual' restaurant, Annie related her encounter with Monsieur Xavier. At some point, she knew she really ought to tell Jack about her search for Fabien, but once again she shied away from it. The story was so inextricably linked to her mum's death, she couldn't face revisiting all the anguish of that time. Especially not now, when she was feeling so happy.

Jack nodded as she finished her tale of the thwarting of Monsieur X, as she now called him.

'Brilliant. That way you didn't let on that you knew about his evil intentions. And he knows you have got friends looking out for you.'

'But I've only got you to thank for not ending up in the white slave trade in the harem of an eastern potentate. There, I really would have to perform the dance of the seven veils... and really reveal all.' And she once again whisked up her serviette to cover her lower face like a yasmak and glanced at him flirtatiously.

The hovering waiter viewed her with alarm.

Jack rolled his eyes to heaven. 'What big eyes you have there, little Miss Red Riding Hood. And what an even bigger imagination.'

'All the better to eat with you, my dear.' She grinned wolfishly.

'Talking of which, would you really like to go to the Negresco?'

Annie couldn't believe her ears. 'Oh dear. Sorry. I suppose I did lay it on a bit thick about how I was sorely tempted to sink into a life of sin, if only to enter the hallowed portals of that august establishment. But it looks so exclusive; it's got to be an arm and a leg job to eat there.'

'Well, yes and no. The actual restaurant is tremendously expensive but they have got a brasserie which is much more reasonable...and much more fun. It's in the shape of a carousel and has hurdy-gurdy music and fairground horses that go up and down while you're dining.'

'Wow, what fun.'

'I've always fancied going myself but never really had

anyone to go with. It's not the sort of place that my French friends would consider visiting. I expect they think it's a bit touristy. They always frequent less ostentatious places, and go to each other's restaurants whenever—'

'I've an idea.' Annie interrupted, fired by the idea of seeing the famed chandelier. 'We could always go into the bar in the hotel for drinks and look at everything there first. That shouldn't be too expensive.'

'Look,' Jack exclaimed, 'stop worrying too much about how much everything costs.'

'Well, you really can't earn much as a waiter and—'

'Whooa there, Accrington Annie. There are lots of reasons I work at Albert's and earning a crust is not the main one. I sold my flat, remember, to finance my trip and I've still got quite a bit left. Albert's was my 'intro' to Nice and speaking French and a way of saying thank you to Lucien's family. Yes, and a way of not eroding my savings too much. Although I wasn't joking about being paid a pittance, the tips are surprisingly good, well, they were in the summer, especially from the Americans. So watch my lips…I'm not hard up.'

'Oh, right,' said Annie, relieved. She had been mainly worried for his sake, aware that so far she had not really paid her way. These things were important to her. 'OK, it's a deal. Let's go there and treat ourselves to a great night out. In spite of what you say about being as rich as Rockefeller, I still insist on going Dutch. After all I wouldn't want to have to pay in kind, would I?' And she eyed him in mock modesty.

Oh, crikes, what have I said, she thought, as she saw a surprised look come over his face. Her embarrassment overwhelmed her. How stupid to hint that she wouldn't want to go to bed with him, however obliquely.

'Although of course I would *love* to pay in kind…' she trailed off…that was even worse.

Beam me up, Scottie.

To cover her confusion and not daring to look at his face, she clumsily groped for her wine, and missed, knocking it straight over Jack's lap.

136

He leapt up. The red wine didn't *quite* cover the *whole* of his groin. But it was spreading fast.

Their usual waiter was on hand to mop resignedly at the formerly white tablecloth, while Jack made hurriedly for the loos to rinse out the offending stain.

Sitting there, shame faced, amidst the debris of the table, she couldn't believe she had done it again. Another glass of bright red wine all over everything. She murmured, 'Pardon,' at the waiter who just shrugged.

And up till then it had all being going so well.

A little later, Jack emerged grinning, holding his serviette carefully over his nether regions.

He stopped her apologies with another grin. 'It's OK. Honestly it is, but...' he hesitated and leant towards her, 'I don't think we better come here again.'

'But what if I do that at the Negresco,' she wailed on the way home.

'You won't,' he reassured her. 'Anyway, we'll just have to stick to white wine...less obvious.'

Approaching her apartment block, Annie once again contemplated the invitation up to her bed...umm...her flat. But before she could devise an innocently phrased request, he pre-empted her.

'Look, I better get straight back home if you don't mind; it's a little parky around the gonads.' He gave a vague gesture towards the huge drenched patch on the front of his jeans.

Bugger. She was just fantasising about the scenario where obviously he would have to get out of his wet clothes as she prepared a steaming cup of coffee, before enticing him into her suspiciously tidy bedroom with a drawer full of condoms.

'Oh right,' she agreed lamely.

'We'll sort out the Negresco visit tomorrow, if that's OK?' And with a tight embrace and a soft lingering kiss that left her wanting more, so much more, he was walking hurriedly, if rather bow-leggedly, away.

Bugger.

Chapter Twenty-Five

Right, Annie resolved, as once again, morning shopping done, she made for the café. I'm going to get that bugger Jack into my bed if it's the last thing I do. He's obviously a nice guy who believes in taking his time, all of which is great. And I'm a nice girl who doesn't leap into bed on the first date, not even with Hamish. But I am getting a little bit randy and perturbed that my alloouer is non-existent. Perhaps I'm being too subtle. Time to ratchet things up a bit.

Sod the Negresco. I'll invite him round for a meal.

With this in mind, she waited for a lull in customers and beckoned him over. Mousy Monique watched from the door with interest.

'Bonjour, Jacques. A pretty delicious little snack of pain perdu if I may say so. Although it was far from little. I'm sure you will get into trouble if you keep giving me such a huge plateful.'

Smiling into her eyes, he gave one of his hugely sexy Gallic shrugs.

As the heat of desire travelled up her body, she thought, he is definitely coming to my apartment tonight. And then...

'Look, Jack, I've been thinking. I really owe you a meal to thank you for that lovely trip the other day.'

'No, really,' he interrupted, 'you don't. In fact Nicole is giving me a hard time about meeting you so I wondered about us all going out somewhere together.'

No way, thought Annie. I feel distinctly uncomfortable with her. Why the heck is she making such a fuss about meeting me again? In fact I got the distinct impression she didn't like me. And the last thing I want right now is an intimate dinner à trois.

'Well, that's nice,' she lied, thinking fast, 'but it would be nice to get to know some more of the family as well. What about asking one of them...in fact,' she found herself rushing into saying, 'you could *all* come round for a meal.'

'That would be great. But not sure about *all* the family. But Lucien liked you a lot. He's a bit of a flirt as you probably noticed, but there's no harm in him and he's great company. Are you sure?'

No. Help. But it was too late. She found herself enthusing about the idea.

And so...

Bugger. Bugger. Bugger.

It was settled that they would all come round for a meal the next night.

Annie paced round the kitchen trying to calm her nerves.

'For goodness sake, stop fussing,' she told herself. 'Why are you so panicky? You have spent two whole days sorting and planning this. You have cooked more difficult meals for more people with a lot less palaver.'

All the dishes were tried and tested. The apartment glowed in the candlelight, the table looked terrific with fresh flowers and gleaming glassware, the wines were well chosen and all the right temperature. And although her colour was a little high from nerves and cooking, she felt she looked good, with just the right amount of cleavage to be suggestive without being blatant.

But it wasn't the meal, it was the mix of people that was causing the nerves. Lucien had a way of looking at her that was so flirtatious it instantly embarrassed her. Whatever happened she must not let his attentions upset her focus on Jack. Jack was the one she wanted to impress.

And why on earth did Nicole want to come and meet her again? None of it made sense.

The doorbell rang. Smoothing her hair with nervous hands, she went to answer it.

Her heart leapt as Jack's smiling blue eyes greeted her. He was wearing her favourite soft linen blue shirt and smart designer jeans which fitted his long legs and hugged his slim hips to perfection. With a wide grin and a flourish, he presented her with an extravagant bouquet of flowers then, as he leaned forward to kiss her cheek, she got the soft lemon scent of his aftershave. Weak-kneed, she clung to his broad shoulders as she returned his kiss.

Then she saw Nicole. She was drop-dead gorgeous in a bright red dress, which suited her dark good looks and slim elegant figure to perfection. The dramatic matching red lipstick had obviously been carefully chosen as had her pervading sensual perfume. She was dressed to kill.

Her cool appraising glance immediately robbed Annie of any vestige of confidence she had in her appearance.

She felt blowsy.

And that's when she started to burble.

She was still burbling over the drinks and nibbles when Lucien turned up half an hour late with a box of Nice's speciality crystallised fruits and a wicked twinkle in his eyes.

One look at his devilish grin and her burble-ometer went off the scale.

She fled to the kitchen to look at her twice baked soufflés, a sure-fire winner usually.

A concerned Jack followed her.

'Are you OK? Look, don't worry about it. Everything smells delicious. Nicole says how wonderful the apartment is…' he began burbling too.

Was it contagious? Why was he nervous?

It was then Annie saw the unopened bottle of Tequila, left by Reen.

She thrust it at Jack. 'Can you do the honours out there? Here's some glasses and some limes.'

'Are you sure?'

'Yup. Sure cure for nerves, Reen says.'

He grinned. 'I must admit getting your guests drunk as skunks used to be one of my strategies when I first started entertaining. Ooops… not that I'm suggesting…'

'Suggest away. But it's not just the guests. I think the hostess needs a little stiff drinkypoos too.' And she held out her glass for the first shot.

In fact the food was superb, even if Annie said so herself. And there was genuine appreciation all round as each trip to the kitchen brought forth even more goodies.

Even Nicole was impressed and took her brother's teasing in good part. Apparently she was not a good cook. However, she was stoutly defended by Jack. He, like Annie, had perhaps drunk a little more than was wise of the Tequila shots. The French brother and sister had politely tried one each, but declined all other offers and as the evening progressed, Annie felt that somehow these two held the balance of power and were much more in control of events than the English pair.

Well, they certainly didn't burble.

She also felt that Nicole was scrutinising the relationship between Jack and her very closely. Surely she couldn't be jealous. To be jealous must mean that she had her eye on Jack. Definitely her manner towards Jack was becoming increasingly flirtatious.

A hot flame of anger took her by surprise. Jack was hers...or rather she hoped he would be. What game was Nicole playing?

She couldn't watch them as closely as she would have liked, as making frequent trips to the kitchen distracted her.

But the biggest distraction was Lucien. To her confusion his wicked gleaming eyes were following her every movement.

She was a totally embarrassed by his obvious admiration of her cleavage. Her top was rather revealing she knew. But Sophie would be cross with her for not flaunting her wares just a little, especially as Annie had deliberately seated herself opposite Jack so he could 'cop an eyeful'.

But somehow the intended recipient of her largesse was being diverted by a much more elegantly dressed Nicole. Whenever his attention strayed across the table to her, Nicole touched his arm to ask him something. Then she kept murmuring comments to him so he had to lean in close to hear what she was saying.

And Lucien seated by her side was demanding more and more attention. She was having to put all her efforts into deflecting his progressively frank overtures. His hand traversed her thigh and had to be forcibly restrained from exploring further than was decorous at a dinner party.

What was the etiquette here? Could one slap a guest round the face? But the mischief in Lucien's eyes told her he was thoroughly enjoying his little game.

As the evening continued in its unexpected fashion and the drink flowed freely, Annie found that the table had virtually polarised. On one side Jack had been mesmerised by a softly spoken, coy Nicole, while she was being captivated by a sparkling and bantering Lucien. He truly was funny and in spite of herself, Annie had to laugh as he mimicked her accent and played her Franglais game with English translations of French expressions. If she hadn't already been so attracted to Jack, she could have fallen easily for this darkly handsome man.

Nicole, although seemingly engrossed with Jack, occasionally glanced across at her brother. Her approving nods seemed to suggest she was delighted with his flirtatious behaviour.

Excusing herself to make the coffee in the kitchen, Annie tried to sort it all out in her befuddled brain. Was Jack being seduced by Nicole before her very eyes at her own dinner party?

She's pinching him from me, and right under my nose. Damn cheek. I've a good mind to go in there and cut her heart out with this cheese knife. And why is Lucien making such a play for me?

Talk of the devil. There he was hovering behind her in the kitchen with a roguish gleam in his eye. Flummoxed by his proximity, she grabbed a pile of plates from the worktop and lurched rather uncertainly to the sink. There she concentrated really hard on rinsing them off.

Although conscious of Lucien's presence behind her, she was taken totally off guard by a gentle hand at her neck softly sweeping her hair to one side. His other hand crept round her waist and, ever so lightly, he kissed the nape of her neck.

'Lucien!' Jack's voice came sharply from the kitchen door. He looked furious.

With a sheepish grin Lucien immediately let her go.

'Oh, thank you, Jack,' sighed Annie with relief. 'I'm just coming in with the coffee.'

Jack continued to glare at Lucien who shrugged, before strolling nonchalantly back to the dinner table.

'Thanks, Jack. Lucien has been a bit of a handful. I've been dying to talk to you all evening but…'

'I know, me too. But actually, Annie, I came in to tell you that Nicole isn't feeling well.'

'Oh no. Really. It's not something she ate, is it?'

'Absolutely not. Everything has been delicious. But she suffers from migraines and she says she can feel one coming on.'

'I'm sorry. Oh dear.' Annie tried to keep her voice sincere while gleefully thinking, great. She's going so I can have Jack all to myself now.

'Oh, Jack, will you take me home please?' Nicole appeared in the doorway with a hand pressed to her head.

'Er…I thought Lucien could take you…' Annie was bewildered. Why was Jack needed?

'No. No. My brother, he should stay and help you. You have gone to so much trouble and your kitchen…,' here Nicole's nose crinkled as she surveyed the chaotic piles of plates and food debris. 'It wouldn't be polite to leave you to clear up all this mess.'

'It's fine. Really…'

But Nicole had gone.

'Where is my coat please, Jack?' she enquired plaintively from the hall.

An embarrassed Jack looked at Annie.

'Why can't Lucien take her home?' whispered Annie.

'No, she doesn't want me.' Lucien was lounging in the doorway. 'I am not sympathetic to her head aches. Not like my friend Jack here.'

'Jack,' came a querulous cry from the hall.

'Oh crikes, Annie. I hate to leave you with all this. It's been a great evening, it really has—'

'Jack. I must go now.'

Annie's shoulders slumped as she admitted defeat. 'It's OK. You take her home.' She went to give him a goodbye kiss.

Jack gave her a tight grateful hug.

'Annie, I really...' He was about to say more but this time the command from the hall was more urgent. He sighed. 'I'll see you tomorrow and thanks again. You are one helluva cook.'

He turned to the figure watching them from the doorway. 'Lucien,' he commanded. 'Time to go.'

Lucien shrugged but Jack's look was insistent as he followed his friend into the hallway.

And, in a short flurry of coats and pecks on cheeks and thanks, they were gone.

Bugger.

Disconsolately she surveyed the room. She'd had such hopes inviting Jack round and it had somehow been high-jacked. The whole thing was a mess, just like the kitchen. Sod it. Tomorrow would do for clearing up.

Angry, tipsy and dejected, she trudged to the bedroom.

But then Pimpy came from her cushion in the corner and whimpered, closely followed by Pugsy.

'Oh sorry, you two. You have been very good waiting this long. Come on, a quick twirl round the park for tiddles, and then it is definitely bed time for all of us.'

Flinging a coat over her dress and changing her heels for flatties, she whisked the doggies out for a brisk walk round the park. The fresh air did her good.

Returning, as she approached the apartment, a figure loomed near the doorway. It was Lucien.

'Lucien? What are you doing here?'

'Oh, Annie. I think I left my keys in your apartment.'

'Really. I didn't notice them.'

Slightly ill-at-ease she climbed the stairs and as she

opened her door, he followed her in. One look at the grin on his face told her the lost keys were a total fabrication. Enveloping her in his arms he began a long passionate kiss.

Angrily, Annie jerked her head away and began to struggle free.

'Stop that at once, Lucien.'

His look of surprise was almost comical. Then he recovered.

'Annie, ma chérie. You are so beautiful when you are angry,' he crooned.

'What a cheesy line.'

'What.'

'A line de fromage.'

'Pardon?'

'Look, Lucien. Whatever you are offering, I don't want it. OK. So sling your hook.'

'My hook?'

'Yes, ton barbe, sling it.'

'Annie...'

'Lucien, just get gone.'

'But...'

'I mean it. Get your coat...you haven't pulled.'

Lucien looked mystified at her words, but her annoyed face and outstretched arm pointing at the door conveyed her meaning very clearly. She saw a flash of anger in his eyes. His pride had obviously taken a hit. Suddenly aware she was alone in her flat with a lustful man, she braced herself and clenched her fists.

There was a moment of stand-off, then with a shrug and a strange smile, he walked out of the door.

She flung herself against it, letting out a deep breath of relief.

What a strange end to a strange evening.

Chapter Twenty-Six

It took all morning to get some semblance of order back into the flat.

Annie's mood didn't help the process. She daren't even take it out on the crockery. Madame Dumont's delicate plates and serving dishes had to be treated with the utmost care.

The more she played back the events of the evening, the more cross she got at the evident games of the brother and sister. For some reason Nicole was determined she shouldn't have Jack, and Annie was convinced that Lucien's attempted seduction was part of her schemes.

She just hoped she got a chance to talk to Jack about it. How aware was he of all the machinations? He was certainly angry when he saw Lucien with his arms about her in the kitchen and he definitely made sure that his friend left when they did.

But Lucien obviously snuck back hoping to have his wicked way. He looked really shocked when she had refused.

He's such a handsome bloke I suppose it doesn't happen very often, she thought. For a horrible minute there, I thought it was going to get really ugly. But I think he realised he was going to have one hell of a fight on his hands. I'm definitely going to tell Jack what I think of that friend of his. How dare he!

She was still livid as, belatedly, she hurried off to the market, ignoring the disapproving stare from an obviously huffy Madame Lafarge. Let her tell Madame Dumont about my dinner party, I don't care.

The market was closing up when she arrived but she headed for her usual stall.

I will have to be careful not to criticise Nicole and Lucien when I talk about the dinner, she thought as she approached Isabelle who was sipping a steaming coffee at the side of her market stall. She knew about the evening as Annie had consulted her about what to cook.

I will just thank her and say how successful the food was.

To her surprise Isabelle just glared at her and pointedly went to serve another customer.

A little bewildered, Annie waited till she was free and began selecting some green peppers.

'Your custom is not welcome here, Mademoiselle,' Isabelle hissed.

'Why not? I don't understand. I came to tell you how good all the food you provided was. It was a great success.'

'Yes, we heard,' said Isabelle sarcastically.

'Really? From Jack?'

'No. You see Lucien was discovered.'

'Discovered?' Annie was totally mystified by Isabelle's words and angry demeanour.

'Oh, you thought your liaison would remain a secret, didn't you?'

'Liaison?'

'With Lucien.'

'With Lucien? No. You are mistaken. There was no liaison.'

'Oh really. So where was he all night?'

'I don't know. He certainly wasn't with me.'

'You English. You look so sweet and innocent...'

'I am innocent.'

'Tell it to Monique, not me.'

'Why Monique?'

'Oh, don't pretend you don't know. Lucien is engaged to Monique.'

'What?' Annie couldn't believe her ears. 'That's not possible.'

But one look at Isabelle's cold, closed face told her it was true.

'Yes, they have been engaged for over a year. They are to be married in the spring. The reception will be at her father's place.' She nodded towards Albert's café. 'I am to be a bridesmaid,' she continued inexorably, accusingly.

'I didn't know.' Annie was thunderstruck. 'He certainly didn't behave like an engaged man last night.' Then she clammed up, realising her remark could be misconstrued. And it was. With a look of disgust, Isabelle stalked away.

What was going on? Had Lucien claimed they had spent the night together? What cheek. Angrily, Annie moved away.

Automatically, she headed towards the café to confront Jack but she saw a perturbed Isabelle rush up to Albert and begin an agitated conversation. There were gestures in her direction and his stern face darkened. As she approached, he moved towards her to block her entrance to his café.

'I don't know what you have heard…,' Annie began.

'Go,' he said and pointed an angry arm away from the café.

For a moment she hesitated, but then knew from the look on his face that he wouldn't listen to anything she said, so walked away, head held high. Whatever they thought, it wasn't true.

In a daze she walked back to the apartment, churning everything over in her mind. Just what was going on? Lucien had obviously given the impression to his fiancée that he was with Annie all night. Why? Surely he wouldn't admit to cheating on her, especially when it wasn't true.

An almost physical blow suddenly hit her in the chest. What had Jack heard? Surely he wouldn't believe it.

But only one way to find out. She had to ask him.

Rapidly, she retraced her steps to the only place she knew she could find him.

A cold wind was blowing as she arrived back at the café. With no idea where he lived, no phone number, it had to be there. Even though it meant facing an angry Uncle Albert.

Her determination wavered as she approached, but convinced of her own innocence in the matter, she steeled herself to go inside. The bulky figure of Uncle Albert barred the way in. So she sat outside, hoping Jack would see her and come to talk.

The late November sky had darkened to a cold grey and she was the only one sitting there. She couldn't see Jack but she couldn't go inside. So she sat there, cold and miserable for a long time as the rain clouds gathered.

No one approached her. She knew she was stupid to stay but didn't know what else to do.

Eventually Uncle Albert came and stopped a few feet away.

'Mademoiselle. You are not welcome here,' he said coldly.

Although intimidated by his manner, she held her ground. 'Whatever you've heard, it isn't true. I want to speak to Jacques.'

'Jacques does not work here anymore. Please leave.'

'What. But I must speak to him. It is important. How can I contact him?'

But Uncle Albert just shrugged and turned away.

'I did not spend the night with Lucien. Whoever has said so, is lying,' Annie cried at his retreating back.

The Patron closed the door and she was left outside in the cold.

Chapter Twenty-Seven

Distraught, Annie paced up and down the apartment.

'Should I ring Sophie?' she asked Pugsy. 'I know your mummy won't mind if I use her phone. This really is an emergency. I have got to talk this over with someone.'

She alternated between bouts of anger and feeling utterly bereft. Her thoughts were going round in circles, as were her steps. The two anxious little dogs ran up and down next to her, threatening to trip her up, so she eventually plonked down onto the ornate sofa. They immediately leapt on to her lap. She gazed at them fondly. They had been bewildered by her sobbing and had tried to comfort her by nuzzling and licking her. In a strange way it had helped. And she had begun to pull herself together for their sakes.

Drained by all her crying, she dragged herself upstairs and let herself into Reen's spartan apartment and phoned Sophie. Her friend's emails were always infrequent and brief, but lately Annie's had also tailed off. She had been reluctant to jinx her relationship with Jack by telling her friend about it. Especially as she knew that Sophie would be a bit sniffy about a waiter from Oswaldtwistle.

But how she longed to hear her friend's voice. It would be so good to talk to her, confide in her. Fingers crossed she would be there.

Philip answered.

'Hallo, Annie.' His warm cultured voice sounded surprised. 'How lovely to hear from you. Although you sound as if you've got a dreadful cold.'

'Cold?'

'Yes. You sound all snuffly. I thought you would escape the British winter ailments out there in the sunshine.'

'Oh yes, well, it's just a bit of a head cold. Um…is

Sophie there?'

'No such luck. In fact I rather hoped it was her ringing to say she was on her way home from the airport. That's why I'm here at her flat. I've got a nice meal waiting. I thought it would make a change to eat in instead of all these fancy restaurants she goes to while she's away.' He tailed off, clearly disappointed. 'She's been in New York for the week. You know since her promotion she has had to travel more and...'

Promotion? Promotion? Did I know about this? Annie asked herself. Perhaps she did, but in her self-absorption it hadn't registered.

'...and we have to make appointments to see each other,' he joked semi -seriously.

He sounded so forlorn, Annie couldn't possibly burden him with her news. And so she set about cheering him up. She had always been able to make him laugh. But he must have been feeling really low to be such a receptive audience for her unsubtle double-entendres and feeble witticisms.

As she went to say goodbye, he said, 'It's good to hear from you, Annie. I thought Sophie said her skinflint relative had barred you from using her phone.'

'Yes, it's true but I've met a lovely lady upstairs who says I can use hers.'

'Oh good. Let me have your number. I'm sure she will want to talk to you when she returns. She's generally a bit drained when she gets back from these trips but she will probably want to update you on the wedding plans, if nothing else.'

Annie gave him Reen's number, carefully explaining that she didn't want to bother her lovely neighbour in the flat upstairs so it was for emergency use only.

'Give Sophie my love when she gets back and say I would love a chat,' she finished.

So Sophie was busy with her life and plans. She knew Sophie hadn't told her about her promotion. In fact, hadn't emailed her for ages. Was Annie out of sight, out of mind? It made her feel worse than ever.

151

She slumped in the cool minimalist apartment and howled again.

It was Pugsy who heard it first. He scampered, paws slipping on the marble floor, yapping excitedly at the door, so when Reen entered in a flurry of gold and perfume he was there at her muled feet beside himself in his welcome.

Annie roused herself and was hugged and cooed over in the same affectionate way as the dogs.

It was only when the taxi driver had finished carrying up all her cases and the kettle was on for a 'cuppa' that Reen took a long hard look at Annie and said, 'OK, Dahling. Tell your Auntie Reen what's wrong?'

Here before her, in this unlikely figure, was the comfort Annie needed. She flung herself into Reen's surprised, scrawny arms.

Too miserable to continue the French pretence, Annie began by confessing to the deception and apologising, but Reen interrupted her.

'That's all right. I know you're not French, Dahling. Don't worry about it. Some rotten man has hurt you, hasn't he? Was it that young man I saw you with?'

'No, it was his friend. But Jack has been seduced by a conniving French strumpet and I can't get in touch with him and I don't know if he believes I've slept with someone, which I haven't, honestly, but everyone thinks I have and...'

'OK, slow down, Dahling. Let's start again. Who's Jack?'

Amidst sobbing and hiccupping and sniffing and tissues, somehow Reen managed to piece the story together.

Annie couldn't have chosen a more sympathetic audience. Reen was outraged at the opprobrium heaped on Annie. And she was in absolute agreement at the utter unfairness of it all. And joined in the besmirching of men in general and Jack and Lucien in particular.

She only disagreed when Annie began to wallow in self-recrimination.

'How could I have been so stupid...?'

'Right,' she said standing up decisively. 'None of this is

your fault but what can't be cured must be endured. What we both need is a little drinky. And I don't mean tea.'

'Oh noo,' Annie wailed again, feeling guilty. 'I think we drank all your tequila at the party last night.'

'I hope you did, my pet. I left it for you. But what makes you think that was my last bottle?' And she flung open a very well-stocked drinks cabinet.

At some point in the evening Ted phoned to check Reen had arrived safely.

Annie heard snippets. 'Pugsy's fine and sends his love. Look, I've got Annie with me. She's in a bit of trouble and. No, no, not that sort of trouble. At least I hope not.' She cast a quizzical glance at Annie, who shook her head emphatically.

'Some bastard man has told nasty tales about her…'

After reassuring Ted that all was under control, Reen poured out more drinks for the pair of them. She even found some nibbles.

Sitting there curled up on Reen's enormous cream leather sofa, Annie was amazed to find that just talking about it all helped.

'I must contact Jack. He's got to know whatever Lucien has said, it isn't true. It's so frustrating not knowing how to get in touch with him, especially now he's lost his job at the café. I feel awful about that. Albert probably sacked him because of me.

'Perhaps I can find Lucien and confront him. I know he has a garage. I should be able to look in a telephone directory and phone around till I find him.'

'Look, Annie Dahling. If Jack cares about you, he will come and find you. I think he will know it isn't true.'

'But you don't know how seductive Lucien is. He could charm the birds from the sky.'

'But he didn't charm you, did he?'

'Well, to be honest, he nearly did. He's fantastic company. Who knows he might have done if…'

'If you hadn't fallen for your Jack first.'

'He's not really *my* Jack, you know. I don't know if he feels about me the same as I feel about him. That wicked Nicole has got her claws well and truly into him.'

'But he will realise in the end, I'm sure, and he knows where you live,' Reen soothed.

'But what if he doesn't come?'

'Well, my pet, it just proves he's a stupid bastard. And doesn't deserve a lovely girl like you. Have another drink.'

She was right. But it was a painful truth.

Just then the phone rang. Reen answered. It was Sophie.

'Oh yes, Dahling, Annie's here,' Reen said, and passed the phone over.

Sophie sounded concerned. 'Philip phoned to say you've got an awful cold and wanted to talk to me. Are you OK? I know you wouldn't ring unless it was something important.'

'Thanks for phoning. Have you just got back from New York?'

'Yes, got back to London this evening. But are you OK? You sound awful. Are you ill or something?'

'Just man trouble,' Annie sniffed.

'Poor you. You're far too soft-hearted you know. Do you want to talk about it?'

Annie did, but not as much as she had done before Reen's comforting arrival.

'Yes and no. I've got a lovely friend here...'

'The lady who answered the phone?' Sophie asked dubiously.

'Yes, she's been wonderful to me. She's getting me a bit squiffy. Helping me drown my sorrows in drink, I suppose.' Annie smiled at Reen who held her glass high in salute.

'Well, go easy, Annie. You know you have never been able to hold your drink. Are you sure you're OK?' Her friend's worried tone nearly started Annie off again.

'Look, it's a long story and it's not my phone. I'll email you tomorrow.'

'Oh no, you won't, Dahling. You will use this phone as much as you want.'

And Reen seized the phone out of her hand.

'Listen. Sophie is it? Don't you worry about your friend. Someone's been nasty to her but she'll be all right. I'll look after her.'

Sophie could be heard asking something.

'Look, Dahling, best if she phones you tomorrow and tells you all about it. I'll make sure she does. But any time you want to phone her, you just use this phone and I'll nip and get her. That tight-fisted French Madame Doodah doesn't deserve her. What sort of person doesn't let people use her phone when they need to? Your friend, Annie, is a lovely girl and we've got to look after her.'

Annie was bit embarrassed by the eulogy that followed, especially as Sophie at the other end was obviously concurring. When she finally got the phone back to say goodbye, Sophie indeed sounded much more reassured and in her signing off whispered, 'She sounds very motherly. A bit of a rough diamond by any chance?'

'Yup. Exactly,' Annie agreed.

Reen filled her glass again.

At some befuddled point in the evening, whilst telling Reen about all the circumstances surrounding her visit to Nice, Annie rather shamefacedly asked if her French act had been believable.

Obviously desperate not to hurt her feelings, Reen gave such an unconvincing affirmative that, even in depths of her misery, Annie had to laugh.

'Oh dear, did I look such a fool pretending to be French?'

'No, Dahling, but you see, everything about you is so English... your lovely red hair... your peaches complexion and those bright blue eyes of yours. Even your figure... well...you are not wafer-thin like these French stick insects.'

Reen was well into her stride by now. 'And then there's the way you talk, it's sort of open and warm...not cool and superior like these snooty madams round here. And', she finished emphatically, 'you don't look people up and down as if they are something the cat's dragged in.'

Reen was obviously biased. But it helped.

Chapter Twenty-Eight

'Don't you just love the way the sunlight plays on the waves?' Just being outside in the bright December sunshine was already lifting Annie's spirits. And she could watch the interplay of light on the bay forever.

As Reen tucked her arm through hers, Annie smiled down at her petite friend.

'Yes, Dahling, but it's not very warm is it?'

'Oh, I thought it was OK.'

'You need to come down to the Costa del Sol. It's much warmer down there.'

As they strolled along the Promenade with the two dogs, Annie was catching up with all Reen's news about the jacuzzi and Ted. She was also tactfully foiling all her friend's attempts to pair her up on a date with her only unattached son, Troy.

They did some food shopping and found a cosy café well away from the market area, before heading back to the apartment.

She resisted Reen's invitation to join her in some 'nice tinned soup', as she was miles behind on her diary work and hadn't posted a disc of pages off for some time now. She didn't want to compromise Sophie if her boss, the arrogant Adam Jarvis, started to complain about paying for transcribing that wasn't getting done. Also, absorbing herself in the hectic, promiscuous life of his Grandma Nina, would take her mind off the waves of misery that every now and again engulfed her.

She couldn't believe how, in the space of one night, she was once again a stranger in this town with no friends. In fact worse than that, she now seemed to have actual enemies, if the look on Uncle Albert's face was anything to go by. But the biggest hurt was losing contact with the one person who mattered to her the most.

Round and round her head swirled the conflicting thoughts about whether Jack would believe the tales told about her. Would he come to visit her to find out the truth? Or was he too much in thrall to the manipulative Nicole?

As the late afternoon light faded, her gloom was interrupted by a gentle knock on the door.

Jack. Her heart leapt and she rushed to open it.

Reen, a shimmering sight to behold, dressed up to the nines and reeking of perfume, struck a pose in the dim hallway.

'Right, get your glad rags on, girl, we're hitting the town.'

'Oh, thanks, Reen, but I'm not really feeling up to it,' she said trying to conceal her disappointment.

'No excuses. You've got an hour to wash your hair, get some slap on and doll yourself up a bit.'

'But…'

'No buts. And it's my treat.'

'But…'

'And if you haven't got anything to wear, I can lend you something. I've got loads of shiny evening tops and—'

'No, no that's OK,' Annie said a little too hastily. 'Er…I don't think anything would fit me.'

'Well, I've got some nice gold lurex stoles if you need to brighten up your outfit. And some lovely sequinned bags. Just yell. I'll be down in an hour.'

'Where are we going?' Annie called after the shiny retreating figure on the stairs.

'I've booked a table in that posh place you said you wanted to go to. Thought it would cheer you up a bit.'

In a way it did. And Reen's flamboyant style perfectly matched the rich opulent decor of the main salon. The chandelier was as magnificent as the book said it was. And Reen's delight in her surroundings was infectious.

'I think champagne cocktails to start with, don't you?'

How could a mere Annie hope to demur. The drinks were delicious and accompanied with lots of small dishes of canapés, to Reen's outspoken glee.

'Right, now to powder my nose. I always like to look at the loos. You can tell a lot about a place from how good the toilets are. Come on.'

Reen blatantly ogled everything on the way to the loos.

'Oooh look. Is that a padded leather lift?' Reen peered in. Annie decided to bank down her embarrassment gene and just go with the flow. She would probably never come back here again, so what the hell.

'Oh, Dahling just look at these loos. Aren't they posh?' Reen enthused loudly. 'I wonder if I could do something like this at home. And oooh look…the men's loos are even better,' she called peeking in the door.

Annie looked hurriedly around but there was no one in the vicinity.

'Yes, you're right. They're a sort of Napoleonic war tent with the sinks in…like war chests.'

'My Ted would love this. I'll have to bring him here to see it.' Reen advanced unashamedly into the men's for a closer inspection.

'Someone's coming,' Annie hissed and they fled giggling like a pair of schoolgirls.

The interior of the Brasserie was, as Jack described, like a merry-go- round. It was circular, bright and colourful with pink padded stalls to sit in. And every now and then, the fairground mannequin in the middle wound the hurdy-gurdy organ and the fairground horses did indeed go up and down. There was a simple gaiety about the place that charmed Annie into forgetting her woes, for a while.

Obviously it would have been nicer to be here with…but she stopped her disloyal thoughts and concentrated on enjoying her meal, her fun-filled surroundings and the generous nature of her companion.

To Annie's surprise the staff weren't snooty and Reen's enthusiastic delight seemed to charm them all.

'Oh, we'll have to start with a salade niçoise, won't we, Dahling? Unless you fancy something else?'

'No, that sounds wonderful.'

'Now, I know we should have this Bully Bussy stuff…,' Reen indicated an item on the menu.

'Um…Bouillabaisse.'

'Yes, but it says here in the English bit, it's fish soup and I'm a bit wary of that. Had it on the Costa once…ill for days I was. Both ends.'

Annie nearly choked.

'So I'm just going to have the steak, I think. Can't go wrong with a good steak.'

'I take it you don't want the tartare,' Annie said, eyeing the listening waiter.

'Ah no, is that the raw one?'

'Yes.'

'No fear. I want my steak done proper. No blood at all in the middle. You do the ordering, Babes. You speak French.'

So Annie did. And then Reen ordered the wine.

During the course of the meal she found herself telling Reen about her mum.

'How she would have loved it here. The funny, magical quality of this place would have appealed to her so much.'

Under Reen's sympathetic probing, she began to tell her about her mum's life-changing visit to France during the long ago summer of her youth. How she fell in love with France, and Fabien, before coming back to spend her life in a terraced house in Accrington.

'I didn't know any of this stuff till I found a blue box tied up with ribbon after her…after she'd gone.'

She described her surprise at the contents and the conclusions she had drawn.

'That notebook, the strip of photos, and the yearning postcards from Fabien of Nice, those are the reasons I came here. I just hope that somehow I can find Fabien. It's possible he's my father. Just think, I could be half French.'

Reen's sharp look, expressed her doubt better than words.

'Yes, I know it sounds silly,' Annie admitted, 'but I might

be. That's one of the reasons I tried to pretend I was French when I first met you. I suppose I'm as bad as my mum. In her imagination she was always pretending to be French as well.'

Reen listened alertly. 'You say your mum was ill for a long time.'

Annie paused to let the shadows disperse, before nodding.

'Oh, Dahling, I don't want to pour cold water over your search, but don't you think, if Fabien was your father, she would have told you?'

'Yes, I have thought of that.' She sighed. 'But Mum was on a lot of morphine towards the end and did keep talking about Paris and someone called Fabien. I didn't know who he was till I found the box. Was she trying to tell me? I don't know.'

The waiter hovered to pour the last of the wine.

'Another bottle of that, please,' said Reen automatically. 'So how are we going to find Fabien then?'

It was lovely that Reen said 'we'.

'If you've got any ideas I would love to hear them but I've already asked someone to help me.' This led on to the tale of Monsieur Xavier.

Reen listened wide-eyed.

'Cor, Annie pet, you don't half get yourself into fixes.'

'I know. I know. My friend Sophie worried about me being too naïve. She said I was too nice for Nice. But now I know what his intentions are, I can be very careful.'

Reen pursed her lips. 'Are you still going to see him?'

'I'll meet him in the café, that's all. Oh no, I can't now can I?' It hit her again with a thud. She would probably never go back to her epiphany café again.

Her eyes welled up.

'Now then, Dahling. Drink up and let's have a look at the puds should we? But if you ask me, I don't think you should meet that Monsieur X again.'

'But he's my only way of finding Fabien.'

'No, we'll think of something. Don't you fret. Now what about this Coupe Royale, that sounds nice, doesn't it? I'm not

160

having the Tarte Tatin because it couldn't possibly be as nice as the one we made. And I think we need something to finish us off. How about a Drambuie, or a nice Peach Brandy. My Ted always finishes with a whisky. He collects all these different single malts and stuff but I'm not fussed myself. I like a nice liqueur. I'll ask them what they've got, should I? And see if they've got some of those nice glacé cherries.'

Next morning Pimpy's barking and a knocking at the door woke her from a deep drink-induced sleep.

Jack?

She was just frantically combing her tangled hair when she heard Reen's distraught voice through the closed door. She rushed to open it.

'Is everything all right?' she asked a visibly upset Reen.

No, it wasn't.

It all tumbled out as Annie invited her in and made her a coffee.

An early morning phone call from Tarquin in London had woken Reen with bad news. His heavily pregnant wife, Tracey, had been rushed into hospital with 'complications' and it looked as if she would have to stay there for a while. Reen went into medical details that meant nothing to Annie but the upshot of it was there was no one at home to look after the twins aged two, little Tristram and Tricia.

Before Reen asked, Annie offered. 'You go. I'll look after Pugsy till you get back.'

'Oh, you are a Dahling and no mistake. I feel awful asking you again.'

'You didn't ask, I offered. Of course you must go and help your Tarquin.'

'It's just he can't really stay off from work. And the twins are bit of a handful at the best of times. And Tracey's been running around, worrying about getting stuff ready for Christmas. She's one of these that has to make everything perfect. If you ask me I think she's been overdoing it. Well, at least if I'm there I can get the presents but I'm not as daft as her…shop-bought mince-pies and Christmas cake is just as good if you ask me. I warned Tarquin she was overdoing it and…'

'Look. You go and get packed and leave Pugsy with me. I'll take him for his walk and by the time I get back, you'll be ready to go.'

'Bless you, Annie.' The hug was heart-felt.

'It's all right. Really. After all, what are friends for?'

Chapter Twenty-Nine

Hunched against the cold, Annie trudged back from her new shopping haunt. It was a small supermarket. Not as personal as the market, of course. Although she'd vowed never to go there again, she really missed all the small interactions and pleasantries.

And she really missed Reen, but she was under strict instructions to phone her each evening from her apartment just to reassure her that both she and Pugsy were fine.

Reen sounded anything but fine. Late last night when she phoned, the twins were still playing her up.

In the little local supermarket, seeing some of the festive treats on offer, it suddenly hit her, Christmas was looming. Unless Jack came round, which she now accepted was extremely unlikely, she would be alone for Christmas.

Although she always knew she would be spending the six months on her own and so would miss all the festivities, the reality hadn't really hit her before. And this would be her first Christmas without her mum. Even in the hospice, they had managed a surprisingly cheerful atmosphere.

Head down, not even the sight of the twinkly bright sea, could lift her spirits, she plodded back home.

'Ah Bonjour, Mademoiselle Annie.' A friendly voice addressed her.

She smiled before she realised who it was.

Monsieur Xavier was enquiring after her health.

'I was worried because I haven't seen you at the café for quite some time now. Are you well?'

'Oh yes, Monsieur. Quite well.'

'It's Henri, remember,' he chided gently.

'Of course, Henri. I'm sorry.'

'You look a little tired. Perhaps you would like to join me for a coffee?'

Oh sod it. What harm could it do? Here was someone to talk to and if he had been looking for her perhaps he had news.

'Thank you, Mon...er...Henri. That is most kind of you. Perhaps you have news of Fabien?'

'Ah, we will discuss it over coffee. Shall we go?'

'Er, not the café in the market please, Henri,' she said hurriedly.

He looked at her sharply. 'Ah, perhaps not then. Would you prefer the place where we had lunch?'

'Yes, that would be nice, but only coffee please. You are too generous to me.'

That relieved her conscience. If she stipulated only coffee, she couldn't get dragged in to anything too expensive. And it was morning and broad daylight, so what could go wrong?

They were shown to the usual table at the back. Aware now of his reputation, she worried a little about what the waiters thought.

Oh no, Reen was right. I should have said no. But it was too late now. I'll just have to brazen it out.

'So tell me what have you been doing with yourself?' Henri enquired.

'Oh not a lot, really.' She wondered if he was probing why she didn't want to go to the market café. What could she say if he asked outright?

'I see you have both little dogs again.'

Trust him to notice.

'Yes, my friend has gone to London for a few days.' She daren't reveal she'd gone for quite a while.

Had he noticed that her conversation was more guarded, more stilted? She must seize the initiative.

'I was wondering, Henri, if you have any news about finding Fabien?'

'Alas no, not yet. I have many friends and acquaintances on the search. Indeed we know of many Fabiens, but none so

164

far, who studied at the Sorbonne during those dates.'

'It is disappointing but thank you so much for trying. I am very grateful.'

'You mustn't let it distress you, my dear Mademoiselle Annie.'

'Oh no, it's not that…' she stopped. She so nearly fell for it, pouring out what was really upsetting her.

He reached out and patted her hand.

'What is it? Perhaps I can help.'

What could she say? She had to invent something quickly.

'It is news from England. My friend is very upset.'

'Your friend Sophie?'

'Oh, you remember her name.'

'But of course.'

'Oh well yes. She is…well, it's a bit personal.' She couldn't think of anything quickly enough. And it was disconcerting to think he would remember every detail, so she daren't lie too much. Anyway, Sophie was always so disparaging of any of her attempts at subterfuge. 'You are a hopeless liar, Annie, so don't bother.'

'Sorry, Henri. I'm not very good company today.'

'Not a problem, Mademoiselle.'

Henri sat back. He plainly wasn't charmed by her today. After some brief desultory comments about the weather, so useful for gap filling thought Annie, Henri called for the bill.

He escorted her outside in his usual courteous manner. They were just about to part, when Annie was compelled to apologise.

'I'm so sorry I was a bit miserable today.'

'Not at all, Mademoiselle.'

'You will still keep looking for Fabien, won't you?'

'Of course,' he murmured as he turned to go.

On an impulse Annie put her hand on his arm to restrain him.

'No, Henri.'

He looked surprised.

She gazed frankly into his face. 'This is very important to

me and you are my only hope. I need to know if you really mean it or you are just being polite.'

He looked back into her eyes, and for a moment Annie thought she saw the real man behind the urbane façade.

'Promise me,' she said urgently her hand still on his arm. 'Really promise me.'

There was a moment's pause. Then he said, 'I promise you, Annie.'

'I believe you,' she said, looking straight into his eyes. And she did.

He smiled, a genuine smile. 'Au revoir, my dear Annie.' And bent forward to kiss her lightly on each cheek.

As she watched him go she felt her mood lighten. That promise seemed sincere.

Then she became aware of a still figure in the bustling crowd nearby. She looked up. Jack was standing watching her.

She was just about to rush over when she saw a look of shock, bewilderment, and then horror sweep over his face.

Oh no. He must have seen that transaction between her and Henri Xavier. Seen them emerging together from a restaurant, her hand on his arm, the brief exchange and smile, then the kiss goodbye. His face told her what he thought about it.

'No,' she cried. 'No, Jack, it's not what you think.' But her words were lost in the crowd and with one more look of agonised disbelief he hurried away.

Chapter Thirty

It was a quiet and very lonely Christmas. Yes, of course, Annie's friends remembered her and sent cards and lovely presents which she opened diligently on Christmas morning. The two dogs had great fun with the paper, and the little treats she'd bought them.

The presents she received were so thoughtful they made her cry. Some of her library friends had sent her books and their little notes told her about the further exploits of Bloody Brian and said how much they missed her. Her Accrington library ladies had sent glittery cards with nice verses in them. Mrs Slater had sent her some nice lace hankies and Mrs Enwright had sent her a lovely bright blue hand-knitted cardigan. She hugged it to her and wept a little. It was so wonderful to be remembered.

In much posher wrapping, there was a pale, duck-egg-blue cashmere scarf from Sophie. To her surprise, there was a beautiful pearl necklace and drop pearl earrings from Philip. Were they real, Annie wondered? Had Sophie chosen them, but the handwriting on the cards was definitely Philip's. The gold glittery evening bag from Reen made her smile.

But nothing else did. For the past two weeks she had felt herself surrounded in a fog of gloom. But she knew she would have to fake a cheerful attitude as, just before lunch, she climbed the stairs to phone everyone in England as instructed by Reen.

Sophie was busy, just back from church with the future in-laws, and helping with the traditional turkey dinner.

'This time next year, you will be doing this yourself,' Annie commented.

'Oh god yes, don't remind me,' Sophie didn't sound too

sure about it, and lowering her voice she whispered, 'Or I might whisk us away somewhere to the sun. Anything to avoid the bloody Brussels sprouts.'

Annie chortled and realised with a shock, it was the first time she had laughed for ages. Ever since Jack had seen her emerge from that café with Henri Xavier. His look of horror and dismay was seared on her brain. It was often the last thing she saw at night before attempting to sleep, and the first thing as she woke each morning to drag herself through another endless day. If she didn't have the dogs, she wouldn't bother getting up, still less going out. The affection the two little dogs showed her was the only small crumb of comfort in her day. It was as if they knew how despairing she was.

Sophie chatted on about her Christmas in a cheerful manner, but Annie had the distinct impression that she knew Philip's family were listening.

She asked about Annie's Christmas. Somehow Annie managed to convey she was enjoying a quiet time with the two dogs, some good books and a lot of bright winter sun.

As Sophie was called away for pre-dinner drinks, she whispered, 'I hope you are OK, Annie love. I know I really miss you. Can't wait to have a proper chat. I'll try and phone you one evening when I'm on my own.'

Annie gulped back her lonely tears as she answered, 'I would love that, Sophie.'

'Merry Christmas, Annie love.'

Reen eventually answered the phone just as Annie was about to ring off. She was frantically sorting a festive lunch for the fractious sounding twins after they had returned from seeing their mum in the hospital. At last, Ted had joined her from Marbella to help. He had phoned Annie and offered to drive up to the UK via Nice, so he could stop off and get Pugsy in case he was too much trouble. The relief in his deep, growly voice was obvious when Annie reassured him there was no need.

'Thanks, Annie pet. Reen knew you would say that but we thought we ought to offer. She's got her hands full with the kids and everything. To be honest, the twins are a bit rough with poor little Pugsy. They don't mean to be of course, but they do tease him a bit and he has to go and hide under the bed when they come and visit. So it is best if he stays with you…as long as you don't mind.' Annie reassured him again. He sounded a lovely man. Even if he was an East End gangster, he certainly loved his family.

His voice could be heard booming in the background as Annie wished her friend Happy Christmas.

'And, Reen, thank you for my lovely glittery bag. Very swanky.' Where had that word come from? But it was obviously the right one because she could hear the pleasure in Reen's voice.

'Glad you like it, Dahling. It will brighten up any outfit, that will.' She broke off to shout, 'Tristram, Tricia, get away from that tree. Tarquin, keep an eye on them. They'll have them baubles off if you're not careful.'

'Are you OK, Reen? You sound a bit frazzled.'

Sounding tired, but determinedly cheerful, Reen replied, 'You know I'm not a good cook, Dahling, and Tracy has got all this high-tech equipment in her kitchen. Me and Ted are a bit lost with it all. We normally go out with our friends in Marbella for Christmas dinner, nice place on the waterfront, in the sun. But never mind. I'm sure I'll get the hang of it.' She sounded very doubtful, quite wistful, and slightly tiddly. Annie managed to entice Pugsy into yapping for her on the phone, which tickled her.

'Got to go now, Dahling. You keep phoning us, so's I know you are all right. And help yourself to anything from the drinks cabinet for as much Christmas tipple as you want.'

'Merry Christmas Reen.'

'Merry Christmas, Annie Dahling.'

With a sigh of relief, Annie finished her phone calls. She prided herself that she had managed to keep up a cheerful façade for them. She daren't do otherwise. If she unlocked the floodgates of home-sickness, they might not close.

Christmas afternoon, she went out with the dogs for a

stroll in the bright cold sunshine, wearing her new scarf and pearls. Then came back and curled in front of fast-talking French TV till bedtime eating the English chocolates someone had sent her. Then she cried herself to sleep, feeling totally sorry for herself.

So that was Christmas.

Then it was the New Year. Not any new year, but a new century.

2000. The actual Millennium.

From her window, Annie watched festive crowds of people heading to the Promenade for the spectacular display of fireworks. They promised to be even more amazing this year to celebrate this millennium milestone. There was no way she was going to join all that jollity, not on her own.

She was just turning away, when she saw a smartly dressed older lady, hurrying along, clearly all on her own. I wonder if she's a widow, Annie thought. Like my mum, alone for all those years. Alone like me.

Then like a thunderbolt it hit her. But that lady is not giving up and skulking at home feeling sorry for herself. And neither did Mum. OK she had me, but when I left for Uni, she got on with life, volunteering at the hospital as well as her part-time job at the library. She even took on delivering all the library books to infirm people, like I used to do.

Never, not once, in all those years, did she give up, or indulge in self-pity. And she had a darned sight more to cope with than this.

'For god's sake,' she could hear her mum's cross voice saying, 'buck up, our Annie. I'm so disappointed in you. There you are, living in France, like I always longed to do, in fact on the bloomin posh Riviera, and yet moping around as if the world had come to an end.

'OK, you've had your heart broken. It happens to us all. In time it will mend. And brooding over it won't make it heal any faster, in fact it will prolong the agony. So come on, Annie girl. Show some grit, some backbone. What can't be cured must be endured. Snap out of it. Get out there. Stop hiding. Life will find you anyway, so why don't you go out and face it head on.'

The voice in her head was so clear. 'Yes, Mum,' she said out loud.

She was right. It was a new century, one her mum would never see. It should be alive with new opportunities. That's what they are all saying. As long as the millennium computer bug doesn't wipe everything away as some are predicting.

Suddenly she was ashamed of herself. Her mum was right. How dare she wallow in such self-pity?

Squaring her shoulders, she said out loud, 'OK. New century here I come.' Then went to dress up warmly, ready to face the music, the New Year, and all the fireworks.

Chapter Thirty-One

Next day, New Year's Day, an emotional Reen phoned her to say she was a Grandma to baby Tarantella. The baby was a bit premature and would have to stay in hospital for a while but otherwise everything was fine.

Annie enthused about yet another 'T' name...such a big name for such a tiny baby. She wondered to herself, if the baby had been born on Christmas day, would she have been called Tinsel.

Reen was apologetic for lumbering Annie with Pugsy for so long but hoped to get everything sorted in a couple of weeks so she could come and collect him.

In fact it took over a month before an exhausted Reen finally climbed the stairs late one afternoon back to her apartment and her beloved Pugsy.

Both were delighted to be reunited.

Reen looked worn out. At last she had been able to leave Tracey and her exhausting young brood. But not before she had managed to sort out a motherly cleaner to come in and help. And most important of all, she had pulled every string she could to get the hyperactive twins into a play school three mornings a week.

'I don't know how Tracey does it. I really don't,' she said, flopping down on the leather sofa and sipping a reviving tequila cocktail. 'She seems to want to be Super-Mum, cooking and cleaning and entertaining her little ones and going out to coffee mornings with other mums and dressing 'em in designer clothes. And keeping a perfect house. You've never seen such a palace...cream carpets and suite...with kiddies!!! I ask you. It wore me out just keeping an eye on them every time they had Ribena.'

She shuddered at the memory.

'It was a darn sight easier for me when I had mine all those years ago... even without these disposable nappies. I stayed at home for a while after each of them but then just left them with my mum and went back to work. She wasn't far from the yard and I popped in all the time whenever it was quiet but I needed to be there helping Ted or the business would have folded. Don't get me wrong, I loved my kids to pieces, but it didn't seem such hard work as they make it these days.'

There was a long pause. Reen, curled up on the sofa with a devoted Pugsy on her lap, looked unseeingly out of the window to the clear blue Mediterranean sky. 'And...well... you see... Tracy just doesn't like the way I do things. I could see how much everything I did irritated her. I just couldn't do things her way, no matter how I tried. In fact the more I tried, the more I seemed to do it wrong. Proper upset me at times, although I think I managed to hide it. It got a bit fraught sometimes and poor old Tarquin got pulled both ways, so, in the end I think it's best I left.'

Reen looked so forlorn, it pulled Annie's heart strings. She knew Reen was just thinking out loud and just wanted an uncritical listener.

'I suppose it would have been easier if I wasn't her mother-in-law. But her proper mum is in Florida. Selfish cow. Do you know she hasn't even been over to see her new grandkid yet? She didn't want to come in the winter 'cos it was too cold. It was bleedin cold for me as well. My sciatica has been playing up something rotten.'

Reen rubbed her bony back.

'And I can't go back home to Spain yet. The bleedin' builders haven't done a stroke while we were away. I bet they got on with another job while our backs were turned. The place is still full of dust. Ted's gone to give 'em what for. If I got my hands on 'em, they'd know it.

'Oh, Babe,' she suddenly laughed at herself. 'I sound a crotchety old so-and-so don't I? I'm sorry...bending your ear like that. I don't know what came over me. It's all been pent up all that while. You shouldn't be such a good listener you know.' She shook herself. 'Right. I'll make you a drinky and then let me hear all your news.'

'Nope,' said Annie gently removing the tequila from Reen's grasp. 'First you are coming down to my place. I've cooked you a nice meal to welcome you back and we can have a cosy chat over a nice bottle of wine…no more tequila.'

To her surprise Reen burst into tears.

'Ooh…Annie, Dahling…that would be lovely. You are so thoughtful. Oooh. I don't know what's come over me.'

As Annie put her arms round her friend's thin, shaking frame, Reen rested her head on her shoulder and sobbed.

'You know, I don't think anyone has done anything for *me* all the time I've been away.'

Later, as they ate together in the cosy crammed apartment downstairs, they had a real heart-to heart. Reen visibly relaxed. Annie could see the toll the six weeks had taken on her friend who, after all, was no spring chicken. It was not only the physical hard work of looking after twins in their terrible twos, but also feeling the unspoken criticism from her daughter-in-law about everything she did…and didn't do.

It all poured out. Annie could see Reen felt better afterwards, if slightly disloyal. But Annie assured her that she understood the family dynamics that meant you could criticise and still love.

Annie in turn brought Reen up to speed with her news. That fateful cup of coffee with Henri Xavier then Jack's expression as he saw them together.

'Oh, Reen, you warned me not to have anything to do with Henri. And worst of all, I can't shake the feeling…you see, it was the restaurant near the apartment, so was Jack coming round to see me? Did I totally scupper any chances we could get back together?'

It was Annie's turn to sob on Reen's comforting shoulder.

The release of so much pent-up emotion seemed to do them both good. Annie knew that, as unlikely a pairing as they were, somehow during their brief friendship a real fondness and trust had emerged.

As she kissed Reen good night, she said, 'I'm so glad you are back.'

'So am I, Dahling. So am I.'

Next morning, Reen urgently knocked on her door.

'It's your friend Sophie on the phone. She seems very upset.'

Annie raced up the stairs, full of foreboding.

Chapter Thirty-Two

'Oh Annie, I'm such a fool,' wailed Sophie.

'What's happened? Has the wedding fallen through?'

'No, not yet, but it will.'

'Why?'

There was a fresh outburst of sobbing down the line before Sophie could bring herself to confess, 'I'm pregnant.'

'Wow. Right. That's a bit early, but no reason to call off... Unless...oh Sophie...'

'Yes. You've guessed. It's not Philip's.' There was almost a touch of bravado in the statement. Then Sophie crumbled into tears again.

Annie didn't know what to say. 'Are you sure?'

'Oh yes. Believe me I've peed on so many sticks hoping and hoping but no sodding luck. I'm definitely up the proverbial duff.'

'Does Philip know?'

'No, not yet.'

Annie sighed. 'OK, Sophie. Yes, it sounds a mess, but all is not lost. Tell me the full story. Whose it is and how did it happen?'

'It's Adam's.'

'Your boss Adam? But you've always said what an arrogant swine he is.'

'Oh yes, that's true, he is.'

'Did he force you...?'

'Oh, Annie. You are so naïve. I've been having an affair with him for over three years.'

For a moment Annie was stunned into disbelieving silence. 'You can't have been. You never told me.'

'I knew you would disapprove.'

That's true, thought Annie, but nevertheless felt hurt that her best friend hadn't confided in her. Suddenly it clicked. 'Of course. Three years. You mean ever since you broke up with Jean-Pierre?'

'Yup, you've guessed it. I was feeling low, away on a business trip with Adam. He made a move, I thought 'what the hell' and it all started from there. No excuses. Knew he was married. Don't even like him very much, but...' here a guilty giggle broke through,' oh Annie, he's fantastic in bed, and I sort of got hooked.'

'But...but even after you were engaged to Philip?'

Here a fresh wail broke out. 'Yes. I know, I shouldn't. What am I going to do?'

'Oh, Sophie. Look, let me think. I wish I could come over...'

The phone was seized from her hand by a listening Reen.

'Sophie. Annie's friend, Reen here. She will be on the next plane.'

'Reen,' Annie protested, 'I can't just go.'

'Yes you can. I don't know what's going on, although I can guess, but it sounds as if your friend needs you. You've helped me out often enough. It's time I repaid your kindness.'

'But...'

'No buts.' Reen turned to speak directly into the phone again. 'Sophie, I take it you would like Annie to come over to see you.'

There was a muffled response.

'Thought so. Then that's settled. As I said she will be on the next plane.'

And she was, arriving in a cold, bleak Manchester. A taxi ride later to Sophie's city-centre flat and she was hugging her tear-streaked friend.

After scant preliminaries of coffee and yet more hugs, Sophie began to tell all.

'I know I should have finished it when I got engaged to Philip, and for a while I was good, I really was. But, Annie, we do so many business trips together, so many anonymous

177

hotels, it was too easy, too tempting.'

'Philip has never guessed?'

'No, that's what makes it so awful. He's such a sweetie, so trusting.'

Annie supplied more tissues as Sophie broke out into more sobs.

Her friend was curled into a ball on her sofa with lank, unkempt hair and no makeup. She looked so vulnerable and lost, so unlike the confident assertive person who had waved her off to Nice, it tore Annie apart to see her like this.

As her friend's tears subsided for a while, Annie asked gently, 'Do you mind me asking two important questions. How do you know it isn't his? And how far gone are you?'

'Well, as you know, I've been on the pill for yonks, and my doctor suggested I really ought to go on a lower dosage, which I have done. So when I told Philip, he started using condoms just to be on the safe side. Not because he doesn't want kids or anything, but he knew the wedding was a big deal for me, so he joked about me fitting into my gorgeous wedding dress. And anyway, we haven't sort of got it together for a while now. I've been away so much with this latest big deal. When I got home I've been so tired, and Philip is such a gentleman…'

'You didn't think to use protection with Adam.'

Sophie sighed and shook her head. 'Ironic isn't it? I'd decided no more…but I was telling him…and we sort of got carried away. It was a farewell fuck.'

Annie said slowly, 'OK. So how far?'

'Two months. Stupid me, I thought my periods had gone erratic because of the different pill, all the irregular hours I've been doing, all the stress of the wedding and stuff. It was Philip who said I should go to the doctor because I've been so tired, he thought I might be anaemic. Doctor asked if I might be pregnant, did a test anyway and…boom.'

'Where is Philip by the way?'

'In London for a few days, thank goodness. I didn't know what to do, so I phoned you. Thank you so much for dropping everything to…'

'You would have done it for me...in fact you did do for me...with Mum. Luckily Reen was there and was more than happy to repay the favour and look after Pimpy for me.'

'She sounds a right character on the phone.'

Annie smiled fondly, 'She's that all right, with the proverbial heart of gold.'

The phone rang.

'That will be Philip,' said Sophie dully. 'I'm not going to answer it. I can't.'

'OK.'

They waited, and heard Philip leave a cheery message, saying his meeting was going well, he hoped she was OK and he hoped to talk to her later.

They both looked at each other. His voice made the reality of the situation more urgent.

'So what's the options, Sophie? You must have been thinking about them.'

'Yes,' sighed Sophie. 'They have been going round and round. My head's in a whirl.'

'Would it help to talk them through?'

'Oh yes. I've been longing for you to get here. You'll know what to do, won't you?'

'Actually, stop there, Sophie. I won't. But we can discuss it and that might help, but I'm definitely not going to tell you what to do. Only you can decide that.'

Sophie looked surprised, then slumped down again.

'Yes, of course. You are right. But you will support me in whatever I decide, won't you?'

Annie nodded slowly.

'Promise!'

'Promise,' said Annie, hoping this answer wouldn't compromise her too much. 'So option one is...?'

'I have the baby. I somehow pass it off as Philip's. If we have mad, rampant sex when he gets back, then I might just about get away with it.'

'OK,' Annie said slowly. 'Then as the baby grows up...'

'I know, I know. Adam is tall, black-haired, brown-eyed, and, of course, Philip is so fair.'

'It would be a dreadful secret all your life.'

'I know. But I can't face being a single mother, Annie. I've told you. I'm never going to go back to poverty.'

'It wasn't poverty, Sophie. You exaggerate.'

'We were bloomin hard up. The shame of those free school meals. I could never go on school trips and those awful cheap, scratchy clothes. No, I've worked bloody hard to escape all that and I'm not going back. I know myself too well, I'm just too selfish, Annie. That is definitely not an option.'

'So that leaves…'

'Abortion.'

The finality with which Sophie said it, told Annie the decision had already been made.

She hugged her friend who burst into fresh tears.

'Annie, surely you can see that anything else is too risky. There's no other way out. I daren't lose Philip.'

'Can I be blunt, Sophie?'

'OK,' said Sophie slowly.

'Is it Philip himself, or what he's got, that you don't want to lose?'

'Um…why do you ask?'

'I'm going to be cruel here. If temptation comes its way again, after you're married, what then?'

'I'd like to think I wouldn't…'

'Not 'think', Sophie. You've got to be sure.'

Clasping her friend's hand in hers, Annie looked earnestly into her pale face. 'I said I was going to be cruel, and here it is. Your dad had affairs and eventually left you and your mum. Look how it's affected you all your life. You of all people have got to think about it. Could you do that to your kids?'

Sophie looked stunned. 'I hadn't thought of that. Oh my god, you mean that I'm as bad as my dad?'

'I didn't say that. But whether you have this baby or not, you've got to think seriously about your marriage to Philip. Do you really love him? Will you be faithful to him?'

'That's a bit blunt.' Sophie blew out her breath. 'Phew,

where did this tough new Annie come from?'

Annie said nothing. But it did seem that her experiences of having to be so self-reliant, facing up to some hard situations on her own, had given her more confidence, more certainty about what mattered in life.

Sophie was thinking. 'I'm not sure what I really feel about Philip. I care for him a lot. But who wouldn't? He's such a courteous, kind man...a gentle gentleman. I feel so guilty about how I could betray his trust. I'd hate for him to find out because it would hurt him so much...and he would no longer respect me.'

'Respect you? As opposed to love you?'

'Oh, Annie, I think he adores me. Even if I told him, he would probably forgive me. But I couldn't bear to see the hurt in his eyes.'

Annie nodded.

Sophie looked stricken but determined. 'So that why it's got to be an abortion. You do see that, don't you?'

'I suppose so.'

'Oh please say you agree, Annie. Your opinion is so important to me.'

'Is it? Why?'

'Of course it is. You've always had a much stronger moral compass than me. I've never told you half the things I've got up to because I've always been worried you would go off me.'

'Go off you? Don't be silly. You're my best friend...you matter to me. No matter what you do I will always...well, I will always love you. You silly sausage.'

'Really?'

'Of course. That's what friends are for. Even though you can be infuriating at times. And you bully me a lot.'

'But only for your own good,' the old assertive Sophie defended herself defiantly.

'That's what you always say,' grinned Annie.

'OK, yes I know I have a tendency to tell you what to do,' Sophie admitted with a smile, 'but to be honest, only when you let me. When you really put your foot down, I know I must back off.'

'Have you seriously worried that you and me would fall out?'

'Oh, Annie, I'm always worried that if people got to know me, the real me, they wouldn't like what they found.'

Annie hugged her tightly. 'I will never, ever stop being your friend,' she said fiercely. 'In fact more than that…you are the nearest thing to a sister I will ever have. You can't get rid of me that easily you know, we are bonded for life.'

Sophie really sobbed now. 'I've been so worried about what you would think.'

'I think whatever you decide, is the right thing for you to do. I can tell you've made your mind up, and so if it matters that much to you, you have my agreement and I will stick by you no matter what. OK?'

'OK,' Sophie breathed a huge sigh. 'You know me so well. I *do* know what I'm going to do. It wasn't an easy decision. But I've already set the wheels in motion.'

Annie waited.

Sophie continued. 'This morning, I phoned that bastard Adam and told him the situation. At first he blustered and said it might not be his, but I helped him see that his wife might not like some of the things I could tell her. That shut him up. So he agreed to pay for a private abortion. He even knows the name of a good clinic. Huh, what does that tell you?'

'He's a shit of the first water?'

'Yup. Anyway I've made an appointment for ten o'clock tomorrow morning. You will come with me, won't you?'

'Of course.'

They sat quietly together on the sofa.

The phone rang again.

Annie raised an eyebrow.

'No, not yet. I'll phone him back soon, or else he will worry. But first I'm going to get a bit of Dutch courage down me. Let's open a bottle.'

'Sophie, should you…I mean…'

'Drink, because I'm pregnant?' Sophie gave a hollow

laugh.

'No, actually I meant if you are going to the clinic in the morning, you don't want a hangover.'

'Listen, Annie, I already feel so bad about myself, a hangover couldn't make me feel any worse.'

Chapter Thirty-Three

She was wrong. After the operation she did feel much, much worse.

Back at the flat, Sophie sobbed as if her heart would break into Annie's tear-soaked shoulder.

'There, there.' Annie rocked her backwards and forwards stroking her hair, not knowing what else to do. 'Oh, Sophie darling. It'll be all right, you'll see.'

'What's the matter? Oh, Sophie, my love, what's the matter? Are you ill?'

In shock they both looked up and there was Philip standing in the doorway. His pale grey eyes were full of shock and concern. He dropped his small suitcase and came rushing over.

Kneeling in front of Sophie, he gently pulled her away from Annie and hugged her so tenderly, it provoked a fresh outburst from his distraught fiancée.

'Sophie, my darling girl, please what is it?' Taking in her pale drawn face, his voiced notched up a worried tone. 'Are you ill? Oh, my darling, please tell me what's the matter.'

She just buried her head deeper into his chest.

He looked up helplessly and seemed to take in Annie's' presence for the first time.

'Annie, when did you get back? What's going on? Help me out here, please.'

What could she say?

Sophie lifted her head and pleaded with Annie with her eyes.

Annie took a deep breath, 'It's OK, Philip. No, Sophie isn't ill. She will be fine.'

'So what's the matter?'

He was beginning to sound exasperated.

With a wail, Sophie struggled to her feet and fled into the bedroom, slamming the door.

Philip got up from his knees and just stood there.

'Right,' said Annie, 'the first thing I'm going to do is make us all a cup of tea, then I'll tell you what's going on.'

As she went to the kitchen, her mind raced furiously. Then she realised what all this was about.

'Sophie,' she knocked gently on the bedroom door. 'Here's a cup of tea.' Peering in, she saw an agonised face looking up from a tear-sodden pillow. 'Here you are. Now. I'm going to talk to Philip. It's OK, it really is. I'm going to leave the door open because I want you to hear everything I'm going to say. If at any point you want to stop me or disagree with me, then just yell out and I won't say any more. OK?'

Sophie looked so woebegone, Annie bent down and whispered, 'Just trust me. OK?'

Sophie nodded despairingly.

'OK, Philip, here's your cuppa. Did you hear what I said to Sophie about wanting her to hear what I said?'

Philip nodded glumly.

'I'm not sure where to begin, but first of all, as I said, Sophie is not ill. But she is overwrought and exhausted and...I think, terrified.'

Philip looked up shocked. 'Has someone been frightening her?'

'Not *someone,* Philip. I think, deep down, *life* terrifies Sophie. I think she was so hurt as a child, she's terrified of it happening again. I think all this toughness she shows, is a way of keeping the dark at bay.'

Concerned, Philip looked towards the bedroom, where the sobbing had stopped and they both knew Sophie was listening to every word.

'Philip, I know she's told you about her privileged early life. The lovely house, the pony in the paddock, the private school, the feeling of security and above all, a father who adored her, gave her everything she wanted. Then, as you probably know, almost overnight it vanished, and vanished forever.'

Philip nodded.

'Think about what all this did to her. Not only did she go to live in a small terraced house in a run-down mill town with a vengeful and embittered mother, she went to a rough and tumble school, she lost her beloved pony, but, most of all, she lost the love of her beloved father. The divorce was so acrimonious; her mother blocked any of his moves to see Sophie again. And, to be honest, he seemed to give up trying to see her heartbreakingly quickly. He then went on to have another family, another little girl that he adored, to whom he gave everything, including a pony. I think he is now on his third wife and third, supposedly adored, set of children.

'From what I can make out he is a weak, plausible man, and a serial philanderer. In fact, the exact opposite of you.'

Philip was listening intently and from the silence in the next room, so was Sophie.

'I just wonder if Sophie thinks you are too good to be true.'

'What?'

'Her father was just the first man to hurt her. I think she's been so hurt by some really bastard men, she has real trouble trusting anymore.'

'I would never hurt her, I hope you know that.'

'I believe you. I really do. I hope Sophie does. But her problem is...oh, what do I know? But because you are so kind and considerate and I think you love her so much...'

'I do,' he said quietly.

'I think deep down, she is really insecure, and lacks a feeling of self-worth because her father rejected her. To her it seemed as if he didn't love her anymore so, basically, she thinks she is unlovable. That's why men let her down. And why she thinks she doesn't deserve a man as good as you.'

There was silence from the bedroom. Then a huge heartrending sob.

Philip immediately leapt to his feet, but Annie restrained

him.

'Look, Philip, I don't know if I'm right but that's my reading of the situation. Sophie is in the middle of...I don't know what to call it, a severe case of pre-wedding nerves.'

Philip crumpled back onto the sofa. 'She wants to call it off, doesn't she?'

'I don't think she knows what she wants.'

He buried his head into his hands. 'I knew she couldn't really want an old fart like me. I knew she was too good to be true.'

Annie gave a little laugh. 'Actually it's the exact opposite. She's a very true person, trying to be good.'

Philip looked bewildered.

Annie went and put a consoling hand on his arm. 'Or put it another way, right now, Sophie is a really mixed up person who is desperately trying to do the right thing, but doesn't know what that is.'

She called into the bedroom. 'Sophie, I'm going to suggest that Philip comes back later, maybe tomorrow. It will give you some thinking time. Then you can talk it out together. Is that OK?'

Silence.

Philip looked distraught. 'She doesn't want to see me again, does she?'

He raised his voice, 'Do you, Sophie?'

An urgent voice replied. 'Yes I do, Philip, I really do. But Annie's right, just give me a little time. Please, just a little time.'

He looked around as if not sure what to do, then with a resigned shrug he turned to Annie.

'Is that why you are here? She called you because she was having a crisis?'

Annie nodded.

'Good. I'm glad you came. Thank you. If anyone can help her, it's you.'

Annie hugged him. 'I'll do my best. But...Philip, whatever decision she makes...'

'I know, I know. I'll just have to accept it won't I?'

He picked up his abandoned suitcase and walked forlornly to the door.

Annie couldn't bear to see the pain in his eyes.

Chapter Thirty-Four

A much calmer Sophie emerged after he'd gone.

'Thank you. Thank you. That really saved my bacon there. I didn't know what to say when he came in and found me sobbing. Your explanation was inspired.'

'No, it wasn't. It was true. Having an affair with that shit of a man means deep down that's all you think you are worth.'

'I suppose so,' Sophie said slowly.

'Sophie, did you listen to what I said?'

'Yes, but…'

'No, I mean really listen.' Annie's exasperation was rising. 'Think about it. Really think about it. And think about what Philip said.'

Sophie nodded. 'He actually said I was too good to be true. Shows how little he knows.'

'Oh, for goodness sake. That's exactly the sort of thinking that's got you into this mess. I meant it when I said you had a very low opinion of yourself. How can I convince you that you are not a bad person?'

Sophie shrugged. 'But I am. Look what I just did to Philip. I think…I think, oh, Annie, I think I've just broken his heart.'

She choked.

Annie just said flatly 'So?'

'What do mean 'so'? Did you just hear what I said?'

'Yes, but what do you care?'

'What. Of course I care.'

'Why?'

'He's a lovely good man…one of the nicest…no, in fact, the nicest, most decent, loving man I've ever met, and I've just hurt him so deeply…'

'So?'

'Why do you keep saying 'so' like that?'

'Because if you truly were as horrible as you make out, you wouldn't care one bit. You'd just move on and break someone else's heart. Believe me, Sophie, with your allure, you could cut swathes through the entire male population if you wanted.'

Sophie sat stunned.

'Is that what you want, Soph? Have affair after affair? Break men's hearts before they break yours? Punishing all the good ones for what the bad ones have done to you?'

'No.'

'Of course not, and do you know why. *You are not your father*. I know you worry you will turn out to be as shallow as him, but you are not. You have great depths of love, and loyalty, and compassion, which he couldn't even comprehend, let alone act upon.'

'But…'

'No buts. He would never have sat by my dying mother's bed for hours holding her hand. He would never have sat and held *my* hand afterwards and supported me through those dreadful weeks, living my agony with me, being there, strong, calm, decisive and so caring. No, at the least sign of any real emotion, any hurt or heartbreak, he was off like a shot, wasn't he?'

Sophie thought about it, then nodded slowly.

'Furthermore, he hadn't the backbone to fight adversity like you have done. He didn't push himself out of that tiny terraced house to university, like you did. No, he swanned through life without one deep thought in his selfish, handsome head.'

Annie grabbed her friend by her shoulders. She had to get through.

'Listen to me, Sophie, your father abandoning you says more about him than about you. You are *not unlovable*.

'You have been deeply loved and returned that love. My mum knew what a fine person you were. You loved her as deeply as she loved you. You know that don't you?'

Sophie managed a hesitant, 'Yes.'

'So you were worthy of her love, weren't you?'

'Yes.'

'So why aren't you worthy of Philip's?'

'Because I have wronged him... Oh, Annie. Oh, I see what you mean. All those years I never visited her. I just couldn't bear seeing her suffering.'

'I know. And she knew. And she still loved you. And she was right. You came when things were at the worst. You didn't have to, but you did. That was pure unselfish love, wasn't it?'

The memories were painful for both of them.

Sophie looked drained.

'Right, that's enough from me for now. You look exhausted. Go and have a rest now. A good sleep. Then, when you wake up, have a good think, and then you'll know what to do.'

Chapter Thirty-Five

Sophie didn't emerge till late the next morning. Annie was quietly sitting on the sofa reading a book she had found. She looked up and gave her friend a careful scrutiny.

'How are you?'

'Feeling much better, much calmer. I've been lying awake for hours going over everything you said.'

'Look, Sophie, I believed what I said, but who knows if I was right.'

Sophie went over and sat beside her. 'So many things you said clicked into place. Oh, Annie, you were right about everything…absolutely everything.'

Embarrassed by her friend's praise, Annie got up, 'No, the only thing I really know about is that a cuppa makes everything seem better. Want one? I've just made a pot.'

'Oh, Annie, you are the only one I know that still makes tea in a pot, not a bag in a mug.'

'Tut. No wonder the world in going to hell in a handcart. Do you fancy a late breakfast? Nice bit of toast and jam?'

Sophie laughed 'Yes, I reckon that will just hit the spot.'

They busied themselves in the kitchen. Soon a pile of hot buttered toast and jam was being gleefully tucked into.

For a moment Annie longed for some crunchy pain perdu, but quickly smothered the thought.

Suddenly the phone rang.

Sophie started, then groaned. 'That'll be Philip. I can't answer it yet.'

It was Philip. The answer phone clicked on.

'Sophie. It's me. I'm coming round. If you don't want to see me, I'll understand, but I hope you'll hear me out before you finally decide. I have something important I want to say.'

Philip sounded very serious, before tailing off, 'Um…I'll see you soon.'

Annie looked at Sophie. 'So, have you decided?'

'Yes and no.'

'What's the yes and what's the no? And I hope it's not that you're not good enough for him.'

'Well there is a slight residue of that but…OK, don't go on at me again. It's just I don't know if I really love him. I really don't.'

'OK, let's look at what you've said so far.' Annie put two more thick slices of brown bread in the toaster. 'If you care about him, which you clearly do, if you can't hurt him, which you say you can't, if you are frightened of losing him which you say you are, and losing his respect, which clearly worries you…perhaps you do love him. Perhaps this is what real love is, not passion, not lust but the enduring sort…you know, proper love.'

Sophie looked thoughtful. 'Yes. You're right about all that. I know I really do care for him deeply. But…I would really like some passion. That's what's bothering me, I think.'

Annie buttered the hot toast and offered a piece to Sophie. 'If you are talking about in bed, I'm sure with the right amount of encouragement and guidance…'

Sophie giggled, slathering on the strawberry jam, 'Well, yes. I think I could definitely do that.' Then she sighed. 'It's not just that. Yes, I know I want the big house…yes, I admit the pony paddock, but I still want a bit of excitement as well. Fussy aren't I? I wish he wasn't quite such a stick in the mud.'

'Is that what you think he is?'

'Yes. Don't you?'

'No, actually. I think 'still waters run deep', as my mum would say.'

Sophie munched her toast thoughtfully.

The doorbell rang. She jumped. 'Oh, he's here quicker than I thought. I look a mess.'

'No you don't. Just wipe the jam off your cheek though.'

Sophie went to the mirror, rubbed at her face and scraped

her fingers frantically through her hair.

The doorbell rang again.

'He's got a key. Why doesn't he use it?'

'Because, Sophie dear, he doesn't know whether you want to see him again, does he?'

'I suppose not.' Sophie began pacing up and down.

'Well, should I let him in?'

'Oh yes, of course.'

Philip stood on the doorstep looking pale but determined.

'May I come in?'

'Yes, of course. Sophie is feeling much better this morning and she *does* want to see you.'

He sighed with relief. Then straightened his shoulders and with a steely look in his eye, he went into the kitchen to confront an equally pale Sophie.

'Philip...I...'

But he cut her short.

'Before you tell me what you have decided, Sophie, I have something important I want to say.' He took a deep breath before continuing.

'I know I said whatever your decision was, I would accept it. But in fact I won't.'

Sophie gasped.

'Hear me out. I know you think I'm a boring old fart... no, I admit it, I am. *But I don't want to be.* I'm a product of my background, my posh conventional schooling, my parents' expectations. They have been on at me for years to settle down with one of their friend's daughters...a lovely, sweet girl, whom I'm fond of in a way, but deep down I yearned for more. But I'd been going out with her for years and sort of resigned myself to it.

'Then I met you at that wedding and I was blown away by your vibrancy. I fell in love with your laugh, your boldness, your sheer seizing of life by the horns. You were everything I was not and I knew I wanted you in my life forever. And I still do.'

Sophie's eyes were wide with wonder and sorrow. 'But, Philip, that girl you saw was not as good as she should have been.'

'I know you have probably had a racy past. A girl like you could hardly avoid turning men's heads. And I've been thinking about what Annie said yesterday, about you being hurt. I won't ever do that. If you marry me I will promise to be true, till death do us part.'

Sophie went to say something but Philip hadn't finished.

'And Annie mentioned you needed security. Yes, I'm offering that as well...but this is the bit I want to say... *Security needn't be dull.*

'That's exactly what I want you to shake me out of. I heard you say to Annie on the phone that you wanted to go away at Christmas to avoid the bloody Brussels sprouts. Believe me, so do I. Save me from the Brussels sprouts of life, Sophie. Marry me tomorrow at a register office, let's flout convention. Let's start as we mean to go on.'

Sophie's face was a picture.

Philip looked exhausted.

'I can't say any more, my darling Sophie. I just knew I had to fight for you. But if the answer's still no, then now I will accept it.'

'What a fight, Philip. What a glorious, wonderful, amazing fight.' Sophie's eyes shone.

'You mean...'

'Yes, Philip. I had already decided I wanted to marry you before you said all that but I'm so pleased I didn't tell you. You were magnificent, my love.'

Sophie entwined her arms round Philip's neck and kissed him. They were still kissing as Annie quietly let herself out of the flat to go for a very long walk.

Chapter Thirty-Six

'So are they going to have a Register Office do?' asked Reen as Annie finished recounting the events of the past week in England.

'I think Sophie considered it for at least a couple of hours before the lure of the long white dress, the marquee on the lawn and the horse-drawn carriage to the church, pulled her back from the brink.' Annie smiled, sipping her margarita.

She had arrived back gratefully to the bright sun of the Riviera after the gloom and rain of Manchester, and been immediately whisked out by Reen for a meal back at her 'posh place'. Reen clearly loved it there and the waiters seemed to recognise them from their last visit. Perhaps Reen's generous drinks order and lavish tip last time had much to do with it.

Annie hadn't wanted to tell the whole story, but Reen already knew about Sophie's unwanted pregnancy and obviously wanted to know what had happened, so Annie gave her the edited highlights. She didn't feel too disloyal as she knew the two would never meet.

'Talking of weddings, as you know my Tyrone is getting married to Tina in September and Ted and me would love it if you would come out to Spain to join in all the festivities.'

'Oh, Reen, that's lovely of you, but are you sure?'

'Of course. The whole family know about you and they are dying to meet you. Of course you will be staying with us, so no need to worry about anything. You'll be getting an official invitation, of course, so don't forget to leave me your English address.'

'Reen, I would love to meet your family. I feel I know them already.'

'Well, Babes, you'll be meeting one of them tomorrow.'

'Really?'

'Annie, Dahling,' Reen suddenly looked quite emotional, 'you see the villa is finished now, well, most of the building and dusty stuff. So my Ted wants me back home with him to help with all the finishing touches. I told him I had to wait for you to get back, of course, but when I said you were coming home today, he set off driving straight away to fetch me and Pugsy home. He's a big softy really, not that you'd tell if you saw him, and I know he's missed me a lot. And to be honest, I've missed him and all. This is the longest time we've spent apart in nearly forty years of marriage.'

How wonderful, Annie thought.

'Anyway, Babes, that's why I brought you here. It's a sort of farewell meal and a thank you one. I couldn't have stood it here without your company. And I knew my Pugsy was in safe hands with you when I had to keep going away. You've looked after him so well.' Reen rummaged in her gold bag and brought out a crumpled tissue.

She wasn't the only one getting emotional. 'Oh, Reen, I feel the same way. I've loved knowing you and hearing you clip-clopping over my head.'

'What…clip-clopping?'

'Oh. It's what I call the sound of your mules on the marble floor.'

For a minute Annie wondered if Reen would be offended.

'Oh, Dahling, that's so funny. Clip-clopping like horses, only they're mules, ain't they?' Reen burst out into peals of laughter.

Annie had never thought of it like that before. 'Oh, you're right,' she giggled. The smiling waiter topped up their glasses yet again.

It was a funny, sentimental, and slightly sad last evening together.

Next day, Ted arrived in his big green Range Rover. Annie heard his deep rumbling voice on the landing. As she opened the door, she saw the deep barrel chest it came from.

He was as large as Reen was petite. He stood there, broad shouldered, with his big arm around Reen's frail shoulders, his massive girth just about contained in a startling crimson floral shirt. Dark mahogany brown like his wife, deep laughter lines around his twinkling brown eyes like hers, and a similar infectious grin. Annie liked him instantly. It was just as well because she was seized in a bear-like hug and heard his chortle reverberate around his chest.

'So you're Annie are you?' He beamed as he released her. 'Yes, she is just as pretty as you said she was, Reen.'

Annie blushed.

'And yes, there she goes. My Reen says you always go pink if anyone says anything nice about you. Well, prepare to be permanently pink whenever I'm around.'

Annie didn't know where to put herself.

'Now, Ted,' said Reen digging him affectionately in the ribs, 'leave the poor girl alone. Come upstairs, have a cuppa and get to know each other while I finish my last bit of packing. Oh, and bring little Pimpy up so she can say goodbye to Pugsy.' She dropped her voice to a hoarse whisper, 'It'll keep his mind off the long car journey ahead.'

Annie smiled at the thought of Pugsy being aware of his impending journey but scooped up Pimpy anyway.

Over coffee she realised that Ted knew everything about her. He knew about what had happened with Jack, and with Henri Xavier.

'Listen, if that old lech comes bothering you at all, you just let me know. I'll be up here like a shot and soon sort him out. Nobody messes with one of my Reen's favourite girls.'

'Thank you.' It was strangely reassuring to know this. Although he looked like a giant cuddly bear in the besotted way he treated her and Reen, she definitely got the impression he could handle himself if need be.

He leaned forward, his shirt straining at the buttons. 'Now I've been thinking about how you can find this Fabien fella.'

Annie sat up alert.

'Why don't you put an advert in the local paper, like a

'lost and found' thing they have in England.'

'Well. I'm not sure…'

'Look, I know he's not exactly lost, is he? But you could say, *Is there a Fabien out there who knew*…er, what's your mum's name again?'

'Grace, Grace Makepeace.'

'*Who knew a Grace Makepeace in summer nineteen* whenever it was? There you are. Bob's your uncle.'

'I have thought of that, but I'm not sure it would work.'

'Why not?'

'What if he suspects what it's about? And he's probably married with a family, so might not want to own up.'

'Hmmn. See what you mean.' He sat back and thought for a minute. But he was determined not to give up on his idea. 'What if you was to say something like *'he might hear something to his advantage'*. Or even offer a reward for information about him. A reward would do it. People would soon grass him up then.'

Annie wanted to let him down gently. 'But I'm not keen on the idea of contacting him under false pretences. If he felt cheated or anything, he could just deny he ever had a relationship with my mum so he couldn't possibly be my father. I couldn't prove he was.'

'OK. See what you mean. But there's always a blood test you know.'

'How could I get his blood if he doesn't want to give it?'

Ted looked stumped.

'Hang on,' said Reen who had been listening to the whole thing while giving the place a final tidy up. 'You've got something there, Ted.'

'I have?' Ted beamed.

'A blood test. If you don't find this Fabien, you could always check when you get home.'

'How?'

'You know the man you always called your dad, get his blood and your mum's and they can see if they are a match with yours.'

'But Mum and Dad are dead, I thought I'd told you.'

'Oh, I know, Dahling, you did. But the hospital or your doctor will have their blood types and as far as I know, you can tell if they are your parents from that.'

Annie's eyes widened.

Reen came to sit on the sofa, perching next to Ted, who immediately put his arm round her. 'Ted, do you remember that palaver with our Ruby's nipper? Tom swore blind it wasn't his cos it had red hair, but they did the tests and it was. Red hair can suddenly emerge like that apparently. She was livid with him for suspecting she'd played away. I can't quite remember how they knew but it was definitely something to do with matching blood.'

Annie nodded slowly. 'Yes that makes sense. Stupid of me not to think of that before.'

'No it's not, Dahling. I suppose we are all a bit romantic at heart, ain't we? All perhaps dreaming we are related to royalty or have some exciting ancestors or something. With your mum being so in love with France and that, it was only natural for you to fancy you were half French. Wouldn't it be nice to be different? You keep looking for your Fabien, Babes, but have plan B ready for if you can't find him.'

'Yes, Reen, you are totally right. I need to stop fantasising and just grow up.'

'Dahling, you are grown up. The way you've handled things recently, your friend, that whole nasty Lucien situation, Mister Xavier, then being here on your own over most of the winter, I've seen a big difference in you since I first met you and I'd say you face things differently now. Don't you think?'

'Yes,' said Annie after a pause, 'perhaps you are right.' Certainly looking back on how she handled the Sophie situation she felt proud of how confident she was.

Although the Jack-shaped ache in her heart was still there, she had survived. And, she fancied, she had now got over him.

Although sometimes, just sometimes, she caught herself yearning for a glimpse of his long, lithe figure hurrying towards her apartment as she sat on her little balcony. And if ever someone was sitting on 'their' bench, she held her breath just in case it was him. And if she was sitting in the sun sipping coffee, a longing so deep came over her, all her limbs turned to jelly. But she was fighting these feelings… and soon she would be back in England and all these little triggers would stop and she could really move on.

Ted was talking and recalling her from her thoughts.

'Now I hope you don't mind, but me and Reen have been talking and we can't stand that old crone downstairs not letting you use her phone. And we both worry in case that Mr X bothers you, so we've got you this.'

His giant hand unfolded to reveal a mobile phone.

'Oh, but I couldn't possibly…'

'Knew you'd say that but we would be right offended if you said no. And don't you worry about the cost or anything, we've loaded it up with, well, enough to see you through. And I've got the number so I can keep topping it up every week or so. Just use it whenever you want.'

Annie was too overwhelmed to speak.

'I've got my Reen one as well, haven't I, Reen? he boomed, even though she was only a few feet away.

'Yes, Dahling, you have. So we can talk to each other whenever we like. Now don't go offending him by saying no, will you?'

'No, Reen I won't. You're right. It would be nice to stay in touch. I'd really like that.'

'Every day if you like,' Reen said shyly. 'If you're not too busy, of course.'

'No, a nice chat every day would be great. Then I can find out how the villa is getting on.'

'And she can check you're OK. And make sure that Mr X knows you've got a mobile phone now and if we don't hear from you, I'll be up here…'

'I know,' grinned Annie, '…like a shot.'

He grinned back. 'That I will.'

An hour later she waved off a tearful Reen, a beaming Ted and a dejected Pugsy who somehow *did* know he was going on a long journey and had evacuated his bowels on the pavement in protest.

'I'll sort it,' Annie said grabbing the poo bag from Reen. 'Have a safe journey. Phone me when you get there.'

'I will, Dahling. I will.'

Chapter Thirty-Seven

'Right, Pimps, my flower, that was a lovely walk wasn't it? Didn't the sea look wonderful today? That is something I will really miss, and you of course. But not long now till I go home, and I'm really looking forward to it.'

Annie sighed as a sudden wave of homesickness hit her. These were happening increasingly frequently.

'How silly, Pimpy. Who would have thought I would miss Lancashire when I'm living in a gorgeous place like this. It's probably because I haven't got enough to do. To be honest, now I have finished the Nina dairies, I'm itching to get on with…well, something. They were certainly absorbing while I was writing them up, and I got quite fond of her, poor thing. All that money, all that high life and fun times, and she was obviously deeply unhappy. I think she was really searching for love, and all she got was sex. Loads and loads of meaningless bonking. From what I can gather, any number of men could have been Adam's grandfather. Good luck to him, the sod. Let him trawl through all her lovers' initials and see if one of them really is an aristocrat. Blue blood doesn't make him a nicer person. So glad Sophie has nothing to do with him anymore. Still, that was a very nice cheque he finally sent me, wasn't it, Pimpy? Auntie Sophie reckons it was hush money, not that I would have told anyone, but it has definitely helped the finances. So let's spend it on a few excursions.'

Annie went into the bedroom to get changed out of her walking clothes and Pimpy followed her, circling round her feet. Fondly, Annie bent down and ruffled the little dog under her tummy. Pimpy rolled over in ecstasy as she always did.

'I know you are missing little Pugsy, aren't you? But you'll be all right if I leave you while I go on one of my little trips. Got to make the most of my last bit of time here, haven't I? Besides, I have to go out today as it's Madame Lafarge's day for snooping…oops…sorry, cleaning the apartment. So you just settle down and have a nice snooze for the rest of the day now your walkies are over, your evacuations sorted…crikes, I remember how much I hated picking that up at first. Ugh. But now, doesn't bother me a bit. Shows how much I've changed doesn't it? Definitely a new me has emerged, I think.'

Since Reen had gone she had given up on searching for Fabien. She had decided that when she got home she would look into Reen's idea about matching blood groups to ascertain her parentage.

Abandoning this futile hunt for Fabien had made it recede in importance somehow. She was calmer, more confident and happier in her skin, as the French would say. She and Reen chatted every day, and with the mobile phone, she could keep in contact with Sophie more often.

Her friend sounded so happy. She and Philip seemed closer than they had ever been. She hadn't told him about her affair, because she got the distinct impression that Philip didn't want to know about her past. It was the future that concerned him the most and plans were well on track for the wedding. Sophie had already lined up some bridesmaid fittings for when Annie got home.

Furthermore, Annie had nearly convinced herself that she had no more feelings for Jack. Apart from when she awoke each morning with an ache of misery, realising she would probably never see him again. And, not wanting to open old wounds, she totally avoided the old town and market area. To her annoyance, yesterday, the deep roar of an old car had caused her heart to flip and she turned, hoping to see the sleek shape of Elspeth thundering by.

That's why she knew it would be good to go home, away from these triggers, these memories of what might have been.

'So what do you think, Pimps, where should I go today? If I've not got long, I'm going to see and do everything. Yup, new me, Pimpy. Seizing life by the proverbials. So I think it's the train again. Done all points east…Cannes, of course, Port Grimaud and even St Tropez…très chic, if a little chilly this time of year, but definitely all places to toss airily into future conversations…that is when I start talking to people again, and not just you, my doggy friend.

'Today I fancy it's Monte Carlo or bust. So let's see, I'd better get a bit poshed up as I fancy another look at the old casino and a window shop at all the fancy doodah shops then…'

Pimpy gave an answering yap as she often did to these conversations, but then scooted off towards the door with an excited little bark.

'What's the matter, Pimpy?'

Under the door had appeared an envelope. Curious, she hurried to pick it up. It was unstamped and addressed to Mademoiselle Annie Roberts.

'How strange, Pimpy. Who can it be from?'

All the post was delivered into Madame Dumont's locked mail box downstairs, where it was retrieved by Madame Lafarge and anything relevant was forwarded on. Annie was definitely not to be trusted with such an important task, as the disagreeable concierge made quite clear.

She tore it open. A business card fell out from a short folded note written in French in a flowing hand:

Mademoiselle Annie

I may have found your Fabien. He is a business acquaintance of mine and fits your description of someone who studied in Paris during the summer of 1969. Although it is difficult to tell all these years later, he looks a little like the photo you showed me. I have not broached anything about this with him, so he knows nothing about you or your quest.

He eats his lunch at 12.30 most days at a small restaurant called Chez Gérard in the Rue Riquier behind the old port.

I enclose his business card.

I trust you find what you are looking for, chère Annie.

Your friend

Henri Xavier

What? Oh my crikes. Totally breathless, Annie had to sit down quickly on an ornate hall chair. Her mind whirled as she picked up the business card and turned it over in her hand.

There was his name, Fabien Jourdan. According to the card he was the Proprietor of Jourdan's printing company and a location flag in the small map showed an area above the Port.

Totally shocked, she gazed at the letter and card in wonder and disbelief. Here it was, out of the blue, a lead, a suggestion that perhaps her mum's Fabien did exist and still lived in Nice.

She felt her pulse throb erratically as she gazed uncomprehendingly at his business card. Fabien Jourdan. Could it be true?

In agitation she began pacing up and down the hallway. Her heart was all of a flutter and she felt lightheaded. Flopping down on the sofa still clutching the letter, she forced herself to take deep breaths.

Her mind was racing. What to do? What to do? Should she go and see him? Stupid question, of course she should. This was her chance to find out the truth at last. But, faced with an actual meeting, she shrank back in fear. What would she say?

She looked at the letter again. As far as she knew, Henri Xavier didn't know where she lived. The only people in Nice who did were Jack, Nicole and Lucien. How had the letter found her?

But she had no time to ponder that.

She must find that restaurant and somehow discover if this was the right Fabien…and if so what then?

Chapter Thirty-Eight

Shaking inside, she checked her appearance yet again in a shop window, before walking past the small restaurant once more and peering inside. It was busy and it seemed to be filled with mainly businessmen either chatting to colleagues or eating alone, reading their newspapers.

Checking her watch, she tried to summon up the courage to go in but, every time she approached the door, blind panic set in and she veered off. Twice a waiter had leapt to open the door for her and looked puzzled as she walked away clutching the blue box containing her mum's postcards and photos. She had studied the photo repeatedly before she set off and memorised the laughing features of the young man. Could she match them up to someone in the restaurant?

Right, deep breath. This time she really must go in. Weak-kneed, she pushed open the door and rapidly scanned the male diners hoping she would be able to recognise Fabien from the photo. But no.

A waiter approached. 'Can I help, Mademoiselle?'

She cleared her throat nervously. 'Yes, I'm looking for Monsieur Fabien Jourdan. I believe he dines here?'

A tall, middle-aged man sitting nearby looked up curiously, having heard her request.

He half rose in his seat. 'C'est moi, Mademoiselle.'

She stared at him. Yes, it was the boy in the black and white photograph. Older, more thick-set, the face fuller, and, of course, in colour, but nevertheless, the same man. She stared, dumbstruck.

He stared back, his courteous smile changing to one of puzzlement.

'Do I know you, Mademoiselle?'

'Perhaps,' she murmured still rooted to the spot. This was him, she was sure.

A concerned waiter looked at her face and pulled out a chair at Fabien's table.

'Mademoiselle,' he gestured.

She somehow forced herself to sit down.

Fabien continued to stare as if trying to place her face.

'A drink, Mademoiselle? The menu?' The waiter was asking.

'Oui,' she managed to say, 'Some water and...a glass of red wine please.'

Fabien was still looking at her curiously.

'I'm so sorry to disturb your meal, Monsieur,' Annie began, then stopped. How to proceed from there?

'Your accent,' Fabien said, 'it reminds me of...someone. May I ask where you are from?'

'From Lancashire in England...a place called Accrington.'

His mouth gaped in astonishment. 'Of course. Grace Makepeace. Are you related? You are so like her.'

'Yes, Monsieur. I am her daughter.'

'Of course. Of course. Your colouring is different but I should have recognised those blue eyes anywhere. This is amazing, after all these years.' He sat stunned, just looking at her.

She was vaguely aware of someone pulling out a chair at the table behind her so pulled hers in a fraction.

'Grace Makepeace,' he said in wonderment, a dreamy look coming over his face. 'So many years ago...' He looked eagerly over her shoulder towards the door. 'Is she here?'

Annie looked down. 'Alas no, Monsieur. I...I'm sorry to say she died last year.'

'No, vraiment? But she is so young,' he looked shocked.

'Yes, she was. It was cancer.'

'Non. That is so shocking. So young, so full of life.' He kept shaking his head in disbelief.

'The Gauloises got her in the end, I think.' Annie felt he needed an explanation.

'Gauloises. Ah yes, she started smoking them when we met. At first she coughed so much, it made me laugh. I told her to give up, but she persevered.'

'Yes, unfortunately, she persevered too long.'

'I am so sorry, Mademoiselle. I myself gave up many years ago. My wife nagged and nagged so…' Here he gave a very French shrug.

'But you are here, Mademoiselle…?'

'Annie, Annie Roberts.'

'Ah yes,' he nodded. 'Of course, Roberts. Yes, that's the name she said in her letter.'

'Letter, Monsieur?'

'Yes,' he sighed, 'the last letter she ever wrote to me.'

'What did it say?' Annie leant forward eagerly.

Just then her wine appeared, and a menu.

'Um, I'm not sure I will be eating.'

'But of course, you must join me. It is my privilege to meet the daughter of such a special person. What would you like?'

The last thing Annie felt like doing was eating but it would be strange to sit and watch him have his lunch without joining in. 'Thank you, you are so kind. Umm, what are you having?'

'Alas, just a simple omelette and salad. My wife says I must watch my weight, so I do.'

'The same for me then, if you please.'

Fabien nodded to the waiter, who disappeared. As he turned back to her, he stopped, as if struck for the first time at the strange coincidence of it all.

'So, I don't understand. How did you find me after all this time? You have a message from your mother perhaps?'

'Yes and no. Oh, Monsieur Jourdan. It is a long story.'

How did she start? Then she realised she was still clutching the blue box. 'You see, after she died, I found a box…this box.' She opened it. His eyes widened in recognition as she took out the two old postcards and the strip of photos.

'May I?' he asked as he picked them up. 'Ah yes, ah yes,'

he sighed, looking at the photos, 'so young and so much in…' He was clearly going to say 'in love' but caught himself just in time. 'I remember so well, these photos. We popped into a booth in the Gare du Nord. It was the day she was supposed to go home, but she decided to stay. It was my last week at the Sorbonne before I came back here for the summer. We spent the whole wonderful week together. It was a very special time, Mademoiselle Annie. Grace was a very special person to me.'

'And you were special to her.'

'I have often wondered…' he began, then sighed again. 'Such a shame that circumstances kept us apart.'

'What circumstances, Monsieur?'

He looked surprised, 'But surely you must know.'

'No.'

He looked puzzled, turning over the postcards. 'Your mother never told you?'

'No, Monsieur. All I know is from these postcards and photos.'

'And my letters?'

'I haven't found any letters.'

'Ah, perhaps she destroyed them. I can see why. Your father? Is he a jealous man?'

'Um. He died when I was seven years old, so I don't really know.'

'Vraiment? Oh, such a shame.' He mulled this over. 'I wonder why she never wrote and told me. Seven years you say…I didn't marry till I was thirty…' She could see him turning it all over in his mind, thinking of the possibilities.

The waiter appeared with her omelette.

It looked delicious, but Annie wasn't hungry. Fabien had stopped eating his lunch, clearly still pondering everything she had told him.

She waited a while, playing with her omelette and sipping her wine, wondering where to go from here. She felt they were at a crucial stage of the story.

'Monsieur, you said circumstances kept you apart. What were they?'

'Ah, this is a little delicate. Can I ask if you have any brothers or sisters?'

'No, I am an only child.'

'And can I ask how old you are.'

'I will be thirty in April.'

'Ah, then perhaps you know…'

'Know what?'

'Mademoiselle Annie, this is very difficult for me, very delicate. Did your mother never tell you about…?'

'I know my mother and father had to get married because she was pregnant with me.'

He breathed a sigh of relief. 'Ah, so you know the circumstance that kept us apart was you, my dear Annie.' He gave a sad smile.

Annie squirmed. How could she broach the subject and ask if it was possible her mother was pregnant when she left Paris?

'Monsieur…'

'Please call me Fabien.'

'Thank you. You say my mother wrote you a letter…'

'Ah yes, ah yes. Many letters over that long hot summer. She was so depressed to be back in Accrington and not France, but then so happy to be going to university to study French. Can I say, to hear you speak French, your accent, it is so charming, just like hers. How I loved to hear her funny expressions. If she didn't know the words, she made up phrases and sayings, so charming. She called them Franglais.'

'Yes, Fabien. She made them up for the rest of her life.'

'I still can't believe she has died. Such life, such vitality she had.' As his eyes filled with tears, he took out a red handkerchief and blew his nose.

Annie reached across and patted his hand. Possibly the hand of her father she thought. 'I know. I miss her every day. She would have loved to be here, in France. I know she would have loved to see you again. Keeping these postcards all these years, locked away. I'm sure you were locked away in her heart as well.'

He nodded, eyes once again filling up.

211

Somehow she must broach the subject of their affair. 'I know that August nineteen sixty-nine was so special for her, because she adopted a very French way of doing things later, after my father died. She once gave my friend and me a French weekend...'

'August?' Fabien interrupted her. 'No, not August. It was July.'

'July? The postcards say the summer of nineteen sixty-nine, so I assumed that meant August. Are you sure it was July?'

'Mais bien sûr. I remember so well. I had to get out of my student room by the end of July and be back in Nice at the beginning of August.'

'But...'

'Yes, yes, I remember now that Grace felt very naughty to take that extra week to stay with me in my student room. But after I had to leave my room we had nowhere to stay, of course, and anyway she had to be back for August to start a summer job in the factory.'

Annie was in a whirl. If it was July then...

Fabien continued, 'He wasn't very happy she delayed her return so she said in one of her letters.'

'Who?'

'Her boyfriend. He lived in the same street as her and he had arranged for her to work in the same factory as him for the summer, because she needed money to go to university.'

'Her boyfriend?'

'Ah yes. She told me about him. She felt so guilty about betraying him with me. But she said she would finish with him as soon as she got back to Accrington, which she wrote she had done. He was very upset apparently. But of course working in the same factory it was difficult to avoid him... and eventually she felt so sorry for him...'

He looked embarrassed, 'He was of course, your father.'

'My father?'

'But yes. She told me everything in her final letter. She poured out her heart. She was angry and upset. She had loved starting university and then was devastated to find she was pregnant. For a while she wasn't sure what to do, but... She said he was a good man, a hard worker who would be a caring husband. His ideas and education didn't match hers, but that was because he hadn't had the opportunities. The main thing was he adored her. He seemed to accept that he loved her more than she loved him. One day she hoped she would learn to love him as he deserved.'

Annie sat there re-arranging her thoughts.

'So, she still loved you when she married my...father.'

'Oh yes, she told me so.' He sighed. 'It was a very passionate letter.'

'Have you still got it?'

'Alas no. Eventually, I had to destroy it. It is not the sort of thing you want your wife to discover. I think perhaps my letters to her were destroyed also.'

Annie nodded, turning over the postcards in her hands. 'But, it seems she could not bear to destroy everything.'

Fabien patted her hand. 'I'm glad. It means I have met her daughter who is just as pretty and wonderful as she was. You have brought it all flooding back. Our youth, our happiness, so much love, so much hope.' He wiped his eyes again.

'Oh dear, Mademoiselle Annie, so many memories you have stirred up. I can't believe you came all this way to find me.' He suddenly looked puzzled. Annie could see the inevitable questions forming in his mind. She had to stop him in this train of thought. Soon he would want to know why she wanted to find him. He must not guess the deep underlying reason why she had gone to so much trouble to see him. She must try to convince him it was a passing notion.

'I was in Nice anyway...um...staying here helping someone for a while.'

'Oh. But how did you find me, and know I was here?' He indicated the restaurant.

Suddenly she felt exhausted. This could get complicated and she really didn't want to get deeply into any more explanations. He wasn't her father and that was that. All her expectations seemed so foolish now.

Trying to seem nonchalant, she nibbled a piece of bread. 'Oh, it wasn't difficult,' she lied. 'I found your surname in one of my mother diaries. So it was quite easy to track you down after that...telephone directories, you know. Then... um...when I asked about you, someone told me you ate here, so I thought I would just look you up. I know that's what my mother would have wanted. You were very important to her.'

'Ah yes.' The slight frown was still there between his eyes but he was prevented from probing further by the waiter coming to clear their plates. He glanced at his watch. 'Oh alas. Look at the time. I'm late and I have an important meeting. I'm so sorry, I'm afraid I must be going.'

He made a sign for the bill, 'Can I contact you again?'

'Of course. I have a mobile number,' she said pulling it out of her bag.

'Ah good.' After he paid the bill he wrote it down on the back of his business card. 'You are in Nice for a while longer?'

'Yes, nearly another two weeks.'

'I will be in touch. Oh, Mademoiselle Annie, my dear, I'm not sure I will be able to concentrate on work this afternoon. You have overwhelmed me with so many emotions. Au revoir, my dear, dear girl.' He kissed her fondly on each cheek.

'Au revoir Fabien.'

Pulling out his handkerchief once more to surreptitiously wipe his eyes, he walked rapidly out of the restaurant.

Chapter Thirty-Nine

Annie just sat, gazing into space, trying to comprehend all that had happened. Her thoughts were in a whirl. So Fabien wasn't her father after all. She wasn't half French.

Like a stick of Blackpool rock, she was Accrington all the way through.

She sighed. This was the end of her foolish romantic notions and she wasn't sure how she felt about it.

As a waiter bustled past, she looked around for the first time to take in her surroundings. The place wasn't as big as she first thought, an illusion of space being created by the long mirrors along each wall. As she glanced in the one by her right shoulder, she froze. A familiar figure was sitting with his back to her at the next table, hunched over a coffee. Quickly she looked down before Jack could see she had noticed him.

Her heart leapt. Jack. After all this time. What was he doing here? It couldn't be coincidence, surely? He must have followed her. Why? Her shoulders locked in shock. What had he heard? Or seen? In a whirl she replayed her actions with Fabien.

With a groan she realised that Jack would have seen her talking to a middle-aged man, clasping his hand on the table, giving him her mobile phone number, kissing him fondly goodbye. The last time he had seen her, she was kissing Henri Xavier goodbye. With a plummeting feeling of dread, she knew exactly what conclusions could be drawn from her encounter.

As he shifted in his seat behind her, suddenly this tight feeling of dismay was replaced with white hot anger. How dare he follow her, judge her, convict her.

Enraged, she leapt out of her seat and quickly turned round to face him. He looked astonished as she bent over to hiss in his face.

'How dare you follow me! How dare you spy on me! How dare you believe the worst of me!'

Jack was about to say something when she cut him short.

'Leave me alone.'

'Annie, wait...'

But she didn't. She fled out of the café and didn't stop until she got home.

There she flung herself on her bed and howled. Howled for the loss of her dreams, howled for the loss of her mother and howled for the loss of Jack.

All these were gone forever.

As the light faded, she could cry no more. Drained, she sat on the edge of the bed. Poor Pimpy had curled up next to her, and howled in sympathy. Now she too was exhausted and had fallen asleep. Annie stroked her soft head as she stirred awake.

'So sorry, little one. It's OK. It's OK. I've just got to grieve a bit. I'll eventually accept all this, but I can't at the moment. It's just all too depressing.'

Her mobile rang.

The last thing she wanted to do was answer it, but if it was Reen she would worry. So she dragged herself off the bed.

'Hallo, Reen.'

'Hallo, Babes. You sound funny. Are you OK?'

'Yes, I'm fine.'

'No, you're not. Don't you try to lie to me. What's happened?' Reen's voice was sharp with worry.

Annie gave in. Why try to pretend everything was all right when it wasn't. 'Don't worry, Reen. It's just I've been to meet Fabien. He's a lovely man, but he isn't my father.'

'Oh, Babes. I'm sorry. I can hear how upset you are.'

'I know it's silly to be so upset, but it's really got to me.'

She didn't want to mention Jack. That was too distressing. That he should have spied on her and misconstrued everything cut to her heart and she couldn't bear to talk about it, not even with Reen.

'No, Dahling. I understand. It's the end of a dream isn't it?'

'Yes,' she nearly began sobbing again.

'Right,' Reen's voice was sympathetic but practical, 'you tell me all about it. It *will* help, you know. How did you find out he wasn't your father. Did he say so?'

'No he didn't have to. Thank goodness. It would have been too embarrassing to ask. But the dates were all wrong. All the postcards referred to the summer, so I assumed it was August. But in fact it was July. So it was too early for me to be his child as I was born on April twenty-third and…'

'Oh, I didn't know that, Dahling. That's St George's Day.'

'Yes, Mum said she nearly called me Georgia. It's William Shakespeare's birthday as well. We always joked I could have been Wilhelmina.'

'Ooo, that's a mouthful and no mistake,' Reen laughed.

'Yes, plain old Annie was quite a come down, wasn't it?'

'But it suits you, Dahling. The others wouldn't.'

Annie sighed.

'You mustn't sigh, Babes. You are what you are, and what you are is lovely. Would it have made a big difference if he had been your father?'

'I don't know.'

'Has he got a family?'

'I don't know, but he's definitely married and his wife sounds a bit…well…a bit of a dragon. No, that's not fair. It's just the way he talked about her. She obviously cares for him and forced him to give up smoking, makes him eat salads for his lunch, so she sounds quite a strong personality.'

'So if he had been your dad, how complicated would that have made it?'

'Quite a lot, I suppose.'

'Course it would, Dahling. Can you imagine a wife

suddenly confronted with her husband's grown-up daughter?'

'Hmmn, I suppose you are right.'

'Yes, I am. Right from when you wanted to find him, I was worried. I was worried either way, to be honest. I never for a minute supposed you were half-French, but I was more worried if you were. It would make you question everything you've ever known.'

Reen was talking really seriously now.

Annie had never really thought about it. 'I suppose so.'

'I *know* so, Dahling, believe me,' Reen said, vehemently. Then there was a slight hesitation. 'Right, I'm going to tell you something only my family know. OK? It's a bit personal. I found out that the man I thought was my dad, well he wasn't. My mum had an affair, while she was married, and I was the result. My dad never suspected. She only told me after he'd died. And I had to re-think everything. Shook me up for a long time, I can tell you. She wanted me to meet my real dad, but I wouldn't. The one who loved me and brought me up was my real dad.' There was a break in her voice as she asked, 'Did your dad love you?'

The question startled Annie. 'I think so. I suppose so.'

'Well he did, I can tell you.'

'How do you know?'

'Because, believe me, you would know if he didn't. The fact that you took him for granted and never questioned it, means he did.'

Annie was thrown by this thought.

'Look, Dahling, most of the time we just take our parents for granted. Just assume they love us, just assume they are there. Until they are gone, then you realise all sorts of things, and wish you'd said all sorts of things…and of course then it's too late.'

Annie sat there silently, processing all this. Reen was right. She hadn't really considered all the ramifications of searching for a new father, when she'd had one all along.

'So, Dahling, about your dad, your real dad, what was he like?'

'I'm just sitting here trying to remember him. As you

218

know he died when I was seven and Mum was such a big personality, I've not really thought about him much. I'm ashamed to say I don't think I knew him. He worked nights at the factory, so he slept all day. My main memory as a kid is having to be quiet all the time. I suppose that's why I read a lot. But I once asked Mum why he couldn't work in the daytime, and she said he got more money working nights. And I do remember a row about her wanting to go out to work and he wouldn't let her because he said it was his job to provide for us.'

'He sounds a very proud man.'

'Yes, so many things are falling into place now. Mum smoked while he was alive, they both did, but it was only after he died she began smoking Gauloises. The local corner shop used to get them in especially for her.'

'How did he die?'

'Oh, it was nasty accident at work. As far as I know, a piece of machinery wasn't fastened securely, came loose and fell on him. Hit his head. They all said he wouldn't have known anything about it. It was an awful time. Lots of people came round to say nice things about him. I think he was really well thought of. Mum really cried a lot and I do remember her saying 'I'm sorry' again and again at the funeral. Looking back, I wonder if she felt guilty at not loving him more.'

'Could be.'

'It was in all the papers, and the firm admitted liability and Mum got quite a lot of compensation. I think she bought our house with that money and the insurance. Oh, and also a little car…a French car of course, a 2CV.'

Annie began putting more and more pieces together.

'Yes, the more I think of it, she only became 'French' after he died. It's funny, I've never really thought about all those early years when Dad was around. He was sort of a kindly but shadowy presence in the house. I think he left all the child rearing stuff to my mum. He never read to me, or talked to me much. I wonder if he was always aware that he wasn't as clever as my mum. I wonder if he felt guilty that she had to give up her university dream because of him getting her pregnant. Although of course it takes two to tango as they say, and Mum must have been as much to blame…if you can call it blame.'

'He sounds like a really nice man.'

'Oh, Reen, I'm beginning to see that. Poor bloke. I'm feeling horribly guilty that I didn't really know him.'

'Don't upset yourself, Dahling. You were only young. Can you remember what he looked like?'

Annie gave a little laugh. 'He was just me Dad.' Then she closed her eyes and tried to picture him. 'Let's see, he had brownish hair, lovely blue eyes, I think. Quite tall. Nice smile. Yes, I do remember how I liked it when he smiled, but I don't think he did very often. Wait a minute… I've just had a really vivid memory of him.' Annie gasped as intense but long forgotten images floated across her eyes.

'Oh my goodness. We were on holiday at a caravan park place. There was a disco in the club house and Mum and he got up to dance, and I was mesmerised. He could really dance. His face came alive and some women behind me were going nuts over him…about how gorgeous he was, how sexy, what a great mover he was. Stuff like that. Actually, my mum was a good dancer as well, but he…yes…he just had got such a feel for the music. I loved watching him. Yes, he danced all evening. I fell asleep at the table and I can remember snuggling into him as he carried me home. He was grinning and humming. How strange, I had totally forgotten about that.'

She sat still, reliving the music from that forgotten night so long ago.

'From the way those women were talking, he must have been quite sexy. When I get home, I must look out all the photos of him.'

'Yes, you do that, Dahling. He sounds the sort of dad you could be proud of.'

'Oh, Reen, you are right. Oh thank you.'

'Night, night, Dahling.'

Chapter Forty

It was a restless deep-thinking night. The talk with Reen had helped her so much.

As Annie lay in bed, listening to the sounds of Nice through the open window, more and more memories of her father surfaced. She had very few of them together as a family except when they were on holiday on various caravan sites in Wales. Then there were days on the beach, paddling in the sea, sheltering from the rain, eating ice-cream but most images were of her parents dancing. All night they twirled before her.

Sometimes her dad would lift her into his arms and dance with her round the floor. It was wonderful to feel his strong arms around her, snuggle into his chest, and look up into his laughing face. Yes, those images were coming back so strongly, she could almost see him. She could hear the music and feel the giddy sensation of it all.

Often she would stretch out, tired after all the holiday activities, on a rough, beer-soaked banquette as her parents twirled and entwined together on the dance floor. Then falling asleep, in spite of the loud pulsating music, she was carried back, cuddled into her dad's broad shoulder, to the caravan in the dark before being tucked up gently into bed.

As an adult, looking back, she wondered if she was seeing great sexual chemistry between her parents, which had probably led to her conception. But perhaps they had not much in common in everyday life.

Thinking about it, she also had a distinct impression that her father played with her, laughed with her, teased her and tickled her more when her mum wasn't around. Yes, his play was always boisterous, whereas with her mum she mainly read and talked.

With hindsight, she now wondered how difficult must it have been for him. He undoubtedly knew about Fabien. Grace must have given it as a reason for their break-up when she got back from those heady weeks in Paris. Then their relationship probably re-ignited one night before she left for university, leading to their decision to marry when she came along. Perhaps he always knew he was second best, that his wife loved another man more than him. Her mum must have cared for her dad because she seemed to have hidden her French longings while he was alive. They only resurfaced after he died.

Long into the night she lay there, thinking things through, but it was difficult to analyse their relationship from such a distance and seen from a child's view.

But the more she considered it, the more she realised it, Reen was right, her dad did love her, and now she knew it.

How foolish to hope that a stranger could love her as much as he did. As lovely as Fabien seemed, he couldn't have replaced all those years.

As she replayed their lunchtime meeting over and over in her mind, she went hot and cold thinking she might have actually asked him if he were her father. Imagine the embarrassment all round. She would have been mortified to have found she had got it so wrong. He looked a sentimental man. Would he have felt guilty at letting her down? Thank goodness he had no idea of the real reason she had found him.

On balance, she was glad she had met him. It was wonderful to know that he had loved her mum as much as she loved him. His memories were of a shared passion, young, romantic and hopeful.

Which brought her back, in ever-decreasing circles, to her own situation with Jack. What was he doing there in the restaurant? He *must* have followed her. How else could he know she was there? Perhaps he just happened to see her and followed her on a whim. How much had he seen? Was it possible he could have watched the whole encounter through the mirrors on the wall? If so, there was so much there he could have misconstrued if he wanted to. It did look bad, especially after seeing her with Henri Xavier. Had he heard any of their conversation? He was sitting back-to-back with her so he could have listened in easily and gleaned that she wasn't having a liaison with Fabien. But the café was noisy so perhaps…

These tumbling thoughts were driving her mad.

'Stop. I don't care.' Sitting up in bed, she shouted out loud and put her hands over her ears to drown out all these turbulent thoughts.

'It doesn't matter what he thinks because he doesn't matter to me anymore,' she told herself fiercely.

But it didn't work. He *did* matter. Oh, how he mattered to her.

'This is so stupid,' she railed. 'I hardly know him. He certainly doesn't know me if he believes I would sleep around. I have got to stop thinking about him.'

Easier said than done. All night she berated herself for still yearning after someone, after something, that wasn't to be.

'It *mustn't* happen to me like it happened to Mum. Let's face it, hers was a holiday romance. Who knows if it would have stood the test of time? Would their relationship have lasted with her living in a different culture? She would definitely have gone to live with him in France as I couldn't see Fabien preferring Accrington to Nice. And the memories of that heady time in Paris forever blighted her relationship with my father, a good decent man who did the best he could for her.

'No, I am not going to repeat history. Jack is *my* holiday romance. Nothing more. Brought on by a combination of being somewhere exotic, surrounded by so many different sounds, sights, smells. A feeling of being unanchored in strange exciting seas. In my case, I latched on to the familiar, someone from home. In Mum's, she longed for the unfamiliar. My romance with Jack hasn't been as intense as Mum's. We haven't even had sex.

'Mum knew Fabien shared her feelings. I have no way of

knowing what Jack felt about me. I think he liked me, but I can't be certain of any more than that. And he certainly has been very quick to believe the worst of me.

'Anyway, I am going home soon to real life, older and wiser. I will put all this behind me and forget about him.

'Let's face it, I haven't even got anything, *anything at all*, to put in my blue box under the bed. A couple of meals, a couple of kisses, a party and a wonderful drive into the hills and to Cannes. That's it.'

As the first bright flickerings of dawn crept through the window she realised that none of these exhortations were working.

So she gave up. Totally exhausted she dragged herself into the kitchen and, after a cup of tea, threw on some clothes and took a surprised Pimpy out for a very early walk.

The sun's rays were casting their golden glow over a calm sea. It was a magnificent sight. The turquoise sky was suffused with streaks of red and the dispersing clouds were tinged with silver.

Despite her misery, she was transfixed by the beauty of it and only gradually became aware of a figure slumped on their bench. A figure, who, on seeing her approach, turned to face her.

Chapter Forty-One

For a moment Annie's steps faltered. Her heart gave a spontaneous lurch as she caught her breath.

Then her pride kicked in. If he was there to berate her, just let him try. But Jack's look was beseeching, his face pale and he stretched out his hands in supplication.

She approached the bench, then, head held high, she just waited.

'Annie, I have been waiting all night to tell you I'm so sorry. I can't tell you how sorry I am. Please forgive me.'

Still she waited. This man had put her through hell. There was no way she was forgiving him this easily.

'I know everything now. Oh, Annie, I'm so ashamed. I should have trusted my instincts. I should have trusted *you*.'

'You mean you don't believe I slept with Lucien.'

'No, I *know* you didn't. I doubted it at the time and...'

Coldly, Annie cut him off mid-sentence. 'And you don't believe I meet middle-aged men for money.'

'Absolutely not.'

'So why did you follow me yesterday and spy on me?'

'Oh, Annie, I wasn't spying on you.'

'So how did you know I was there?'

'Henri Xavier told me.'

'What? Oh, I get it.' Cold anger seized her. 'You thought I was meeting one of my fancy men and came along to gloat at what a slut I was...'

'No. no. Oh, Annie, no.' He looked anguished. 'I knew that wasn't what you were doing. He told me you thought you were going to meet your father. And I wanted to be near you just to see...well, just in case you needed anyone...in case you were upset or anything...' Jack's voice trailed off.

'Were you sitting behind me all the while?'

'Yes.'

'So you heard everything?'

'More or less. Yes.'

She stopped. This was too much to take in. Why would Henri Xavier tell Jack anything about Fabien?

Disconcerted and profoundly perplexed, she turned around to face the sea. But her agitation was too great to stand still. She began a fast-paced walk along the promenade. Jack fell into step by her side.

'Annie, can I ask? I heard him say he met your mum in July and you sort of pressed him on that so was it important? Did it mean…?'

'Yes. He can't be my father.'

His eyes searched her face. 'Are you very upset?'

Suddenly drained of all emotion, Annie slumped onto a nearby bench.

'I'm not sure what I feel right now.'

He sat down beside her, his face full of such distress, Annie had to turn away. She was still angry with him but this fury was being eroded by his evident misery.

'Annie, love, you look exhausted.'

Her eyes welled at the concern in his voice. All her damped down feelings of attraction were resurfacing despite herself. But she wasn't done yet.

'Of course I'm exhausted. I've been trying to figure things out all night.' Turning to confront him she couldn't contain her rage. 'You say you went to the café to check I was OK. Big deal. You haven't checked I was OK for weeks now…in fact since *the last century*. Why suddenly all this concern when you really haven't given a damn for the whole sodding winter?'

'I know. I know. I feel so guilty. I'm so sorry. I *have* thought about you all the time, wondering how you were. I can honestly say, I have thought about you every single day.'

Annie looked long and hard at his anguished face.

'Look, Annie, I've been a stupid naïve fool. All I can do is agree with everything you throw at me. All I can keep saying is I'm sorry. I really am.'

'Right, let's start at the beginning. You now say you don't believe I slept with Lucien?'

'No. I now *know* you didn't.'

'How do you suddenly *know* when you obviously believed the worst before, didn't you?'

He hung his head, shamefaced. 'Yes and no. It didn't seem like you, so I didn't want to. I really didn't. But Nicole told me Lucien said he had spent the night with you. At the time, I could see no reason why he would lie about something like that. I knew he fancied you. You saw how angry I was when I saw him making up to you in the kitchen. That's why I insisted he left with Nicole and me. But, as we were walking back home, he just disappeared and I suspected he had snuck back. I wanted to go and check you were OK, but Nicole, bloody Nicole, had a bad headache...so she said, so I had to take her home. After I had deposited her safely back at her apartment, I went back to our flat to find no sign of Lucien. This wasn't unusual. Even though he was engaged, he had a string of girlfriends so I just hoped he was with one of them.

'I was really torn about whether to race back to your apartment. But then I thought, what could I do? If he was there, you presumably had invited him up. In which case it was none of my business.

'Next day, Nicole told everyone he'd been with you. I argued that I didn't believe it and she laughed at me and said I was a naïve fool. She asked if I'd ever known any girl refuse Lucien. And I had to confess I hadn't. I had seen him at work more than once and I know he can charm the birds from the trees. I knew he was smitten by you. When I confronted him, he had the grace to look shamefaced but said he did go back to see you.'

She nodded. 'Yes he did. And I gave him short shrift. He did look very surprised but eventually I persuaded him I meant it when I told him to sling his hook.'

'Yes, I have confronted him since and I now know that's what happened, but it's not what I was being told at the time.

Oh, Annie, I couldn't feel more guilty if I tried. As I said, my gut instinct was to come straight round the next day to talk to you about it. Then I thought, if he *had* stayed the night, what right had I to complain...or...say anything? I mean, I *thought* we were sort of going out, but...then again nothing had been said or anything. Annie, I really didn't know what to do, what to believe.'

Slowly she nodded her head. She had never thought of it like that. Now she could see why he might not have come round after the party. If she *had* slept with Lucien, would it have been any business of Jack's? Their relationship wasn't established as such, both of them still negotiating, aware of their mutual attraction but unsure of how deep the feelings were on the other side.

However, as she faced him, she deliberately kept her tone cold, 'So what made you change your mind?'

He ran his fingers through his hair and his shoulders slumped down. 'I've only just put all the pieces together properly and what a fool I've been. I've been had for a right mug. It's no excuse really, I know. I've had my suspicions about so many things for a while now, but the blinkers finally fell off yesterday morning. After a massive row with Nicole about her giving Henri Xavier your address, I immediately went and confronted Lucien in person. He could see I wasn't in the mood to be fobbed off. How I didn't hit him I'll never know...but he confessed it was a lie, he hadn't spent the night with you. He confessed a lot of things. It's all fallen into place now...you see...'

'Wait a minute. You need to go back a bit. This is all too confusing. Why did Nicole give Henri Xavier my address? And why did you come to that restaurant yesterday.'

'OK. You're right, it must seem confusing. Things have happened fast since yesterday.' Jack looked relieved that she was giving him time to explain.

'First, Annie, please forgive me for what I thought was happening with you and Henri Xavier when I saw you together outside that restaurant. Sod's law. It was the day I had, at last, decided to come and see you...just for a chat. I knew Lucien hadn't seen you again and anyway I reasoned that anything that had gone on wasn't really my business. I just hoped we could perhaps be friends, if nothing else. I missed you, kept thinking about you…then I saw you with Henri Xavier. Oh, Annie, I was so shocked, so horrified…'

'I know. I saw your face.'

'Now I know you just wanted his help to find Fabien.'

Annie shrugged. 'I realised it looked bad, but you could have asked me. I tried to run after you to tell you…'

'I know, I know. I can't believe I've been wrong about so many things.' He leapt up from the bench and began pacing.

'Sit down and tell me why Henri told you about Fabien.'

'Apparently Henri's been trying to find you for a couple of weeks now. Wisely you never told him where you lived and obviously you haven't been to any of the usual cafés or places he always used to see you.'

Annie didn't want to reveal she had been deliberately avoiding all her previous haunts so just said, 'I've been back to England for a while.'

'Oh, that explains it.'

'So why did he come to you to find me?'

'It wasn't me, it was Nicole. I think he keeps his ear to the ground and he'd sort of heard about the scandal with you and Lucien from one of his friends…'

Annie felt her face freeze. 'So half of Nice believes I slept with an engaged man.'

Jack grimaced, 'I'm not excusing him, Annie, but he was put up to it.'

'What?'

'I've been such a fool, a gullible stupid fool.' Jack gave a hollow laugh. 'I can't believe I once accused you of being naïve, an innocent abroad. Serves me right. They landed me hook line and sinker.'

'Who?'

'Lucien, Nicole and all her family.'

Annie's heart leapt. 'Nicole?'

'Yes, forgive me for abandoning you that night of your dinner party. That's such a huge guilt. Lucien confessed all when I had him by the throat yesterday morning.'

'What?'

'Yes, it does sound a bit macho doesn't it? I surprised myself but I can't tell you how livid I was. Anyway, Lucien said he really fancied you and couldn't believe you turned him down when he came back after the dinner party. So I think he told everyone he had spent the night with you partly to save face, especially as he was under specific instructions from Nicole to seduce you.'

Annie gasped.

'Oh yes. You haven't heard the half of it, Annie. He daren't confess his failure to Nicole, so he went off to one of his girlfriend's and pretended he'd stayed with you.'

'But he's supposed to be engaged to Mousy Monique.'

Jack laughed, 'Is that what you call her? Yes, she is a bit mousey, but apparently she's always, but always, had a crush on Lucien from way back. Her father, Albert, you know, the Patron from the café, is not a man to be messed with. If your only daughter wants something, you get it for her. He has invested heavily in Lucien's garage and, one way and another, bound Lucien up so tightly, he had to promise to marry Monique. In spite of everything he's done, I do feel a bit sorry for him. He doesn't love her and has numerous girlfriends which she knows about, but she won't let go. Incidentally, I've found out all the girlfriends are warned off pretty nastily so I worried about you. You didn't get threatened did you?'

'No, just a cold shoulder from everyone I'd ever met in Nice, that's all.' The hurt in her voice must have come through because Jack looked aghast.

'Oh, Annie, love...' he went to embrace her. But she pulled back. It was too soon for any reconciliation.

'Sorry,' he mumbled, turning away. They sat side by side in awkward silence as the sun was rising into an azure blue sky. The white buildings curving round the bay glowed pink in the early morning light. The wind had lost its winter's edge and Annie could feel the promise of spring in its warmth.

Although there were still a million questions tumbling

through her mind, gradually the truth was emerging and she realised the tension in her shoulders was beginning to lift.

Chapter Forty-Two

'Look, Jack, do you mind if we stroll on for a bit. Pimpy is missing her walk.' Annie felt the need to move. It was proving too much to take in and she was hoping she could piece it all together if they walked.

Jack leapt up. 'Yes of course.' He looked as if he had so much pent-up anxiety, he also needed to move in order to release it.

The sun was behind them, casting long shadows as they paced side by side, Pimpy trotting happily slightly in front. The heavy morning traffic raced along, brought to a halt at intervals by traffic lights when pedestrians streamed across both ways. Some were clearly going into the city for work, others coming on to the Promenade for their morning exercise. Annie remembered how fascinated she used to be with all the activity on this broad walkway. Now it was just part of her daily life.

Her mind was darting backwards and forwards, sorting out everything Jack had said. For the moment, she shelved the Henri Xavier questions. First she had to come back to the burning injustice of Lucien's lie. The unfairness of this had gnawed at her all winter. Everything else could wait as she got to the bottom of this falsehood that had had such a devastating impact on her life in Nice.

'So you say Nicole put Lucien up to it. Why? Why would she want him to seduce me? Why daren't he confess the truth?'

He sighed. 'I think it goes back to when I first came to know the family.' He ran his hand through his hair in his familiar gesture when troubled. 'I admit it. I was bowled over by Nicole. To my embarrassment, I think I was awestruck by how sophisticated she was. I'd never met anyone like her. And, of course, she could see it and played up to it. Let's face it, she liked having someone at her beck and call. I was always there, babysitting her son Sébastien, helping her decorate her apartment, and all sorts of little jobs. She loved going for drives in Elspeth, loved the prestige of it, I suppose, and I felt great, taking a gorgeous looking woman around. The family embraced me and I really did feel I was wanted and, I confess, I was flattered. A bit like you wanting to be French, I really felt I was part of Nice. I suppose I was acting the part a bit, but it felt good.'

Annie nodded. She remembered how confident and how very French he was when she first met him.

He gave a rueful grin. 'I can't tell you how tickled I was that you thought I really was French.'

In spite of herself, Annie smiled back at him. Some of the anguish lifted a little from his face and his eyes held a ray of hope. She turned away, annoyed with herself.

As if knowing he wasn't out of the woods yet, Jack continued, 'Anyway, when I met you, she noticed...well let's say, I wasn't as attentive and she didn't like it. That day I took you for a drive, she came looking for me to run an errand, and I wasn't around. She wasn't happy. Then the night of André's birthday party, she was clearly jealous of you.'

'Me? Why?'

'Oh, Annie love,' he laughed. 'You were such a hit, and so funny and vibrant. You looked gorgeous and all the fellas couldn't take their eyes off you, including me. She could see there was definitely something between us...well, that is, I thought there was.' He suddenly looked confused, unsure about what he had revealed.

Annie lowered her eyes. Definitely there was a real attraction between them that night. She could feel his arm round her waist, could remember the spark in his eyes. So she hadn't imagined it. He had felt it too.

Jack ran his fingers through his hair. 'Let's just say, she didn't like what she saw. Lucien confessed that she told him to play up to you and get me drunk. Which he did. So I couldn't walk you home.'

'I did wonder… It did seem a bit strange the way he was plying you with drink.'

'Shows how stupid I was. Never noticed a thing. I think the original plan was for him to walk you back, but there was no way Mousey Monique was going to allow that to happen. I was so relieved when I found you'd had a lift. To think they would just have let you wander back through all those dark streets on your own…I'm so sorry.'

'Don't worry. It all worked out fine. But I can see it all fits now. I did have my suspicions but thought I was imagining things because I couldn't see why.'

Jack's voice revealed his anger. 'No, you are too nice to realise the lengths a jealous evil woman would go to. It has amazed me. And Nicole hadn't finished. Oh no. She really wanted to scupper things between us, so got herself invited to your dinner party, and Lucien, of course. And I fell for it, like the idiot I was. Looking back, you clearly wanted a chance for us to get together. Oh, Annie, I have played that dinner back in my mind a thousand times…'

'You and me both,' said Annie flatly.

'Nicole, she just…well she just…'

'Vamped you?'

'Yes that's it. Now I know her and have seen her operate on others, she's like a snake charmer, she just mesmerises you.'

'I know. I saw it.'

'And she wanted Lucien to do the same to you. But you didn't fall for it in the same way I did, did you?'

'No, he was charming of course, and it was very flattering, but I just didn't fancy him.' She didn't add 'because I was already hooked on you.'

'I remember how angry I was when I saw him in the kitchen with his arm round you.'

'Yes. I was pretty angry too when he came back, furious that he thought I was that sort of girl.'

He groaned. 'I know, and deep down I knew you

234

weren't…but…'

'But what?'

'Shoot me down in flames if I'm wrong, but you did seem to want to invite me up to the apartment a couple of times soon after we met. Or was I imagining it?'

Annie blushed. 'No, I will admit, I did quite fancy… But that's because…'

How could she say any more without revealing just how much, and how quickly, she had fallen for him.

There was that spark again in his eyes. His familiar grin lit up his face.

'Believe me, I really wanted to…well, to come up,' a wicked grin lit up his face, 'but I was worried it was too quick and I was misreading the signals.'

All she could do was nod. It was true. Once again, she was having to re-evaluate things, see situations from his point of view.

Both deep in thought, they walked on for a while.

'We were so good together at the beginning, weren't we?' He turned to look at her. 'And I've made a right mess of it all since, haven't I?'

She was beginning to wonder if it was all his fault, after all. But there was still so much more she needed to know.

'So how have you found all this out?'

'It's been a gradual process. Once Nicole had got me in her clutches again… But first Annie, it's important you know, I haven't had an affair with her. I think she's just a needy, manipulative person who couldn't bear losing one of her minions, and believe me, she's got loads of them. Let's face it, her own brothers dance attendance on her and they should know what she's like better than most. She can range from frightening bouts of fury, to weak and vulnerable in a matter of seconds if she's thwarted.'

Annie had seen the way she operated at the dinner party, so could well believe it.

Jack grimaced. 'She's the power behind the throne…and it's a very shady throne, as I've found out. After I left the café…'

'Incidentally, why did you leave?'

'I didn't like what they were saying about you and Lucien so I defended you, and had a stand-up row with Uncle Albert. I think I left seconds before I got the sack.'

He grinned, 'I'd had enough anyway. It had served its purpose of getting me integrated into Nice. And I had become increasingly fed up with Uncle Albert treating me like a servant. One of the main reasons I hadn't quit earlier was because I loved seeing the look of delight on my favourite customer's face when I served her a plate of pain perdu.'

He gave a cheeky glance sideways at her face and she instinctively smiled. Yes, it had been such a treat for her as well. His grin had been as welcome as the food.

'Anyway, after I left, I was at a bit of a loose end so I began to help Lucien and the family, setting up computer systems for them, stock control and stuff like that. I soon found out they've got fingers in all sorts of local businesses, cafés, hotels, food supply companies. It all seemed OK at first, then some things just didn't add up. I offered to computerise their accounts and Lucien just laughed at me and shook his head in disbelief that I could be so naïve. The proverbial pennies began to drop about just how shady everything was.'

He shook his head as if he still couldn't believe his gullibility.

'And it all came to a head yesterday morning.'

Chapter Forty-Three

Jack came to a sudden halt. They had walked a long way along the Promenade by now. Clasping the railings, he gazed with unseeing eyes out across the bay. Annie noticed his knuckles were white as he sought to control his anger.

'So, yesterday I was working in their office when I heard Nicole on the phone to Lucien. She didn't know I was there and there was a nasty tone in her voice. It was almost gleeful as she explained she had passed on your address to Henri Xavier.

'I was so shocked I must have gasped because she turned round and looked at me almost defiantly before ending the call. I told you I'd had an angry morning, well, that was the start of it. I asked her why she would give him your address, knowing what an old lech he was. She just shrugged and gave a spiteful laugh, asking why I should still care about a slut like you.

'Oh, Annie, I felt my whole body go rigid with anger. I suddenly *knew,* I knew with every fibre of my being that you were innocent. The proverbial scales fell from my eyes and I saw her for what she was. A spiteful, nasty, cunning, unscrupulous, scheming...words fail me to describe that woman. I tried to say some of this and she just walked away, laughing at me. I've never felt such a fool in my life...and I never will again.'

His face was white with suppressed rage. He could scarcely catch his breath as he continued. 'I raced off to confront Lucien at the garage because I wanted the truth about what he'd said about you. He could see how livid I was. Annie, I grabbed him by the front of his overalls and gave him the full force of my fury.'

He shook his head. 'I've never done anything like that before in my life. But it worked. That's when he told me the truth about everything, the party, your dinner, and everything. It just spilled out, like he was glad to get it off his chest. I know you think he's a cheat and a liar, but underneath I think there's a decent bloke struggling to get out.'

Annie gave him a withering look.

'Don't look like that. Hear me out. You saw the best in Henri Xavier and I think there's good in Lucien. He's trapped. He doesn't want to marry Mousey Monique but whatever he does, she won't let him go. And the families round here are very powerful. It's a 'you scratch my back, I'll scratch yours' community as I found out as I was doing all that computer work for them. No major crime or anything, it's just the way things are done.'

He shrugged. 'Annie love, I realised it's miles away from what we know.' For a moment he was lost in contemplation, before continuing to unburden himself.

'After I'd calmed down a bit, I told him I would be moving out from our flat. And I did yesterday afternoon.'

'Where did you go?'

'There're hotels agogo. The ones in the back streets round the port aren't expensive. I wanted to leave immediately but I knew Henri Xavier had now got your address so I had to find him before he got to your apartment. So I raced off. Some bits were making more sense but—'

She chipped in, 'You couldn't work out why Henri didn't know my address. If I really was an escort he would know it, wouldn't he?' Annie couldn't keep the ice out of her voice.

'I know, I know.' He looked so ashamed.

'Well, carry on.'

'I got to your apartment block just in time to see him leaving. So I grabbed him. I think he was quite shocked but I was in no mood for messing. He didn't get a word in until I told him what I thought of his sordid little game. How dare he trap a decent girl like you into such a sleazy operation. And if he thought you were friendless and defenceless, he'd got another think coming. If you had come to any harm, he'd have me to deal with.'

Jack looked a bit embarrassed, 'It all sounds very he-man doesn't it, but...well I told you it was an angry morning. I don't know where it all came from.' He blushed as he glanced at her.

Annie nodded. How much of his actions were prompted by wanting to protect her and how much by guilt at believing the worst about her. But it did sound rather thrilling that, once roused, he had really leapt into action.

And all for her.

But she kept her tone neutral. 'What did Henri say?'

'Well, to be honest, he just looked a bit stunned at all these accusations. Wasn't too keen on the scene I was making, but he could see I didn't care. Then he began saying nice things about you...he really likes you, you know. He protested he had no ulterior designs on you but was acting in your best interests. For reasons of confidentiality he wouldn't say how.

'There was no way he was getting away with that and I said so. Then the old codger sort of softened...well, he gathered I cared about you and gradually I got it out of him. How he was helping you find a Fabien who might be your father. He told me about the restaurant where you might be meeting him.

'I was stunned and frankly disbelieving. Then I remembered you asking at André's party about anyone called Fabien. I thought it a bit strange then.'

'I didn't know you had heard me.'

'Yes, I didn't let on because you'd told them you were a writer.'

She blushed, 'Yes, it was a little porky so I had a reason to ask about any Fabiens.'

'Why did you never tell me you were looking for...well, your father?'

'My *possible* father. Everyone thought it was a wild goose chase so I didn't want you to think I was a bit crazy. I nearly told you that day out in the hills but it meant talking about my mum, which always upsets me, and we were having such a good time, I didn't want to spoil it. Also I felt a bit embarrassed that I had already innocently met Henri for lunch before you had told me about him. Felt a bit foolish. I would have told you eventually, but we never got that far, did we?'

'No. We were just getting to really know each other, weren't we? Oh, Annie, have I cocked it up for good between us?'

His eyes searched her face. There was such yearning there. She had to lower her eyes so his need wouldn't totally overwhelm her. Could she forgive him? Or had the hurt been too great?

'It's not too late to make amends, is it?' He had stopped and reached out his hands in supplication.

Suddenly, weary from all the conflicting emotions and torrent of information, she sighed, 'I don't know, Jack. I think I'm going to go back to the apartment and try to get everything straight in my mind.'

He nodded forlornly. 'I understand. May I walk back with you?'

'You don't have to.'

'But I want to, Annie.'

They slowly walked back, each deep in thought.

As they approached the apartment block Jack said. 'Can I ask a favour?'

She hoped he wasn't going to ask to come up, 'I'm not sure.'

'Oh no, I wasn't going to ask to come up. I still have to remove Elspeth from Lucien's garage.' His voice was vehement. 'I want nothing more to do with them...any of them.' The embers of his anger still shone in his eyes.

'No, it's something else. I couldn't help noticing in the restaurant that you now have a mobile phone...'

'Oh yes, Ted bought it for me.'

'Ted?' He looked worried.

'Reen's husband is called Ted.'

'Clippy-cloppy Reen from upstairs?'

'Yes, she's gone back to Spain now and wanted to keep

240

checking I was OK, especially with Henri Xavier lurking.'

'Yes, I'm not happy he now knows your address. Please can I have your mobile number, and I want you to have mine, so you can call me if you need me?'

'OK.' She fished her new mobile out of her bag and he swapped the numbers on to the phones. 'You don't think Henri will come round, do you?'

'I don't know. I did try to frighten him off but he may come round and try to extract a reward for his labours in finding Fabien.'

'I don't think so. I think he's nicer than you may suppose.'

Suddenly Jack laughed. 'It's believing the best of people that's got us both in a fix, hasn't it. Two innocents abroad, that's us.'

'Soon be time to go home.' She sighed, half in sadness and half in longing.

Arriving at her apartment door, Jack blurted out. 'I'm so glad I managed to catch you this morning. I was hoping if I waited by our bench you would eventually come by. In fact I haven't slept all night and I was going to wait there forever till I saw you.'

He gave a rueful laugh. 'It sounds a bit dramatic, doesn't it? But I didn't dare come to your apartment because you told me to leave you alone.'

He bent down and stroked Pimpy.

'Thank goodness for your little dog. I knew eventually you would take her out for a walk and I just hoped you would let me explain everything then. It's been such a relief to get all this off my chest. Thank you so much for hearing me out.'

'It's certainly been a lot to take in,' she said wearily and turned to go.

'Annie…um…about us. Are we broken?'

'I don't know, Jack. I really don't.'

Chapter Forty-Four

Annie's phone was ringing. She groaned.

After an exhausting day yesterday, processing all Jack's revelations and explanations, she had eventually become clear in her mind about the facts of the situation. But the feelings of it all were a different matter. How did she now feel about him?

So it had been another wakeful night of turmoil and uncertainty as her head advocated she had nothing more to do with him, while her heart yearned for him to hold her. Oh, how it yearned.

It felt as if she had only just dropped off to sleep when the insistent ring of her mobile had awoken her. Wearily, she dragged herself out of bed to answer it.

'Hallo, Reen,' she said automatically.

'I'm not Reen,' said a familiar voice, in French.

'Oh.'

'Please excuse me, Mademoiselle,' the voice continued, still in French, 'I don't expect you know who I am, but my name is Jack Armitage. I am English, from a place called Oswaldtwistle.'

Bemused, all Annie could say was, 'Oui?'

'This must be strange, receiving a phone call from me, but please allow me to explain. I used to work as a waiter in a market café, and one day last September I saw you sitting there with your little dog, and, Mademoiselle, please permit me to tell you that your smile lit up my heart.'

She gasped. Jack's voice was so deep and sincere it took her breath away.

He rushed on as if worried she would not hear him out. 'I thought at the time that this girl with a magical smile, sitting in the sun, sipping her café au lait, couldn't possibly look at a mere English waiter. But I have eventually plucked up all my courage and I wondered… Do you think it might be possible that we could become acquainted?'

Annie could hear him hold his breath as he waited for her answer.

'Oui, Monsieur Armitage, I think it might be possible.'

A huge sigh of relief filled the airwaves.

'Magnifique. As it is such a beautiful spring day, do you think we could, perhaps, meet for a first date?'

Once again, Annie answered, 'Oui, Monsieur, it might be possible.'

'Fantastique. I have a grand old car called Elspeth and have told her all about the girl with a magical smile and she would love to meet you. Is it possible that you would like to meet her?'

'Oui, Monsieur, it is possible.'

'Merveilleux. There is a beautiful drive from the coast of Nice along the famous Corniche towards Monaco. Is it possible the girl with the magical smile would like to accompany me and Elspeth along this route and perhaps have lunch somewhere together?'

By this time, Annie couldn't keep the smile from her voice as she answered, 'Oui, Monsieur, it is possible.'

'Formidable. Is it possible, Mademoiselle, that I could pick you up at a certain bench on the Promenade in an hour's time?'

'Oui, Monsieur, it is very possible.'

'Merci. Merci beaucoup, chère Mademoiselle. Is it possible we will have a lovely day of getting to know one another?'

'Oui, Monsieur, I think it is very possible indeed.'

'Au revoir, Mademoiselle Annie.'

'Au revoir, Monsieur Jack.'

How could she refuse?

Any doubts she had were dissipating in the bright sunshine as she waited by their bench on an animated

Promenade. Jack was right. It was a beautiful day. The spring sun had some heat in it and she felt it warm on her back as she stood watching for the familiar shape of Elspeth. It also seemed to be having an effect on her emotions as slowly the icicles of her isolated winter melted away and she felt an optimistic lightness of spirit.

Could they really have a fresh start? Far too soon to tell. She must not allow herself to be charmed by the sunshine… or the man.

A toot of a horn alerted her to Jack's impending arrival. Despite her best intentions, her traitorous heart gave a spontaneous somersault as he swung the Jag's long, sleek shape into the side of the road. Impervious to all the irate hooting from behind, he leapt out of the car, ran round the bonnet, and ceremoniously opened Elspeth's passenger door for her.

'Mademoiselle, your carriage awaits.'

Instinctively she felt her face flush in response to his warm eyes and glowing smile. Annoyed at her heightened colour, she ducked her head as she slid into the shiny leather bucket seat.

'Merci, Monsieur,' she murmured.

'May I compliment you on the elegance of your attire, Mademoiselle?' Jack said, glancing at her carefully chosen bright blue top, as he pulled away into the busy lanes of traffic.

She grimaced.

'Too much?' he asked with a grin.

'Yes, way too much flannel…but still very nice.'

'Well you see, as this is our first date, I was trying to make a good impression. If you thought I was a gent, you might not be too hard on me when you find out I'm just a lad from Lancashire trying to woo the most wonderful girl he's ever known.'

There was a catch in his voice, a barely suppressed longing.

She couldn't help but respond. As she did so, she felt her body unfurl like a spring flower in the sun. The tension began to lift from her shoulders as she turned to smile at him.

'Luckily I have a soft spot for lads from Lancashire. And what girl doesn't like being wooed.'

Jack's face lit up and there was long sigh of relief. Then he deftly manoeuvred the big car through some narrow back streets leading to the legendary Corniche road.

It was a magnificent drive as they climbed up and out of Nice. The sea was at its bluest as it reflected the cloudless sky. Iridescent sparkles of sunshine danced on its restless ripples.

As they ascended out of the town, Annie began to glimpse the rocky outlines of the surrounding hills through the car windows. They were soon roaring round tight curves. Once again, she felt a thrill of excitement as the pulsating growl of Elspeth's engine throbbed up through her body. It was so deeply, deeply sexy. Try as she might, she couldn't stop her gaze straying to Jack's strong tanned hands as he drove the big car round the winding road. She noticed he was wearing a white shirt, pressed and pristine, and new tan chinos. Also the subtle tang of his lemon aftershave permeated the car.

Of course. It was a first date and he had made a special effort to dress to impress. But she felt she really must fight her attraction to this man who had believed the worst of her.

As if aware of the building tension in the car, Jack slowed down as they approached a small lay-by.

'Would you like the full film star experience?'

'Um, sounds good to me,' she replied, bemused.

'Good. I see you have the requisite scarf.'

Puzzled, Annie looked at the gorgeous cashmere one Sophie had given her for Christmas laying in her lap.

'I think it's warm enough for this don't you?' Jack grinned as he brought down the roof on the car. 'And if it does get a bit chilly, you can always wrap your scarf round your hair a la Audrey Hepburn.'

She smiled, 'Actually I think the famous Corniche driving scene in the movies was with Grace Kelly and Cary

Grant.'

It certainly was the most romantic film she could think of…but she shut that thought down swiftly. 'I agree. I think it will be warm enough and so much nicer with the top down.'

It would certainly help to dissipate the heat she felt in her limbs. At least she hoped so.

Jack nodded, his blue eyes sparkling with anticipation of the drive ahead.

As she settled back in her seat, Annie imagined gliding round the famous Corniche bends, the sun on her face, a slight breeze ruffling her hair and the whole vista of the Riviera coastline unfolding before her.

It was a bit like that, but much noisier and windier. And much more exhilarating.

The tortuous bends snaked before them with breathtakingly sheer drops to the sun-drenched sea below. Clinging on to her seat as the car whipped round the tight corners, she couldn't help laughing at the thrilling white-knuckle joy of it all.

He shot a delighted glance at her face.

'This is just how I dreamed it might be when I set off last spring,' he roared above the growl of the powerful engine. 'No, actually it's better. Are you enjoying it, Mademoiselle?'

Was there still that little frown of apprehension between his brows? Was he hoping to recapture that carefree teasing fun they had when they first met?

'Yes, Jack. It is fantastic. I absolutely love it.'

'Good. There's a little village just off the main route I discovered during one of my explorations. Would you like to stop and have a coffee?'

'Great idea.'

It was a perfect spot. From the terrace of the café perched high amongst the rugged hills, they had distant glimpses of the sun-speckled sea beyond the red-tiled roofs of the little village as it sloped down the steep escarpment.

The peace and quiet was a welcome change from all the engine noise. But it did accentuate the slightly strained silence that had descended between them as they sipped their coffees in the sunshine.

After all the first-date bantering, they were both reluctant to broach any other subject in case it opened old wounds.

Eventually Annie said, 'You know, Jack, I understand you are trying for a fresh start and I'm really pleased you asked me out for a drive today. It's wonderful but we can talk about…stuff…if you want.'

He sighed. 'Thanks. I just wanted today to be light and fun but there is too much, what the Americans call 'baggage' between us, isn't there?'

'Yes, just a bit.'

His face looked troubled again as he seemed to be casting about for a safe topic of conversation.

She decided to help him out. 'Right, let's start with a catch-up on where you are living now. Did you manage to move out OK?'

Looking relieved to be getting things out into the open, he ran a hand through his hair, tousling it in an achingly familiar gesture.

'Yes, Lucien wasn't there so I packed up everything. To my surprise I hadn't got that much more than when I came. Just some more summer clothes, a few French CDs and a few books. I somehow expected there to be more. I thought I had put down deeper roots than that. But no. It all seemed so,' he searched for the right expression, '…nomadic. Is that the word I'm looking for? Anyway, Lucien gathered what was happening when I took my case to the garage and he saw me load it into Elspeth. He looked so shamefaced he couldn't meet my eye.'

Annie saw a brief interplay of emotions cross his face, hurt, bewilderment, sadness, anger.

He looked at her with pained eyes. 'Half of me wanted to go and shake his hand and thank him for all he did for me when I first arrived here, but the other half still wanted to punch his lights out for all he's done to you. In the end we just sort of nodded at each other as I drove away.'

Clenching and unclenching his fists he looked as if he

was about to say more, but Annie wanted to keep the tone light, so asked, 'Have you found somewhere to stay?'

'Yes, I'm not in Nice any more. I want to be away from that lot, so I've found a little hotel in the hills. Much cheaper and very pleasant, although I do miss the sight of the sea.'

'Yes, I'm going to miss that too.'

They both gazed at the distant sapphire blue peeping through the stone alleyways.

'Shall you be sorry to go back?'

She had a think. 'Yes and no. Now I've found Fabien and talked to him, I am more ready to return.'

'Can I ask? Were you very disappointed he wasn't your father?'

'Oh, I don't know. I keep churning it over in my head, keep going over the meeting.' She slowly sipped her coffee, trying to articulate her feelings. 'I thought I would know instinctively the first time I saw him if he was my father; there would be a connection, a sort of natural strong bond.'

'And...?'

'And there wasn't. I didn't feel anything other than all the horrible nerves. He's a lovely man, I can see that. And he clearly loved my mum as much as she loved him, but I somehow knew he wasn't my father. My instincts had already told me...' She shook her head.

'So you are not too let down then?'

She paused to analyse her main feelings. The long phone call with Reen had helped her re-evaluate her relationship with her real father. Realising now how much he loved her, she felt a deep regret that she hadn't really known him. Her mother's big personality had somehow blocked him out. And she was becoming increasingly aware of how much her own life had been dominated by her mother's dreams.

But this wasn't the time to delve into all these thoughts. She was determined to keep the mood light.

'No, not let down really. I think I mainly feel relief. Of course, the romantic fantasist in me still thinks it would be nice to be half-French with all that alloouer,' laughing, she tossed her head in a mock-provocative manner, 'but it's not really me, is it?'

'Darling, Annie, you have alloouer by the shed load, but it's the natural Lancashire sort.'

Surprised by the depth of emotion in Jack's voice, she turned away, knowing she couldn't face her conflicted feelings for him, not just yet.

Keeping her tone deliberately light, she said, 'You mean mixed with a bucket-full of common sense and down-to-earth practicality.'

'Yes, you do have those qualities, when you are not going into one of your romantic flight of fancies or trying to be something you're not.'

She blushed, knowing just how foolish some of her notions had been.

But leaning forwards he added more seriously, 'But you also have imagination, resilience, kindness, and…'

She waved her hands at him. 'Jack, you can stop soft-soaping me now. I know it's supposed to be our first date but you really don't have to woo me with all this nice nonsense.'

'I am not soft-soaping you, Annie Roberts. Although I never met your mum, from what Fabien said, you have the same vivacity, humour, good looks and atrocious use of Franglais phrases.'

Annie giggled. 'Yes, I have definitely inherited that.'

He sighed. 'I'm so pleased you can laugh about it. After watching you walk up and down past the restaurant so many times before you went in, I was so worried. Perhaps I shouldn't have listened in to your conversation with him, but I just knew I had to be there to pick up the pieces…either way.'

'Oh, Jack, I hadn't realised you would be nervous too.'

'Of course. I…care about you a lot. I hope you know how much.'

'I'm beginning to.'

He clasped her hand across the table and looked deep into her eyes. There was no disguising the depth of emotion there.

But Annie still wasn't ready. He may be sure of his feelings but she wasn't. Yes, she loved being with him and she certainly felt the return of the old excitement but she had been too bruised to fall under his spell again so quickly.

She slowly pulled her hands away.

With an almost imperceptible nod of understanding, Jack reluctantly let her go.

Chapter Forty-Five

To break the uncomfortable silence that followed, Jack asked, 'Another coffee? Or do you want to set off again.'

Annie looked round. It was so peaceful and she knew that if they returned to the car now, they wouldn't have the opportunity to talk. Feeling instinctively that they needed to clear the air further, she said, 'It's so lovely here, should we stay a little longer.'

'Yes, of course.' Jack caught the waiter's eye and indicated 'same again'.

Annie returned the conversation to safer ground.

'Talking of Fabien, can you imagine if I had been his daughter…? Just think of the complications. And, of course, I forgot to ask if he had any children.'

'His wife sounds,' Jack grimaced, 'well, a bit tough, don't you think?'

'Yup, are you kidding? I wouldn't fancy his chances in introducing her to a long-lost daughter, would you?'

They both laughed.

'I'm so glad that, in the end, I didn't have to actually broach the possibility that he might be my father. The minute he said he met Mum in July, I knew. How stupid am I? This whole thing rested on my supposition that it was August, late August really, they spent together. All the references to summer in the postcards and I just thought…' She shook her head. All this time, all this turmoil, all based on a silly assumption.

Jack's voice was gentle. 'You say your mum always hankered after being French. Do you think that influenced you into thinking…?'

'Oh, undoubtedly. It added fuel to my suspicions. I even

remember her telling me she wanted to call me Marie-Anne but my dad vetoed it as too poncey.'

'So you sound as if you are becoming reconciled to not being French then.'

'I suppose so.' She sighed. 'Deep down I know I'm Accrington through and through.'

'Nowt wrong with that, lass.'

'No, there isn't. In fact the more I think about it, I wonder if I was too influenced by Mum's French act. Being absolutely honest, I think being French was more her dream than mine.'

He nodded. 'Did she ever visit France again, after that summer with Fabien, I mean.'

'No, not even when she could. I offered to take her, and some of her friends often suggested it, but somehow she never went. She was a dreamer and I think she preferred her romantic memories to the reality.'

'Are you a dreamer too?'

'Probably. Comes from a childhood full to busting with books. After Dad died Mum got a job at the library, just mornings, so she could always pick me up from school. But, of course, in the holidays I used to go with her and she would park me in a corner with a book and there I would quite happily stay until she finished at lunch time. Libraries are a sort of sanctuary to me.'

'Will you go back to library work, do you think?'

'I've no idea. I wish I did. I thought coming away would help me decide what to do with my life.'

She contemplated the view with the distant sea sparkling as far as the horizon.

'I do feel different. This has been a sort of watershed. Since university I have been fitting in my life around Mum, looking after her, taking her to hospital visits and stuff like that. I enjoyed the job at the library but I originally only took it to be near her. Because I'd known the people there all my life, they were like family to me. They were wonderful in letting me have time off for her chemo sessions and whenever she needed me. I felt very supported all through those awful last months.'

She dashed away a tear. Although it still felt very raw, she realised she was ready to talk to Jack about it.

There was a long silence. Jack said quietly. 'I didn't know any of that about your mum's illness or anything. Thank you for telling me.'

Of course. That's what he was doing. He was trying to get to know her. Really get to know her.

With a flashing insight, Annie realised how much of herself she had kept hidden from him. He only knew the aspects of her life, of herself, that she had wanted to reveal to him. He knew none of the important stuff about her mum, her search for Fabien, and the reasons for continuing to meet Henri Xavier, even after she knew about his shady intentions. No wonder he had been so shocked and bewildered. No wonder he was ready to believe all those lies about her.

Perhaps she shouldn't be blaming him as much as she had. And this day out was an attempt on his part to really get to know her, the real Annie.

In spite of all the recriminations she had thrown at him, he obviously still wanted to know her. Feeling a jolt of guilt, she realised he could just have walked away, but no, he had persevered and was now trying to get to know her better.

Looking at him with renewed respect, she determined to open herself up to all his questions. It was only fair.

Clearly trying to understand her past, he asked, 'So even though you had all that support, you still moved away from Accrington after…?

'Yes, after she'd…gone.'

'I bet that was a wrench.'

'Not as much as I thought it would be. I make out my friend Sophie bullied me into selling up and moving to Manchester, but, if I'm honest, deep down I yearned for a fresh start. Difficult to explain, but I realised how cramped, how claustrophobic Accrington was. Everyone knew me from childhood, and my mum, of course, and I would always be Grace's child. Don't get me wrong, they were all wonderful and caring and rallied round me…lovely, lovely people, but, I suppose, too much baggage drags you down. You become what they expect and the real you gets stifled somehow.'

He was looking at her keenly.

With a shudder she shrugged her shoulder as if throwing off the weight of all those years.

'I'm forever grateful to Sophie. I hope I would have had the courage to eventually do it myself but Sophie was right to prise me away when she did.'

'To the buzzing metropolis of Manchester.' He grinned.

'Yes. It all felt a bit overwhelming at first. But I immediately felt freer, younger. I met up with some old friends from Uni and started to socialise again.'

'And another library job.'

She laughed, 'I know, but chalk and cheese.' She leant forward eager to impart her enthusiasm for what she had discovered at the university.

'The university library job was much more varied and challenging, and their use of computers was bringing me up-to-date with modern research techniques. It was good to talk at a deeper level to the staff and lecturers, and of course, I loved helping the students delve into all the subjects they were researching. It was heady stuff. And of course there was all the social life of parties and clubs and stuff. I loved it.'

'So remind me what happened?'

'Bloody Brian.'

'Brian?'

'I was gutted when they made me redundant. The head of staff was really upset about it too, but last in, first out. Everyone said it should have been Brian that went. He's a right slacker, always having time off, but slippery as an eel.'

She didn't really want to talk about all the upset she had felt at the time. It seemed a world away from where she was now. Closing her eyes for a moment, she felt the sun's warmth on her face. This was so relaxing sitting chatting to Jack over a coffee in a pretty mountain village. She turned to look at him and felt the familiar thrill tingling down her spine as his eyes met hers. His blue eyes crinkled into a smile and she felt a charge of intimacy between them. With a jolt she realised, it was exactly how it used to be between them... before his betrayal. Was she ready to forgive him yet?

Confused by this swirl of conflicting emotions, she forced herself to look away.

'Sorry, I've been rabbiting on about me...'

'Only because I asked you. It's important on a first date to get to know each other. Really to get to know each other,' he said significantly.

Was there a slight reproach in his voice or was she imagining it? It sparked a momentary flare of anger. OK, she acknowledged she hadn't told him everything about herself so she was guilty of the sin of omission. But how much greater was his sin of commission in assuming the worst of her.

As if on cue, a cloud passed over the sun and she shivered, remembering her long lonely winter. And how much Jack had hurt her.

Aware that the atmosphere between them had somehow changed, Jack shifted uncomfortably in his seat, and signalled for the bill.

Chapter Forty-Six

With a slight frown, Jack stood up and stretched. Annie could see the pent-up energy rippling along his taut arms. In spite of her best intentions, her heart skipped a beat as she looked at his taut torso, his broad shoulders and long lean legs. Remembering her initial flare of attraction to him all those months ago, she sighed. Where had it all gone so wrong?

The waiter left the bill on a small silver dish. She noted that Jack left a generous pile of coins. He always tipped well.

With a bow, he gestured towards Elspeth. 'So, Mademoiselle Annie, where do want to go next?'

With a pang of regret, she realised that he had warily returned to his slightly forced 'first date' formality. But perhaps this was a good thing. Lulled by the intimacy of their chat, for a while she had believed all was well between them. But she knew her wounds still weren't healed.

He opened the car door with a flourish as she approached Elspeth. 'We could carry on round the Corniche to Monaco, if you so desire?'

She grimaced. 'Yes, if you do.'

'You don't sound too keen. Have you been before?'

'Yes, a few times on the train. Amazing marble-lined station all underground, so impressive...but...'

'What?'

'I feel very provincial there. The shops are mega-expensive, all the women are mega-thin and everyone is mega-rich...unless of course they are normal plebby tourists like me, gawping at them.'

He laughed. 'Yup. Even dear old Elspeth felt intimidated by all the Porsches, Rolls Royces and Ferraris. We could go up into the hills some more or down to the sea again.'

'Hmmn. I can see loads of hills when I go back to Lancashire, but it's a bit of a trek to the sea. And neither Fleetwood nor Blackpool are quite like anything you get here.'

'Oh, I don't know. Blackpool has a prom, a bit like the one in Nice. And it has a Tower as well.'

'True, true, not quite as much sun though.'

'OK. But sometimes, in the baking heat of the Riviera summer, I have found myself longing for a bit of cooling Lancashire drizzle.' He grinned, 'Oh my goodness, wash my mouth out. What have I said?'

Annie found herself nodding in acknowledgment. They had both relaxed back into their familiar banter, united by their common Lancashire roots. Was that all that had drawn them together initially? Had they both been feeling a little adrift in this sophisticated, unfamiliar country and so had clung to each other? Or was there something more, something deeper? If only she knew.

He started the engine and Elspeth roared into life. Annie's eyes lit up as she felt the beat of the engine stir through her blood. She had to admit she loved the exhilaration and glamour of driving around in the grand old car. Jack glanced at her face and smiled as if he knew exactly how she felt.

'OK, the sea it is.' He pulled away down the narrow, labyrinthine streets towards the gleaming azure Mediterranean stretching before them. 'In fact I know a nice restaurant on the quay at Villefranche...or we could go through Monaco to somewhere like Menton near Italy.'

'I've been to Menton so I quite fancy Villefranche. I've looked down on it from the train a few times, but it's so close to Nice, I've never got round to going there.'

'It's quite small and unspoilt and has a rather quaint painted chapel. It's not spectacular in any way, but I like it.'

'Sounds my sort of place.'

As they plunged down the mountainside, once again the dramatic views took her breath away. Each twist and turn revealed a different vista of jagged inlets, perched villages and wild scrubby vegetation clinging to the rocky outcrops.

It was too noisy to talk properly and they soon lapsed into companionable silence, Annie enjoying the scenery and Jack engrossed in the driving.

As they neared the coast, he turned down a steep hill. They passed through several tunnels before emerging onto a pretty little harbour lined with clusters of pale pink and ochre buildings whose faded shutters were closed against the midday sun.

Jack parked deftly between some bollards on the quay. With a final roar, he switched off the engine and a wonderful peace descended.

'Here we are.'

The small bay was fringed with restaurants and a tempting smell of garlic and fish filled the air.

As they clambered out of the car, Jack asked, 'Before we eat, would you like to see the painted church first?'

Annie's stomach gave a loud rumble.

'Oh, sorry about that,' she said, blushing.

He grinned. 'I'd forgotten just how insistent your stomach was. So, I think we have our answer, don't you? May I recommend this restaurant for your delight and delectation?' They were approaching a charming old fashioned establishment with tables by the water's edge.

'Perfect,' said Annie, hastening her steps as a couple began making their way to the last remaining table for two in the sun. 'Quick grab that one,' she hissed.

A beaming waiter, as if divining her intention, swiftly pulled out a chair for her, thus blocking the other couple.

'Monsieur, Mademoiselle,' he said in a loud voice, bowing slightly as they approached. 'This is the reserved table you requested, is it not?'

Jack replied with a grin, 'Merci, Antoine,' as the waiter ostentatiously pulled out the other chair for him.

Muttering angrily, the other couple walked away to occupy a shady table nearby. Antoine winked as he made a fuss of draping the snowy white serviette on to Annie's lap.

'The usual for you, Monsieur?' he asked.

'Oui, merci. Alas, once again I am driving so a Perrier for me.'

'And for you, Mademoiselle?' The young waiter positively beamed at her.

Flustered by all this attention, Annie couldn't think for a moment.

'Perhaps you would like your usual red wine,' Jack said, then eyeing the gleaming white tablecloth, he teased, 'Or perhaps something…safer…'

She laughed. 'How ungallant of you, Jack Armitage, to dredge up my spillage record. In fact, as I'm thinking of having fish anyway, I quite fancy a white wine.'

Antoine smiled. 'Of course.' He whisked away to fetch the drinks.

'I take it you know him.'

'How did you guess? Although I've never had such VIP treatment before. I've been a few times but always on my own and I think he's delighted that I've brought someone with me this time.'

Annie was aware of the unspoken presence of Nicole. She knew he had often driven Nicole to places along the coast, but obviously not here. Glancing around, she delighted in the ambience. Their little table was right by the water's edge and she could see the old town climbing up the hillside in front of them. It looked a great place to explore, but only after they had eaten.

'I love it here,' he was saying. 'It wasn't too far to come if I only had a half day off from the café and wanted to escape for a while. It's been really quiet through the winter and being on my own I got chatting to Antoine about…well, all sorts of things. You know…life, the universe and this and that. We got quite deep at times. There aren't a lot of opportunities for him in this village and, of course, the restaurant is a family business, as so many of them are. He would really love to go and study art at college. He's the one who told me I must visit the little church there.' Jack turned and indicated a small white building just beyond the quay. 'It's full of paintings by Jean Cocteau.'

'And has Monsieur seen it yet?' asked Antoine who had silently appeared with the menus.

'No, Antoine, and please call me Jack.'

'No, Monsieur.' Antoine gave a discreet nod with his head, indicating the nearby table occupied by the disgruntled couple.

'Of course,' Jack nodded. 'No, I haven't managed to visit the church yet. It's always closed when I go.'

'Ah yes.' Antoine shrugged. 'It's the winter, and the lady who looks after it is a bit...well, she's very artistic and she keeps artistic hours, I think.'

Jack laughed. 'But I will try again today, I promise.'

Antoine turned to Annie, his face alight. 'When Jean Cocteau was painting in there, he often used to dine here.'

'It sounds wonderful,' said Annie. 'I do hope we get to see them.'

'I hope so too.' And with another small bow, Antoine left them to peruse the menu. He reappeared almost immediately with their drinks and, with a wink, he set out a wonderful array of olives, and delicious small canapés.

'Merci, Antoine. Cheers, Annie. Here's to sunshine and wine and...was Jack going to say 'us'? But after a small hesitation he said, 'and life.'

They chinked glasses. The wine was refreshingly cold and tasted citrusy with a hint of elderflowers.

'So what do you fancy?' Jack said indicating the menu as Antoine appeared, pad poised to take their order.

'Ooh everything looks so good. I just fancy fish and garlic really.'

'So what do you reckon, Antoine?'

'May I recommend the Sole Meunière?'

'Yes that sounds lovely.'

'I'll have the same.'

As Antoine bustled away Annie's mobile rang.

She grimaced an apology to Jack. 'Sorry about this. It will be Reen checking I'm OK. Do you mind if I take it. She'll only worry if I don't.'

'No, that's OK. Please go ahead,' said Jack, turning away

and tucking into the nibbles.

'Hallo, Reen,' Annie said as quietly as she could to avoid disturbing the other diners. 'And before you ask, I'm fine.'

A smoker's laugh, so reminiscent of her mother's, came down the phone. Reen could be heard clip clopping around the house as she talked.

'How's the weather?'

Reen always asked that and seemed pleased when she learned it wasn't as hot in Nice as it was in Marbella.

'Actually it's gloriously sunny here, Reen. Might be nearly as hot as you. In fact I'm sitting outside just about to eat my lunch at a little restaurant in Villefranche.'

'Ooh, Dahling, that sounds lovely. You sound really perky this morning.'

Annie glanced at her watch and could see it was in fact afternoon but she knew Reen was not an early riser in Spain. Her night life was definitely more riotous at home than it had been in Nice.

'Yes, I am, Reen. I'm having a smashing day.'

Jack looked up clearly pleased by this remark.

'Has that Mr X been anywhere near you?'

Annie hesitated. To tell the truth would lead into a long story, best saved till another time.

'No, Reen, everything is fine.'

'OK, Dahling.

'How about you? What are you doing?'

'I'm just in the middle of finally sorting the guest list for Tyrone and Tina's wedding. The invitations look dead classy. All gold embossed with flowers and cherubs. You'll be getting yours as soon as you get back to the UK. Just give me a ring when you arrive home and I'll pop it in the post.'

'Oh thanks, Reen. I'm really looking forward to it. It will be good to see you again.'

'Can't wait, Babes, but don't forget you are welcome here anytime. Ted's just nodding. He agrees as well.'

Annie's eyes filled a little at the warmth in her friend's voice.

'Thanks, Reen. You are both wonderful to me.'

261

'Get along with you,' said Reen dismissively. 'Just as long as you are OK.'

'Yes, Reen, I am.' She looked across at Jack, 'I definitely am.'

'OK, bye, Babes.'

'Bye, Reen.'

Annie turned slightly misty eyes towards Jack.

'Sorry about that, but she is so lovely to me. I had to take it. She's invited me to her son Tyrone's wedding in September in Marbella.' She giggled. 'Knowing Reen it should be amazing. Did I tell you all her family's names begin with a T so her son Tyrone is marrying a Tina? I'll have to really bling up for it. What a contrast it will be to my other wedding in August. Do you remember my friend Sophie?'

'The one who got you the dog sitting job in Nice?'

'Yes the very one.' Why did it tickle her so much that he remembered what she'd told him all those months ago? 'Well I'm the chief bridesmaid at her wedding. I've been really rubbish at it, she says, but she doesn't hold it against me. Anyway, hers is a real posh elegant do, not Lancashire you note, but far more up-market Cheshire.'

'Right, you need to fill me in a bit more about Sophie. And also Reen's family. You obviously really hit it off.'

Annie laughed, 'Oh, she's such a treasure, but where do I start?'

Just then lunch arrived.

Over a long, lazy lunch by the little harbour, Annie filled him in on Sophie and their shared childhood. Obviously she omitted completely her recent trip back to the UK to help her out. She knew from her frequent phone calls all was well between her and Philip. More importantly, the wedding plans were proceeding perfectly well without any input from the chief bridesmaid.

Updating Jack about Reen led inevitably on to that lonely time during the winter when Reen went away. Annie couldn't keep the pain from her voice as she spoke about being all on her own for Christmas and the Millennium. Although she hadn't meant to make Jack feel guilty, he clearly did.

'I feel awful. To be all on your own. And your first Christmas without your mum. Oh, Annie, I'm so sorry.'

'Yes it was awful,' she acknowledged,' but looking back, it gave me good thinking time. I decided I could wallow in self-pity or I could get on with my life, on my own if need be. It toughened me up.' Here she looked at him, wanting him to know this. 'So a new century means a new me, and I do feel more resilient.'

Jack disconsolately picked over the remains of his meal.

'I feel exactly the opposite,' he mumbled.

'What?'

'I felt so good when we first met. Now, after all I've learned about myself, I feel, well, I've lost all confidence in myself, my ability to judge people, my integrity, my—'

'Woah. Stop right there. Your integrity is intact.'

'It is?'

'Yes. You didn't like what you found out about what Nicole and her lot were doing and you wouldn't be part of it.'

'True, but…'

'And the minute you uncovered their lies, you were shocked to the core, weren't you?'

'Yes, of course.'

'Because like me you have an innate faith in people and dishonesty is so unexpected, it actually shocks you.'

He nodded. 'You're right it did. I still have trouble believing that Lucien, my supposed friend, would betray me like that. I just feel such a fool.'

'Join the club. How do you think I feel about fantasising that Fabien was my father?'

'But you didn't let down someone you really, really care about like I did. Leave her to endure a dreadfully lonely time on her own. Spoil the best thing that's ever happened to me.'

He grasped her hand.

'Annie? Can you ever forgive me?'

Was she ready yet? But somehow sitting in the sun, sipping the fresh white wine, chatting like old times, opening up to him like never before, Annie felt the final shards of ice in her heart melting. She knew her feelings were as strong as ever. Her heart was screaming yes, but was her head?

As she pondered her answer, she saw Antoine was about to clear the plates. He swiftly swerved away as if guessing the intensity of the moment.

'What a lovely bloke,' Annie said following him with her eyes.

Jack groaned. 'Look, I know you've got a thing about waiters…'

'No I haven't,' she protested quickly, 'just you.'

Yes, it was true.

Just Jack.

Chapter Forty-Seven

She hadn't meant to blurt it out, but like a thunder clap, she realised it was true.

Just him. From what they had shared earlier and from what they had said today, she felt she really knew him. And she loved him.

In spite of everything, here was an honest, true man, who admitted his failings, clearly cared for her and wanted to protect her. He had persevered in spite of rejection, was a wonderful companion with whom she could share her innermost thoughts. They had a similar sense of humour, sense of honour. They enjoyed the same things and seemed to want the same out of life.

And, seeing his twinkling blue eyes and his devastating smile, she knew she fancied the pants off him. Literally.

All barriers were down now.

She looked at him frankly and grinned, 'Ooops.'

His expression had changed from one of amazement to one of delight and finally a roar of laughter.

'That's a pretty big ooops. What an admission. Really. You really have a thing about me?'

'I suppose so.' She clinked the wine glass. 'In vino veritas, I believe the saying is.'

'No, that's not it. You haven't had enough vino, so that's no excuse.'

'I suppose not. So it might just be the sunshine, it might be the ambience, or…' She leaned forward, 'Or it might just be you.'

'I can't believe it. After all I've done.'

'After what? After you apologised profusely, have been totally guilt ridden, have lambasted yourself without mercy, and yet still persisted in spite of all my frostiness.'

'No, not frostiness. You were never frosty. I can't imagine you ever doing frosty.'

'Well, that's nice to know.'

The conversation tailed off as they sat there hands clasped and beaming at each other.

'Of course,' Annie prompted, 'you haven't yet said you have 'a thing' about me, so perhaps—'

'What!' he roared, causing heads to turn. 'Of course I do. Annie, I love you. Absolutely I do. Really, really love you.'

There were gasps all around as their fellow diners stopped what they were doing and stared.

'Well, that's nice to know.' She smiled.

An astonished man behind her nearly choked.

'Les Anglais,' said his companion with a shrug. 'So very restrained and polite.'

'Oh dear,' Annie giggled. 'I suppose that was a little underwhelming as a response. But truly it is nice to know.'

'Surely you realised before.'

'Yes, I suppose I did. But I've been fighting my own feelings about you for so long…I just never thought we would actually get it together.'

'Well, I hope we have now.'

There was little cough and there was Antoine with two sparkling glasses of champagne.

'May I present you with these on the house? And may I say how pleased I am for you both?'

All around them polite applause rang out and they turned to see a ring of beaming faces and glasses held high in salute.

Exultantly Jack leapt to his feet and bowed. 'Thank you, everyone, and thank you, my dear friend Antoine, whose wonderful welcome has melted the heart of my darling Annie.' He clasped a surprised Antoine in a fierce embrace. Then, seizing hold of his glass of champagne, he roared, 'Vive la France!'

Annie just stared, unable to believe her eyes as, all around them, people rose to their feet and joined in his heartfelt salute.

Shouts of 'Vive la France, Vive la France' resounded round the bay.

Flushed with jubilation, Jack hauled her to her feet and gave her a long passionate kiss.

'Vive L'Amour,' someone shouted and this too was repeated wholeheartedly by the standing diners.

Annie was convulsed by a range of feelings, astonishment, embarrassment, joy, hilarity...but mainly embarrassment.

Her first proper kiss with Jack and everybody was watching.

Jack, too, seemed suddenly aware of what was happening and released her.

'Umm, sorry about that. I think I got a little carried away there.'

'Les Anglais,' said that same women with a very Gallic shrug. 'Always so very restrained and polite.'

The journey back to Nice was very different from that morning's leisurely drive out. With Annie's hand firmly gripping Jack's thigh as he roared through the gears, they couldn't get back fast enough.

Parking near the apartment, his eyes held a question as he switched off the engine.

'Would you like to come up for a coffee by any chance?' Annie asked sweetly.

'That's very kind of you, Mademoiselle. Are you sure?'

'I am very sure, Monsieur.'

'In that case it would be churlish of me to refuse.'

'It would indeed.'

With fake nonchalance they strolled to her apartment.

Then ran urgently up the stairs.

Rushed headlong into the apartment.

And tumbled passionately into her bed.

Chapter Forty-Eight

Much later, exhausted and fulfilled, Annie nestled into Jack's chest. Then suddenly burst into peals of laughter.

'I can't believe that scene on the quay. What possessed you? Vive la France, indeed.'

'I know, I know. I can't believe I did that either. I was so elated, I just wanted to hug the world.'

'Can you believe you hugged Antoine before me?'

'Oh yes, don't remind me. We are going to have to go back and apologise, you know.'

'I think everyone was as delighted as you were. You made their day. *We* made their day. Although that skinny Frenchwoman just kept raising her plucked eyebrows and shaking her head at *les Anglais*.'

Annie lay back and stared at the bedroom ceiling. It was early evening and the lights from the Promenade played across the darkening room. She felt so contented and sated and loved.

Kissing the top of her head, Jack squeezed her to him.

'Oh, Annie, my darling, I still can't believe this. I really thought I'd blown it with you. And the more despairing I became, the more I realised how much I missed you, wanted you, loved you. Thank you for having me back.'

'No,' she said sharply. 'No more of that. I'm not having our relationship founded on guilt and forgiveness. You said… oh crikey, was it only this morning…? You said, fresh start, and you wanted to get to know me?

'Well, fresh start it is…' she giggled, 'and you've certainly got to know me, haven't you?'

'Oh yes, oh yes,' he breathed, as he bent to kiss her.

Her body tingled all over at the tenderness of his lips,

which gradually become harder and more passionate.

'Mmmn. Would you mind terribly if I got to know you again?'

'Les Anglais,' she giggled as she pulled him closer. 'So very unrestrained but very polite.'

Next morning Annie stretched luxuriously on the crumpled bed as the sun streamed through the window.

'What a wonderful way to wake up,' she murmured, lazily disentangling her limbs from Jack's.

'You mean the sunshine,' he teased.

'Of course. What else? I'm really going to miss it when I go back. But the more I think about it, the only other thing I'll miss is Pimpy.'

She giggled, feeling guilty about the very swift walk Pimpy had last night. But there were far more pressing demands on her time and her body awaiting her in the apartment.

'Poor little thing. She has been such a lovely companion. I can't believe that this time next week, I'll be back in my little flat in Manchester and probably preparing for one of the many bridesmaid fittings that I know Sophie has got lined up for me. But it will be good to see her again. Although it will mean wall-to-wall wedding plans.'

'Have you booked your flight yet?'

'No, I really must get on to it. But so much has happened lately, it has sunk to the bottom of my list. I'll have to get out all Madame Dumont's knick-knacks before then. She arrives back mid-morning. There's a flight at tea-time that will be perfect as I don't think it's wise we spend too long together. It's plain she doesn't approve of me in some way, and she's so dainty, it makes me feel like a lumbering elephant next to her.'

She rolled over and contemplated a grinning, tousled-haired Jack. 'And besides, I want to go before Madame Lafarge, the nosy concierge, tells her about my overnight visitor, which is strictly forbidden.'

'Will she know about me?'

269

Annie looked at him with astonishment. 'Jack, she's a *French concierge,* she knows everything. I should imagine I will be gossip fodder for months to come.'

'Do you care?'

'Not in the slightest. But I don't want to hang around to see the pursed lips and frowning and tutting and stuff.'

'You sound as if you are really ready to go back.'

'Yes, I am. It sounds strange, but I'm actually looking forward to it. Don't know why? I've got no job, no prospects, the weather will be worse, but...'

'Yes?'

'It will feel more real than this. I suppose knowing all this was only for six months, it's felt like a holiday somehow, a bit of a fantasy. But I now know living like a French person was my mum's dream, not mine. I think I have well and truly got it out of my system. I can't wait to reconnect with my friends and stuff. Going back will be real life, and I feel an urge to get on with it.'

She saw Jack was nodding vehemently.

'Yes, exactly how I feel about going back. Like you, no job to go back to but I've got lots of ideas swirling around in my head about something I fancy doing. And I feel I've got a heck of a lot of stuff out of my system too. I know I've learned a lot about people...and myself.'

'And me.'

'Oh yes, I've definitely learned a lot about you,' he growled, seizing her in a bear-like embrace.

'Let me finish. I meant I've learned a lot about me too. And I feel...'

'No, I feel,' he said...and did.

'Jack,' she giggled. 'I'm trying to have a serious grown-up conversation here.'

'Oh, sorry. OK, I'm listening.'

'But you'll have to stop doing that or else I won't be able to concentrate on what I'm saying.'

'Spoil sport,' he muttered, but stopped.

'Anyway where was I? Oh yes, going back... Hang on. Did you say you were going back as well?'

'Of course I am. Did you think I would stay here without you?'

'Well…you don't have to.'

'Woah, if you think I'm letting you go back without me, you've got another think coming. I know you and your penchant for waiters…'

She thumped him on his wonderful tanned, toned chest.

'Not just any old waiter. Oh crikes, I can't wait to see Sophie's face when I tell her I've fallen for a waiter.'

'Ah, but I'm not just any old waiter as you so eloquently put it. But I'm certainly glad I waited for you.'

Her groan at his pun was stifled by yet another passionate kiss.

'So you really are going back to rainy old Manchester?' she tried to hide her delight.

'Yup. Love the place. Pouff,' he gave one of his incredibly sexy Gallic shrugs.' What's a bit of rain to tough old Lancastrians like you and me? And I do have an idea whereby we might acclimatise ourselves slowly to the English climate.'

He lazily traced a finger round her belly button causing ripples of goose pimples.

'How do you feel about driving back with me and Elspeth? We could follow the spring up the centre of France.'

His hand slowly wound a circling path down her body as she gasped with anticipation.

'We could take our time,' he murmured as his hand reached lower and lower.

'Mmmn.'

'Till we reached our destination…together.'

'Yes, oh yes.'

Chapter Forty-Nine

Malaga Airport. September 2000

'There's our suitcases.'

'Thank goodness for that. Last off the plane it looks like.' Jack heaved their two bags from the noisy carousel.

Annie sighed with relief. 'I don't know what we'd have done if they had gone missing. All my wedding finery, the presents and...'

'All your bling,' Jack teased.

'It's not bling. It's just been carefully chosen with Reen in mind. It's just a little bit more colourful and shiny than my normal stuff.'

'Actually, I love it.' He paused, to give her a swift kiss before wheeling the bags away.

She went pink. Even after being together for over six months now, she still couldn't get over how demonstrative Jack was. All his friends had told her that his trip abroad had really brought him out of his shell. And his Gallic shoulder shrug was widely admired.

And it certainly worked for her. It was so sexy. A fact of which he was well aware. Often it was deployed as he suggestively wrapped a large white waiter's apron around his naked body as he served their evening meal. Or poured her a glass of wine with a flourish and a rakish grin. She blushed, remembering the times the meal had gone cold by the time they had got round to eating it.

She noticed the hubbub of noise in Malaga airport increased, as did the heat, as she hurried after his broad-shouldered figure.

'Sounds like a lot of people waiting out there,' Jack said

with a nod towards the approaching exit doors.

'It does sound like a bit of a crowd. So we'll just look for someone little and very tanned wearing something bright and shiny, next to a large big-chested man wearing a very colourful shirt.'

'Ok.'

The doors opened and a cacophony of colour greeted their eyes.

'Crikey,' Jack exclaimed. 'They are *all* tanned and shiny and bright and…'

'Yoo hoo,' a piercing cry cut through the clamour and a little hand could be seen waving above the shimmering crowd.

A burly figure shouldered his way towards them towing a tiny, strappy-topped and very familiar figure.

Annie felt a lump of emotion swell in her throat. 'That's them,' she said just before she was enveloped in a fierce, highly-perfumed hug. Tears prickled her eyes. Oh, how she had missed her warm-hearted friend. She returned Reen's hug, squeezing her tightly.

Laughing to cover their emotions, the two friends pulled apart and gave each other a warm appraisal.

Yes, there she was again, Reen, in all her golden-muled, mock-ocelot legginged glory, her eyes sparkling as brightly as the sequinned logo on her crimson crop top.

Reen nodded her head, obviously approving of Annie's bright turquoise top, white cut offs and strappy silver sandals.

Suddenly Annie was twirled around and found herself deep in a flowery broad-chested squeeze.

A deep voice rumbled, 'Good to see you again, Annie.'

Then two pairs of bright eyes twinkled at Jack, waiting nearby with cases and looking a bit shy.

'So we meet again, Jack,' Reen said approaching him. 'Right, let's have a proper look at you, now your face is not being hidden by my kissing friend.'

Over the last six months Jack and Reen had spoken frequently on the phone where they had established a relaxed, teasing relationship. But this was the first time they would actually meet properly. Obviously that time in Nice outside the apartment when Annie had winded him against the wall as she kissed him, didn't really count.

Reen looked him up and down, then with a raucous laugh, reached up and seized him in a warm embrace, covering his face with bright red lipstick kisses.

'Lovely to meet you at last, Jack, Dahling.' And with a wink at Annie she said, 'Yes, you're right, Babes, he's a proper bobby dazzler.'

Embarrassed, Jack extricated himself, only to be seized again by Ted in a firm manly hand shake followed by a hefty slap on his shoulder.

'But you've got to promise me you won't ever mess my Annie about again,' Reen wagged a stern finger at him.

A bit taken aback, Jack looked at the fierce little figure in front of him and her big beefy husband.

'No. Never. Let's face it, Reen, I wouldn't dare.'

With a mighty laugh Reen hugged him again.

Ted grabbed their bags. 'Right let's go. Tyrone is parked where he shouldn't be, so we better get a move on.'

Talking all the time, Reen hustled them out into the blinding sunlight and towards a large, white Range Rover with darkened windows parked on a busy corner.

They scrambled into the cool interior as Ted stored their luggage in the boot. Their anxious driver swerved off swiftly before they even had time to buckle up.

'Just in time, Ma. That cop had got me in his sights,' exclaimed Tyrone as he forced his way into the steady stream of white taxis.

'I told you it was risky parking just there,' Ted rumbled. 'Why didn't you go where I always go, just a bit further up there?'

And a friendly argument arose about the relative merits of illegal parking spots as they drove away from the busy airport into the heat of the Spanish sun.

'That's enough, you two,' Reen quickly silenced them both. 'Now, Tyrone, I want you to meet Annie and Jack.'

'Hi, you two.' He raised his hand from the wheel in

greeting.

'Hi, Tyrone,' they chorused together.

Annie caught a pair of twinkling brown eyes looking at her in the rear view mirror.

'Right, should we come to an understanding?' he said. 'I won't believe everything Ma's told me about you, if you don't believe everything she's told you about me.' He winked.

'Well,' replied Annie, 'how about we only believe all the good things we've heard.'

'That sounds about right to me.'

'So, are you all ready for your wedding?' she asked.

There was a shrug of his broad shoulders. 'You're asking the wrong person. Surely you should know that. Ma's the one who's sorted it all. Ask her.'

So Annie did.

And the rest of the journey was spent talking flowers and favours and food and all the final flurry attached to the wedding while Ted and Tyrone sat silently in the front. Occasionally Tyrone would catch her eye and she could see the indulgent smile in his eyes as Reen outlined yet another piece of wedding outrageousness.

Yes, she was going to like Tyrone very much. She hoped the rest of the family would be as nice.

Chapter Fifty

'Here we are,' Ted announced.

Full of curiosity Annie leaned forward and peered through the darkened windows of the car. She could see high white walls covered at intervals in crimson, orange and deep-red bougainvillea. Ornate columns topped by rampant lions stood either side of intricate gold, wrought-iron gates. Facing her on the wall there was a large plaque with *Tedreen Villa* writ large in bold ruby red.

She daren't look at Jack. He had been warned what to expect and they had both vowed not to catch each other's eye, whatever they saw.

But rampant lions!

The golden gates opened automatically and they drove in, parking outside a large, white villa under a grand portico entrance.

The doors opened suddenly and a small, round body came rocketing out, barking excitedly.

Pugsy. Annie picked him up into her arms for an ecstatic cuddle. 'Hello, Pugsy, my little friend. So you *do* remember me. Poor Pimpy missed you so much when you'd gone.'

But Pugsy was wriggling, wanting to be put down so he could welcome all these other lovely people, most of whom had only been gone an hour but still needed the full barking welcome.

'He's been so excited about you coming,' Reen said indulgently as she picked him up away from all the milling feet. 'Now, in you come.'

They were whirled into the cool bright interior to be greeted by marbled columns and a pair of life-size ceramic leopards guarding an arched entrance to the huge lounge.

They were assailed by colour. Large bright paintings of raven-haired flamenco dancers, huge red flowers and rampaging elephants adorned the walls. Blue, green and yellow easy chairs, settees covered with a multiplicity of orange oriental-silk cushions, highly patterned rugs on the marble floors, all vied for attention. There were whirring ornate ceiling fans, billowing gauze curtains at the large open patio door and, in the distance, could be heard the squeals of excited children splashing in the pool.

And these were just the first impressions.

'Hello, you must be Annie and Jack,' said a cheerful voice and a pretty, petite, dark-haired girl emerged with a gold tray of champagne flutes.

'Oh good girl, Tina,' Reen said with a smile. 'Ted, will you do the honours with the champers.'

Ted dropped their bags in the hall and took the champagne from the tray.

'Hello, Tina,' Annie said smiling. She felt she knew her already. With her bright eyes, tanned limbs, clingy emerald green crop-top, short white leggings and gold mules, she was looking at a younger version of Reen.

A cork popped. There was a rush to catch the fizzing liquid.

'Welcome,' said Reen, offering them both a sparkling glass of bubbles.

And Annie knew they were.

It was a hectic afternoon as they were introduced to the rest of the family.

The three Taylor boys, Tarquin, Tyrone and Troy were spitting images of Ted, but all had their mother's sense of humour and vivacity.

Tina and Tyrone snuggled up to each other and had a sort of pre-wedding glow, sneaking secret smiles at each other now and again.

Troy was on his own. Tall, very good looking, he was resplendent in a Hawaiian shirt covered in brightly-coloured birds and an expensive gold watch on his wrist. Annie remembered that Reen desperately wanted to pair her up with her one remaining single son. But looking at Jack laughing with Ted, Annie had no regrets. And besides, her name didn't begin with the requisite letter 'T'.

Tarquin's wife, Tracey, was very pretty but had a slightly petulant frown and Annie could well imagine her giving Reen a hard time last Christmas. She pursed her lips as Reen stopped the twins, Tristram and Tricia, dripping wet from the pool, wreaking havoc by jumping on the furniture. Luckily the new baby, Tallulah, seemed very placid and just smiled from her baby chair at all the noise and chaos surrounding her.

Annie couldn't help notice Tracey's frown of disapproval as some white-uniformed caterers emerged from the kitchen and began to set out a large buffet lunch in the shade by the pool.

'I knew she wouldn't approve,' muttered Reen, filling up Annie's glass, yet again. 'Probably thinks I should be flying around the kitchen doing it all myself. Well bugger that. I'm no good at cooking... apart from cheese soufflés and Tarte Tatin of course...all thanks to you.'

Annie laughed. 'Crikey, Reen, you've enough on your plate at the moment without the hassle of feeding a small army in your home.'

'Course I have. Now come over here and let's have a good natter.' She led the way outside to a large, garden swing-seat. 'Tell me what's been happening. I've been so busy with all this wedding lark, I feel I've lost touch a bit since you got home.'

Annie grinned. She had been expecting an interrogation about her and Jack's relationship, especially now Reen had met him properly.

But she wanted to deflect her friend from anything too personal. Although it had been six months now, she still felt her cocoon of happiness was quite fragile. Knowing how hurt she'd been in the past, she couldn't shake the feeling that it was all too good to be true. She daren't commit her heart totally, just in case. And she knew an astute Reen would pick up on any doubts she may harbour.

So, knowing it was impossible to avoid, she followed her friend to the shady garden seat and prepared for Reen's Spanish inquisition.

Chapter Fifty-One

Settling down next to Reen on the padded white seat, Annie was careful not to dislodge too many of the blue, jewel-encrusted cushions. It was a lovely shaded spot, from which they could survey all the garden activities as they talked.

For a moment Annie's eyes were distracted by the Greek columns surrounding the huge barbecue area and the plastic pink flamingos scattering the lawn.

'So, Babes, you and Jack, tell me all about how you are getting on.'

'Not much to tell really, Reen. You know about our lovely drive home through France.'

'It sounds wonderful, Dahling.'

'Oh, it was. We motored round some lovely little places, well off the beaten track and stayed in some sweet little hotels. It was so romantic. We really got to know each other.' She stopped, feeling a blush creep up her body as she remembered those amazing nights of passion and love and exploring and fun.

Reen grinned and nodded.

'No, I mean we talked a lot and…everything,' Annie finished lamely hoping her friend would get her drift and enquire no further. However, sensing Reen was longing to probe further, she swiftly changed the subject.

'Of course it was sad to say goodbye to Elspeth. She was such a gallant old gal, but needed quite a bit of expensive T L C by the time we got back.'

'Elspeth?'

'His lovely old Jag, Elspeth the E type, remember?'

'Oh yes.' She could tell Reen would much rather talk about her and Jack's relationship than a car. But she wasn't sure how much she wanted to reveal about it, even to her lovely old friend.

That journey home was too intense and precious. Their love had blossomed and bloomed as they talked and laughed and planned. The misunderstandings in Nice had finally been ironed out, resolved and put behind them. The whole journey had set the tone for their continuing relationship, companionable days and romantic nights.

Sensing the searching questions looming, Annie ploughed on, talking on the much safer subject of Elspeth.

'I hadn't realised that Jags of that vintage are worth quite a bit, even when a bit knackered. But Jack needed the money to finance his current project. Do you remember me telling you about that on-line mapping idea he had whilst we were driving back?'

Reen nodded absently, clearly not remembering any of it.

So Annie cut it short. 'Well, as you know, he started his own little IT company and it's doing really well. He's got a swish office in the centre of Manchester, lots of screens and keyboards and stuff. And his staff are a lovely enthusiastic bunch of people.'

Somehow it was important that she convinced her friend that Jack was financially secure as well as a wonderful person. It was vital that Reen should wipe any memories she had of those times in Nice when Jack was definitely persona non grata. She desperately wanted Reen to approve of him, respect him and, above all, like him.

Reen nodded again but her eyes had glazed a little. She reached down by her side for the bottle of champagne and, despite Annie's protestations, topped up her glass before refilling her own.

The catering staff were laying out platters of salads and salmon and cold meats. From the kitchen Annie could smell the aromas of baking bread…and was that chips?

She turned to ask, but Reen was already launching into her next round of interrogation.

'So, Babes, what about you. Have you found a job?'

'Actually, Reen, I have some big news.'

'Oooh, Babes.' Reen's eyes shone. With a thump, Annie realised her friend was thinking of engagement and weddings and romantic news. Not job news. For a moment she felt almost cross. It was far too early to be talking engagements and such. The fact that she and Jack had found each other, were happy together, was enough. Or it was for her.

'Right, Reen, the big *job* news. Do you remember me telling you about bloody Brian, the one who should have been made redundant instead of me? Well, he went off long term 'sick' with a bad back caused by carrying too many heavy books. Poor lamb.' She made a face. 'Everyone knew it was fake and that he was playing the system yet again but nothing they could do. But it was great for me because they called on me to cover for him. I know you think being a librarian is all about stamping books in and out, but it's not. There's so much new IT stuff going on, the job is really changing and evolving to keep up with this new century, the twenty-first century.'

She knew Reen wasn't a big reader, never used a computer and had no idea how diverse the job of a modern librarian was. Nevertheless her friend was loyally hanging on her every word, so she plunged on.

'So, the really big news is…' she hugged herself in delight, 'Bloody Brian got caught out. Big time. Supposedly off with a bad back, but he was photographed leaping for joy in the winners' enclosure at Aintree. He was only in the background, but it was unmistakably him, large as life on the back sports page of a national newspaper. One of my friends spotted it. I heard all the cheering in the staffroom and they came and dragged me in to show me.'

She grinned at the memory.

'So they've sacked him, interviewed me and I got the job. I start full time beginning of October.' She didn't add that there were five other strong contenders for the job, but walking in with her new-found confidence and her posh Nice clothes, she knew she had wowed the interview panel. Her time in France had definitely made a difference to how she felt about herself, and it showed.

'Oh, Babes, I'm so pleased for you. They are lucky to have you.'

'Hmmn, do you think that you are perhaps just ever so slightly biased?'

'Me? Never, Babes. If my Troy wasn't already courting…' Reen sighed.

'Oh, is he? You never told me.'

'That's because we only found out last night. Dropped it like a bombshell just as we were about to eat.'

'Is it serious?'

Reen nodded. 'Think so.'

'What's her name?'

'He hasn't told us.'

'So you fear the worst?'

'What?'

'You know…her name might not begin with a T.'

'Oh, Dahling, as if that mattered. If she was the right person for him, I'd cope. In fact, do you want to know a secret?'

'Go on.'

Reen indicated the vivacious woman who was gazing with adoring eyes at her soon-to-be-husband.

'Tina over there…her real name is Sharon.'

'What?'

Here Reen had to delve into her pocket for a tissue before she could continue. Dabbing her eyes she whispered, 'But she thinks so much of my Tyrone, she changed her name to Tina for him. All official like. Now that's what I call true love, don't you?'

'Yes, Reen, I do.'

Reen blew her nose clearly overcome by her future daughter-in-law's consideration for the family's traditions.

'Just hope my Troy has found someone as golden. But he's not invited this new girlfriend to the wedding. He seemed to think it might be a bit too much.'

'As if, Reen.'

There was pause as they both looked towards the sound of uproarious laughter coming from the men. The Taylor boys were obviously teasing Jack but he had said something back at them that creased them up. It was great to see them all getting on so well. Especially as Jack had seemed a bit tense over the past few weeks. She had tried to put it down to his anxiety at the prospect of meeting all these new people at the wedding. Strange though. He had been perfectly relaxed about meeting Sophie for the first time, and he had thoroughly enjoyed her wedding last month.

It just niggled her a bit that there was something bothering him and she couldn't work out what it was. But it definitely added to her sense of insecurity. She just hoped it didn't presage anything wrong between them. Certainly Jack was still as loving, if anything more so, but might that also indicate something? Was he being extra nice to her before he gave her some bad news? She fervently hoped not, so was determined to carry on being an optimistic ostrich, until she was forced to take her head out of the sand and confront whatever secret was troubling him.

'Your Jack seems to be coping OK, doesn't he?'

'Yes, he does.'

'So you are living together then? How's that going?'

Annie grinned. She knew she couldn't escape any longer. The whole point of this tête-à-tête was for Reen to ask her how she felt about Jack.

'Yes. He had sold his flat to fund his trip, as you know. So it made sense to move in with me. It helps with bills and things and...'

'So it's purely practical then, is it?'

'Of course, Reen, what else?' Annie teased. Then unable to resist any longer, she confessed, 'and of course, it's wonderful. We get on so well, it's just...wonderful.'

Reen beamed. 'So you really love him then.'

'Oh, Reen, I daren't say that.'

'Why ever not?'

'Just in case. Silly, I know, but I don't want to admit it, I think. Let's just say, he's wonderful.'

'So what's so wonderful about him?'

'Everything.' Suddenly all her pent-up feelings gushed

out of her. 'He's so caring and funny. I can't wait to get home each evening to see him and we talk and we share so much. And he's very loving,' she blushed. 'So very loving. I never knew…well…it could be so wonderful.' She looked across the pool at Jack, who, sensing her gaze, turned and grinned. 'And just look at him, he's so gorgeous. And, oh yes, when he's had a few, he's a fantastic dancer.'

She gave a sheepish grin. 'Yes, I confess I'm a bit smitten. And all my friends like him too. Actually Sophie really, really likes him and even asked him to be an usher at her wedding. Philip just agreed, so I know he likes him as well. I've met his family and friends and we get on great.'

'So everything seems to be going really well, so you must be just waiting for him to propose.'

Annie was shocked. 'Oh no, Reen, it's far too early for that.'

'Nonsense, Babes…if—'

'Please, Reen, don't jinx it by saying that. I'm holding my breath in case it all goes wrong.'

'Why should it go wrong?'

'Oh, I don't know. Don't you see, it's all too good to be true? I can't really relax just in case it's not meant to be. I could be living in a fool's paradise.'

'Don't be silly, he plainly adores you.'

'Do you think so? Do you really think so?'

'Of course, Babes, plain as the nose on your face.'

But Reen was prevented from saying any more by the caterers ready to serve lunch.

Did he adore her?

As Annie saw Jack coming to fetch her, wickedly waving a bottle of champagne, she crossed her fingers and wished it could be true. She really, really wished.

Chapter Fifty-Two

After a large and very liquid buffet lunch, Reen escorted Annie and Jack upstairs to their sun-filled room. It vibrated with bright yellow and orange curtains, coverlets and cushions.

She opened their patio door onto a large veranda. 'Look over there, in the distance. That's Gibraltar. Can you see it?'

Jack by this time looked as if he was having trouble focusing on his feet, let alone Gibraltar, but manfully agreed it was a wonderful view of the giant rock.

'Good. I gave you this room because I knew you would love to see it. Now, make yourselves at home. Feel free to pop down to the kitchen if you want a cuppa or anything. Or the jacuzzi is there if you want a nice bubbly relax. I'm just going to rest my eyes for five minutes. Got to get my beauty sleep before the big day tomorrow.'

'This is a beautiful room, Reen. Thank you so much for inviting us and...' Annie began.

'No more of that, Dahling. Of course you were invited, and you too, Jack.'

'Please let me finish, Reen, and for putting us up here with your family. We really appreciate it, especially as you've got so much to do with...'

'Babes, you are part of my family now, so of course you must stay with us.' She lowered her voice to a whisper, 'and they've all told me how much they like you. Knew they would.'

Annie hugged her tearfully. 'And I love them too. You are a treasure, Reen, a real treasure.'

Reen disentangled herself and patted her arm. 'So are you, Babes. Now I've got to get orf quick for my shut eye before Ted starts snoring...oh, too late. Never mind, I'll just dig him in the ribs. That usually does it.'

Off she tottered towards the deep reverberations coming from her room.

Annie closed the door quietly. The whole house had gone for a siesta and this was the first time she had been alone with Jack since they arrived.

'So what do you make of all that?'

But Jack was already flat out on the bed, slumped amongst the sunny mounds of cushions. He gave a tipsy smile and with a sleepy arm patted the bed next to him.

'Sorry, Annie, love, but I'm going to have to close my eyes for a while. You did warn me and honestly I tried not to drink too much but...'

She laughed, 'I know. I know. Oh, how I know.'

Snuggling up beside him she quietly watched the sun filter through the gauzy nets at the window till her eyes drooped.

'Drinkies.'

Reen could be heard tapping at the bedroom door.

'The sun's over the yard arm. Come and join us by the pool whenever you are ready.'

Her footsteps clip-clopped down the stairs, accompanied by the tinkling of ice in her glass.

Annie opened her eyes to see a pinkish glow in the sky from a spectacular sunset.

'Oh crikes,' Jack groaned, as he lifted his head from the pillow. 'I was flat out.'

'Me too.'

'It surely can't be drink time again.'

Annie laughed and gave him a hug. 'I did warn you. It's always drink time at Reen's. Seriously, are you OK?'

'I think so, although it was a bit like entering the lion's den.'

'Or the leopards'.'

'What?'

'Did you not see those huge ceramic leopards guarding

the hallway?'

'Oh yes, I was thinking of those rampant lions at the gate. She really has got a thing about big cats hasn't she? Well, big game generally. That huge rampaging elephant painting. And did you see the big fake elephant's foot by the door with brollies and golf clubs in?'

'And that bar in the Greek temple at the top of the pool.'

'And the pink flamingos. And…'

'No, this isn't fair, we must stop it. She is the most warm-hearted person I have ever met.' 'Yes, I agree.'

'And I love her family. You seem to be getting on well with her boys.'

'Yes. They really are terrific. You can stop worrying. I am loving it. And you of course.'

He pulled her close and gazed into her eyes, 'Especially loving you.'

His kiss was long, slow and lingering. 'Hmmn. Have we time for…?'

'Oh, Jack, I'm not sure. I think we ought to be going…'

Too late. His kisses had travelled to just that spot at the base of her neck that shot tremors all over her body…and…

Reen cast a knowing smile as they later emerged by the pool, slightly damp from a shower.

She waved at the well-stocked bar. 'Now what's it to be? Margaritas or tequila or…

'Oh, Reen, go gently with us please,' Annie begged. 'Is it possible to have a nice cup of tea?'

There was roar of laughter from the Taylor boys, swiftly stopped by Tina.

'Absolutely right, Annie. I could murder one as well. And you,' she poked a grinning Tyrone sharply in his chest, 'are going to have a sober night tonight. You are *not* going to be hungover tomorrow…and that goes for the rest of you too.' She stared fiercely round them all.

'Sorry, Reen, but can I suggest one drink maximum for everyone tonight?'

The look on Reen's face suggested she was already too

late. But gamely putting her glass down, she agreed. 'Yes, Tina, Dahling, you are absolutely right. We all want to look our best tomorrow, don't we?'

'Yes, Ma,' came a somewhat sheepish chorus.

Annie turned away with a smile. Tina was taking no prisoners and her stance and demeanour was so similar to her future mother-in-law, it was uncanny.

Suddenly there was ring at the gate and the intercom buzzed.

'That'll be the caterers,' said Reen.

'I'll get it, Ma,' offered Tyrone.

'No you don't. Troy, can you let them in?'

Puzzled, Tyrone looked at Tina who just shrugged.

Reen whispered to Annie, 'As it's his last night as a free man, they are cooking his favourite meal.'

'Oh, what's that?'

'Bangers and mash with onion gravy, followed by spotted dick and loads of custard.'

Annie tried to stifle her gasp. 'In this heat.'

'Why not, Babes?'

The evening was a tremendous success, even without drink, well, a few beers didn't seem to count as they were taken with food.

Annie got into a close conversation with Tina who ran her own hair salon in Marbella and was an avid book reader.

She also noticed Reen taking Jack to one side and having a long, intense conversation with him.

'What was that all about?' she asked as they eventually escaped upstairs to bed.

'What?'

'Your chat with Reen.'

Jack looked decidedly shifty. 'Oh nothing much. You know what she's like?'

'I do. It looked as if she was giving you the third degree.'

'No, just sort of asking about…my job and stuff.'

A very endearing feature of Jack, Annie thought, was the

fact that he was a really bad liar. But he obviously didn't want to tell her.

She tucked in next to him, knowing she would eventually get it out of him. She just had to bide her time.

Still, it was intriguing. It looked almost as if they were plotting something.

Chapter Fifty-Three

The music was loud, the drinks were flowing and a riotous time was in progress.

'Now that's what I call a wedding,' Annie sighed as she flopped down on a slender gilt chair beside Jack. 'Eat your heart out, Sophie. As lovely as yours was, you couldn't top that.'

Jack grinned. 'Yes. As chief bridesmaid, I feel you derelicted your duty in not suggesting the pink and purple doves released from a gilded cage.'

'Really?'

'Or the Cinderella coach drawn by white horses festooned with feathered head dresses.'

'Oh dear, how very remiss of me.'

'Or all the men in white frock coats with pink and purple cummerbunds and bow ties.'

'In Cheshire?'

'Or the chocolate fountain…'

'No, stop. The whole thing was wonderful. Yes, very different from Sophie's do. But hers was lovely as well. Her parents managed to be civil to one another. The great and the good turned up and were not too stuffy. And I enjoyed it, even though I got a bit stressed about getting everything right.'

'It was a brilliant day and you looked gorgeous.'

'Thanks. That dress was rather elegant wasn't it. And I managed not to fall over in those heels. Even when you twirled me round that dance floor all night.'

She paused, remembering the closeness and intimacy of those long romantic dances during the wedding evening. Jack's body hard against hers as they swayed rhythmically together.

She was hoping for more of the same tonight.

Looking round at all the noisy revelry amongst the gold and crimson balloons, the gaudy wedding streamers and the flashing disco lights, Annie grinned.

'This has been so much fun. My face aches from smiling all day. I loved it.' Leaning over to give him a big kiss, she said, 'But I tell you what, Our Jack, in amongst all this bling, there is so much love. So much love.'

She sighed and nestled into his shoulder. He was looking tousled and gorgeous, his silver wedding tie was loosened and his white shirt was unbuttoned at the collar revealing that V of brown chest that turned her on so much.

Jack grinned and put his arm round her bare shoulders. He was a little bit tipsy she could tell.

As the evening wedding party had progressed, the magnificent ballroom had got warmer and warmer, in spite of the valiant efforts of the air con. All Reen and Ted's family and friends were exuberant dancers and she had been whirled around the dance floor all evening. The floor was full of children. The girls were flouncing and strutting around in their pretty party frocks. The little boys had long since discarded their posh waistcoats, and now, with shirts hanging out, they were just chasing around or doing some sort of spacewalk dancing.

But as wonderful as it all had been, Annie was feeling a little disappointed. In spite of all her pleading, Jack had steadfastly refused to join her on the dance floor. He was an effortless and very sexy dancer and she wanted an opportunity to hold him close and smooch. Just like at Sophie's wedding.

At the beginning of the evening he had engaged with everyone, laughing and teasing 'all the soft southerners' as he called them. But for the last half hour he had looked really tense and there was also some sort of conspiracy going on between him and Reen. Every now and again she would glance across at him meaningfully and he would shake his head and turn away.

What on earth was going on?

Just then the band began a lilting romantic waltz. The ballroom seemed to vibrate with an air of expectancy and she saw Reen looking across at them with a huge grin.

'Come on, Jack. This sounds lovely. I really fancy a dance with you.'

But when she tugged his arm, he almost shrank back from her.

'Jack. What's the matter?'

'No, no…um, not yet. I've just got to go to the loo.' He leapt to his feet and a little unsteadily wove his way through the guests towards the gents.

Crossly, Annie folded her arms. At this rate he would soon be too drunk to dance at all. Right, she decided, the very first dance when he gets back, she was pulling him out there on to the floor, whether he liked it or not.

Tapping her fingers, impatiently waiting, she eventually saw Jack appear with a look of quiet desperation on his face. Just then the band struck up a silly dance tune. With a grin Annie recognised The Birdie Song. It was a favourite at weddings for getting everyone to embarrass themselves on the dance floor by flapping their arms like chickens.

With a whoop of laughter, she pulled him into the middle of the flapping throng and began to join in all the gyrations, waving her arms up and down and waggling her bum as if laying an egg. Jack looked appalled.

Suddenly the band stopped mid beat. One of the whirling spotlights stopped and searched them out. Everyone round them melted away leaving her and Jack isolated and illuminated in the middle of the floor.

Stunned, she looked round.

'What…? she began, turning to Jack.

Crimson-faced, he was glaring at Reen, who just shrugged and continued directing the spotlight to focus on them.

Then his shoulders came down and he grinned as if accepting his fate.

Sinking down on one knee, Jack retrieved from his

pocket a small jewellery box. He snapped it open to reveal a simple diamond ring nestling in its plush interior.

'Annie Roberts, would you do me the honour of becoming my wife?'

She just gasped, too shocked to think, 'Umm...'

'Please, Annie,' Jack begged. 'I know this is a ludicrous tune for a proposal. It was supposed to be that last romantic song, not this one. But I sort of chickened out. A bit like you really.'

Annie realised she still had her arms out in mid flap and her bum in mid wiggle. Blushing fiercely she straightened up.

'Annie? Yes or No?' Jack pleaded, his eyes serious.

'Put the lad out of his misery,' Ted's voice boomed. Then came a loud 'Ouf' as Reen had obviously dug him sharply in the ribs.

Snapping out of her suspended animation, Annie found herself yelling, 'Oh yes, yes. Yes, of course, yes. Oh yes, Jack, yes.'

'I think he's got the message,' someone shouted before the whole room erupted into cheers. Jack just had time to raise himself from his knee, slip the ring on her finger and fold her in his arms for a kiss before they were caught up in an avalanche of hugs and congratulations.

A beaming Reen came to their rescue. After a long tearful hug and smothering them in kisses, she ushered them through the throng to a quiet corner of the room. A relatively quiet corner. Not to be thwarted in its jollity, the band had struck up the same catchy tune again and the floor was once again filled with flapping arms and hopping feet.

'Oh god, you do realise that that's going to be our tune from now on, don't you?' Annie groaned before she became overcome with giggles. 'What on earth possessed you, Jack? A public proposal? A spotlight?'

'I'm so sorry, Annie. I blame Reen. It was her idea.'

'Reen. You consulted *Reen* on how to propose. *Reen!* Reen of the purple and pink doves, the Cinderella coach, the...'

'I know. I know. But she was giving me a hard time about you feeling insecure in the relationship and it was time I made an honest woman of you and…'

In spite of the heat, Annie went cold. 'Wait. Stop one minute. Are you telling me, you only proposed to me because Reen forced you into it?' She began tugging to get the ring off.

Jack gently folded his hand over hers to stop her. 'No. You daft thing. Of course not. I've known for weeks now I was going to propose today. Why do you think I came out here with the ring in my pocket? It was supposed to be a surprise but Reen winkled it out of me. Then she suggested our first romantic dance tonight would be the perfect time. I had no idea she had told everyone, and the spotlight and everything. When the time got near, I got really nervous about it. I think when she saw I'd chickened out of the waltz one, she was waiting for us both to be on the floor at the same time…you dragged me on for that Birdie dance so she just went for it.'

He enfolded her in his arms.

'Annie, I'm so sorry. I hope it didn't spoil it.'

'Well, it was certainly the most unusual proposal a girl has ever had.' She was still in shock.

'But you do like the ring, don't you?'

She looked at the perfect solitaire diamond sparkling on her finger.

'Oh Jack, it's beautiful. It really is. It fits and everything.'

'I know. I sized it up from one of the other rings in your jewellery box.'

So he really had been planning this for a while.

'And you do know why it had to be today, don't you?' He was grinning.

'Um…' She wracked her brains and had to confess, 'Nope.'

'Well, it's exactly a year ago today that I first saw you, my girl with a magical smile. You came in looking all French and elegant, with your little dog, so very chic and sophisticated. Then you sat down in the sun and gave that most amazing smile. I was transfixed by it. And when I approached, you looked at me with your gorgeous blue eyes and said in the most appalling Lancashire French, 'Café au lait, s'il vous plait'. I think it was at that moment I lost my heart to you.

'And I want to stay lost with you for the rest of my life.'

His kiss was deep and tender. As she emerged, he smiled. 'Yes, there it is again, that magical smile.'

'Well, what do you expect? I'm having one of my epiphanies.'

As he glanced over her head, his laugh turned to a startled groan.

Annie had been vaguely aware the Birdie song had obviously unleashed a desire for participation dances and she had heard a riotous Hokey Cokey going on behind them.

Now she twirled round to see a beaming Reen, feathered fascinator defiantly askew, leading a snaking line of conga dancers in their direction.

'Can we escape?'

'Don't think it's possible, do you?'

'Nope.'

'And you do realise Reen is going to want to organise our wedding, don't you?'

'What?'

'Can we escape?'

'I don't think that's going to be possible either, do you?'

'Nope.'

'Do you want to?'

'Nope, not really.'

'Just as well. Here she comes.'

Fantastic Books
Great Authors

CROOKED
CAT

Meet our authors and discover
our exciting range:

- Gripping Thrillers
- Cosy Mysteries
- Romantic Chick-Lit
- Fascinating Historicals
- Exciting Fantasy
- Young Adult and Children's
  Adventures

Printed in Great Britain
by Amazon

65868958R00180